"[A] wonderful follow-up to her extraordinary fantasy debut, *Mélusine* . . . every bit as original and satisfying as its predecessor." —*Publishers Weekly* (starred review)

"Fascinating . . . In the course of escalating adventures that will leave your knuckles white and your mind ablaze, these half brothers manage to find (or rediscover) some small measure of order in a very disorderly world. Monette brings their story to a strong conclusion, but I'd gladly follow her into the labyrinth again—with or without their company." —*Locus*

"Monette creates an interesting world with fascinating and complex characters . . . a fun read." —*SFRevu*

"An engagingly intelligent fantasy." —*Library Journal*

Praise for

Mélusine

"A lush novel, rife with decadent magic, debilitating madness, and dubious deeds, told in a compelling entwined narrative. The setting is richly imagined, a sprawling city at once strange and familiar, and the characters are vivid and alive." —Jacqueline Carey,
New York Times bestselling
author of the Kushiel's Legacy series

"Open this book and fall under its spell . . . a spellbinding, gut-wrenching, breathtaking quest that resonates with truth and heart." —Joan D. Vinge,
Hugo Award–winning author of *Psion*

"Brilliant and original . . . Monette writes with a deftness that never loses its way among the intricacies and anguishes of her plot, world building, and characters." —Jo Walton,
World Fantasy Award–winning author of *Ha'penny*

"If *Mélusine* weren't four-hundred-plus pages long, I might have tried to finish it in one gulp—it's that good, and it moves at a commendable pace for a character-driven novel with a complex, twisty plot."   —*Locus*

"Set in the wondrous city of Mélusine, Monette's extraordinary first fantasy novel focuses on two captivating characters from two very different worlds. [Monette] is a highly original writer with her own unique voice."
—*Publishers Weekly* (starred review)

"An exciting debut by talented new writer Sarah Monette."
—Cecilia Dart-Thornton,
author of the Bitterbynde trilogy

"While Monette's story engages, her characters deserve a standing ovation. Mildmay's off-color personality and often wickedly funny narration keep the story and the other characters fresh."   —*Booklist* (starred review)

"I was hooked from the very first page . . . lush and mesmerizing, so carefully constructed that I often found myself rereading passages as if letting the smoky flavors of a good red wine roll over my tongue . . . I couldn't have asked for a more satisfying book."
—*GLBT Fantasy Fiction Resources*

"Elegant, joyously written . . . an exquisitely painful romp, a return to an old kind of fantasy with a gleaming new edge."   —*Interzone*

The Mirador

Sarah Monette

ACE BOOKS, NEW YORK

THE BERKLEY PUBLISHING GROUP
Published by the Penguin Group
Penguin Group (USA) Inc.
375 Hudson Street, New York, New York 10014, USA
Penguin Group (Canada), 90 Eglinton Avenue East, Suite 700, Toronto, Ontario M4P 2Y3, Canada
(a division of Pearson Penguin Canada Inc.)
Penguin Books Ltd., 80 Strand, London WC2R 0RL, England
Penguin Group Ireland, 25 St. Stephen's Green, Dublin 2, Ireland (a division of Penguin Books Ltd.)
Penguin Group (Australia), 250 Camberwell Road, Camberwell, Victoria 3124, Australia
(a division of Pearson Australia Group Pty. Ltd.)
Penguin Books India Pvt. Ltd., 11 Community Centre, Panchsheel Park, New Delhi—110 017, India
Penguin Group (NZ), 67 Apollo Drive, Rosedale, North Shore 0632, New Zealand
(a division of Pearson New Zealand Ltd.)
Penguin Books (South Africa) (Pty.) Ltd., 24 Sturdee Avenue, Rosebank, Johannesburg 2196,
South Africa

Penguin Books Ltd., Registered Offices: 80 Strand, London WC2R 0RL, England

This is a work of fiction. Names, characters, places, and incidents either are the product of the author's imagination or are used fictitiously, and any resemblance to actual persons, living or dead, business establishments, events, or locales is entirely coincidental. The publisher does not have any control over and does not assume any responsibility for author or third-party websites or their content.

THE MIRADOR

An Ace Book / published by arrangement with the author

PRINTING HISTORY
Ace hardcover edition / August 2007
Ace mass-market edition / August 2008

Copyright © 2007 by Sarah Monette.
Cover art by Judy York.
Cover design by Judith Lagerman.

ISBN: 978-0-441-01618-1

ACE
Ace Books are published by The Berkley Publishing Group,
a division of Penguin Group (USA) Inc.,
375 Hudson Street, New York, New York 10014.
ACE and the "A" design are trademarks belonging to Penguin Group (USA) Inc.

PRINTED IN THE UNITED STATES OF AMERICA

10 9 8 7 6 5 4 3 2 1

For Sarah Wishnevsky

Part One

Chapter 1

Mildmay

So to begin with, General Mercator was dead.

There'd been rumors for months that he was sick and then that he was failing and then that he was dead, but the news had come for sure that morning. General Mercator'd been in charge of the Bastion for longer than I'd been alive, so I guess it wasn't no surprise that nobody in the Mirador quite seemed to know what to do now that he was dead.

So Lord Stephen had cancelled all the committee meetings and soirées and stuff that was what the Mirador normally did with its time. Me and Felix had gone back to the suite, and Felix and Gideon had talked the thing to death, because that was how Felix was, either you couldn't get him to say nothing, or you couldn't get him to shut up. They'd been reading since dinner while I played hand after hand of Hermit's Pleasure, but all at once Felix shut his book and said, "Do you want to go see *Berinth the King* tonight?"

"I don't mind," I said. Mehitabel was in it.

"Well, I don't mind either," he said—teasing me, but only a little. "It's a nice change from arguing with Edgar and Simon about the nature of the stars."

"You could wear your new coat," I said, hoping I could keep his mind off me. "The one Rinaldo says—"

"Is an affront to seven hundred years of aesthetic philosophy. I could, couldn't I?" He loved to wear this red-violet color that clashed with his hair something awful. He said enough people stared at him, they should suffer for it. The new coat, aside from the color, had gold bullion around the cuffs and down the lapels. "Loud" don't quite begin to cover it.

A little pause, and he looked at Gideon. "Do you want to come?"

It wasn't no big secret that you could hardly get Gideon out of
the suite with a crowbar and an ox-team. I don't blame him—
powers and saints, if I'd had the choice, I'd've been right there
with him, and I don't know which one of us had the worse deal. I
mean, there's me with the obligation d'âme and being the guy that
offed Cerberus Cresset, and then there's Gideon being Kekropian
for one thing, and having had his tongue cut out by the Duke of
Aiaia for another. And then there was the fact that he was sleeping
with Felix and everybody and their dog knew it. And the Curia
wouldn't let him take the Cabaline oaths. No, I don't know why.
Felix and Gideon were both so pissed off about it that I didn't even
want to ask. So, anyways, he didn't go out much, and like I said, I
didn't blame him.

But Felix kept trying, first one way, then another, and mostly
Gideon said no, but sometimes he said yes. And tonight, he
gave Felix a crooked sort of half-smile and nodded, and got a
smile back, too.

"All right," Felix said. "Let's go see *Berinth the King*."

Mehitabel

After the worst rehearsal in the history of the world, I went back
to my dressing room. Well, *fled* back, to be perfectly honest,
and if I had a plan at all, it was to make faces at myself in the
mirror until I felt better.

But when I got to my dressing room, there was someone already there. He was about my age, Kekropian-dark, not like the
people in Marathat with the leaven of Tibernian blood, well-
dressed and as sleekly self-pleased as a cat with a songbird
pinned beneath one plump paw. He would have been perfectly
cast as Uriel Glabney in *The Siege of Kerchesten*.

I drew myself up on the threshold like every outraged cuck-
old in every comedy de Ferric ever wrote and said, "You have
the wrong room." Corinna's taste in men was frequently ghastly.

"Oh, I don't think so," he said. And paused. And smirked.
"Maselle Cressida." Cressida was the code name I'd had in
the Bastion, when I'd been a spy; anyone who used it was therefore a spy from the Bastion himself, and oh didn't that just put
the hatpin through an already foul day.

The door swung shut behind me, and I heard the bolt thump
home.

I could have screamed, like a good little bourgeoise, or fainted, like the ingenue I was getting too old to play. I said, "Who are you?" and made sure I said it crossly.

"Come now, maselle," he said in Kekropian. "Surely you do not believe I will give you my real name. Why don't you call me Vulpes?"

The Midlander word for fox. So he knew about Mildmay. "Very well, Messire Vulpes," I said and swept him a curtsy, more to relieve my feelings than out of any real hope it would annoy him. "Now that I know who you are, may I ask what you're doing in my dressing room?"

"*Lieutenant* Vulpes, please," he said finickingly. "And I should think that would be obvious, Maselle Cressida. I have come from Major Goliath."

"Of course you have," I said, all weary irony; *he* couldn't tell that my mouth had gone dry. "General Mercator is dead, then?" I had prayed—actually *prayed*—that when Mercator died, his spymaster Louis Goliath would be caught in any purging Mercator's successor decided to do. Clearly, I was not that lucky.

"General Parsifal's *caefidus* arrived this morning."

Gemma Parsifal. A great many people must still be smarting from the debacle of Malkar Gennadion, if Gemma Parsifal had been appointed to the generalship.

"What do you want?"

Vulpes shrugged fussily and said, "Information."

"What sort of information?"

"*Useful* information. Will anyone bother us in here?"

"No," I said. "And if you're waiting for me to invite you to sit down, you're going to be standing an awfully long time."

"Temper, temper," he said and wagged a chiding finger at me, sitting down on the less rickety of my two chairs. I wanted to force-feed him that finger, and the hand it was attached to, but he was a wizard. I'd never even get close to him. And coming as he did from Louis Goliath, anything I did to harm him would only rebound tenfold onto my own head. Or someone else's.

But I didn't have to roll over and show my belly, either. And there was some value in playing the thing grimly out—no shortcuts. "Can you prove that you are what you say you are?"

"And what is it that I say I am, Maselle Cressida?"

"A creature of Louis Goliath's."

His smile disappeared, and I was glad to see it go. "I am no one's creature, maselle. But I am here on Major Goliath's behalf. Will his seal be sufficient proof?"

"It will do," I said negligently, as if he bored me.

He took a folded half-sheet of paper out of his pocket; he had lifted the seal cleanly, and it was Louis Goliath's signet all right, that thing that looked like a badly drawn wheel but was really a spiderweb. "And I have a token for you."

He was smirking again as he handed me a grubby slip of paper. I gave it only a glance, only enough to know who had written those straggling words. Nothing more.

I inspected the seal with far greater care, then gave Vulpes a long, slow, considering look, the sort my grandfather had used to spectacular effect on wives and children and intransigent players. It made Vulpes fidget. "Oh very well," I said, turning away from him indifferently. "I don't suppose you have either the skill or the balls to have forged Major Goliath's seal." And then, as if I'd forgotten about him entirely, I sat down at my dressing table and began repinning my hair.

Vulpes's face, as reflected in my mirror, was a treat. I'd learned a lot about wizards from observing Felix Harrowgate over the past two years, and one thing I'd learned was that wizards were completely unprepared to have an annemer ignore them. They didn't know what to do with it—especially wizards who had spent any amount of time in Mélusine, where the Cabaline wizards were marked by their rings and barbaric tattoos, and where the common people were deathly afraid of them.

I'd found, though, that compared to old-school Eusebian wizards, Cabalines were a collection of indolent and good-natured tabby cats. And Vulpes, for all his swagger, was not a Eusebian of the old school. He was not Louis Goliath.

If he *had* been Louis Goliath, he would have had the sense to outwait me. I was the one with a performance of *Berinth the King* that evening; *I* was the one who had to placate *him* to get him out of my dressing room. But he let himself be rattled into forgetting that. He said, in a hard, falsely nonchalant voice, "I believe you know Gideon Thraxios?"

"I do," I said. I did not turn away from the mirror.

"What do you know *about* him?"

"He's a refugee from the Bastion. His tongue was cut out, so I assume he's one of those cultists." I made sure I continued to sound bored, half-distracted, as if it all meant nothing to me.

"And?" Vulpes prompted, confirming my suspicion that he had come from the Mirador. He knew perfectly well what "and," or he wouldn't be trying to make me tell him.

"I didn't realize your curiosity was vulgar," I said—dear God, if I sounded any more bored I'd have to pretend to fall asleep. "He's Felix Harrowgate's lover."

"Is it a relationship of long standing?"

"They've been lovers for as long as I've been in Mélusine. Nearly two years."

"Is the relationship a, er, happy one?"

I slewed round to stare at him, the gesture just exaggerated enough to sting. "In what sense, lieutenant? As the knight and his lady in a romance? Or are you asking me if Messire Thraxios is sexually satisfied?"

He was too swarthy to show a blush, but I knew I'd offended his prudish Eusebian soul. He said stiffly, "Do they quarrel?"

I didn't try to bite back a shout of laughter. "Do they *quarrel*? You realize that's the same as asking if Felix has a pulse?"

He glared at me. "Do you think their quarrels are serious?"

"Meaning, do I think Felix would ever throw Gideon out? Not a chance."

"What about Messire Thraxios? Might he leave?"

"Where would he go?" I said callously.

"I . . . see." He changed the subject briskly: "Why has Messire Thraxios not sworn the Cabaline oaths?"

"Surely you're better qualified than I am to answer that question."

"But I'm asking you, Maselle Cressida. Why?"

"I don't know. I try not to have anything to do with Cabaline politics."

"That will have to change."

"You would do better to cultivate a wizard."

"Who says I'm not?" His smile was sharp and ugly. "But still, maselle, I have asked you, and I should like you to answer."

"And I did. I told you. I don't know."

"Oh, come now. Your lover has told you nothing? I find that hard to believe."

I said lightly, "Mildmay doesn't like to talk about what he calls 'hocus-stuff.'"

"Then you will have to induce him." But at least he seemed to believe that I didn't know anything, for he stood up, saying as he moved unhurriedly toward the door, "I will expect you to be a good deal more informative next time, Maselle Cressida."

"But what do you want to know?" I said. The exasperation in my voice was quite real; I only hoped it was adequate cover for the equally real desperation that was cold lead in the pit of my stomach. "Why Gideon hasn't become a Cabaline—"

"You have a wide *acquaintance* among the court," he said with a sneer. "Use it. Go trawling. I will tell you if you find anything interesting."

The door shut behind him with a small, decisive snick. I waited, but when a full minute had passed and he had not popped back in like the Necromancer in the pantomimes so popular in the Lower City, I concluded he had really gone. *Then* I let myself look at that grubby slip of paper and touch the inky blotches of Hallam Bellamy's fingerprints.

I'd let Mildmay believe Hallam was dead, and God forgive me, sometimes I wished he was. They had broken his fingers, cut off both his thumbs; I was trying not to wonder how he'd held a pen at all.

SO SORRY TABBY was all he'd written, in sprawling, clumsy letters I didn't need my spectacles to read, that and a squiggle that was a sad travesty of his wizard's sigil. I sagged down across my dressing table, pillowing my head on my forearms. Once you sell your soul to the Bastion, you never get it back.

Mildmay

The cult of Felix worked like usual on the Empyrean staff. The ushers fell over each other to get us into the second-best box. The best box was for the Teverii, just in case one of them decided to come. Lady Victoria never did. Lord Stephen came for premieres, and he'd come to see *The Tragedy of Horatio* three times. Lord Shannon came a lot. Small favors—tonight the Teverius box was empty. Which meant Felix was in a good mood. He was telling a story about the lady in the box opposite and who the father of her third son was supposed to be. Gideon grinned, and he must've said something, because Felix laughed out loud. They'd forget I was here in a minute or two. We might go backstage after the play, if Felix was feeling nice, and then we'd go back to the Mirador. They'd go into their bedroom, and

I'd go into mine. I'd lay there and pretend like I didn't have a clue what was happening on the other side of the wall.

Mehitabel wouldn't be alone tonight 'less she wanted to be.

By the time the curtain went up on *Berinth the King*, it was too late for the story to save me from my own stupid head. The best it could do was distract me for a while, but everything was waiting for me when the play was over, right where I'd left it.

We did go backstage for a minute, but it would've been smarter of me not to. You get in moods sometimes where you have to prove to yourself that the world is a pile of shit. So Felix and Gideon hung around in the stage-lobby while Felix flirted with Corinna Colquitt—she knew it wasn't going no place, but it didn't do her no harm to be seen flirting with him. And Gideon just watched, smiling a little. Madame Colquitt wasn't no threat to him.

I went back to Mehitabel's dressing room. Something about the play had pissed her off. I knew that as soon as I walked in the door, just in the way she was pulling the pins out of her hair. Probably Madame Dravanya, because so far as I could tell *everything* about Madame Dravanya pissed Mehitabel off.

So I went and opened my stupid mouth. "Surprised I beat the rush."

"What's *that* supposed to mean?"

"Usually, I can't see you for all the boy-toys."

Her back was always straight—it was the way she carried herself, like a queen—but I saw it go stiff. She didn't turn around, just gave me a look like pure black murder in the mirror and said, "If I didn't know better, I'd think you were jealous."

Meaning, don't pull this shit on me. Because, powers and saints, we'd *had* that fight, gone round and round 'til we were both dizzy and sick with it. And what it all came down to was, I couldn't marry her, and she wouldn't've had me if I could. I knew I should be glad she was willing to have anything to do with me at all—even if it was mostly fucking—and, you know, if I didn't like it, wasn't nobody forcing me to keep showing up to get kicked in the teeth. I just, I don't know, I wanted her to want me for more than my cock, and I wasn't sure she did.

Right now, from the look on her face, she didn't want me at all. "Were you like this with Ginevra, or did she pander properly to your masculine vanity? Before she dumped you, of course."

My breath hitched in like she'd hit me, and, powers, I kind of felt like she had. And sacred bleeding *fuck* I must have caught her on the raw, because she'd never said nothing *that* nasty to me before, and we'd never talked about Ginevra at all. Mehitabel'd always pretended like she didn't know, even though we both knew she did.

I opened my mouth, shut it again. Mehitabel said, "You call me by her name in bed sometimes. When you say anything at—oh for God's sake! Would you just go away already?"

Somehow, it seemed like good advice. I went.

Mehitabel

Mildmay shut the door behind him carefully—a tidy-minded man, he was—and I made a face at my reflection. "Oh, very well played. What will you do for an encore, kick him in the crotch?"

It wasn't that I'd lied—he did sometimes call me Ginevra. It was just that I'd never meant to tell him. Unless of course, I thought, disliking myself intensely, I'd just been saving it. Because I knew exactly why I'd said it. I was scared and angry and needed to lash out at *someone*. And Mildmay was safe. I knew he'd forgive me. The worst of it was that I actually felt calmer, better able to attend to tonight's business with a clear head.

Corinna and Susan between them had the Empyrean's ushers and prompt-boys well trained, and I hadn't hesitated to take advantage of that. The prompt-boys in particular loved the sense of intrigue—God only knows what stories they told each other about our goings-on. So there'd been no difficulty in finding out which boxes were being used tonight.

Lionel Verlalius had come, but he'd brought his fiancée—an insipid creature and I hoped he'd be as happy with her money as he thought he would. Barnabas and Harcourt Malanius were in their family box, but I *really* wasn't in the mood for a threesome, and picking one over the other wasn't worth the resulting aggravation. Arthur Lelius, Rudolph Novadius . . . Felix, who was not himself a problem—or even a factor—but I hadn't needed an exasperating and time-consuming scene to know that Mildmay *was* a problem.

I'd been right about that.

But the prompt-boy had also told me that Lord Peter Jessamyn was attending the play, and I'd spotted him myself: Peter Jessamyn, sitting alone and meek as an anchorite's cat in the box he and several other wizards had gone shares in for the season.

Peter Jessamyn was ideal for my purposes; I'd sent him a primly worded note in the first intermission, to which he'd responded, equally primly, in the second. And since Peter could hardly be expected to be enthusiastic with Mildmay playing Eofor Henning all over the place, I'd cleared the stage the quickest—and dirtiest—way I could. I'd told the doorman to stop everyone else.

I was glad of the knock on the door; feeling guilty about something you've done on purpose is a terrible waste of time. And I liked Peter: middle-aged, nondescript, soft-bellied and soft-handed, and a keen and cynical observer of the Mirador's politics. Also a considerate and imaginative lover. Not as good as Mildmay—*no one* was as good as Mildmay, who sometimes seemed to forget that he, too, had a right to climax—but a charming bed-companion. And he liked having me on top.

We went to The Harpy's Kiss, where Peter had thoughtfully bespoken the Rose Room and a late supper. We talked about the play while we ate; Peter nearly made me choke with a wickedly accurate imitation of Susan Dravanya, and I retaliated by describing, and even acting out bits of, the mimed and furious cat-fights that were an inevitable part of life backstage. "One of these days, Drin *is* going to murder Bartholmew and then go shooting out on stage with his hands covered in blood. Because it will never occur to him to wash them."

"Well, as long as he waits until the fifth act," Peter said reasonably and grinned at me over the rim of his wineglass.

I grinned back. It was easy with Peter. We enjoyed sex with each other; we enjoyed gossiping with each other. He appreciated the cachet of being my paramour—Mildmay's scornful cant term "boy-toy" echoed unpleasantly in my head—and I quite liked having a lover who wasn't high-profile, who didn't have to please anyone but himself. And who didn't *want* anything from me except bone-rattlingly good sex.

We managed that all right, and in the aftermath, lying together companionably to wait and see if Peter was going to be good for a second round—sometimes he was, and sometimes he wasn't—it was easy for me to trace one of the swirls of his tattoos and say, "Did these hurt very much?"

"Oh, you know. Not much more than setting yourself on fire."

"Why do you *do* it?"

"Become a Cabaline? Well, the alternative is to be a heretic and get set on fire for real."

I shuddered and I wasn't entirely faking. "You could leave."

He shook his head. "Wouldn't want to. And being a Cabaline is worth a little pain."

"Why? I don't understand why anyone would want to . . ."

"You're annemer. You can't understand."

"Try me. Why is it better to be Cabaline than to go to the Coeurterre or the schools in Norvena Magna?"

"You really want to know," he said, half skeptically.

"It puzzles the living snot out of me," I said promptly, and he laughed, distracted.

"Different wizards will give you different answers, of course, and the Virtu has a good deal to do with it, too."

"I don't understand *that*, either."

"My sweet, if you want me to explain thaumaturgic architecture to you as well, we're going to be here all night."

Thaumaturgic architecture was his specialty; he probably wasn't exaggerating. "No, I don't," I said firmly. "Just tell me why *you* wanted to be a Cabaline."

"That question's not much better. But all right. When I was young, I thought I wanted to be powerful, and all I knew about power, growing up in Breadoven, was that the Mirador had it. By the time I was actually ready to swear the oaths, I knew I wasn't powerful and wasn't going to be. So one answer to your question is that becoming a Cabaline offered protection. The warding spells, you know. And a chance to do my work in peace. And . . ." He was frowning. "I don't think I can explain the rest of it. But I suppose I like feeling that I'm part of something much larger and much older than myself."

"You're right," I said, smiling at him. "I am no wiser than I was." A lie, since protection was a very good reason indeed for Gideon to want to become a Cabaline. I kissed Peter's nose. "Are there lots of wizards who feel that way—I mean, did you have a lot of competition?"

"Competition?" he said blankly.

"Well, they don't take everyone who asks, do they?"

"Powers, no!" That was genuine, appalled horror; I let myself laugh.

"So how do they decide? And who does the deciding anyway?"

He told me about the Curia and the complicated systems of sponsorship and patronage and the list of criteria—some of which seemed exceptionally nebulous and vulnerable to interpretation—and I listened and wished I could take notes.

When I'd heard enough, it was very easy to shut him up. And it turned out he was good for a second round after all.

Mildmay

Oh, I was in a shitty mood. It was just as well Felix and Gideon wouldn't have noticed me if I'd got up on the table and started dancing, because I *would* have picked a fight with Felix, just because I could. That kind of mood.

I went into my room and threw myself on the bed. I sat there and stared at the wall—the other side was Felix and Gideon's bedroom and Kethe knows what they were doing in there, I didn't want to—and spun my butterfly knife, first one way, then the other. I'd used to do it for practice, when I was a knife-fighter—and for swank, too. And then it got to be a habit, and I'd never got around to making myself quit.

And powers and saints, it was better than thinking.

But sometimes, no matter how much you don't want to, you get to thinking anyway. And after a while, a thought got in my head. If I was calling Mehitabel Ginevra—and no matter how mad she was at me, she wouldn't make up something like that—then there was something wrong. Something very fucking wrong.

And it wasn't Mehitabel's problem, neither.

See, Ginevra was dead. She'd been dead for indictions. We'd been lovers, and we'd crossed Vey Coruscant, who was boss of Dassament and a blood-witch besides. And when the Dogs got on my track, Ginevra walked out on me, walked straight back to her stupid poet. And a decad later, she was dead. Somebody'd told Vey Coruscant how to find her. And the cade-skiffs had dragged her out of the Sim with her throat cut.

All at once, I had to move or I was going to start screaming. It was past the septad-night so I wasn't likely to meet anybody else wandering around. I let myself out of the suite and started walking. I didn't care where I was going. Truth to tell, I didn't notice. I was thinking about Ginevra, like a knot you can't untie and you can't fucking leave alone.

I hadn't realized it had got so bad. I know how stupid that sounds, but blessed saints, if I'd *known* I was calling her Ginevra, I wouldn't've fucking done it. I'd known I was still dreaming about Ginevra, but I'd kind of got used to it—got to where it seemed like it was normal, and maybe that was the problem.

I was dreaming about a dead girl maybe two or three nights in the decad. That couldn't be good, could it? I mean, I ain't big into dream-casting or nothing, but you didn't fucking need to be. And so what I was doing while I limped around the Mirador was trying to figure out how to shut it down. Which, yeah, I should've been working on a long fucking time ago, but I couldn't do nothing about that.

"So what *is* the big fucking deal?" I said out loud in the Buried Rotunda because there wasn't nobody around to hear. It wasn't like I'd never known anybody dead before. And sure, I'd loved her, but I couldn't hardly remember her no more. I mean, I remembered things about her, but I didn't remember *her*, and I knew it.

Well, what did you do when somebody died?

You went to their grave. But I didn't know where she was buried. Probably out in the Ivorene where I'd never find her.

You made offerings, burned a lock of their hair or something of theirs you still had, to a saint or the god they'd particularly followed or Phi-Lazary or Cade-Cholera. But I didn't have nothing. Not *nothing*.

You got together with other folks what knew them and had a wake, but even if any of Ginevra's friends were still alive, they sure as fuck wouldn't want to talk to me.

You settled your debts with them. You did things they hadn't gotten finished. You found answers to questions they'd been asking.

And there, finally, I caught hold of the end of something I could use. Because there were questions, oh fuck were there questions, and they all clustered around when Ginevra had died. Somebody'd sold me to the Dogs. I didn't know who. But it got me out of the way real neat. Somebody'd sold Ginevra to Vey Coruscant. I didn't know who'd done that, neither. I didn't know if it was the same person had done both. Or not. And I didn't know which idea I hated worse.

And well, fuck, Milly-Fox, if you got questions, then you need to talk to somebody with answers.

I knew right where to go, too. There wasn't no problem about that. The *problem* was that it meant going down in the Arcane and, well, me and the Lower City weren't exactly on speaking terms no more.

How bad you want them answers, Milly-Fox?

But I knew ways to go—secret or forgotten or just not used—and I figured I could get where I was going without getting lynched.

I could probably even get back again.

Felix

Gideon sighed, his body tensing in climax, his hands knotting in the sheets. He was very good; he never tried to touch my head when I did this for him. I swallowed copper-salt warmth, my throat muscles working around him, and then eased slowly back, kissing his thigh, the line of his hipbone, buying myself what time I could.

Gideon touched my shoulder gently, almost shyly. :Do you want to . . . ?:

Neither of us ever said the word.

I *didn't* want to, particularly, but saying so would only lead to another of our increasingly frequent, futile arguments, and I wanted that even less.

I went carefully, slowly, biting the inside of my lower lip when the urge for power got too strong. Gideon was sacrificing as much of his autonomy as he could in submitting to me—and he could not think of it in any other way. I could not be so ungrateful as to tell him it wasn't enough, especially when the one time I had dared hint at the ways of tarquins and martyrs, his revulsion had been all too palpable.

Gideon thought submission was demeaning. I knew it disturbed him that he enjoyed it, that I could make it good for him. He never asked me to submit in return, and it was something I could not offer. The words jammed and died in my throat even in imagination.

He achieved no more than half-hardness, although I kissed

the knobs of his spine, stroked him, used clever caresses I'd
learned at the Shining Tiger. Finally, he said, :Don't bother
about me. Once is all I'm good for tonight.:

:Are you sure?:

:Please. Just go ahead.:

My teeth sank into my lip until I tasted blood. Bright pain kept
my hands gentle against Gideon's hips as I thrust and strove and
finally climaxed. We cleaned up silently, and then, finally, I could
escape into sleep.

In my mental construct of Mélusine, Horn Gate was now
bound open by wisteria vines. It led to the Khloïdanikos and
nowhere else. I kept the other gates closed and tried to ignore
the so-called Septad Gate, where even in my construct, the truth
bled through and the Sim exited the city. The Khloïdanikos was
the only oneiromancy I was interested in.

Thamuris and I had been meeting for two years, and the
Khloïdanikos's geography was warping itself very slowly around
us. Horn Gate had a stable location now, a brisk walk past a ruined orchard wall to the bench which Thamuris and I had chosen
as our meeting place.

I stopped, as I always did, to check on the mostly dead perseïd
tree that stood against the ruined wall. I didn't know if the tree
still retained any symbolic connection to the waking world, but it
had been linked to Mildmay, to the huphantike that Thamuris had
cast and that I, in my blind arrogance, had enacted. It might have
been superstition or it might have been penance—either way, I
could not enter the Khloïdanikos without making sure that the
perseïd still had some life in it, even if only a bare handful of
green leaves.

I had learned not to hope for more.

The tree looked as bleak as ever tonight, and I did not linger.
Thamuris was waiting, stretched out on the bench and staring up
at the stars. He preferred the Khloïdanikos at night, when myriad paper lanterns stood beside the path, hung from the bridges,
floated on the koi pond, nestled in the branches of the perseïd
trees. The moon did not wax and wane here, but bloomed always
full and beautiful in the sky; the stars, against the velvety blackness of the sky, glittered in constellations that neither Thamuris
nor I could recognize.

The astrologia of the Khloïdanikos was an abiding mystery,

one we returned to again and again. "Any progress?" I asked, by rote.

"Well," Thamuris said, swinging upright with an ease he hadn't had in the waking world for three years or more, "I found Astrape."

I goggled at him unbecomingly. "You're joking. Where?"

"Where Hydrastra should be."

"You *are* joking." But I looked south, to where the cluster of seven stars should have been, and sure enough, recognizable now that I knew what I was looking at, there was the bright cruel light of Astrape, named for the lightning the ancient Troians had thought she governed.

"And Hydrastra?" I said after a moment.

"Yes. Where Astrape should be."

"So they put the sky in upside down."

"And backwards. It's harder to tell, but I'm pretty sure *that*"—and he pointed to the west—"is the upside down mirror image of Arktidion."

"This is going to give me a headache," I said. "Have you a theory yet as to *why*?"

"It seems to me that it might have something to do with, um . . . well, with why the Khloïdanikos has remained extant— remained *stable*—for centuries."

"Which is certainly a question deserving of an answer. Go on, Thamuris. Tell me."

For all that he was a Celebrant Celestial, Thamuris was self-deprecating to the point of insecurity about his intellectual abilities. I had learned to tread carefully, not to say things that would sound condescending or as if I were merely humoring him when I listened to him.

He said, "From what Khrysogonos and I have been able to find, which isn't much, the weakness of most oneiromantic constructs was that they needed periodic reinforcement. Otherwise they collapsed into the dreams of the person who made them or—if I understood the passage correctly, which I may not have—just dissolved back into the waking world. Or both, maybe. The monograph I've been reading is written in a dialect I'm not very good with."

"Either, or even both, would make a certain amount of sense. But what does it have to do with this lunatic sky?"

"Well, those stars aren't going to collapse back into the waking world, are they?"

"No," I said, looking at Astrape so egregiously out of place. "And you couldn't just *dream* them, either. It must have taken a great deal of work."

"Oh yes," Thamuris said. "And I think it works like . . . like an armature. Once they set the stars, it didn't matter if the garden shifted a little here and there. Because those stars—"

"They're not a dream," I said. "They're thaumaturgic architecture."

"If you say so," Thamuris said doubtfully.

"No, really. It makes sense. And you're right. It explains why the Khloïdanikos doesn't seem to need . . . anything. And why there are ghosts."

"You lost me."

"Think about it! The stars—to get them like that, they must have picked a particular day, mapped them all out, transposed them. It's why the moon doesn't have phases, either. There's *one day* in the Khloïdanikos. Well, one day and one night, but you know what I mean. So everything that happens in it, happens at once."

"Now I'm getting a headache," Thamuris said. "So why haven't we run into ourselves, then?"

"Who's to say we won't? I think it's a very *slow* day, and since we can find either night or day . . . I don't know."

"You think I'm right, though?"

"I'm sure of it. Those stars are what keep the boundary. And that's why we've never found the walls, either."

"Sorry?"

"When we went looking for the boundaries. We didn't find them, because they're up there." I jabbed an emphatic finger at the night sky. "The gardens can go on forever, as long as they've got that sky overhead."

"That's . . . very odd."

"It's *brilliant*. I would never have thought of holding a boundary that way." I sat a moment, contemplating. "Do you suppose we can work out what day they used?"

"The astrologists have charts—I know that much. I can send Khrysogonos to plague them. Does it matter?"

"Probably not. But I *would* like to know just how long this has been . . ." Not "here," because this wasn't a place. Not exactly. "Has been extant. It might help us figure out how and why the Khloïdanikos *does* change. Because it does."

"Yes," Thamuris said. "And I admit, I have been wondering a little if the boundary is, um, permeable both ways."

"What do you mean?"

"I can't explain it. Not yet. Let me marshal my thoughts first."

"You don't have to mount a defense against me."

"I know." But his smile was nervous, fleeting. "You're just . . . you can be a little overpowering, you know. And I don't . . . I should go."

"Thamuris!" I caught his wrist, and then flinched back. I was usually careful not to touch him, for I could feel the consumption in him when I did. I risked a smile, half in apology. "I know I get excited about things. But I've never wanted to make you feel . . ."

"Crushed beneath your advance?" he said dryly. "It's all right, Felix. Just let me take things at my own pace."

"All right. If you're sure—"

"It's who you are. I don't expect you to change."

He couldn't know why that made me wince—an echo of Gideon I did not want, a reminder of my own foolishness in believing it could be true—and I said hastily, "I'll try to remember not to browbeat you in the future."

That got a proper smile. "Don't make promises you can't keep. But I really do need to go. Xanthippe wants to show me to a healer visiting from Theodosia."

"But I'll see you Jeudy?" I couldn't keep the anxiety out of my voice.

"Of course," he said and strode away with a vigor and briskness he only had here, in this garden of dreams.

I stayed until the Mirador's dawn, watching the twisted constellations in the Khloïdanikos's immutable sky.

Mildmay

Felix hated the Lower City. For him, it was all about hate, the way he hated Pharaohlight and Simside, the way he'd hated his keeper and his pimp. He didn't get why I missed it, didn't get how I could ever have been okay with my life there. And he didn't get that I'd been brought up to hate the Mirador the same way he hated the Lower City. He hadn't lived in the districts where the Mirador went witch-hunting. He'd only seen that from the Mirador's side, where it got called "necessary purging"—and you want a phrase to spook you the fuck out? Think about that one for a while. Nobody in the Mirador really understood that Cerberus Cresset being the Witchfinder Extraordinary was a reason for somebody to want him dead. And I was only in the Mirador because of Felix. Last fucking place I'd ever thought I'd end up. He didn't get that, either.

I was sort of wishing I did hate the Lower City the way Felix did, because then walking through the Arcane wouldn't've hurt so fucking much. Wouldn't've been like a list of things I couldn't do no more, places I couldn't go, people I couldn't talk to. And, you know, it did hurt. And it hurt worse because I couldn't tell nobody about it. Nobody who'd listen to me could understand what I meant. And the people who'd understand were never going to fucking listen. They'd say I'd made my choice and it was too fucking bad if I didn't like it.

Three hookers and two pushers gave me the come-on in the three blocks I walked down Rue Souterraine between the back alleys of the Limerent and the Goosegirl's Palace. I guess they figured my money was good anyway.

The bouncer on the side door of the Goosegirl's Palace recognized me straight off. I knew him, too. Tiny d'Orisco. Biggest guy I've ever laid eyes on—six and a half feet tall and almost as broad.

"You," he said.

"Me," I said and waited, not in grabbing distance. I could hurt Tiny in a brawl, but he could hurt me way worse.

"Whatcha want?"

"Talk to Elvire."

Tiny grunted. He gave me the sort of look he gave drunk guys just before he bounced them, then stuck his head in the door and yelled at one of the eunuchs to tell Elvire that Mildmay the Fox was on the doorstep.

"If she tells me to joint and gut you, you know I'll be happy to oblige," Tiny said while we were waiting.

"I know," I said. She could, too. I was betting she wouldn't, because the thing I knew about Elvire was that she was a junkie for information. She wouldn't turn me away if she thought I had something she could use. I hoped, anyway.

And the eunuch came trotting back and said as how madame would see me, so I'd won the toss.

Elvire's look wasn't much warmer than Tiny's, but she waved me to a seat. "What do you want?" She had that perfect flash voice that nobody knew if she'd come by natural or been trained like Felix had. I'd heard Felix slip a time or two, but never Elvire.

"I don't want to make trouble," I said, "and I ain't here 'cause anybody sent me."

She gave me the hairy eyeball. "I see. And how do you suggest we prove that?"

I very nearly said, *Why don't you get out the thumbscrews?* but I was afraid she'd take me up on it.

"Look," I said. "S'pose I tell you what I want. Then you can decide what you think." She gave me a grudging sort of nod. I told her what I wanted.

"That's old information," she said. "You only want this for yourself?"

"Swear it on anything you like."

"What makes you think," she said—and she still sounded like a plate of icicles, but she couldn't quite sound as bored as she wanted. Elvire loved the hunt. "What makes you think that anyone will remember?"

"C'mon, Elvire. It ain't *that* old, and there were people watched Vey Coruscant's doings pretty close."

Elvire signed herself against hexes. "Is it true you killed her?"

"Yeah. Thought that was common knowledge."

"Rumor is rumor," she said. "What do I get out of this—aside from the pleasure of having you in my house?"

"I'll pay you what I can, but it ain't much." Felix would give me all the money I wanted, but he'd want to know what it was for.

"To think the day would come when I would hear Mildmay the Fox say that." She gave me a look like curdled poison. "I don't need your money. Is it true that Felix Harrowgate is also Methony Feucoronne's son?"

"Yeah."

She smiled. I wondered how much somebody was going to pay her for that, and I wondered why the fuck they wanted to know. "I will look. Do you expect me to send you billets-doux in the Mirador?"

"I ain't that dumb," I said. "I'll come back on Huitième and ask."

She nodded. I'd given myself away—never, *never* let anybody know how bad you want something when you're bargaining. But it was sort of okay with Elvire. She'd jack up the price—more secrets that weren't mine to give, most likely—but she wouldn't lie to me, whether she hated me or not. As far as things like that went in the Lower City, she was trustworthy.

That far and no farther.

Chapter 2

Mildmay

I thought we were going to make it out of court okay. Felix wasn't stopping to pick a fight with nobody, and nobody seemed minded to pick a fight with him. But just as we got to the door, one of the pages comes trotting up and squeaks, "Please, my lord, His Lordship wants you."

Although all the hocuses and flashies pretend like everybody's title means the same, there's only one "His Lordship" and that's Stephen Teverius. "Thank you," Felix said, and the two of us turned around and hiked all the way back down the Hall of the Chimeras to the dais, where Lord Stephen was waiting.

"My lord," Felix said and bowed, and I stood there and racked my brains trying to think of what he could've done this time to make Lord Stephen mad. It turned out, though, it wasn't nothing to do with Felix specially, just that somebody had to hold the baby—meaning the Bastion's messenger. He was what the Bastion called a caefidus, somebody who had sworn oaths to the Bastion but was annemer, not a hocus. Kind of like the obligation d'âme and kind of a shitty hole to be stuck in, if you ask me.

Felix had other things to do Lundy afternoon and started to say so, but Lord Stephen said, "Don't argue. Simon Barrister will talk to them for you. *You*'re going to be nice to Messire Perrault this afternoon. Don't lose him."

Felix opened his mouth, shut it again, and said, "Yes, my lord."

Lord Stephen waved the messenger forward. He was a middle-aged Grasslander, dark and with lines on his face like he frowned a lot. Good hands. "Lord Felix has graciously agreed to put himself at your disposal this afternoon," the Lord Protector said. He watched the two of them shake hands like he wanted to be sure it happened, and then left.

Mr. Perrault said, "I hope I do not inconvenience you, Lord Felix."

"Not a bit," Felix said. "What would you like to do with the afternoon?"

Mr. Perrault looked a little sheepish, but he brought it out anyway. "I should very much like to walk around the Mirador with someone who knows it."

"Nothing could be better," Felix said. "Just a moment."

He flagged down a pageboy and dragged him aside. It wasn't a long message, whatever it was, because in less than a minute the boy went haring off and Felix came back. He picked up the conversation right where he'd left it. "Roaming around the Mirador is my favorite hobby. Anything of special interest?" He started toward the door, Aias Perrault keeping step and me a couple paces behind, just like always.

Mr. Perrault laughed a little. "Considering that I cannot find my way from my room to this hall without the guidance of an adolescent boy, I scarcely feel qualified to say."

"People say us and the Bastion are on the same plan," I said. Because they did.

Mr. Perrault looked at me funny, like he hadn't thought I knew how to talk, but he said, "I do not know. Certainly, if it is true, it is not helpful."

"The Mirador is strange," Felix said. "Wizards who've lived here for twenty years get lost occasionally. And although it and the Bastion might once have been twins, they are no longer. Let's start at the top." He'd led the way to one of the narrow, twisty staircases that went to the Crown of Nails, the Mirador's highest ring of battlements. Oh fuck me sideways, I thought. I hated those stairs.

At least it was a pretty day. I sat down in a patch of sun, and Felix pointed out interesting bits of Mélusine to Mr. Perrault: the two cathedrals to Phi-Kethetin, the one in Spicewell, and the big fucking brick one up in Dimcreed. Ver-Istenna's dome. The Vesper Manufactory. Bercromius Park, which the Bercromii were hanging onto like bear-baiting dogs. Last open land of more'n about a septad-acre in the whole city. You could get in for a deca-centime on Cinquièmes, and a tour of the house was another septacentime. Only place in the city where the Sim looked like a river instead of just like death.

And then the other flashie houses in Roy-Verlant and

Lighthill and Nill, and Mr. Perrault said, "A strange name for a city district. I understand the word means 'nothing.' "

Felix gave me an eyebrow.

"Nighthill," I said, " 'cause it's on the west."

"My brother doesn't speak in riddles on purpose. The extended version would be that 'Nill' is a contraction of 'Nighthill' and the district was so named because it is, as you can see, on the west side of the Mirador."

"I see," said Mr. Perrault. "And which part of the city is it that you call the 'Lower City'—it is all lower than the Mirador, yes?"

"Um," said Felix. "That's not exactly what 'lower' means in this context, although"—and he waved an arm out vaguely southeast—"the ground does descend toward the St. Grandin Swamp as you go south. The Lower City is the oldest, poorest, and most crime-ridden quarter of Mélusine. I don't suggest going there without a, er, native guide."

"I have no intention of leaving the Mirador," Mr. Perrault said. He gave Felix a funny look. The pause was just long enough for me to know what he was going to ask next: "Is it true you yourself are from the Lower City?"

Felix had seen it coming, too. "Both of us are," he said, like it didn't cost him nothing to admit it. "Mildmay retains the native dialect."

Thank you so very fucking much, I thought.

"I meant no insult," Mr. Perrault said. I couldn't tell if he was talking to me or Felix. "As the child of sharecroppers, I have no high place from which to throw mud. I was merely curious."

"Curiosity is popularly agreed to have killed the cat," Felix said. I couldn't tell if it was a real warning, or if he was just fencing to see what Mr. Perrault would do.

What Mr. Perrault did was laugh. "Do you have any idea of the stories that are told about you in the Bastion?"

I don't think he could've shocked Felix more if he'd done it on purpose.

"Messire Gennadion made no secret of how he had contrived to break the Virtu," Mr. Perrault said, "and your Lord Protector has made no secret of how it was mended. Can you blame me for being curious?"

"How appalling," Felix said, and he sounded like he meant it. "I hope you don't believe everything Malkar said about me."

"I myself never met him—my duties keep me mostly away from the Bastion—but I know there is still debate over how much Messire Gennadion should have been listened to."

"The correct answer being: *not at all*. Malkar would never tell the truth if a plausible lie was available. I assure you, from fifteen years' experience of him, you should not believe anything for which he was your sole authority."

"Such as the idea that you are the linchpin of the Mirador's strength?"

"*Me?*" Felix burst out laughing. "Good gracious, no. I'm nothing more than a troublemaker. Ask Lord Stephen. Ask Lord Giancarlo."

"Messire Gennadion swore that your destruction would be the downfall of the Mirador."

"Did he?" Felix's mouth twisted. "I imagine he wanted to believe so, since it would provide a magnificent rationale for his desire to . . . destroy me. But it's certainly not true. Oh, I grant you that I'm the most powerful wizard in the Mirador, and I do sit on the Curia, but if I died tomorrow, the Mirador would go on without so much as a wobble. I'm afraid Malkar was merely telling you all what he wanted you to believe—an art he excelled at."

"But why did he want you dead?"

"I'm sure he hated me as much as I hated him. I'd given him reason."

"You are frank."

"About Malkar? I have no reason to be anything but. As I said, I hated him."

"And yet—"

"I know, I know!" Felix threw a hand up, like he was warding off a blow. "And yet I was his apprentice and his lover. If you had known him, Messire Perrault, you would understand that these were reasons to hate him."

"From what I know, I have never considered him anything other than reprehensible."

"I see. What you wanted to know was if I am like him. I am not."

Mr. Perrault actually went back a step, and I didn't blame him. Felix looked about ready to bite. I supposed I'd have to step in if things got really ugly, but I was hoping like fuck it didn't come to

that. Because I didn't want no part of this conversation. Didn't
want to think about Malkar Gennadion at all.

Or, to give him his real name, Brinvillier Strych.

Brinvillier Strych had been Mélusine's nightmare for a
Great Septad, since he killed Lady Jane Teveria. By burning her
to death in the middle of the Hall of the Chimeras. I'd heard
they'd had to replace some of the mosaic, but I'd never yet been
bored enough to see if I could spot the patch. The Mirador had
caught Strych, and they *said* they'd killed him, but it didn't
seem like that had worked so good. He'd got out somehow—or
maybe he really had died and had found a way back—and gone
north to the Norvenas, where he'd fucked up Mavortian von
Heber's life. And when it'd been long enough, he came back.
This time round, he called himself Malkar Gennadion, and he
found Felix in a Pharaohlight brothel and bought him and
trained him and got him into the Mirador.

And used him to break the Virtu.

Which Felix had fixed again, later, after we'd been all the
way across Kekropia and back. And I figured Felix was right
about Strych hating him, because that had drawn him back to
Mélusine, so as to be able to lay a trap for Felix.

Only he caught me instead.

And what he did to me . . .

Well, look. There's this thing in the Arcane called the Iron
Chapel and it's where you go for a meet if you want to absolutely guarantee that nobody's going to come across you by
accident. Because people don't go there. Nobody knows anymore who it's a chapel *to*, although we all got our ideas.
There's a grate in the middle of the floor, iron, probably older
than most of Mélusine and rusting to pieces one flake at a time.
People tell stories about what happens when the grate rusts
through, and they ain't the sort of stories that end with hugs
and kisses and happily-ever-after. But, I mean, since each bar
is as thick around as my arm, it ain't nothing I'm ever going to
have to worry about. Somebody built that fucker to *last*.

You don't touch the grate. But if you lay down on the floor
and look through it, you can see this kind of crack in the stone.
Not dressed. Nobody made it or meant for it to be there or nothing like that, and how far down it goes . . . well, your guess is as
good as mine. If it wasn't for the grate, somebody would've

found out by now, but I'll tell you right now they wouldn't be coming back to talk about it. The sewermen call it Mélusine's cunt, and there are days when I figure they ain't so far wrong. Because for sure if you try to fuck with Mélusine, you ain't getting your cock back.

And that's what the inside of my head was like, around where my memories of Strych should've been. I didn't know, and I didn't *want* to know, and I most especially didn't want to talk about it.

Lucky for me, Mr. Perrault backed right the fuck down. "I am sorry. I have been tactless."

"No, you have a right to wonder," Felix said. "I imagine I would wonder, too. But Malkar is not an edifying topic of conversation. Let's go in." He turned and started back down into the Mirador, and me and Mr. Perrault followed him.

Mehitabel

Rehearsals weren't getting any better.

Jean-Soleil, our impresario and part-owner of the Empyrean, insisted on doing a modern comedy after *Berinth the King*. I had nothing against Trevisan's *The Wrong Brother*, but I wished Jean-Soleil wouldn't bother—as I wished every time we did a comedy. Performances went well enough, but comedy was the Cockatrice's forte, not ours, and I thought we looked as stupid trying to compete with them as they looked performing tragedies to try to compete with us. Madeleine Scott, she of the famously henna'd hair, was the only real tragedienne they had, and she must have been nearly forty, for all that she tried to hide it.

And the Empyrean's company was not suited to comedy; the rehearsals brought out the worst in all of us.

Both Levry Tannenhouse and Bartholmew Hudson looked hungover, and I wondered if Adolphus Jermyn at the Cockatrice had been throwing out lures to Bartholmew again—he was watching Jean-Soleil with the "give me one good reason" expression we'd all gotten so tired of. Drin Baillie was sulking— ostentatiously and with one eye on his audience, as always. He'd made a pass at me just before rehearsal started, although perhaps calling it a pass was being too kind. Drin believed himself another Seigneur Christophe, misled by the reactions of middle-aged burghers' wives and shopkeepers to his profile, and he did not seem to realize that both Corinna and I knew exactly what he meant when he leaned close and murmured that he'd been dreaming of our kisses.

I'd fended him off with an elbow and said, "Clarisse got tired of you and you don't have another girl lined up." And I'd laughed, hard and deliberately, at the look of wounded reproach he gave me. Nothing but brutality would discourage Drin, and I had great faith in his self-love; once he was satisfied that everyone had noticed how he was suffering, he'd bounce back.

Susan Dravanya, the Empyrean's first tragedienne and my personal bête noire, was sulking because she felt comedy was beneath her. Susan was extremely beautiful, pale-skinned, and she rimmed her pansy-brown eyes with kohl and put belladonna in them to make them lambent. She had a deep, throbbing, mellifluous voice, and when well-coached in a role like Pasiphaë, Berinth's mad queen, she could make an audience's hair stand on end. But she had no comic timing, and she was as stupid as an owl. Every break we took was filled with that deep, throbbing, mellifluous voice complaining like a spoiled child denied a sweet.

For my part, as I waited in the wings for my entrance cue, my mind was more on Vulpes than the play. And I hated him for it.

I hated him for waking up the person I'd been, for resurrecting a past I'd thought safely buried and forgotten when I left the Empire behind me.

I should have known better. Should have thought things through. But I'd let my wishing do my thinking, in my Aunt Charmian's phrase, and now I was paying the price, for Vulpes had started the game three moves ahead, and it would take a stroke of luck bordering on the miraculous for me to catch up to him.

I desperately wanted to upend the situation and rid myself of him. But I couldn't. Just *couldn't*. I didn't know what they'd do to Hallam—I'd always been agonizingly careful *not* to know. Used every shred of my acting ability to keep Louis from guessing I was discontent. When I ran, there was no warning, no clues before or after. And they hadn't caught me. So there'd been no point in hurting Hallam, and I knew Louis Goliath, the spider.

He never did anything without an eye to its effect, never did anything petty or spiteful. It was one of the reasons he scared me to death.

But it was different now. The Bastion had no reason to trust me, and they knew it. Vulpes would have a way of communicating with Louis—wizards were clever about that sort of thing—and if I gave him any reason to be dissatisfied with me, Hallam was the one who'd suffer.

I remembered the last time I'd seen him, half a year before I ran. They'd cropped his hair, and for a moment all that registered was the staring bones of his skull, the great dark misery of his eyes. He was nothing but bone under lusterless skin, crippled, captive, chained by the spells of the Bastion like lead around his heart. He could never be freed, for even if the stress didn't kill him, those spells would, and I knew it would be a slow, suffocating death. Louis'd been very careful to explain it to me in the immediate aftermath of Hallam's capture.

Louis knew we'd been lovers; I could touch Hallam at least, trace the line of his cheekbone, give him a fragment of tenderness. But I was careful not to appear sympathetic, to say harshly, "God, Hallam, I *told* you not to run." And those dark eyes lowered, and he whispered, "I know. I'm sorry."

I hoped he'd understood later, when I'd run myself. Hoped wearily that he'd forgiven me.

Of course, I'd also hoped that my leaving the Bastion would be the end of it, and we could all see how well *that* had worked.

I pinched the bridge of my nose, half-listening to Bartholmew and Jean-Soleil shriek at each other like barrow-wives. It would be so easy, if only I didn't love Hallam. If I could say to Vulpes, "He's no concern of mine," and mean it. And I'd tried. I'd tried everything I knew to cut him out of my heart, to cauterize the raw bloody mess I'd let him make of me. And I couldn't. Couldn't get rid of the love. Or the guilt—for I should have stopped him from running, should have confessed my own plans, gotten him to wait, to be silent, to pretend acquiescence. But I'd protected myself, curled up in an armored ball like an armadillo, and he'd suffered for it. And the fact that I hated myself for it now meant absolutely nothing. Didn't change anything. Didn't redeem anything. It was just something else I had to live with as part of who I was.

And then Bartholmew started Act Two, and for a while I could be someone else.

Mildmay

Felix dragged Mr. Perrault all over the Mirador that afternoon. I limped along behind, feeling like I'd felt when I was a kid, and Nikah and Leroy would let me tag along after them, so long as I didn't get in trouble and didn't bother them. And it was worth it, too. Every once in a while, Felix would throw a question back at me, but mostly he talked. That was typical.

Mr. Perrault said "yes," and "no," and "fascinating," and not much more, but I could see the way he was forgetting to be stiff and formal. The cult of Felix in action. Once, during the winter—after Felix'd started drinking too much—his friend Edgar St. Rose had bet him that he couldn't work that trick on one of the Tibernians, the guys that Lord Stephen had had to let in to get the Mirador repaired and now couldn't get shut of. Felix had done it in less than half an hour, and I don't think I'd ever hated him quite as much as I did that night, watching him melt that poor guy with a smile he didn't even *mean*.

It hadn't lasted, of course, but it had worked for that half hour, and Edgar'd had to pony up a septagorgon. And it was working now on Mr. Perrault. When Felix could be bothered to do it, it most always worked. I thought that was why he generally couldn't be bothered, 'cause it was too easy, and it bored him, and maybe because it made him feel like a whore again.

We went most everywhere in the dayside of the Mirador, but I noticed Felix was being careful about where we *didn't* go. We didn't go up under the roofs anywhere, and he kept out of the Tiamat and the Grosgrain, where they were still working on the damage from the fire. I didn't know if it was along of not wanting to show Mr. Perrault—and the Bastion behind him—just how slow repairs were going, or along of him feeling guilty. That fire had sort of been his fault. Or at least that was how some people saw it.

Now, most of those "some people" were Thaddeus de Lalage, and I didn't think Felix should give a rat's ass what Thaddeus thought. But Felix wasn't built that way. Him and Thaddeus had been friends once, and I didn't think it was that Felix wanted to be friends again—the things he said about Thaddeus weren't no nicer than the things Thaddeus said about him—but it was like he couldn't quit caring. Even when he knew it wasn't doing him no good.

I was just as glad not to have to smell like smoke the rest of the day. And also glad not to have to listen to Felix going off about the Tibernians and how they weren't helping at all, just hanging around like vultures waiting for us to die.

And that was the other reason—now that I thought about it—Felix had taken that stupid bet. He really didn't like the Tibernians, most especially their hocus, and having them here itched at him almost as bad as it did at Lord Stephen.

So I figured he was probably being nice to Mr. Perrault on purpose, and I wasn't as surprised as I might've been when it turned out he'd put some thought into it. Along about sunset, Felix led Mr. Perrault to the Seraphine, where it turned out somebody'd put together a sort of little soirée. Hocuses, mostly the people Felix got along with—"friends" might be pitching it a little strong—plus a handful of Kekropians: Andromachy Sain, Elissa 'Bullen, Isaac Garamond, some others I didn't know. None of 'em with the Mirador's tattoos, and, I mean, nobody'd want to put Thaddeus in this kind of situation, but Felix *liked* Eric Ogygios, whose spine was all twisted from what his masters in the Bastion had done to him. He had a tongue on him like a cheese grater, and he hadn't forgiven the Bastion nothing. Eric would've made poor Mr. Perrault's life a misery, and Felix must have been tempted to invite him. But he hadn't.

All the same, though, he wasn't doing the Bastion no favors. These weren't people who were going to be sweet-talked into taking the offers of amnesty Mr. Perrault had brought. I'd seen Isaac Garamond all over Lord Giancarlo like a cheap coat, wanting to know how the oaths worked and what he'd have to do and when the Curia would be listening to petitions again. Which they weren't right now, along of the tantrum Felix had pitched over Gideon, but they couldn't hide from it forever.

And, you know, even the hocuses like Elissa Bullen who weren't all that excited about putting their souls in hock to the Mirador, even if the protection you got in return was the best to be had—Miss Bullen was talking about going farther west and maybe settling in Vusantine, not about going back to Kekropia.

Gideon wasn't here—I mean, not that he would've come—and neither were Simon and Rinaldo. And I bet Felix had been tempted to invite them. They'd probably still be in the Bastion if I hadn't got dumped in their cell when Strych got tired of me.

I wished they *were* here, though. Because at least they didn't mind talking to me, and they didn't look at me like I was going to bite them or give them plague or something. And even more than wishing they were here, I wished I was there, that I could just disappear like a hocus in a story, go off to Simon and Rinaldo's suite and play Long Tiffany until Felix was done. Felix teased me sometimes by calling me a duenna, and truth to tell, that was pretty much how I felt, like some old maid chaperone along to keep everybody else from having a good time.

The hocuses were happy enough to ignore me, though. It was easier on them. People didn't go around using the obligation d'âme no more, and the whole Mirador was pretty spooked by the fact that Felix had. It was worst for the hocuses who were trying to be friends with him, because the only people in stories who did the obligation d'âme were the bad guys, like Porphyria Levant. I'd thought more than once that Felix would be pretty fucking convincing as the bad guy in a story, but the obligation d'âme didn't have nothing to do with that.

I picked out a chair and settled in to watch. Dominic Jocelyn had a crush on Felix the size of a buffalo, and was trying hard to be witty to impress him. Felix was being nice and not letting on that he knew, but him and Fleur were giving each other these looks behind Dominic's back. Elissa Bullen and Charles the Dragon were doing everything but standing on their heads to make Aias Perrault happy, and he was even letting them.

I watched, and they let me alone, until Isaac Garamond came over and said, "Messire Foxe, we had hoped you would join us."

For fuck's sake, I thought, *why*? Mr. Garamond was maybe an indiction or two younger than Felix, about my height, sleek and bright-eyed like an otter. He wasn't one of my favorite people, but I didn't have what you might call a reason for it. I said, "Thanks, Mr. Garamond, but I'm okay over here."

"It must be very dull," he said.

"I'm okay," I said, instead of either agreeing with him or lying.

He looked at me, one of those hard looks like a trepan, and said, "I feel certain, Messire Foxe, that you are a more interesting person than you choose to appear."

Oh powers, what does this prick want? I didn't know what to

say to get rid of him without being rude, so I ended up not saying nothing at all.

He smiled and said, "As you wish." He went back to the hocuses. Whatever he said made them laugh.

Mehitabel

After the curtain went down on *Berinth the King*, my dressing room collected the usual flock of courtiers and gentlemen—what Mildmay called "flashies." Also, "boy-toys."

I swatted that thought irritably aside and took stock of my admirers—not for their talents in bed or their scandal potential, but whether they might know something Vulpes would find "interesting."

Most of them deserved to be called boy-toys; they hardly had two thoughts in their heads to rub together, much less anything to say that *anyone* would find interesting. I was thinking that Ashley Demellius might be the best of a bad lot—he was a featherwit, but also a gossip—when the door opened and like the saturnine answer to my prayers, Antony Lemerius came in.

He didn't bother to hide his impatience with the young men blocking the door, and I carefully didn't smile at the haste with which they got out of his way. Antony wouldn't find it funny.

I shifted my weight, dropped my shoulders a little, became the Mehitabel Parr Antony would want. Antony, thank God, was bored by stupidity rather than threatened by intelligence; he'd been one of the first to transfer his favor from Susan to me. But his sense of his own dignity was smothering, like the air on a really humid day in the Grasslands, and if you didn't measure up, he'd have nothing to do with you.

He was very like his father, whom he hated in the particularly venomous fashion reserved for those whose good graces we must cultivate. And his father, Philip Lemerius, was one of Lord Stephen's cronies. If there was anything stirring in the Mirador's inner circles, Antony would know about it.

And even if I didn't get a thing out of him, Vulpes couldn't accuse me of not having tried.

Set in the proper role like a custard in a form, I turned from my mirror, rationed out a smile of delight, and extended one hand toward Antony, letting my wrist carry the motion. "Lord Antony," I said, as he bowed over my hand, his lips brushing dryly against my skin. "I did not know you would be in attendance this evening." Carefully implied, that I would have dispensed with my untidy rabble of beaux if I *had* known.

"A last-minute impulse," Antony said, straightening but keeping his gaze on my face. "Rewarded sevenfold, if I may say so. You were magnificent."

"Thank you," I said. I didn't simper—Corinna did that, although I was trying to break her of the habit—but did lower my eyes briefly before meeting his again, as if I were modest enough to be a little flustered by the compliment. Susan always took praise, no matter how lavish, as no more than her due.

It took maybe a quarter hour to get the last and most ardent of my admirers to take himself off, but I was finally able to close my door with only Antony and myself on the right side of it. If it had been Peter, or Mildmay, I would have leaned dramatically against the door and said, in my best imitation of Susan, "At last, we are alone." As it was, I said merely, "Now we may be more comfortable," and crossed the room—a matter of five paces—to where he sat on the lumpy chaise longue.

I sat down beside him, slightly sideways, knees together, spine perfectly straight, letting the long skirts of my dress cascade and pool around me. I lowered my eyes, demure as an ingenue, and said, "What is your pleasure this evening, my lord?"

I held still when he brought his hand up to my chin, allowed him to tilt my head up. "You are my pleasure," he said, dark eyes burning, and leaned close to kiss me.

It isn't easy to participate in a passionate kiss when you want to giggle. But we could have come straight out of those luridly sentimental Ervenzian novels that Corinna devoured by the hundredweight: dialogue, stage business, and all. I quashed my sense of humor and indulged Antony in his desire to master me.

My sense of humor was controllable. What got away from me was the realization, as Antony's hands moved to grip my skull, that he was serving, in a horrible, only half-metaphorical way, as a proxy for Vulpes. It wasn't Antony who had made himself my master.

Antony pulled back. "Mehitabel?"

Oh God. He'd felt that sudden revulsion. I said, "I'm sorry. My head's a little sore. Aven's headdress is very uncomfortable." All of which was perfectly true, if not precisely germane.

His frown deepened. "I'm sorry. I had no intention of hurting you."

"I know," I said and softened my expression. "It's all right. Truly."

His face cleared, although he said, "I shouldn't have forgotten myself like that."

I remembered, with sudden and visceral vividness, a day in the summer when Felix had, for reasons best known to himself, let Mildmay off the leash. Mildmay had come to the Empyrean, sat quiet and good as gold watching our rehearsal, followed me, uncomplaining as ever, back to this dressing room when we were done. He'd listened as I raged about Susan and her vanity and her petty games and her monumental stupidity, and when I'd finally run down, like an overworked clock, he'd said, "You done?"

"Bored?" I'd said waspishly. "Yes, I suppose so."

"Hang on." He hadn't smiled, because he never did, but I'd seen the lightness in his eyes and trusted him.

He'd tipped the chair under the door handle, pointed me to this chaise longue, and proceeded to make love to me with his hands and mouth, and finally, when he had me so wild I was swearing at him in every language I knew, he fucked me, hard and deep, with all the power he usually kept carefully in check.

It wasn't until afterward that I realized I'd been screaming like a hunting cat and that everyone in the building must have known exactly what we'd been doing.

Corinna'd made Mildmay blush like a rose, leering at him in the stage-lobby, but he'd said as he was getting into the hansom I'd flagged for him, "I don't take it back." And for a man as shy and private as Mildmay, that was something remarkable.

He had made me forget myself. This genteel clinch was nothing. I murmured something vague and soothing, and encouraged Antony to try again. This time, I kept my mind on what I was doing, and predictably, after another round of restrained passion, he invited me back to the Mirador for the night—and to attend court with him in the morning.

I wondered, though I'd never ask, what Philip had done to annoy him this time.

I had no illusions about my place in Antony's life, no matter how courteously he might give me unnecessary help in rising from the chaise longue, how tenderly he might drape my wrap around my shoulders. I was a means to an end for him, just as much as he was for me. There was no doubt he enjoyed the sex, but what mattered to him was the next morning, when he could walk into the Hall of the Chimeras with me on his arm and see his father go dull crimson with rage. As it happened, Antony's priorities suited me just fine.

He'd clearly expected to get what he wanted, for he'd brought his carriage. His driver looked a little rumpled, and I suspected he'd taken advantage of *Berinth the King*, a notoriously long play, to find some company for the wait. I couldn't fault him—God knew there couldn't be anything much more boring than the life of a nobleman's coachman, being treated as an extension of the horses, three-quarters of the job comprised in waiting.

Antony, of course, would never descend to the crass vulgarity of necking in a carriage; we sat in constrained silence for several minutes before he said, "You're . . . friends with Mildmay Foxe, aren't you?"

His hesitation over the word "friends" told me that he knew exactly what Mildmay and I were to each other.

If I hadn't needed to stay on his good side, I would have said, *Something like that*, and let him twist. I said, "Yes."

Antony said, obviously choosing his words with great care, "It is said, in the Mirador, that Lord Felix and his brother burn offerings in the crypt of the Cordelii."

I'd expected that sentence to end rather differently from how it did, and there was a more than slight pause before I said, "To the best of my knowledge, that isn't true. I can't imagine Felix doing such a thing."

"Ah," said Antony, and in the darkness of the carriage, I couldn't tell whether it was disbelief or disappointment or something else entirely.

My curiosity got the better of me: "Why do you ask?"

The sound he made was as close as I'd ever heard him come to a nervous laugh. "I, ah . . . no reason, really."

It wasn't even worth calling that a lie. I waited, and he caved so fast I knew he wanted to tell me, even though it embarrassed him. "It was just that, if it *was* true, I was going to ask if you thought he'd be willing to show me the way."

"To the crypt of the Cordelii?"

"For my research," he said with prim stiffness, as if I'd accused him of necrophiliac urges.

"Of course," I said. Antony was a historian—he had studied in Vusantine as a young man and would probably have stayed among the scholars of the great and venerable Library of Arx if his father hadn't summoned him home. He was working on a history of the reign of Laurence Cordelius and spent most of his time in the Mirador's scattered and chaotic libraries.

"But if you think the story untrue . . ."

"I'm sure they don't burn offerings, but that doesn't necessarily mean Mildmay doesn't know where the crypt is. It can't do any harm to ask him."

"Would you?" he said, with a kind of eager gratitude I'd certainly never gotten from him in bed.

"Of course. I can ask him tomorrow."

"It's very kind of you."

"It's no trouble," I said. In fact, I was glad to have something neutral to talk about, considering the things we'd said to each other the last time we spoke. "What is it you're hoping to find?"

And the rest of the way to the Mirador, Antony was all too glad to tell me.

🜂

It was a good thing—I thought sometime later—that I didn't mind the color of Antony's bed canopy, because it was certainly all I got to look at. Not that he was an inconsiderate lover, but he knew where I belonged, and it was underneath him.

Afterward, though, he relaxed—as much as Antony ever did relax—and began to talk, like a boiling kettle venting steam. He hated the Mirador's politics, in the same way—and sometimes in the same breath—that he hated his father, but his hatred seemed to force him to watch, and the malevolent precision of his observations was always fascinating.

And tonight it was more than that: Stephen Teverius was contemplating marriage.

"You're joking," I said, even though I knew he wasn't.

"No," he said, but he wasn't offended. "His councillors have been encouraging him to remarry since—well, essentially since the moment Emily stopped breathing. But even Father had almost given up hope that he ever would."

"Do you think he means it?"

"That kind of fakery isn't in Stephen's nature. He means it— if they can ever find a young woman who meets their criteria."

"Criteria?"

"Extensive criteria," Antony said. "Listening to them discuss the matter, you would imagine they were buying Stephen a horse."

"Suddenly, I am very grateful to be beneath their notice."

"Yes, you are," he said grimly. "You are indeed."

Mildmay

Near the septad-night, Fleur came over to me and said, "He's drunk, isn't he?"

"M'lady?" I said. I should have stood up, to be polite, but it just didn't seem worth my while.

"Your brother," she said. "He's drunk."

I looked at Felix. He was sprawled out in one of the chairs. Isaac Garamond was leaning on the left chair-arm, talking to him, but Felix was grinning up at Edgar like he'd won the moon in a raffle and had clearly just said something snarky beyond belief.

Yeah, if you knew what to look for, he was drunk.

I said, "So?"

"He never used to get drunk."

No, I thought, liquor looks pretty damn boring next to phoenix. But I just said, "People change, m'lady."

"I was wondering if there was a reason."

"Sorry?"

"A reason he's started drinking too much. Is there something wrong?"

Something wrong. Powers and saints. Did she want a fucking list? "Sorry," I said. "I don't know what you're talking about."

She stared at me. "You can't be that stupid."

Depends, sweetheart. How stupid do you think I am? I didn't say nothing.

"I want to help," she said, fierce but kind of whispering. "Surely you can understand that."

"Well, you can't," I said, too sharp and too ugly, but it was true. Maybe I was stupid, but I knew what Felix would do to me if I spilled my guts to Fleur, and I wasn't anywhere near stupid enough to let myself in for that. Not when it wouldn't do no good anyhow.

"Your jealousy isn't helping him, either."

Powers, I wanted to hit the silly bitch. But I couldn't, so I just kind of stared at her. Because, I mean, what the fuck do you say?

"I don't want to take him away from you," she said. "Can't you see that?"

I wished, mightily, for the roof to cave in and get me out of this. "Lady Fleur, I don't own him. You want to try and help, you go on ahead. Just don't come crying to me when—"

—he rips you a new asshole. Powers and saints, for a moment I thought I'd actually said that out loud. But I'd managed to get my fucking mouth shut in time. Small fucking favors.

Not that what I *had* said wasn't bad enough all on its own, and she was getting ready to pin my ears back for it when a voice called, clear as a fucking bell, "Fleur, is my little brother annoying you?"

Felix was coming toward us. I knew that look in his eyes, and my heart and stomach all turned to mud.

"Of course not," Fleur said. She was a terrible liar.

"Perhaps I'd best take him home before he starts, then," Felix said. I'd've been happier if he'd just belted me one. He said good night all around, with one of his killer smiles, and walked out like he owned the world. I followed him.

He tore into me as soon as we were out of earshot, his voice low and mean. I didn't try to talk back. I couldn't beat him that way, and anything I said would just make it worse. I especially didn't say, though it lumped in my chest like a knot sealed with lead, that, just once, I wished he would take my side instead of theirs.

Gideon'd already gone to bed when we reached the suite. Felix ordered me off to bed like a thief-keeper would a stupid, useless kid, and I was glad to go. I fell asleep pretty quick—too tired to stay upset. Walking all over the Mirador'll do that for you.

And of course I dreamed about Ginevra. Again.

Felix

The door closed behind Mildmay, and I let my breath out explosively. Alcohol wasn't enough tonight, and the black, mindless fury was building. I looked at the closed door of my bedroom. Gideon was probably awake; I could go in and pick a fight, but I knew how it would end, and Gideon did not deserve that.

Silently, carefully, I let myself out of the suite. I'd promised myself a year and a half ago that I wouldn't go near Gideon unless I could be gentle, and there was no gentleness in me tonight.

I went to the Arcane. The guards at the Mortisgate pretended they didn't see me; that was better for all concerned. The denizens of the Arcane also pretended they didn't see me, but that was common courtesy. Uncommon courtesy—I was not the only Cabaline who came to the Arcane, but I was the only one who ventured farther than the Gargoyle's Bride, the import shop where you could buy Myrian amber at half the price it cost in "respectable" shops.

And for most purposes, the Gargoyle's Bride was deep enough. But not for mine.

The Two-Headed Beast was not in the lowest reaches of the Arcane, but I could hear the Sim from its doorway, a dancing, rushing, roaring howl, just at the edge of perception. Once inside, the door shut behind me, the sound was gone, drowned beneath the noise of the Two-Headed Beast itself.

There were candles everywhere, in candelabra and wall sconces, on every table, anchored in their own wax on the shelf behind the bar, casting strange reflections in the wavery and fly-specked mirrors. Jean-Tristan was holding court in one corner, the candlelight kind alike to his aging beauty and paste jewels. Young martyrs knelt adoringly at his feet; Jean-Tristan might be nearly fifty, but he was still as terrifyingly compelling as a chimera. I felt the draw myself, but wrenched away.

I was not a martyr any longer.

Sylvienne and her girls were spread like orchids across the broad staircase that divided the room in two: black velvet and fake pearls and rice-powder pallor on the fair ones, while the dark girls had kohl on their eyelids, subtle rouge on cheekbones and temples so that they glowed like bronzes. Even if I had been janus, that sweet poison would not have been what I wanted.

Sylvienne gave me a wary nod as I passed, one tarquin to another, unspeaking.

The upper level of the Two-Headed Beast was darker, all nooks and crannies and curtained alcoves and oddly shaped small rooms. The sweet smell of orange and clove incense was heavy in the air, not quite hiding the underlying musk of sweat and sex. I looked over the men leaning against the bar, sitting at the tables, in the mismatched chairs. There were women, too, hungrier than Sylvienne's flowers, feral, savage. It was hard to tell the predators from the prey; I supposed grimly that we were all predators, one way or another. And we were all prey.

There were signals, which I had learned in the Shining Tiger both to deploy and to interpret. The boy sitting alone, skinny, ferret-faced, probably not more than nineteen: his hands were folded on the table in front of him, and he wore red at his throat—a tattered kerchief, badly dyed, but you did the best you could with what you had. I understood that, and did not hold it against him.

It was not done for a martyr to approach a tarquin, not unless the martyr knew and wanted what he would get if he did. I had seen one of Jean-Tristan's martyrs do it once, deliberately, after a quarrel. Jean-Tristan had slapped her to the floor, as fast and vicious as a striking snake. And then he had helped her up again, quite tenderly, and kissed her until her mouth was red with her own blood.

That dark, skinny boy was sitting still, not making eye contact. Not merely curious, then, and not a thrill-seeker come slumming in the bear-pit. Some martyrs were excited by the waiting; from how *very* still he sat, I thought he might be one of them.

I crossed to the table, waited until he began to look up, then caught his chin with one finger and pushed his head up the rest of the way so that I could see his eyes: clear and bright, the pupils normal. Drugs were easily come by in the Two-Headed Beast, and I would not accept a martyr dosed on phoenix.

He held my gaze, though I could feel the tension in him, like a lute string, and when I released him, he looked down at once. He had lovely eyelids, smudged with kohl, and long veiling lashes.

I sat down across from him, placed my own hands flat, palms-down on the table. His breath hitched. I said, low and hard and fast, "I do not want to know your name, and you do not need to know mine. I will not kill you or cripple you. Do you require other assurances?"

His throat bobbed, and he said in a husky whisper, "No,

m'lord." He might know my name anyway; it didn't matter as long as he never said it.

"Good," I said. He looked up, hopeful. And I smiled at him. "My pleasure tonight is the Red Room. This is your last chance to decline."

But he shook his head, and I saw the tremor go through him.

I tossed a demigorgon across the table. "Find out when it will be available."

He was quick in his obedience, eager to please, and I approved. I was in no mood for a fight, not when I wouldn't be able to trust myself to remember the limits I had promised. Not tonight.

Before I could stop myself, my fingers had gone to the little wash-leather bag in my inner pocket. It was stupid to keep carrying it about, even more stupid to be so deathly afraid of opening it. Its contents could not harm me; it was mere superstition that made me imagine Malkar's spirit might linger in the rubies he had worn all the years I had known him.

Until I killed him.

And it was not—unfortunately—that Malkar's spirit *could* not return. I was apostate from Cabaline orthodoxy in admitting the possibility, but I had seen the ghosts of the Mirador. I had laid the spirits orthodoxy claimed did not exist. When it had occurred to me, some months after we had returned to Mélusine from the Bastion, that Malkar might . . . might come back, I had wished I could dismiss the idea as nightmarish fancy. I had *tried*. But he had been a blood-wizard, worse than a necromancer, and I could not silence the voice in my head whispering that Brinvillier Strych had died, too, and that had not stopped him. And who might he have been before he was Brinvillier Strych? How old *was* he, when my magic set his heart alight in his body? How many times had he cheated death?

That he was physically dead, there was mercifully no doubt. I had taken the rubies from the still-smoldering ashes of his body. But I did not know about his spirit, his essence . . . his miasma, for surely if ever a man had a miasma, a palpable cloud of cruelty and self-will wrapped about him, that man was Malkar Gennadion. And that was what I feared more than anything, that that miasma might endure past death. That he might find a way to parlay it again into agency, into control.

I had studied, piecemeal, clandestinely, not wanting to discuss my fears—not with Gideon, and certainly not with any of my Cabaline brethren, who would merely sneer at my overactive and heretical imagination. Gideon would not sneer, but if Malkar was a miasma, I did not want to make Gideon breathe it. He had suffered enough in my company.

So the process had been slow, frustrating and frightening, and even now that I thought I knew what I needed to do, I found myself hesitating, drawing back as if committing to the idea would somehow give Malkar's spirit the strength I feared it had. I did not admire myself for dithering, and it was that tension that was preying on me, shortening a temper that was never amiable in the first place, making me reckless, wantonly cruel, hateful even to myself.

And so I came to the Two-Headed Beast, in search of an outlet for all this fury.

My outlet came pattering back then. "The Red Room is free now, m'lord. If it pleases you . . ."

"Oh, it does," I said, and looked him over slowly, once, before I stood up.

I made him precede me down the narrow staircase to the Red Room, gratified by his nervous glances over his shoulder. On the landing, the intricately carved panels of the Red Room's door indecipherable in the low light, I caught him by his kerchief, pulled him to me. He choked a little, but did not struggle, and I kissed him as a reward, deep and hard, not loosening my grip. He responded eagerly, his mouth pliant and welcoming beneath mine. He tasted of gin and mint.

I raised my head after a time, said, "The key."

He fumbled for it, and if I had been another sort of man, I would have punished him for that, for the seconds it took him to press the key into my waiting hand. I merely kissed him again, bit his lower lip not quite hard enough to draw blood, and then released him completely, stepped around him, and unlocked the door.

My hand at the small of his back guided him into the Red Room. He stopped moving when my touch left him, and he stood perfectly still, save for a fine shiver, as I locked the door.

I left the key in the lock and walked round in front of him. "Undress."

He was quick but fumbling, and I did not bother to hide my

amusement. When he stood naked, I reached out, brushed the silky skin of his pectoral, ran a slow caress down to his navel, feeling his stomach muscles twitch beneath the lightness of my touch.

He had scars, clean thin lines marking his shoulders, his thighs, crisscrossing his spine with a geometer's precision. To this ferret-faced boy, they were beauty; to tarquins such as myself, they were desire. The ruined skin of my back seemed to burn beneath my shirt, though that was mere morbid fancy. I traced one of the lines across the front of his left thigh, watched his sex jerk with his indrawn breath.

I moved away then, out of the boy's line of sight, to the long table that held the Red Room's selection of erotiques. Other rooms offered silk ribbons, peacock feathers, little jars of various unguents—the petty toys for those who wished to play at power, or those whose cruelties were subtle, serpentine. In the Red Room there were manacles, blindfolds, lengths of chain, hard gags, fine-bladed knives, choke collars, clamps both delicate and brutal, a seven-tailed cat lying curled in obscene splendor like a dragon sleeping among its hoard. The oil was unscented, glowing in a decanter once used for sherry. Next to it was a pitcher of water and a pile of cloths.

I made my choices, returned to the boy, restrained him.

At the Shining Tiger, Merle and Justin had held me down while a patron plied a riding crop. I couldn't remember his name, but I remembered the way the pain had burned in toward my bones. This martyr didn't make a sound for the cat cutting his shoulders, dancing on his inner thighs. It was the blindfold that undid him, making his breath catch in a whimper when I showed it to him.

I was intrigued, heat unfurling in the pit of my stomach, and I tied the blindfold around his head with exaggerated caution, not wanting his reaction to be muddied by the pull of so much as a single strand of hair.

It was worth it, for he could not quite keep himself from trying to wrench away, even though he knew as well as I did that it was useless. I pressed myself against him to feel the quivering he could not control, to let him feel my arousal. I guided him to the floor, positioning him the way I wanted him, supported on his chained forearms and on his knees. He panted, his breath rasping in his throat, his head turned as if he was trying to see me through the black padded silk of the blindfold, and pleaded breathlessly.

I pulled back. "What do you want?"

"M'lord?" Bewilderment.

"You keep saying 'please,' " I said patiently. "What is it that you want?"

"Oh—!" A sob, hastily bitten back.

He didn't know; lost in the darkness, clouded by pain and sexual heat—I doubted he would have been able to tell me his own name. But I asked again, "What do you want?"

"You!" The word burst out of him. "Please, m'lord, please, fuck me, touch me, anything, just please, please—"

"Your enthusiasm is very gratifying, however crudely expressed." I ran my hand over his flank, delighted by the way he leaned desperately into my touch. I unstoppered the oil and slicked my hands. There were certain kinds of pain I chose not to inflict.

I teased him for a time, making him work for what he wanted, making him sweat. The sweat would keep his whip-weals alive for him.

When I was ready, both of us effortlessly slick with oil, I wrenched him onto his whip-marked back. He landed hard, his mouth open in a scream he had no breath to voice, and I entered him, not letting him arch off the floor, my fingers clawing into his buttocks, dragging them higher so that he had no choice but to take his weight on his shoulders.

He was fighting me, fighting his own body, and this was what I wanted, this panicked animal helpless strength, this hopeless struggle. I drove into him, snarling with effort, and he screamed like a lost soul, screamed and bucked and climaxed.

"Damn you," I said, although I did not know which of us I meant, and spent myself inside him in mingled pain and relief. I dragged myself away as soon as I could move, washed sketchily, and put my clothes on. Then I returned to the boy where he lay sprawled on the flagstones, removed manacles and blindfold, washed the mix of oil and sweat, semen and blood from his belly and back and thighs. I was careful, though not tender, checking to be sure I had not inflicted more damage than I had intended.

I helped him stand, helped him dress, asked because I had to, "Are you all right?"

His smile was sweet and wholehearted. "Ah, m'lord, any time you want me again, you just come find me."

I smiled back politely, but I wouldn't. I never did.

And we parted. I felt saturated in my own monstrosity, but the darkness, the fury, was draining out of me as I left the Two-Headed Beast, and I could have sobbed with gratitude. It was nearly four in the morning; I went straight to the St. Dismas Baths and scrubbed myself almost raw in the futile effort to wash the reek of the beast out of my soul.

But at least when I walked back through the Mortisgate, the boy's blood was not on me.

Mildmay

I woke up feeling like I'd died in the night and been dug up by resurrectionists with filthy, pox-festered hands. When I went out into the sitting room, Felix was wearing his wet cat look, the one that meant Gideon had taken after him for something he didn't think was his fault. They went at it like firecrackers all through breakfast. I could tell by the glares they were giving each other, even though neither one was saying anything out loud. Finally, Felix burst out: "All right, damn it! Mildmay, *you* tell him. Was I flirting with Isaac Garamond last night?"

"Can't you leave me out of this?" I said.

"Tell him," Felix said.

"I didn't see you flirting," I said.

Gideon snorted. He didn't believe either one of us. He knew I'd lie for Felix.

"Gideon, I *swear*—" Felix started, but Gideon cut him off, and whatever he said was poison mean. It took a lot to make Felix flinch.

"We'd better go," I said. "It's getting late."

The look Gideon gave me was one I could read. It said, *If he didn't do nothing wrong, why are you bailing him out?* But Felix's face went absolutely sunlit, and he said, "You're right. Come on." He was out the door before he even finished talking.

I said, "He really wasn't." Gideon didn't look at me. I got up and followed Felix.

It had been a shitty start to the day, and things only went downhill from there. I really didn't think Felix had been flirting with Mr. Garamond the night before, didn't think he gave a rat's ass about Mr. Garamond, to tell the truth, but when Mr. Garamond found Felix after court, *he* sure was—Mr. Garamond, I mean. He was better at it than poor Dominic Jocelyn, too, and Felix was sore enough at Gideon to start flirting back. I wished Gideon had believed me while I was still telling the truth.

As for me, the day had turned to complete and utter shit the moment I spotted Mehitabel on Lord Antony Lemerius's arm. And then she caught my eye and gave me the little wave that meant she wanted to talk to me later. How many guys do you *need* on your string? I thought. And I knew damn well that if Felix let me, I'd go meet her just like she wanted. Watching Felix and Mr. Garamond, I didn't think I'd have any trouble getting permission.

Mehitabel

I made Antony come with me to meet Mildmay. I wanted an audience, and Antony's scruples irritated me enough to drop character for a moment: "I assure you, he doesn't bite."

Antony bridled, but at least he quit arguing.

Mildmay and I had a system. The only thing he hated more than Felix teasing him was me telling Felix to shut up. So we didn't meet in their rooms, but in the Stoa St. Maximilian, where there were benches to sit on and almost never anyone around. The benches by the north doors were decorated with dragons. I sat on one; Antony, being keenly conscious of propriety, took the one opposite. I checked my watch. A quarter to seven. If Mildmay could come, he'd be along in the next half hour. And Felix might be frequently appalling, but he was almost never so petty as to refuse to let Mildmay go.

I looked at Antony, sitting poker-straight, his discomfort written plainly on his face, and said curiously, "If Mildmay distresses you so, why didn't you ask Felix?"

He gave me a look that was as much offended as anything else. "I am not on intimate terms with Lord Felix."

I heard Felix's breathless, mocking voice in my head: *Darling, I wouldn't take you if you came free with a pound of sugar.* Squelched it, said, "This is hardly an 'intimate' favor. And Felix would understand about your work."

"I want nothing to do with him," Antony said, and I didn't

spoil the magnificence of his statement by pointing out that if
that was the case, he was going entirely the wrong way about it.
Instead, I asked, "Do his proclivities offend you so greatly?"

"Oh, it isn't that, although Father gets quite exercised about
the degeneracy of the court. But the Lemerii do not consort
with wizards."

"Oh," I said, brought up hard against the lunatic schisms of
court society. "Of course."

Another awkward silence. I was about, in desperation, to start
him talking about the Cordelii again, when I was saved by my
other problem. Mildmay came through the door, with just enough
hitch in his eyebrows to tell me he'd had another argument with
Felix. The frown vanished from his face almost before I'd seen it,
and he nodded at Antony, his compromise between the obligation
d'âme and his own innate politeness. "Lord Antony," he said.
"What can I do for you?"

"Mildmay," I said; he gave me one of his indecipherable
looks, green and sharp and waiting. "Lord Antony wants to examine the crypt of the Cordelii. We've heard that you know the
way—will you show him?"

There was a pause; although Mildmay's face didn't change,
I knew I'd startled him, and I was glad of it. Then he shrugged.
"Yeah. Sure. When'd you like to go, m'lord?"

"Is now too soon?" Antony said.

"Nah. Suits me fine. Want to come, Mehitabel?"

"Are you kidding?" I said, getting up. "You'd have to beat me
off with a stick."

Mildmay

Nobody talked much on the way to the crypt, which was fine
with me. Felix had picked a fight with Johannes Hilliard at the
end of the committee meeting, because he knew Lord Johannes
would give him what he wanted, and it was either his bad luck or
just exactly what he had coming to him, depending on how you
look at things, that Lord Giancarlo heard him. He had some
things to say about it, too.

Felix didn't fight with Lord Giancarlo—he wasn't that
stupid—so he stood and let Lord Giancarlo chew him out, and
then Felix dragged me up to the Crown of Nails and chewed *me*

out, and we ended up having a fight like we hadn't had in months. He'd finally yelled at me to get away from him and leave him alone. I hadn't waited for him to say it twice.

But there was this little voice in the back of my head saying, he's getting worse. I mean, he was a nasty-tempered prick at the best of times, but these days it seemed like he was going out of his way to find fights. And he was leaving the suite at night, and me and Gideon didn't have the least idea where he was going, although it wasn't hard to guess what he was doing when he got there. And there was the drinking.

He ain't drinking that much, I said to myself. I mean, he ain't getting smashed or nothing.

But that didn't even get a chance to make me feel better before I was thinking, Yeah, but he's getting drunk enough that people are noticing. People other'n me. People who've known him longer'n me, and they don't like it. *They* think it's weird.

And then I sighed because it didn't matter. Felix wasn't going to listen to me, and if he'd wanted to tell me what was wrong, he would have. And maybe the binding-by-forms could've helped—there were stories that sort of hinted it might—but that would mean giving it more of me, and I wasn't doing that.

Fuck this for the Emperor's snotrag, I said to myself. Think about something else, can't you? And that worked about as well as it ever does.

When we reached the top of the white marble staircase that me and Felix had found once, couple indictions back now, I guessed, I snagged one of the candles out of the nearest sconce. Mehitabel and Lord Antony followed suit. The door at the bottom of the stairs was still unlocked.

"How many people do you think know about this?" Lord Antony asked.

"Powers, *I* don't know," I said, and waved 'em ahead of me through the door. Old habits die hard. "I'd bet us and Felix are the first people been down here in at least a Great Septad. Prob'ly more like three."

"Amazing," Lord Antony said. He was trying to look everywhere at once. He started off down the first aisle. About halfway along, he dug a tablet and stylus out of his coat pocket and began scribbling, using one of the tombs as a table.

"He'll be off in his own world until we drag him out of here," Mehitabel said. "Are *all* of the Cordelii really in here?"

"Nah. Just the dynastic line."

"So what's the dynastic line?"

"The kings and their kids and their wives, and I think the grandsons." I remembered something else I thought Mehitabel would like—something that might keep her looking at me instead of her flashie. "And the kings' hearts are down in the Arcane."

"I beg your pardon?"

"Kings' hearts went to Cade-Cholera. They're down in the Arcane, in the Mausolée de Verre."

"You're putting me on."

"Nope."

It wasn't my kind of joke, and she knew it. "What a grisly custom."

"The Mirador had a lot of stuff like that before the Wizards' Coup."

"No, *don't* tell me. Not in here."

"'Fraid of haunts?"

She gave me a smile that was mostly teeth. "Morbidly imaginative. Shall we sightsee?"

"Sure, if you want," I said.

But she only stayed with me a moment before she went off reading plaques. I stopped walking and leaned on a tomb to watch her, the way she forgot to behave like a lady and her eyes got wide.

She came back to me. "Do you know who all these people are?"

"Most of 'em."

"Come tell me about this one. She looks interesting," she said and dragged me over to one of the wall plaques.

The plaque she pointed to didn't look no different from the others. Mehitabel read it out loud:

HERE LIES AMARYLLIS CORDELIA
17 PRAIRIAL 14.1.3 - 11 FLORÉAL 14.6.2
Her waking over,
may her sleep be dreamless.

"Who *was* she?"

"Fuck," I said. "I dunno. I mean, I know about *one* Amaryllis Cordelia, but *she* can't be here."

"Why not?"

"Not in the dynastic line, though that ain't from lack of trying."

"What do you mean? Who was she?"

"Let's sit down," I said and started toward the row of free-standing tombs behind us. "D'you mind?"

"All right," she said, and sat with me on the nearest tomb. "Now talk. Who was Amaryllis Cordelia?"

"Gloria Aestia with guts."

"Felix is right," Mehitabel said. "You *do* talk in riddles."

Powers, how many people was he saying that to? "Sorry," I said. "But it ain't a riddle. She was born into a cadet branch, and she wanted to be queen."

"She didn't make it, though."

"Nope. Bad timing."

She laughed.

"It's true," I said. "Too young to marry Laurence and too old to marry Charles. She got married off to an Emarthius before Charles was old enough to care about girls."

"So what makes her like Gloria Aestia?"

"She seduced them both."

"She *what*?"

"Her husband—poor bastard, I can't think of his name—got some political appointment when Laurence was in his seventh septad, and—"

"Don't give me that septad nonsense," she said.

"Sorry. Laurence was older than forty-two and younger than, um, forty-nine. Charles was about sixteen, and the lady herself was, say, thirty."

"All right. I've got that now. Go on."

"She went after Laurence first, but he wouldn't do her no good. He'd had lovers since he hit his second septad, if you believe the stories, and he knew how to keep 'em where he wanted 'em. So she gave up on him and went after Charles."

"Well? What happened?"

"Ain't clear," I said. "Laurence died when Charles had two septads and four, um . . . eighteen. Maybe it was murder. Maybe Amaryllis Emarthia had a hand in it. Seems like Charles didn't, since they let him on the throne. But he hadn't reached his third septad yet, and everybody knew he was missing some of the top cards from his deck. Laurence had been careful about the way he set the regency up—and maybe that was Amaryllis's fault, too. So by the time Charles came of age, his advisors had most of the power, and that's where the Puppet Kings came from."

"What about Amaryllis?"

"Her and her husband got the boot—not *officially* because of Laurence being murdered, but you know how that is. I don't think they ever came back."

"But here she is," Mehitabel said.

"*If* that's her."

"We have a historian. Let's ask." She called down to the other end of the crypt, "Antony!"

"Mehitabel!" I said in a hiss.

"What? Afraid I'll wake someone?"

"You only think you're joking. And people didn't get buried down here along of being nice to widows and orphans, you know."

"Sorry. I think it was mostly bravado. This place gives me the horrors."

Lord Antony reached us. "You bellowed?" he said disapprovingly.

"Mildmay just told me a very interesting story about a woman named Amaryllis Cordelia who shouldn't be in here. Is that her plaque?" She pointed.

Lord Antony turned and read the plaque and said, "How very peculiar."

"*Is* it her?"

"The dates are right, and I've never come across another Amaryllis in that generation of Cordelii, but not only shouldn't Amaryllis Cordelia be here, she can't be. That is to say, she *isn't*."

"Pray continue," Mehitabel said and gave me a sidelong smile.

"My mother is an Emarthia, a very cadet branch, but she was a favorite of old Lord Rodney's. She spent several summers at Diggory Chase, and took me along two or three times. When I was twelve, I spent the summer doing rubbings in their graveyard—including one of the tombstone of Amaryllis Cordelia Emarthia."

We looked at each other.

"The inscription is the same," Lord Antony said. "I remember the motto. But someone here apparently didn't like thinking of her as an Emarthia."

"Charles?" I said.

"He was completely in thrall to her, true enough," Lord Antony said, "but I've never heard that he was particularly prone to melodramatic gestures."

"But why is she here?" Mehitabel said.

"That's just it," Lord Antony said. "She *isn't* here. She's buried beside her husband at Diggory Chase."

"Then what's this?" I said.

He started pacing up and down, scowl black as a thundercloud. "Someone has erected a plaque to the memory of Amaryllis Cordelia—"

"No, they haven't," Mehitabel said. "It doesn't say anything about her memory. It says, 'Here lies Amaryllis Cordelia.' "

"It's a copy of the Diggory Chase plaque," Lord Antony said.

"Why?" Mehitabel said. "Why would you copy an Emarthius plaque when you patently want to deny her connection to the Emarthii?"

Lord Antony opened his mouth to answer her and then closed it. Then he did it again, like a guy trying to force a rusted lock.

"Look, I know this is stupid," I said, "but what if it's the other way 'round?"

"Riddles, my darling," Mehitabel said.

"No, it ain't. What if the Emarthius plaque is the copy?"

"But that makes even less sense," Lord Antony said. "Why would the Cordelii put up a plaque for her before the Emarthii got one up, when she died at Diggory Chase?"

"Why would they put up a plaque for her at all?" Mehitabel said, and we ran aground again.

"Only people in this crypt," I said, "are kings, their wives, and their children."

"And grandsons," Lord Antony said.

"Yeah, them too. But Amaryllis Cordelia wasn't any of those things. Never mind who did it, *why* is she here?"

"Is it," Mehitabel began, then stopped herself. "No, that's hardly likely."

"What?" Lord Antony said.

"I was just wondering if being the *mother* of a king would be enough. Could she be the next king's mother?"

"Claudius," I said.

"No," Lord Antony said. "Claudius was born nearly a year after Amaryllis died, and I'm afraid there is no doubt he was the son of Jemima Cordelia. It's a good idea, though."

"So that ain't it," I said, "and since I always heard Charles was pretty stuck on Jemima—I mean, he wouldn't've gone around putting plaques up, if this lady died after he got married, right?"

"That's a solid piece of reasoning," Lord Antony said, "and besides, Amaryllis Cordelia has a perfectly legitimate and presumably tenanted grave somewhere else. It really is most peculiar."

We were silent for a minute. Mehitabel was hugging herself, and Lord Antony was looking around nervously. I felt it, too, that sense that somebody I couldn't see might be watching from the shadows. Our candles were burning low.

Then Mehitabel said briskly, "We can certainly ponder it elsewhere. Come on. I'm beginning to feel as if I'm overstaying my welcome." She led the way to the door. Me and Lord Antony were glad to follow her.

I stopped to drag the door closed, which took some doing. Lord Antony waited for me. I hadn't expected that from him. Looking at his face, sort of embarrassed and stubborn, I could see that he was trying to get past that we were both on Mehitabel's string, trying to be a decent person.

I found myself saying, "If you need to come back down here—I mean, if you want, m'lord, I'd be happy to, um, come with you."

"Thank you," Lord Antony said. "I appreciate that." We both knew what he was talking about, and it didn't have a thing in the world to do with the crypt of the Cordelii.

🙠

It was Huitième, and I couldn't quite tell if Mehitabel and Lord Antony had other plans. So I said good night and went back down to the Palace. The looks I got in the Arcane were nasty, and a couple people made hex signs when they thought I wasn't looking. That was almost funny. They were giving me lots of space. Elvire had probably put the word out that I claimed Vey Coruscant.

At the Palace, Tiny was watching a gal cheating two demibeaux at dice. She saw me and the dice fell out of her hand, laying there on the floor like tiny corpses. I recognized her. She'd been one of Elvire's girls four indictions back, but they must have figured she was better at sharping. I even remembered her name.

"Hey, Mirandy," I said.

Her face was suddenly all eyes. She said, "Hey," back, but I saw the way she covered her dice.

"I can't hex 'em, darlin'," I said. "That's my big brother."

"You again," Tiny said before she could figure out what to do with that. "She said if you had balls enough to come back, I should let you go on in." He stepped aside, and I made my own way to Elvire's office.

"Sit down," she said, and I sat and waited. She was quiet for a long time, just looking at me until my back started crawling, then said suddenly, "I'll give you one chance to forget the whole thing."

"Why?"

"All or nothing."

I thought about it, and thought hard. Because her making that offer said as how she didn't like what she found. *And* it said as how she thought she owed me one, and this was it. And that meant something. But it just didn't mean *enough*.

"If I didn't want to know, I wouldn't've asked," I said.

"St. Anarthe preserve you from your own stupidity then," she said. "The only person offering the information you want is Kolkhis of Britomart."

Keeper.

"The *only* person?"

"For what you can pay."

Fuck. "What does she want?"

Her smile was all knives.

"She wants to talk to you," said Elvire.

Chapter 3

Mehitabel

My boarding house was called the Velvet Tears, and it catered mostly to working women who could claim respectability but weren't actually respectable. No manufactory girls here—we were actresses and modistes' assistants and probably, yes, at least a couple of the tenants sold more intimate skills, but they were quiet about it and didn't bring their work home.

When I got back—very late Mardy night or very early Mercredy morning—I found Corinna waiting for me on the front stairs, and my heart sank.

The Empyrean didn't perform two days in the ten of the decad, the Lower City's week. Cinquième was sacred to the five principal gods of the Marathine pantheon, and Huitième was sacred to Jean-Soleil, who went out to Sauvage to visit his wife and children. So I'd had no qualms about accepting Antony's invitation, assuming I could leave the Empyrean to its own devices.

But not only was Corinna waiting for me, she was also more than a little drunk. I turned from locking the front door behind me, and she said, "Tabby. Been waitin' for you."

Corinna was normally very conscientious about her elocution; that dark drawl was a bad sign. "I can see that," I said. "What's the matter?"

"What's the *matter*?" She laughed, and there was another bad sign, because it wasn't her well-schooled genteel chuckle, either, but a raucous bark. I shushed her hastily, for the last thing we needed was the landlady to descend in her wrath like Tammerlion Ferox.

"Come on," I said. "Upstairs." I chivvied her gently into her own room, shut the door gratefully behind me, and watched as Corinna subsided in a slithering rustle of taffeta and grosgrain onto her bed, itself a narrow oasis amidst the racks and piles of costumes, which Corinna was repairing, remaking, and sometimes simply reinventing for the Empyrean. Some of them were part of the effects of the long-defunct Merveille Theater, which Jean-Soleil had bought at auction five years ago, and the rest were the spoils of Corinna's trawling among the secondhand clothes shops of the Engmond's Tor Cheaps. "Now cough it up, whatever it is."

"I went over to the Empyrean after dinner," she said, readily enough. "I'd left the mauve thread in Susan's dressing room when I was repairing Pasiphaë's funeral gown—you know."

"Yes," I said.

"And I found this." She fished a crumpled twist of paper out of her bodice and waved it at me.

"Which is . . . ?"

Another raucous bark of laughter. "Bartholmew's gone to the Cockatrice."

I stared at her a moment. "That can't be all."

"He talked Susan into going with him."

"He did *what*?"

"Susan's gone," Corinna said, half dolefully, half in unholy amusement. "Packed up her bags and left Jean-Soleil this little billet doux."

Susan was stupid and tiresome and as an actress was about as talented as a tent pole, but her beauty and her voice and even the cold refinement of her manners had made her a tremendous draw. If she'd appeared before me at that moment, I would cheerfully have throttled her.

And I didn't understand her. Susan had not liked me, rightly believing that I had designs on her status as lead tragedienne, but she had been sitting pretty here at the Empyrean—adulated and generously paid—and she had known it. What could have possessed her?

I asked Corinna, "So what did she say?"

"Shame, Tabby," she said, drawing herself up and scowling at me unconvincingly. "To ins . . . insin . . ."

"Insinuate."

"Yeah, that. That I'd read a letter addressed to Jean-Soleil."

"In Susan's handwriting. Of course you would. I'd do the same."

"Unladylike, the pair of us," Corinna said. "You want a drink?"

"No. And I don't think you need any more, either. Come on. Why is *Susan* leaving?"

"Well, to hear her tell it, Adolphus Jermyn's going to make her Queen of Tambrin."

I didn't recognize the allusion, and at the moment I didn't care. "But what about Madeleine Scott?"

"Becoming Mrs. Jermyn."

I honestly didn't think I'd heard her correctly. "Becoming Mrs. Jermyn?"

"Oh yes. So naturally, Jermyn's replacing her—can't have *Mrs. Jermyn* treading the boards, you know—and it sounds like he promised Susan the sun, and moon, and two or three stars for good measure. She says he's planning to revive *Edith Pelpheria* for her."

"Oh you have *got* to be joking!"

"Nope. 'S what Susan says." She considered a moment and added, "Silly bitch."

"We knew that already," I said, and we grinned at each other.

"But we're fucked, Tabby," Corinna said, suddenly and utterly serious. "I mean, what're we gonna do without Susan?"

"I don't know," I said.

The worst part was that Corinna wasn't wrong. The Empyrean's reputation was built on Susan. I didn't want to calculate what percentage of our take Susan was responsible for, but it was substantial, and with both her and Bartholmew gone, the troupe was crippled, cutting our income even further, possibly even to zero.

I knew how fast an acting troupe could go under. I knew what kind of mercy Jean-Soleil could expect from his creditors, too. What I *didn't* know was what I'd do if the Empyrean was forced to close. When I first came to Mélusine, I'd taken shameless advantage of Felix's generosity, made easier by the fact that he clearly thought nothing of it—merely looking at me blankly when I offered to reimburse him for the money drawn out of his stipend. Mildmay'd come to me later, and we'd settled accounts; he'd said with a kind of fond resignation that Felix had no better head for money than he did for cards.

But I couldn't do that again. Pride and conscience refused it, and I couldn't tie myself more closely to Mildmay, not when I had no intention of giving him what he . . . wanted? Needed? It was hard to tell with him; he said so little about himself, and watched everything with the same stone-faced glower. And asking merely made him withdraw further.

One thing I knew. I didn't love him.

Another thing I knew. He didn't love me. Not when he was still so haunted by Ginevra that he could call me by her name and never even notice.

A relationship between us was a disaster waiting to happen, and I thought we had enough disasters already. I knew I hadn't called him Hallam only because I had trained myself rigorously, viciously, never to say Hallam's name out loud. *Never.*

And so Felix—an unlikely refuge if ever there was one—was off-limits. I certainly couldn't go to the Cockatrice; the mere idea was enough to turn my stomach. And I was not going to become anyone's light of love, living a parasitical, precarious existence and having always to mind my tongue. My stint in Klepsydra had taught me I needed acting to stay sane, and needed the theater to stay a person instead of merely a façade, a mask.

I needed the Empyrean.

I shook my head, coming out of a most unprofitable reverie with a start. The doomsaying would keep. "Come on, now," I said to Corinna. "You're going to hate yourself in the morning, you know. Let me get your buttons undone, and you can go to sleep."

"But what are we gonna *do*?" she said, catching my wrist.

"We start by talking to Jean-Soleil," I said. "And we can't do that until tomorrow. *Sleep*, Corinna."

She was drunk enough to be amenable. I undid her buttons, helped her out of dress and petticoats while she murmured bits of Bysshe's address to sleep from *Margot and Bysshe*.

"I don't care what cards he's got in his hand," I said finally, extinguishing the lamp. "I wouldn't back Jermyn against Jean-Soleil if you offered me the best odds in the world."

"Hope you're right," she said, already three-quarters asleep, and I slipped out into the hall with a tremendous sense of relief.

And nearly walked straight into the massive and queenly form of our landlady.

"Everything quite all right, Miss Parr?" she said dryly.

"Yes, thank you, Mrs. Angharad."

"I trust Miss Colquitt's indisposition is a temporary one?"

Corinna, you *owe* me, I thought, and managed to turn gritted teeth into a passable smile. "Yes, thank you. She's better already."

"See that she doesn't relapse," Mrs. Angharad said and moved with icy grandeur toward the stairs.

I retreated to my own room and had rarely been more grateful to bolt its door behind me. I didn't need this. Not on top of everything else. "Nothing more tonight," I said fiercely under my breath, undoing my own buttons. "Not one more damn thing."

And it worked—if you don't count the uneasy dreams.

Mildmay

So I didn't get much sleep that night. Too busy thinking about Keeper and just how much I didn't want to get in spitting distance of her.

I never have figured out a good way to explain Keeper—except to people who grew up kept-thieves, and they don't need the explaining in the first place. I still didn't know, all these indictions later, whether I hated her or loved her. But I for sure hated the way she was trying to run me.

I knew what I was to Keeper. I'd figured *that* out a long time ago. I was like one of them clockwork bears. You wound the bear up and put it on the floor and it walked forward, banging its sticks together. Me, you wound me up, pointed me in the right direction, and I killed people. Good old reliable clockwork.

Only my clockwork had got busted somewhere along the way. And I knew exactly how much use Keeper had for busted things. So if she was putting herself to any kind of trouble to get me down in Britomart again, it wasn't for old times' sake, or to see how I was doing, or—saints and powers forbid—to say she was sorry. It was because she wanted something. And I was pretty sure that whatever Keeper wanted, I didn't want to give it to her.

So *think*, Milly-Fox. Not that you're any good at it. Was there any other way I could get at the information I wanted? Anybody who might know, and would tell me if they did?

I went round with it in circles for a couple hours, and most of what I came up with wasn't good for nothing but making cats laugh. But I did think of one thing, and sure it was a long shot, but even in the morning when I looked at it again, it didn't seem like it was completely batfuck nuts to try.

Because Hugo Chandler was a musician in the Mirador now. I could get at him. And Hugo—stupid little rabbit that he

was—had had a thing like a dying swan for Austin Lefevre, the
poet Ginevra'd gone to when she'd dumped me. And, no, it
didn't make me feel better that Austin'd died with her, too.

But he'd let Hugo hang around. I think he liked knowing
Hugo'd slit his own wrists with a spoon if that was what Austin
wanted. And so if there'd been somebody nosing around and
asking questions, or if Ginevra'd said something stupid in company, odds were—maybe not great, but not bad either—that
Hugo would've heard.

It was something to try. If it worked, it'd mean I could stay
the fuck away from Keeper. And powers, that didn't seem too
much to ask.

🙙

When I came out of my bedroom, Felix and Gideon were fighting again. They gave me the same look, like I was somebody
they didn't know and didn't want to.

After a silence that lasted for septads, Felix said, "Good
morning," like a slab of marble.

"I'll be in the hall," I said and ducked out. I couldn't have
gotten away from Felix's voice in my bedroom—and if him and
Gideon were really getting into it, he'd start yelling sooner or
later—but from the hall I couldn't hear a thing. Couldn't've if
I'd wanted to, which I didn't. I sat down against the wall and
started reciting "Rowell's Stand" in my head. It passed the time.

I'd got to the middle of the thirteenth stanza, where Rowell's
wife looks in her mirror and it turns pitch-black, when Lord
Shannon Teverius came into view at the other end of the hall. I
guess right then Rowell's wife and me probably felt pretty much
the same.

I got up as fast as I could. Lord Shannon was nobody to fuck
with, and what exactly his thing was about Felix I couldn't have
told you. They'd been lovers, and Lord Shannon had dumped
Felix when Felix was "not himself." That was how Felix always
put it, like being absolutely batfuck nuts for more than an indiction was just one of those things that happens to everybody
once in a while. And when Felix came back to the Mirador with
his head put back together, he didn't want nothing more to do
with Lord Shannon. Lord Shannon couldn't stand that. I'd seen
the way he watched Felix when he thought nobody was paying
attention, and it was the kind of look that makes your skin

crawl. He looked a little crazy himself. He laid traps for Felix, too, cunning things that Felix waltzed right out of without even seeming to see. Sometimes you could almost hear Lord Shannon's teeth grinding.

He stopped when he reached me. I ain't molly, but I could see why Felix had fallen for him, and why the court molls would just about kill themselves to make him smile. He really was that good-looking. He took after his mother, Gloria Aestia, the Golden Bitch, and looking at him made you understand what had happened to Lord Gareth.

"I wish to speak to Lord Felix." His eyes were perfect Monspulchran blue, and they were staring through me like I wasn't there.

Powers, I thought. "He's, um, busy just now, m'lord, but—"

"Nonsense."

If I was really, really lucky, Felix might throw a fireball at me, and I'd get out of the rest of this freakshow. I opened the door.

Felix turned on me like he was glad to have somebody else to yell at. *"WHAT?"* Shit. Gideon had found the right place to push and the right words to push with.

"It's, um, Lord Shannon. He says he wants to talk to you."

"Now?"

"Yeah," I said and stepped to one side so he could see Lord Shannon behind me.

Felix said, *"Damn,"* not quite under his breath. I'd turned to keep an eye on both of them, and I saw Lord Shannon twitch.

When he wanted to, Felix could do these lightning-fast changes that made me feel like a cat in a room full of people with heavy boots. He did one now, went from acid to honey in the blink of an eye. "Come in, please," he said, his voice low and pleasant. His smile wasn't one of his best, but it didn't look fake.

Me and Gideon both tried to bail right then. "Sit down, Gideon," Felix said, watching Lord Shannon. "Don't leave, Mildmay, but do close the door behind his lordship." I looked at Gideon. Gideon looked back at me. We did what Felix wanted. I stayed by the door and did the best imitation I could of the wall. Gideon picked a chair out of both Felix's and Lord Shannon's lines of sight and hunched down in it like he was hoping he would turn invisible. At least Lord Shannon didn't look happy about it neither.

"Now," Felix said, "what can I do for you, my lord?"

I knew Felix well enough to see the gloat behind his good manners, that nasty little light in his eyes that meant he'd got some poor bastard right where he wanted him. And that's when I got it. Lord Shannon hadn't wanted no witnesses, and Felix had seen it, and made sure we didn't leave.

There was a pause, the spine-crawling sort where you want to say anything just to make it quit. Then Felix said, in a horrible, purring voice, "I don't know about you, my lord, but I have to prepare for court, and I haven't a great deal of time at my disposal. So, please, tell me what it is you want." I hoped he didn't know how much he sounded like Brinvillier Strych.

"I would prefer to speak to you alone," Lord Shannon said finally, and I figured we could call it one–nothing Felix, for making him admit it.

"Well, you can't," Felix said, brisker but less dangerous. "So either say what you've come here to say, or leave."

Lord Shannon looked around, and I thought for a second he was going to bolt. He had that kind of expression on his face, and honestly, if he'd started for the door, I would've got the fuck out of his way and let Felix yell at me for it later. But he stood his ground and looked Felix in the eye and said, "Come back to me."

And powers and saints, that just sat there for the longest time—felt like an indiction at least, maybe two—and then Felix laughed, not nicely, and said, "No."

"Why *not*? Is it because of him?"—with a wave at Gideon, who was trying to look even more invisible—"Or *him*?" And he jerked his chin at me.

I just about fucking swallowed my tongue. But Felix didn't even blink, although he went awful white. He said, "No. It's because of you."

They stared at each other. Right then, I don't think there was anybody else in the world for either of them. And the funny thing was, Felix didn't look mad. He just looked, I don't know, *tired*. And after a long, long moment, just them staring at each other, Lord Shannon said, "I . . . I should go."

"Yes," Felix said. Not mean or nothing.

And Lord Shannon went. I got out of his way, and he didn't so much as glance at me. Small fucking favors.

And all the time Felix was getting ready for court—in a tearing hurry, of course, because he'd already been running late before Lord Shannon showed up—he kept saying, "I can't believe I *said* that." Sometimes he said it like it made him want to cry. Sometimes he said it like he was about to start laughing. Finally, when we'd actually gotten out and were on our way, I got fed up with it and said, "Then why the fuck did you?"

He stopped walking for a second. "Because it was true, I suppose," he said when he started again. "Shannon made his personal feelings quite clear in that ugly little hotel in Hermione. If he hadn't, I'd probably have gone crawling back to him like a dog. That's what he wants, you know," and he gave me a weird, sideways look that I wasn't sure I'd been meant to see and I didn't know what to do with anyway. "He doesn't want me back—he's got that new boy, whatever his name is—he wants me crawling around him the way the rest of them do."

"He don't like you, um, holding out," I said. The "new boy" was Lord Arden Anastasius, and I knew Felix knew perfectly well what his name was.

"Exactly. That's what's driving him mad." He sighed. "I hope he's not going to start spreading that incest rumor again."

I remembered something . . . something Hugo'd said back before I'd walked into the bear trap called Brinvillier Strych. "The 'Lai of Mad Elinor,' " I said. "He was having everybody sing it."

Felix didn't say nothing for a moment, which was answer enough. "It . . . it isn't aimed at *you*."

"Feel better if it was."

"Mildmay—"

"Oh, never mind," I said. "It don't matter."

He turned on me so suddenly that I went back a step. "Don't say that! They're petty-minded bigots, and there's not a thing in the world I can do about it, but it *does* matter."

"Oh, right," I said. "Like it matters that your friends hate me."

A second later, I was wishing I'd bitten my tongue through instead. Felix flinched back like I'd hit him and said, in a very small voice, "They don't *hate* you."

"Oh, powers," I said. "I'm sorry. I didn't mean it. I don't blame you, or nothing. I just get so damn tired."

"Gideon thinks," Felix said, "that you *should* blame me."

"Fuck, I can't help what *Gideon* thinks."

He laughed, but said, "What if Gideon's right?"

In pure desperation, I said, "We're gonna be late if'n we don't hurry."

He looked at me for a moment, and then let it go. "Come on, then. And the unadulterated 'if,' if you please."

Mehitabel

Corinna was sallow and moaning softly to herself when I stuck my head around her door at nine. But she was up and dressed and applying kohl carefully to her eyelids; she'd do fine.

"You don't need to say it," she said without turning from her reflection.

"Yes, well, if you aren't careful, it's Mrs. Angharad who'll be saying it—to the accompaniment of an eviction notice, I suspect."

"Oh damn," Corinna said and grimaced, although I wasn't sure if it was at herself or me or the absent Mrs. Angharad.

"She's going to let it go this time. And next time, you get to deal with her yourself."

"Oh, Tabby. I *am* sorry." She turned and rose, a single grace-ful motion, and crossed the room to lay one small hand apolo-getically on my forearm. "I was just . . . Do you really think Jean-Soleil will be able to find a way out?" At close range, that beseeching look was hellishly effective—and I still didn't know how she did it. Corinna was three years older than me and more than capable of looking after herself.

"Like I said, my money's on him. After all, he'll never let himself be beaten by—"

"Dolly Vermin," she finished with me, grinning. Jean-Soleil's contempt for the impresario of the Cockatrice was legendary.

"Can I have Susan's letter? I'm going to try to catch Jean-Soleil as soon as he gets back."

"Oh, of course! Now where . . . ?" She frowned around her room with its darkly gaudy fabric jungle, then knelt and sorted through yesterday's dress and petticoats as deftly as she had probably once picked the pockets of drunken or sleeping tricks. She emerged triumphant with Susan's battered letter, which I tucked into my own bodice.

"Do you want me to come with you?" she asked, although she was clearly hoping the answer would be no.

"No. Just be on time at noon, right?"

"You got it, lovey. Good luck."

I made one of her gargoyle faces back at her and left with her laughter—her well-bred gurgling chuckle.

The day was brisk but sunny—good weather for the end of Eré, and the five blocks to the Empyrean was a pleasant walk. The brothels, curtains drawn, were still sleeping. The people out on the streets of Pharaohlight at this hour were dairymen and coal carriers, scullery maids and apprentice boys running errands, a woman hawking sachets of dried lavender and sage.

I caught myself thinking—for the first time in years—Hallam would like this. It was true; Hallam had always loved going out into Lamia, talking to the traders—everyone from the merchants from Aigisthos to the peddlers with their cheap ribbons and packets of pins. Even inside the Bastion, he had always been talking to the maids, the cooks, the caefidi, wanting to know where they were from, why they'd come to the Bastion, whether they'd spoken Midlander or Kekropian at home, if they'd left family behind. I'd lied to him, of course, but it was how we'd become lovers, Hallam's hunger for knowledge, for connection, for *touch*, meeting my then quite desperate need for affection. He'd never backed away from my need; he'd given of himself as generously as rain gives itself to parched earth. Even when he'd realized I'd lied to him, as he inevitably had, he hadn't withdrawn from me, but had continued to love me and to share his own abundant warmth.

Stop it, I said to myself, as loud as a shout in the confines of my skull. I'd taught myself years ago not to think about Hallam. It would have killed me if I'd let it, so I'd shoved it all in a box. Closed it. Locked it. And made it *stay* locked.

I had done it, and I would be damned if I was going to do it all over again.

I breathed deeply, straightened my spine, cloaked myself in Mehitabel Parr the actress—not any of those other Mehitabel Parrs who might still dream of Hallam's gentle eyes—and went to meet Jean-Soleil.

I waited for Jean-Soleil on the sidewalk in front of the Empyrean. Although he walked out to Sauvage, Jean-Soleil hitched a ride back to Mélusine with his wife's brother, the mayor of Sauvage, who brought the village's trading goods to the Neuvième market in Gatehouse. Jean-Soleil always returned punctually at ten.

At five minutes of ten, Jean-Soleil's stocky figure came into view, swaggering up Paixe Street as if he owned all of it, and not just the forty-nine feet of sidewalk in front of the Empyrean. His stride faltered as he caught sight of me, and by the time he came up to me, his face was grim.

"I know you're not standing out here just because you couldn't wait to see me again—what is it?"

"Bartholmew and Susan," I said and stopped, hoping he could fill in the blanks for himself.

"Verb, please?"

"Have deserted to the Cockatrice."

"*Both* of them?"

"Here." I gave him Susan's letter. He raised an eyebrow over its crumpled and obviously already read condition, but opened it and scanned the contents.

I knew when he'd reached the part about *Edith Pelpheria*; he snorted and said, "I believe I'd pay to see the silly chit muff Edith." He thought a moment, and suddenly his face lit up like a hundred-candle chandelier. "Fancy a go at her, my Belle?"

"What if it's just a rumor?"

"Then we revive *Edith Pelpheria* with an actress up to its weight. No harm done."

"Yes!" I said, and he laughed. Then my common sense caught up with me, and I said, "We're still a second principal and an ingenue short."

"Don't worry about the second principal," he said over his shoulder, unlocking the theater doors.

"And the ingenue?"

"We hold an open audition. Do you know how many young women in this city are panting at a chance to join the Empyrean?"

"No," I said. He held the door for me and I stepped into the warm darkness of the lobby.

"Neither do I," Jean-Soleil said. "But we can find out."

༄

By noon, when we gathered in the largest rehearsal room, everyone had heard the news. We were a solemn little group. I didn't know about Corinna, but I was thinking about those costumes in her room, made for actors who might not even have gotten the chance to wear them. Corinna had told me the story of the Merveille's ingenue, Argine Pettifer, who had thrown herself into the Sim a week after the theater closed. She was now said to haunt the tenement that had gone in after the building burned down in the fires three years ago.

Morbid and unedifying, I said to myself sternly. Besides which, the Empyrean isn't going to fold.

Jean-Soleil had assimilated the disaster and bounced back so quickly that I half guessed he had been expecting it. The open audition, as he said, was good publicity and easy to reshape as the Empyrean looking for fresh blood. "Not that anyone will *entirely* believe it, but if *Edith* comes off well—which it will— it will be clear that we are not pining for Madame Dravanya."

"No," I said, deliberately audible, and then did a double take, as if I hadn't meant to say it. I felt the mood lighten, and Jean-Soleil gave me one of his twinkly little grins.

"The question is," he said, looking around the circle, "what are we to do in the meantime? I'm afraid *The Wrong Brother* is, er, right out."

We sat and thought. The six of us, with Bartholmew and Susan gone, were the core of the Empyrean troupe: Drin for the heroes and lovers, Jean-Soleil for kings and cuckolds and enraged fathers, me for heroines, Corinna for confidantes and nurses and mothers. Jabez Meridian, our principal comedian, played fools and clowns, and Levry Tannenhouse, a mild, cherubic little man with the shape and general demeanor of a small tame bear, seconded him when necessary and played servants and messengers when not.

"*The Soldier of Ochimar*," Drin suggested.

Jean-Soleil shook his head. "We're looking to replace the Trevisan, not *Berinth the King*. Comedy, Drin my boy. Something to make *Edith* look even more spectacular."

Drin made a face at him, and we all thought some more.

Then Jabez said, "*The Misadventures of Mardette*."

Corinna laughed—and it was the raucous bark from last night. "You must be out of your mind, Jabez. I'm too damn old."

"No, you ain't," Jabez said.

"What are we talking about?" I said.

Jean-Soleil was eyeing Corinna speculatively. "It's called a trouser-farce, Belle. They're an old Mélusinien tradition."

"That didn't exactly help," I said.

"Look," Corinna said, half exasperated, half amused. "You

get a young, pretty, abundantly stacked girl, and you get her in trousers, and a shirt she can spend the play half falling out of, and then you put her in the stupidest, silliest plot you can think of, and pretend that nobody can tell she's a girl."

"Lots of molly jokes," Levry said.

"That's what I started out doing," Corinna said, "but I'm too old. I've hit my fifth septad, Jean-Soleil."

"Couldn't I do it?" I said. Not that I was all that much younger than Corinna, but I had not lived as hard as she had, and I could still pass for twenty-five.

They all looked shocked, and there was a confusing babble of negatives.

"It's not for serious actresses, lovey," Corinna said over the rest of them.

"No reputable tragedienne would dream of appearing in a trouser-farce," Jean-Soleil said. "You'll have to sit this one out, Belle."

"We're not going to *do* it?" Corinna said.

"Of course we are," Jean-Soleil said. "It just takes you and Jabez and Levry, and it's not like it needs complicated sets or anything."

"And it won't take us more'n a day to get up to speed, even with Levry learning his lines," Jabez said. "When's the last time we did *Mardette*?"

"'Bout a septad," Corinna said, and as if that harder laugh had brought it, the Mélusinien drawl was back in her voice. "But, yeah, I could still do her in my sleep. All right, damn you. But they're going to hiss me off the stage."

"No they won't," Jean-Soleil said. "Wait and see."

⚜

Drin had that look in his eye, the one that said he wanted to corner me, although whether it was to make a pass or just to whine I couldn't tell and didn't want to know. I went to ground in my dressing room and discovered I had escaped from wolves to be trampled by buffalo: Vulpes was waiting for me. I wished I could have pretended it was a surprise.

"Good afternoon, Cressida," he said.

"Lieutenant Vulpes," I said and dropped a curtsy. He was clearly wondering whether it was ironic or not, and that was fine with me.

I told him what I had learned from Peter and Antony. I hated being glad to please him, but there was no denying the rush of gratitude and relief when he nodded and said, "Very interesting. And yet—why is Lord Stephen's marriage of such concern? He *has* an heir." And when I didn't answer immediately, he frowned at me. "Doesn't he?"

"I . . . don't know."

"It is a simple yes or no question, maselle," he said crossly, and I thought, If you believe such a thing exists, you don't know anything about Marathine politics.

I said, "As I understand it, Lord Shannon's position is ambiguous."

I was even more gratified by his obvious bafflement than I'd been by his approval. "He's not . . . that is, I understood that Lord Gareth had been *married* twice."

Prude, flinching from the word *bastard*. "Lord Shannon is perfectly legitimate," I said, "but his mother is the only annemer in the history of Mélusine to be burned for treason."

"Oh," said Vulpes.

"I don't understand the legalities of the situation—"

"Find out."

"Beg pardon?"

"I imagine you heard me perfectly well. And I'm sure you know who to ask. And how."

"Yes, of course," I said, and didn't let my voice twist. "But I thought you were interested in Gideon."

"You don't think this is an avenue worth pursuing?"

Insecurity is a terrible trait in a spy. "How should I know?" I said, and I did smirk at his suspicious glance.

"Find out about Shannon Teverius," he said through his teeth and flung himself out the door.

"Have a pleasant day, lieutenant," I said under my breath and prepared for my next move.

I was itchily aware that I had not treated Mildmay very well over the past few days. So tonight I really ought to go up to the Mirador and see Mildmay. And it would be easy to ask him about Lord Shannon, especially with the news of Lord Stephen's plans as an excuse. And I didn't have to worry that Mildmay might tell someone I'd been asking. He wouldn't.

I took a hansom to Chevalgate and tipped a page a demigorgon to find out where Mildmay was. It was the better part of an hour before the boy came panting back to report that Lord Felix Harrowgate was in a meeting of the Sponsors' Board and that the meeting should be done by four o'clock. I had him take me to Felix's suite to wait. Mildmay would just have to cope if Felix and I got into it.

Gideon was there, an ink-smear across his forehead and his fingers knotted in his hair, wrestling with another of his thorny theoretical problems. Despite the Mirador's refusal to admit him, he pursued his researches as fast as Felix brought him books from the Mirador's myriad libraries or the bookshops which lined the side streets off the Road of Horn.

His delight at my arrival was patent; he shoved all his theorems and diagrams out of the way, and unearthed the wax tablet and stylus he used for conversations. *What brings you here?*

"Boredom," I said with a vast mock-sigh and entertained him with a scurrilous and vindictive version of Bartholmew and Susan's decampment, finishing by saying, "So, you see, I have nothing better to do for the next two days than bother my friends and interfere with their work."

The benefit is all ours, Gideon wrote. *Are you waiting for Mildmay?*

"Will I annoy you?"

Not if you will talk to me, he said with a wide-eyed ingenue's look.

"Yes, because *obviously* you're dying of boredom."

He grinned. *No, but it does get a little lonely.*

"With Felix gone all day, I imagine it must."

Even when he's here. He gave me a semidefiant glower.

"Are you fighting again?"

When are we not? He shrugged, although it was an uncomfortable, twisted motion, as if he were trying to get out from under some invisible hand.

"Same old subject?"

It hardly matters. He would far rather fight with me than give me a single scrap of the truth.

"The truth about what?"

I don't know. He stared at the sentence for a moment, then changed the period into an exclamation mark. *Something is eating at him, but he obfuscates it endlessly.*

"Maybe he doesn't know himself?"

No, that's Mildmay.

He caught me off guard. I should have turned the conversation, but I said, "What do you mean?"

He raised his head and looked at me. *The things he claims he doesn't remember.*

"You think he's lying?"

No. I don't think it's that simple. But I think if someone pushed him— But Felix won't, and I see you won't either.

I broke eye contact and didn't answer. After a moment, the stylus started scratching again. *Felix thinks he has destroyed Mildmay.*

"Felix is prone to melodramatic nonsense," I said, parrying desperately.

Is that what it is? Think of Mildmay as you first met him. Can you find that man in him now?

"You should have been a dissector for the Medical College in Aigisthos," I said, still trying to turn the conversation, although it was plainly too late.

Answer my question. It is important.

"Important to whom? I didn't think *you* cared."

His head jerked back a little. *I consider him a friend. Don't you?*

I couldn't find an answer fast enough.

Why are you so surprised? Do you really care so little about him?

"You know that's not true," I said, but it was a weak defense. I was trying to find something better when Felix and Mildmay walked in.

Gideon had the presence of mind to close the tablet and drop it back into his pocket. I got my expression clear before I turned, but the way Gideon looked at Felix was like a man staring into some deeply desired hell. Mildmay gave us one swift, unreadable, green glance. Felix said, "Mehitabel! What are you doing here?" with every evidence of surprise and genuine delight. But he was a good actor, and I wouldn't have liked to bet that he'd missed the signs.

Felix—tall, beautiful Felix, as molly as de Fidelio's dormouse—wasn't as difficult to read as Mildmay, but I'd found that his skew eyes made his face unpredictable. I even had a conceit, half fancy, half uneasiness, that his yellow eye and his blue eye governed different expressions.

I gave Felix and Mildmay the same version of events I had

given Gideon, and when I had finished, Felix said, "Let me guess: this means you want to borrow Mildmay for the night?" The blue eye was gently teasing; the yellow eye had a spark of malice dancing in it.

"If it won't inconvenience your lordship too greatly," I said, giving him an ironic little curtsy—showing offense only made him worse.

"I think I can manage without him for tonight." Felix was looking at Gideon, but he turned his head to say to Mildmay, "Go on. Have fun."

Mildmay did that horrible thing he did sometimes to conversational gambits: let it drop to the floor and lie there twitching. After a very long pause, he said, "That an order?"

For a moment, I thought Felix was going to respond in kind, but then he quite visibly deflated and said, "No, only a wish. I'll see you tomorrow morning."

"Thank you," I said for both of us, and dragged Mildmay out the door.

Felix

:I am impressed,: Gideon said sardonically. :You passed up an opportunity for a fight. Does this mean you won't argue with me tonight either?:

:Not if you keep that up,: I said, groping for the person I was supposed to be. :Arguing with Mildmay's no fun, anyway. No challenge.:

:Am I meant to be flattered?:

:Only if you want to be. Gideon—:

He waited, eyebrows raised.

:There's something wrong with him, isn't there?:

:Yes,: Gideon said gently. :But you know that.:

:Yes,: I said, abruptly too weary to deny it. :Malkar.:

Gideon said nothing; I turned away to stare blindly at the bookcases. "*Damn* him. Even dead . . ."

:It is often said in Kekropia, to comfort the newly bereaved, that the dead person is not *truly* dead until the last person who remembers them dies.:

"Oh." I pressed my fingers to my mouth to try to stem a tide of lunatic giggles. "What a . . . what a *horrible* thought." It was no use; the laughter would not be stopped, and it was nearly a full minute before I could calm myself again.

When I turned back to face him, Gideon said, at his driest, :It is not a theory I subscribe to,: and that nearly set me off again.

But there was a question I wanted to ask, a serious one. :What *do* you believe? About the fate of the dead?:

:You want to talk about theology,: he said slowly, clearly wondering if my interest was genuine.

"I want to talk about the dead. And why they . . . haunt us."

:Literally or figuratively?:

"Sorry?"

:You understood me. Do you want to talk about ghosts or do you want to talk about why Malkar Gennadion continues to plague your brother—and you—nearly two years after his death?:

Gideon's eyes were too damnably sharp. :I suppose I want to be certain they are not the same question.:

:Do you believe you are being haunted by the ghost of Malkar Gennadion?:

His tone was neutral, but the question still stung. "No, of course not!" I said, pacing across the room to stare into the fire.

Into the silence, Gideon said, :But you are afraid.:

"I've been afraid of Malkar half my life. It's a hard habit to break."

Gideon crossed the room to stand beside me. :Mildmay is not being haunted by any but the specters in his own mind. I know the signs of haunting.:

:But he doesn't remember what Malkar did to him. He says so.:

:And how much effort is it costing him to keep Malkar safely forgotten?:

I said nothing.

:Felix—: He touched my arm lightly, as if he was afraid I would only move away from him. :Have you *talked* to him? About Malkar?:

I didn't move away. I couldn't. I couldn't even raise my head. :I kept expecting him to shake it off. To be himself again. And when I realized that wasn't going to happen . . . I don't know what to say! I don't know how to reach him, or even if it's possible. Frankly, I don't know if I have any right to try.:

Because it was my fault. But Gideon didn't need me to tell him that.

He said, :You are the only one who does.: I started to protest, but he cut me off. :*Because* you are to blame—and because you are his brother. Because you were . . . what you were to Malkar Gennadion. You're the only person who can understand.:

:Simon—:

:Mildmay won't talk to him. Do you think Simon hasn't *tried*?:

"I know," I said, my voice barely more than a whisper. "But I'm afraid . . ."

Gideon waited.

"What if he won't talk to *me*?"

Gideon started laughing.

I wrenched away from him. He said, :You must be the only person in the Mirador who hasn't realized Mildmay would walk on knives for you.:

:Yes, but he'd find that much less unpleasant.: I took a deep breath, raked my fingers through my hair. :What do you want, Gideon? Shall I promise to try?:

I could feel his gaze on me, although I refused to look at him. :This is not about what I want, although I realize it would be much easier for you if it were.:

"Stop it," I said and was horrified to hear my voice shaking. "Just . . . *stop*."

He sighed and after a moment moved away from me, back to the table and its piles of books. :What would you prefer to discuss? The weather?:

I struck back viciously. :Why don't we talk about the Bastion?:

:And her refugees in the Mirador? Yes. Let's.:

:Do you think Gemma Parsifal's offer of amnesty is sincere?: I asked, before he could say anything about Isaac, and it stopped him.

:No,: he said bleakly. :The Bastion does not—*cannot*—forgive. It relies too greatly on loyalty.:

:So does the Mirador.: Anything to keep him away from the subject of Isaac Garamond and where I went when I left the suite at night.

:No, not . . . I misspoke. It isn't loyalty at stake. It's *obedience*. And if the disobedient are not punished, then how can the obedience of the rest be commanded?:

I shivered at his tone, dull, flat, as if he was too weary to be horrified at what he knew.

:Once you have run,: he said, grimly pursuing the question, :you *cannot* be welcomed back. There is no abasement great enough to erase your sin. I don't know if Gemma knows she's lying, but she's lying all the same.:

:Then why make the offer?:

:To get us back,: Gideon said and bared his teeth in something that was not a smile. :And to wring every last scrap of information about the Mirador out of us that they can.:

He cut off my protest before it was even fully formed. :Don't think anything has changed. Gemma is far more politically astute than old Jules Mercator, but that doesn't mean that if you scratch her, she'll bleed a different color.:

:You sound as if you speak from personal knowledge.:

:I do.: He gave me no chance to ask further, but said, :The Bastion wants to see the Cabalines fall. They want the Mirador for themselves. And Lord Stephen having been such a great disappointment to them after the disasters of Jane's and Gareth's reigns, they are becoming less and less choosy about the means they employ. I am only afraid that some of the younger wizards may be foolish enough to trust Gemma's pretty words.:

:You could speak to them.:

:What need? Thaddeus and Eric between them will say all that can be said.:

:I am given to understand that Thaddeus tore up his letter of amnesty on the spot and threatened to feed it to Aias Perrault.:

:That's Thaddeus,: Gideon agreed. :Subtlety is ever his watchword.:

:He's probably already urging Stephen to declare war.:

:Expel us all as spies. He'd love to ship me back to the Bastion in a box.:

:You're never going to tell me why he hates you, are you?:

:No,: Gideon said and smiled at me sweetly. :The same way you're never going to tell me anything except exactly what you want me to hear.:

:Gideon—:

:Don't start,: he said fiercely. He sat down, opened one of the books, and bent his head over it in a fashion clearly intended to rebuff conversation.

I stood and watched him for some time before I said quietly,

"I'm going to bed." It took all my willpower not to allow my retreat to be a skulk or a scuttle.

It was much later when Gideon came to bed. Although I was awake, I said nothing, and although he knew I was awake, he did not try to touch me.

Mehitabel

I'd never exactly given up my room in the Mirador; no one had asked me to—it wasn't as if they needed the space—and Mildmay and I found it very useful. Neither one of us had much privacy in the normal way of things.

I was very careful with him—there were too many things I didn't want his terrifyingly sharp eyes to see. He came willingly enough to bed, and once there it was easy. Easy because he made it easy. The gentle expertise of his hands made a lie of the sullen silence he gave to the world. He let me take what I needed— almost flinched away when I tried to give in return.

We'd done this little dance a thousand times, me persisting until all at once he yielded; tonight it irritated me. "What," I said, "you're the only man in Mélusine who doesn't *like* getting sucked off?"

"It ain't that," he said, and added humbly, " 'M sorry."

Perhaps I should have pursued it, but I didn't. I didn't want to talk. Not until afterward, when I could push the conversation where I needed it to go.

I lowered my head and got to work.

Mildmay

After we'd fucked, when I was laying there feeling basically boneless, Mehitabel said, her own voice kind of dreamy, "I hear the Lord Protector is really going to get married again."

"About fucking time," I said.

"Why does it matter? Wouldn't Lord Shannon inherit anyway?"

"That's *why* it matters," I said, tracing the line of her back with one finger.

She rolled over to look at me. "You've lost me."

"Politics," I said.

"Yes, but this really *bewilders* me. I thought Shannon was a legitimate heir."

"Yeah."

She smiled suddenly. "You're teasing me, you devious little shit."

"Yeah," I said. She tried to tickle me, and we didn't talk for a while. But she came back to it: "Why would it be so awful if Lord Shannon became the Lord Protector?"

"He'd bitch it all to fuck," I said.

"Why? I know he's a fop, but—"

"Gloria Aestia. And he's molly. And . . . powers, I don't know." But I remembered the way he'd looked through me like I wasn't there. "He just ain't suited."

"You know," Mehitabel said, "I never *have* understood why Gloria Aestia is such a bugbear in this city. What did she do that was so terrible?"

"Treason ain't enough for you?"

"History—Marathine as much as anyone else's—is full of traitors. You've told me enough stories."

I couldn't argue with that. "Dunno if I can explain it."

"Oh, I have faith." And she could've meant it to be snarky, but it didn't sound like it.

"Okay. I'll give it a go. Gloria Aestia was Lord Gareth's second wife, right? And she was a lot younger than him. And, um, Lord Shannon was awful big for a septad-month baby."

"She trapped him into marriage. That's hardly unusual, either."

"Wait a minute. It gets better. See, it came out at the trial that she'd been Cotton Verlalius's lover a lot longer than she'd been Lord Gareth's."

"So Lord Shannon might not be a Teverius at all?"

"Oh, he's a Teverius all right. Legally, anyway. Lord Gareth made sure of that. But he might not be Lord Stephen's blood-kin any more than whatsisface Verlalius is. The one that moons around you all the time."

Which I shouldn't've said, but she let it slide. "You think the legal fiction wouldn't hold."

"No, but it ain't just that." I struggled with it a minute, and she let me. "Because he looks just like her, you know. And some people figure being molly ain't no better, morally speaking, than

being a slut. And it ain't just that she cheated on Lord Gareth,
neither. D'you know what it was she was aiming to do?"

Mehitabel shook her head.

"Her and Cotton Verlalius and their friends were going to
get rid of Lord Gareth. She'd seen to it that Lord Gareth had
named her regent—she could make him do damn near anything
she wanted. And once she was regent, something was going to
happen to Lord Stephen. And probably Lady Victoria, too."

" 'Something'?"

"Sort of thing that mostly happens to inconvenient people.
And then there Lord Shannon would be. Lord Protector with a
good septad of his minority still to go."

"And his mother pulling strings. I see why you said Amaryllis Cordelia was like her."

"They would've understood each other. And it's worse'n
that, even, her not being Marathine and all—"

"She had a Marathine name."

"She was Monspulchran. Like Simon. Monspulchra ain't far
from here, but it's Tibernian. And she never shut up about how
much better it was, neither. And at the trial, Cotton Verlalius
spilled his guts and said as how she'd wanted to make Lord
Shannon a king."

"And a king would be different from a lord protector *how*,
exactly?"

"King ain't got the Cabinet and the Curia riding herd on
him. It's what the Wizards' Coup was *for*."

"Ah," said Mehitabel. "All right. I can see that Lord Shannon's mother was a nasty piece of work. But do people *really*
think that Lord Shannon would turn into her the instant he took
the throne?"

"Well, yeah. Some people do. But it ain't really . . . I mean,
the problem ain't what people think Lord Shannon would do.
It's . . ." I really didn't know how to make her understand how
bad it would be. "Well, he'd be a shitty Lord Protector anyway.
And we'd be fucked."

"Countries have survived bad rulers before," she said.

"Not when they got Tibernia on one side and Kekropia on
the other."

"You're allied with Tibernia."

"Yeah, we're allied with Tibernia, same way Lord Shannon's

a Teverius. Everyone pretends real hard and it works okay. Mostly."

"What about the envoys?"

"They're new. Weren't no envoys before the Virtu got broke. See, the king is leaning on Lord Stephen to quit pretending and knuckle under for real, and it's only 'cause Lord Stephen's stubborn as a pig that he ain't caved yet. But Lord Shannon couldn't hold out against 'em."

"What would that mean?"

"Well, the Tibernians come in. They take the Protectorship apart, and if they're feeling really full of themselves, they take the whole Mirador apart with it. And then it's just Tibernia and Kekropia going head to head to see who's gonna get to be emperor."

"Emperor?"

"Fuck, yes. It's only the Mirador keeping Aeneas Antipater back. 'Cause the hocuses here, they don't want the king telling 'em what to do. They figure the Bastion's *their* problem. Bastion split off from the Mirador, you know, way back when, and the Mirador wants it back. Like a personal grudge. Do the hocuses out there feel the same way?"

"I beg your pardon?" She sounded startled, almost alarmed.

"Just wondering," I said.

"Oh. I'm sorry. I thought you said something else." She frowned a little. "I think some of them do feel that way, but for most of them it's just part of what they're supposed to do, like obeying orders. But I'm still confused."

"Get used to it," I said.

"But I thought the Mirador *was* doing what the king told them to."

"Darlin'," I said, "it ain't that simple. Why d'you think Felix spends half his mortal life in Curia meetings? It's all politics."

"Everything is," she said and kissed me.

Mehitabel

The Mirador had more clocks in it than any place I'd ever seen. In the Bastion, there was only one clock, a monstrous giant called the Juggernaut, which could be heard everywhere, in every corridor, staircase, and closet. The Mirador had once had such a clock; its name had been Nemesis. It was said to have been haunted, Mildmay had told me, his eyes shining with delight in a good story, and by the reign of King Mark Ophidius, the bells had no longer marked the hours, but rang at odd times and in a jangling cacophony that was said to have driven several people mad, including the wife of Mark's heir. It had been disassembled and its bells melted down. After that, understandably, the Mirador wanted nothing more to do with what were called Titan Clocks, and instead it became infested with small clocks which struck the hours regularly and sweetly—though rarely in time with each other.

Mildmay had gotten—scavenged or stolen, I didn't know and didn't ask—a clock for the room we used, one with a cunning mechanism by which you could have a bell ring at a particular hour. When we spent the night together, he would set it to ring at six o'clock—what he called the first hour of the day—so that he could get back to Felix's suite before Felix was awake.

He woke immediately and completely with the shrill clamor of the clock; I lay lazily in bed and watched him dress, admiring the play of muscles in his back and buttocks—Felix might be breath-stealingly gorgeous, but Mildmay had his own beauty, though I didn't think he was aware of it.

He'd braided his hair and was tying it with a black ribbon I'd given him long ago when he asked, "You going to court?"

"I thought I would." It would keep me visible, and that was not a bad thing—especially since it would be goodness knew how long until I was back on stage again. And I had to keep moving, had to keep working, had to keep the present real so that the past did not paralyze me.

"Would you . . . I mean, could you do me a favor?"

The hesitancy with which he asked—as if he expected me to say no—hurt, and I said unguardedly, "Of course. What is it?"

Stupid to make a promise so blindly, but almost worth it for the way his expression lightened. "It's Gideon," he said, and I relaxed a little. "He don't leave Felix's rooms hardly ever, and him and Felix are fighting, and I thought if you didn't mind, he could maybe come along with you, and then—"

"You wouldn't have to worry about him," I finished. That was practically babbling, for Mildmay, and I'd understood him mostly from long practice and context.

"Yeah." And he was definitely blushing.

I forbore to tease him, remembering Gideon's far more eloquently expressed concern for Mildmay himself.

And Felix between them like the Uleander Tree in *Edwin
and Esterhin*, beautiful and poisonous.

"I'd be glad to," I said, and I wasn't even lying.

Mildmay

That morning, Lord Stephen read out this long thing that,
stripped down of all the flourishes and pretty bits, was basically
fair warning. He was looking for a wife, and anybody wanting to
get a gal married off was going to have a chance to show her to
him. I watched the way people reacted. I saw a lot of quick sidelong glances at Robert of Hermione, standing as usual just behind Lady Victoria. Robert himself was looking glassy and
blank, trying to pretend like this wasn't a nasty kick in the balls
for him.

See, the only reason Robert was anybody in the Mirador was
him being the brother of Lord Stephen's first wife, Emily.
Robert wasn't much of a hocus, and he was about as bright as
ditchwater on a cloudy day—and a nasty-minded little shit to
boot. Oh, and Felix hated him like there wasn't nobody else
around who'd do it right. But Lord Stephen protected him—
even seemed not to mind him, but maybe that was just good
manners—because of Emily. But you couldn't imagine any second wife letting that go on.

It'd be nice, I thought, if Felix would keep his mouth shut for
the next few days, and not give Robert a target. When Robert
didn't like what Stephen was doing—and he hated most everything Stephen had settled with the envoys from Vusantine over
the winter—he looked for ways to make other people's lives a
misery. And him and Felix hated each other so fucking much, it
was like being in the middle of a war.

Fuck me sideways 'til I cry, I thought, and wondered why it
seemed like everything that happened these days was something that was going to make Felix's mood worse.

Mehitabel

Gideon had been reluctant, but Mildmay's clumsy manipulation
had worked; he was even more reluctant to admit to me that he

didn't want to go. We watched together as first the courtiers came in, then Lord Stephen and his siblings entered through the door behind the dais. Lord Stephen took his seat in Lord Michael's Chair, as the throne of the Lord Protector was styled, and then the wizards filed in to perform the daily ritual of loyalty, swearing their oaths to Stephen and committing their magic to the Virtu, which shone like a blue-green star from its plinth. And Mildmay was just behind Felix like a shadow. His part in the ritual—by the Mirador's own laws—was to fail to participate in it. The obligation d'âme meant that his only allegiance was to Felix, making them a separate kingdom of two, with Felix as king and Mildmay as ministers, army, and populace all combined in one. A stormy little kingdom, I thought, with periodic flare-ups of civil war and a magnificently unstable government. And I was glad I wasn't a citizen of it.

I practiced being a swan-daughter, as I did whenever I attended court, tall and grave and distant, and Gideon stood sharp-eyed and aloof beside me. But interested. After court, after Lord Stephen had made the announcement of his plans to seek a bride, it was Gideon who noticed Antony heading toward us. A sharp nudge in my ribs and a nod in Antony's direction, and I could see the inquiry in his raised eyebrows: *friend or foe?*

"Lord Antony Lemerius," I said under my breath. "Harmless."

That got me a sardonic quirk of his mouth, and he moved back a little.

Antony didn't notice him. "Mehitabel," he said. "I was wondering if you would do me a favor."

Not again. I bit my lip against the impulse to laugh and said, "What is it?"

"I, er, I wish to return to the crypt of the Cordelii to test a theory, and I was wondering if you would ask Mr. Foxe if he . . ." He trailed off, looking at me hopefully.

I said, "I can show you the way."

And then I wondered what in the world had possessed me.

"Could you?" Antony said with unmistakable relief.

"I remember the route Mildmay took. When do you want to go?"

"Er, this evening? About nine?"

Not the ideal time for exploring a crypt, but in the great and windowless bulk of the Mirador, it hardly mattered.

"All right." And then a thought hit me, mingled charity and malice, and I said, "Gideon, do you want to come?"

Gideon blinked. He pulled his tablet and stylus out of his coat pocket and wrote in his neat, swift, highly Kekropian hand, *Won't I be in the way?*

"Not a bit," I said brightly, ignoring the appalled expression on Antony's face that said otherwise. "And if you're along we won't have to worry about the candles going out."

He made me a small, ironic bow.

"Good," I said, and to Antony, briskly dismissive, "We'll meet you at nine in the Stoa St. Maximilian." Gideon was happily quick to pick up my cues, quicker than many actors I'd worked with, and we made our exit.

Back in Felix's suite, he was still eyeing me with puzzled speculation. "What?" I said.

He wrote, *Why do you want me along?*

"Can't I enjoy your company?"

It embarrassed him; he looked away for a moment, then wrote, *I hope that you do. But that does not answer my question.*

"Oh, God, Gideon, do you have to analyze everything to death? Look, that crypt isn't a very pleasant place, and Antony is, um, uninspiring company at the best of times."

His eyebrows went up; I said, "I know, I know—that being so, why did I offer?" I didn't know the answer to that myself, so I chose a reason I thought he'd accept: "I didn't want Mildmay to have to put up with Antony on top of everything else he has to put up with all the time. All right?"

He considered me a moment. *It is not a crime to love some-one.*

That depends very much on whom you love. But I didn't say it.

Mildmay

Today was Jeudy in the Mirador's reckoning, and Jeudy afternoons were when Felix locked himself in his workroom and did hocus stuff. Sometimes he told me to clear out. Sometimes he dragged me in with him, because he needed me for one reason or another, because of the obligation d'âme or just because he needed somebody to stand still at a particular spot on the floor. Every once in a while, he'd let me choose if I wanted to come with him or go off on my own. I always stayed with him. On Jeudy afternoons he was like a different person. He never said anything mean, and he'd talk to me sometimes the way he talked to his friends, like I was smart enough that it mattered to him that I understood him. I hoarded up those afternoons like a miser counting decagorgons. And it always seemed to make Felix happy, too.

This afternoon I was expecting him to run me off. But he stopped at the door and raised his eyebrows at me. "Do you want to come in?"

"Um. Sure. I mean, if you don't mind."

"If I *minded*, I would have told you to go away," he said. But there was no sting in it. He unlocked the door. "Come on."

We didn't talk much for an hour or so. He was tangled up in some crazy thing that had him crawling around on the floor with lots of string and chalk. And it seemed like he kept running into the east wall, like it wasn't where it was supposed to be. Finally, he sat back on his heels and said, "Damn. Damn, damn, damn."

"What's the matter?" I said.

"I must look mad," he said and got to his feet. "I'm trying to diagram a *katharsis*."

"A what?"

"It's an old Troian word," he said, coming back to the table with his pieces of string snarled across it. "Translations vary, but it means something between 'purification' and 'purgation.' Both of those seem suitable to me."

"What are you wanting to, um, purge?"

"Oh, this is just hypothetical."

I waited, not asking, *So how come you keep on running into that wall?* Felix hated silence.

"Do you *always* know when I'm lying?"

I shrugged a little.

There was another pause before he said in a low voice, not looking at me, "Malkar had a workroom down in the Warren. No one knew about it but me."

I only realized after I'd done it that I'd made the sign to ward off hexes.

"Exactly," Felix said. "I don't want anybody coming across it by accident and finding . . . well, finding what Malkar left there."

"Sacred *fuck*. And you were just planning to sneak off all by yourself in the middle of the night?"

"I can't . . ." His voice choked off, and it was a moment before he went on. "I don't want Gideon to see it, and I can't think of anyone else who wouldn't laugh at me. The Mirador doesn't believe in ghosts and miasmas."

"I ain't laughing," I said. "Can I help?"

The piece of chalk he was holding snapped in half, like I'd startled him.

"I mean," I said, and I could feel myself blushing, "I can't do magic or nothing, but I can hold a lamp, or something. Or just *be* there."

"Thank you," he said. "That would indeed be a great help. But we'll have to do it at midnight."

"That don't surprise me at all," I said.

He managed about half a grin and said, "Doesn't."

🔊

We played Long Tiffany badly, both of us with our minds mostly somewhere else, until the sixth hour of the night. Mehitabel and Gideon left at some point, and it was only after they'd gone that I realized I'd forgotten to find out where they were going. I was mostly just glad we wouldn't have to think up some fancy story for them. But finally Felix threw down his cards and said, "It's time." He called witchlight as we stepped out into the hall, the little green chrysanthemums circling his head like a crown.

"Could you change the color on them if you wanted to?" I said.

He gave me a puzzled look, but his chrysanthemums went yellow, then orange and red and purple and blue, and then back to green. "Most wizards develop, er, shortcuts for the spells they use most often," he said. The green chrysanthemums began to spin in big figure eights around us both. "Mine for this spell just happens to make them green. Why do you ask?"

"'Cause I'm piss-ignorant," I said and made him laugh. "Just wondered."

"No harm in that. I'd never even thought about it. Malkar's witchlights were always green, and I just never . . ." He snorted. "I'm not going to change them now."

"I like the green. Better than Simon's awful blue globes."

"I'll remember to tell him that. Malkar did globes, too. I learned chrysanthemums from Iosephinus Pompey. He died the year you killed Cerberus Cresset."

"Oh."

Something got into my voice that I hadn't meant to let him hear. He said, "I didn't mean that in a pointed way. It's just that I associate Iosephinus's death with the absolute gibbering panic that possessed the Mirador all autumn. He was *very* old, old enough to remember the end of Lord Malory's reign, and I think he'd just outlived any care he had for what people thought or what the political fashions were that season. He said I was the most promising wizard he'd seen since he was a young man and was learning from Rosindy Clerk, and that it would be criminally stupid not to teach me everything I could learn. I was at least smart enough to listen to him." He shook his head, maybe at the memory of Iosephinus Pompey or maybe at himself.

We were moving out of the everyday part of the Mirador, into the Warren between the Mirador and the Arcane. The bitter smell of the Sim began to crawl up around us. Felix was shivering a little, but his witchlights stayed calm.

Felix argued with the other hocuses—Rinaldo and Edgar and Charles the Dragon and Lunette—about the building of the Mirador. There weren't any records. They'd all been lost or destroyed or never written in the first place. Charles the Dragon insisted that the lowest level of the Arcane had to be the oldest part of it. Charles the Dragon was a great one for logic and being rational and shit, and I didn't much like him. Felix said the Warren was older. Lunette and Edgar agreed with him. Rinaldo said firmly that the mazes around the Iron Chapel were older than anything else in Mélusine, and I thought Rinaldo had the right of it.

But leaving that aside, I agreed with Felix—not that any of 'em ever asked me. The Warren was older than the Arcane. The passages were lower and narrower, and the stonework was weird. The stones lay in these thin, sort of wavery courses, and Felix called them alien. They weren't quarried from either Rosaura or Mutandis, the way the Mirador and the Arcane were. They were from some other quarry, one that had been used up or lost or something. The Warren *felt* old, old and twisted and mean. Mikkary fucking everywhere. I'd never liked it, and I liked it even less now.

Felix stopped in front of a low, ironbound door. It looked like all the other doors we'd passed. He touched it lightly, almost like he was afraid it would burn him. I heard the tumblers shift, and he pushed the door open.

For a moment, I thought he'd been turned to a pillar of salt, like the woman in the old story who looked at Cade-Cholera's face. Then he said, "Someone has been here."

Powers and saints, that can't be good. "I thought you said you—"

"I did say. I thought I was." He sent his witchlights through the door. They settled to roost like crows on the braziers that circled the room. "It appears that I was wrong."

He stepped into the room. My mind was full of all the places I'd rather've been, but I followed him.

It was an ugly room. You could feel the Sim in it, which ain't a compliment. The floor was Rosaura marble, and the bright, wet, blood-red of the mosaic pentagram was Stay Hengist's work for sure. Hengist had repaired the mosaics in the Hall of the Chimeras for Charles Cordelius, and he'd never told nobody how he got his colors. There were manacles bolted to the points of the pentagram, and I didn't want to ask what they'd been used for. Felix's witchlights weren't much use against the dark in this room, but I wasn't going to light the coal in the braziers or the candles in the sconces any more than he was.

"Powers," I said, mostly to prove that I hadn't been struck dumb. "I didn't think there were rooms like this outside of all them stories about evil hocuses."

Felix laughed, but not like anything was funny. "You have no idea of how pleased Malkar would be to hear you say that. He *loved* playing the part of the evil wizard when he could get away with it. He had a monster's vanity. A monster made of vanity." His voice had gone weird and dreamy, and his spooky eyes—even worse by witchlight—were wide and bright. I'd learned the signs. His attention was on his magic now, not on me or the room or even on himself.

If you were going to be a hocus, you had to be able to concentrate like you were made of stone. Simon had told me that once, though I couldn't remember what he'd been trying to explain. But I'd understood, because when Felix was doing magic, it was like he was somewhere else, where nothing—not thunderstorms or screaming fights or even the hullabaloo of a kitchen boy falling down the servants' stair with a tray of china—*nothing* could get to him. It made me understand why they might have started doing the obligation d'âme in the first place and why maybe it had been a good idea when they did. Because if you were going to get like that, you needed *somebody* guarding your back.

"Light your lantern," he said, and I did. When the nice, ordinary yellow flame caught and held, his green witchlights disappeared. The shadows in the room were immediately a septad-times worse. "I'll need you to follow me with the lantern," he said, fishing a piece of chalk out of his coat pocket. "Don't step on the chalk lines, and I'll draw you a circle of protection when I'm done." I couldn't tell if the circle of protection was just the next step or a reward to me for not smudging his lines.

I don't understand magic at all, but I could see that the pattern Felix chalked on the floor was the same one he'd been working on earlier—this time, the east wall was where he wanted it. I followed him and didn't step on his lines. He drew a quick circle across the doorway, surrounded by symbols. He'd told me once that the Mirador didn't believe in runes and diagrams. I thought anything that would keep Brinvillier Strych away from me was a good idea.

Felix went back to the middle of the room, where his chalk and Strych's pentagram seemed to come together, and drew some more symbols. He took a little wash-leather bag out of his inside pocket and emptied it out onto his palm. Dull greasy little lumps of something-or-other, and he put two of 'em in each point of the pentagram, lining 'em up real careful, although I don't have the first idea with what. When he was done and standing in the middle of the pentagram again, he said, "Sit down if you like. This may take a while."

I sat, carefully, and put the lamp where I wouldn't be blocking it. Then I waited.

Nothing happened that I was fitted out to sense, though after a while I could see sweat on Felix's face. But he just stood there, not saying nothing, not doing nothing. I began to think I could see shadows gathering around him, like the darkness was actually getting heavy and would smother him if it got the chance.

All at once, suddenly enough that it scared me, he let out a shout and flung up his arms. Light, whiter and harder than anything I'd ever seen his magic do before, shot out from his fingertips to fill every corner and crack. There was a loud, sharp snap like a firecracker. When I looked, I saw that the manacles in the pentagram had all broken in half, right where he'd put those little greasy lumps. Every candle and piece of coal, even the candle in our lantern, burst into flames, burning so fast and hot that they went out again seconds later.

But there was nothing scary about the darkness they left, excepting of course where we were and what we were doing. I didn't hear nothing strange or feel like anything was reaching for me. And it was probably only a second or two before Felix's green witchlights woke up again. By their light, I saw that Felix's chalk lines had disappeared, and the mosaic glass of the pentagram was all dull and cracked, like it'd been in a fire.

Felix was swaying where he stood. I scrambled up and got to him just before he fell. I had his full weight for a second before he got his feet under him again. "Thanks," he said. "I've been facedown in this damn pentagram too many times already." We staggered together out the door, where he leaned against the wall while I fetched the lantern.

"Let me see that a moment," Felix said. I handed it over. He examined it from all sides, even touching the puddle of tallow with one finger. "That's odd," he said. "No magic is supposed to be able to cross that circle of protection—at least, according to the grimoire I found it in—but that spell certainly did."

"Did it work—your spell, I mean?"

"I think so," he said. "It's a nebulous sort of thing to try to do, but I am at least sure that Malkar's spirit—if there is anything left of it—can't use this room as a focus to . . . restructure itself."

"Restructure? You mean, like, come back? *Could* he have?"

"There are records of such things happening," he said, pushing himself slowly off the wall. We both waited for a moment, but his legs held him. "Oh damn. The rubies."

"The which?"

"Malkar's rubies. I can't leave them there."

He went back into the workroom, moving about as fast as a slow turtle, and picked up his little greasy lumps of something-or-other, two at a time. Strych's rubies. I swallowed hard, remembering like a fever-dream him kicking through Strych's ashes, picking them out.

"How long you been carrying them around?" I asked when

he came back into the hall, the rubies already back in their little bag and it already back in his pocket.

He shrugged. "I won't have to any longer."

"What're you gonna do with 'em?"

He gave me a look, sidelong and very bright-eyed. "Oh I thought I'd give them to the necromancers down in Scaffelgreen. What do you *think*, dimwit?"

"Well, I dunno. Dunno what you're s'posed to do with something like that."

"There isn't exactly an established protocol," he said, real dry but not mean this time. "But I have some ideas."

I didn't want to know. Really didn't.

He closed and locked the door, muttering a word to it that I didn't catch. "*That* will be a surprise for whatever weasel has been sneaking down here." I didn't like the glint in his eye when he said it, but I didn't like the idea of somebody poking around in that room, neither.

We started back up the hall together. "Who d'you think it was?" I said.

"I don't know," he said, "and that worries me. Up until an hour ago, I would have said I was the only person in the Mirador Malkar trusted his hold on sufficiently to bring to that room."

"Could somebody've found it by accident?"

"Not a chance. The spell on that door was specially tailored. I got past it because I helped him cast it—anyone trying to pick it, whether magically or physically, wouldn't do anything but fuse the entire lock mechanism straight into the wall. No. Malkar trusted somebody enough either to teach them the spell . . . or give them the key."

"Powers," I said.

"What really worries me, though," Felix said, "is if there's anything in the Mirador that Malkar told this weasel about, and didn't tell me."

I didn't have any kind of answer to that, but we walked a little closer together, like sheep who hear a wolf howling.

Mehitabel

Dinner that evening was a peculiar meal. Felix and Mildmay were preoccupied with something which they weren't sharing.

Sometimes you could feel the bonds between them, their blood-ties and the obligation d'âme, like a kind of wall—or the borders of a kingdom, as I'd thought that morning—and that was how it was tonight. Felix barely even seemed to notice when I remarked that Gideon and I had plans for the evening and would be out late; I saw Mildmay register the news, but he didn't so much as lift an eyebrow at me. I hadn't intended to keep it secret from him, exactly, but there seemed no point in discussing it when he and Felix were so clearly somewhere else. I could see in Gideon's face when we closed the door behind us at quarter of nine that he was as relieved as I was.

We met Antony in the Stoa St. Maximilian and made our way down through the shadowed and derelict halls of the Mirador. Despite my crack about Gideon's usefulness, Antony had brought a lamp, and I was glad of the homely light.

"So what is this theory you want to test?" I asked Antony.

"I did some checking. And reconfirmed everything I already knew, including the fact that Amaryllis Cordelia never returned to the Mirador after her husband lost his post. Not that she had much time to, since she died in childbirth two years later."

"What was his name?"

"I beg your pardon?"

"His name. Mildmay couldn't remember it."

"Wilfrid, if you truly want to know. Wilfrid Emarthius. But my point is that that tomb has to be a blind. It must be concealing something."

"Ah," I said warily, but Gideon interrupted with a touch at my sleeve. His witchlights illuminated his tablet very nicely: *Who was Amaryllis Cordelia?*

It was a fair question. It wasn't hard to get Antony started, either, and the rest of the way to the crypt, we regaled Gideon with the sordid history of Amaryllis Cordelia.

The door was still unlocked. Antony led the way directly to Amaryllis Cordelia's tomb. Gideon read the inscription and wrote thoughtfully, *Is this a common sentiment for memorials?*

Antony considered a moment, taking candles from the sack he had brought and lighting them to let their wax anchor them to the freestanding tombs nearest Amaryllis Cordelia's plaque. "I know of three or four variations on that same platitude. Why?"

Gideon shrugged, running his fingers over the deeply carved letters of her name, and then wrote, *Only a folk belief common in the Grasslands, that ghosts are the dreams of the dead.*

"You mean someone was trying to avert haunting?" I said.

Possibly. From what you said of her life, I can understand not wanting her ghost to walk.

"It's an interesting idea," Antony said, "but it hardly matters, because she isn't here."

"Do you think it's just a fake, then? Nothing but the slab?"

"I think it's a riddle," Antony said, and the unsettling light in his eyes wasn't all reflections from the candles.

Gideon and I exchanged an uneasy look. "What kind of riddle?"

"What better place to hide secrets than in a crypt?" Antony said, flourishing a crowbar he'd pulled out of his sack.

"Don't answer questions with questions, Antony," I said.

He glared at me. "You need not help if you don't want to, but kindly don't get in the way."

I promptly got in the way. "I want to think this through again."

"What is there to think through? An obviously, *demonstrably* false tomb—it's only logical to assume that it's a hiding place for something."

"But what in the world—"

"That," said Antony, stepping around me, "is what I intend to find out."

The tombs of the Cordelii had been designed so that one *could* open them again without breaking anything, if one really wanted to. I wondered morbidly, watching with Gideon as Antony levered the stone out of the wall, if that had been in case they forgot and buried one of the kings with his heart still in his body. I hadn't meant to help—this felt wrong to me, and I was increasingly sure I wanted no part of it—but I ended up taking one end of the stone, just to keep it from smashing to bits on the floor. I figured we'd be putting it back in another couple minutes.

It was a thin stone, not as heavy as I'd expected; on the count of three, Antony and I pulled it free of the wall and laid it down.

Gideon screamed.

I had never heard him make a noise before, not once since Bernard Heber and Mildmay had hauled him out of the oubliette in Aiaia. At first, I didn't even connect the noise with

Gideon but looked frantically up at the tomb, assuming in some morbid madness that such an awful, senseless sound had to have come from there.

I might have screamed myself; later, I found my memory of the next few seconds vague, until I was standing, with Gideon and Antony, pressed back like cornered animals against the tomb of Geoffrey Cordelius, the same one Mildmay and I had sat on as he told me the story of Amaryllis Cordelia and her ambition.

There was a body in the wall niche, now slumped halfway out; Gideon later confessed that for a moment he had thought the body was a ghoul, like the ones that infested the swamps to the south of the city. It was richly clothed in a gown of what had once been velvet, black stitched with white seed pearls; its hair, long and colorless, was dressed under a cap of the same. The eyelids were open, the sockets clotted and staring. The hands had petrified into claws, and every time I tried to close my eyes that night, I saw them again.

"It wasn't a riddle," Antony said in a dull, dazed voice. "It was the literal truth."

"*Is* it her? I hate to ask, but, really, *is* it?"

"The ring she's wearing." Antony pointed with a none-too-steady finger. The ring, plainly visible on the corpse's dangling left hand, was a huge beryl signet. "It's the Emarthius unicorn holding a rose. That's *her* signet. It's her."

"God," I said.

We have to put her back, Gideon wrote, in straggling, wobbly letters completely unlike his normal handwriting.

Antony and I looked at him in horror.

We can't leave her like that.

"God," I said again, knowing he was right. "Who's going to touch her?"

We looked at each other. I had seen death before. But this thing which had once been Amaryllis Cordelia . . . I bit back the question rattling around my skull: do you suppose she died before or after they put that stone in place?

"I'll do it," Antony said. "It is, after all, my fault." Neither Gideon nor I was moved to protest. Antony carefully lifted the corpse back into its niche and laid it out flat; he put the dreadful claws together over its chest, the beryl signet uppermost, in a parody of peace.

I helped Antony guide the tombstone back into place. It was

harder to lift than it'd been to let down; in the end Gideon had to help after all, bracing it as we lined it up with its tiny grooves. When it slotted back into place, it did so with a sudden thump of finality.

Antony blew out the candles, leaving them where they stood, as if Amaryllis Cordelia's tomb were a kind of shrine. As if the rumor he'd mentioned, about burning offerings in the crypt of the Cordelii, was starting, in a strange backward way, to come true. He collected the lamp, and we left; I looked back once, seeing the inscription stark with shadows. All things considered, I thought that was the kindest wish one could make for Amaryllis Cordelia, and I made it a prayer of my own as I closed the door of the crypt: God grant her sleep be dreamless.

Chapter 4

Mildmay

When we got back from the Warren, we found Gideon, Mehitabel, and Lord Antony huddled around our fireplace like kids who've been told too many stories about the Tallowman to be able to sleep. I think me and Felix felt about the same.

"What is this," Felix said, "a second Cabal?"

"Not exactly," Mehitabel said. "Oh, Felix, this is Antony Lemerius. Antony, Felix." But you could see she'd done it by reflex, like good manners were so ingrained she couldn't ever get quit of them. Her mind was really somewhere else. I didn't think I'd ever seen her look that spooked, not even in Aiaia. "We just . . ." She trailed off.

"We just found something," Lord Antony said, almost like he was apologizing.

Mehitabel gave a laugh that sounded as fake as a four-centime piece and told us about their return trip to the crypt of the Cordelii.

"Sacred bleeding *fuck*," I said.

"Rather," Felix said. "Why would anyone do that?"

"More than that," Lord Antony said. "Who's buried at Diggory Chase?"

"And Gideon wants to know," Felix said, "why it is commonly believed that she was Amaryllis Cordelia."

"Why would any woman agree to that?" Mehitabel said.

The more you thought about it, the more it itched at you. I can't abide mysteries anyway. "And why would you *have* to?"

"It would appear," Lord Antony said, "and forgive me for thinking out loud, that it was vitally necessary to someone that Amaryllis Cordelia's death be made invisible. By the way, I think I know why she's in the Cordelius crypt—you were right, Mehitabel."

"I was?" Mehitabel said. "About what?"

"She was pregnant with Charles's child."

We sat there for a minute, blinking like owls.

"I admit I didn't examine the corpse closely enough to tell, but that dress she was wearing—I knew it was familiar."

"What was it?" Felix said.

"You know the state portrait of Queen Thamasin in the Judiciary?"

Felix, Mehitabel, and Gideon all looked blank. "Oh," I said. "Yeah. You mean the one, *Pregnant in the Sixth Month with His Majesty's Heir*?"

"That's it. We probably wouldn't have it if that first child had turned out to be a girl, but it was Matthias just as expected. The body was wearing an exact replica of that dress."

"Pregnant in the sixth month with his majesty's heir," Mehitabel said.

"It's exactly the sort of grandly greedy gesture Amaryllis *would* make," Lord Antony said. "I suspect her murderers appreciated the irony."

Another silence.

"They couldn't let the child be brought to term," Lord Antony said, "because the laws about minorities and regencies are entirely different if the ruler in question has an heir."

"But—" Mehitabel began.

"Remember that my 'they' are the men who created the Puppet Kings," Lord Antony said. "They wanted power, just as poor Amaryllis did. We know she wanted it badly enough to murder Laurence, and history shows us how much easier it is to murder by committee."

"How do we know she murdered Laurence?" Felix asked.

"Because she was pregnant," Lord Antony said.

"Beg pardon?"

"When Amaryllis Cordelia became pregnant with Charles's child," Lord Antony said, "there were several things she had to accomplish in order to parlay her child into power. After all, merely announcing that she was pregnant by someone other than her husband wouldn't get her very far."

"True," Felix said.

"What she really needed was to marry Charles. At the very least, if a king acknowledges an illegitimate child as his own, then that child can legally be entered into the succession."

"I sense a 'but' coming," Felix said, and I thought it figured that him and Lord Antony would be getting along like a house on fire. Mehitabel liked guys who were good with words, and Kethe knows Felix could keep himself entertained by talking for just hours on end. *Door slammed in your face again, Milly-Fox?* Keeper's voice said sweetly, and I wished my own stupid head would leave me the fuck alone.

"None of that applies to a king's heir," Lord Antony said. "The bastard son of a prince is just that: a bastard son. And her ideal option, to become Queen Amaryllis . . . Charles, as the king's heir, couldn't marry without the king's consent."

I said, because I couldn't stand not to, "And Laurence would never let him marry her."

"Exactly. Laurence set up the conditions of regency several months before his death, and he worked very hard to exclude the possibility of Amaryllis—or any woman—ruling through Charles. Most historians think he was too trusting of his advisors and simply failed to see what scope he was leaving them—but he knew his son, as well. I don't know. In any event, Amaryllis would never have been able to get the king's permission to divorce her husband—she'd have had to petition Laurence for that, too—and marry Charles. I'd never quite understood before why she couldn't just *wait*."

"Oh, I see," Mehitabel said. "Being pregnant, she had only a limited amount of time to get what she wanted."

"So, to her mind," Felix said, "Laurence had to go."

"Yes," Lord Antony said. "If Charles became king before her child was born, he could divorce her from Wilfrid and marry her himself. No problem in the world."

"So she had Laurence murdered," Mehitabel said.

"And then," Felix said. "Well, what *did* happen?"

"I'm still working on the chronology of events," said Lord Antony. "If she was really six months pregnant when she was murdered, something had obviously gone very awry with her plans."

"Something *did* go very awry with her plans," Mehitabel said. "She ended up dead."

"Yes, but I think that was only because she was finally getting what she wanted," Lord Antony said. "They'd have no reason to murder her if Charles wasn't showing signs of caving in."

"Or already had, Gideon says."

"*That* would do it," Lord Antony said. "If Charles *had* divorced her from Wilfrid, that would explain this bizarre need to pretend that she was still alive and still married."

"I'm not following," Mehitabel said.

"All right." Lord Antony sprang up and began to pace. "Imagine you're a councillor of King Charles. The only name I can remember right now is Gorboduc Briskett—so, imagine you're Gorboduc Briskett. King Laurence, whom you served faithfully for many years, is dead. His wastrel son has taken the throne and incidentally handed you an astonishing amount of power. You are, in a vulgar phrase, sitting pretty. I imagine you know, or strongly suspect, that Amaryllis Emarthia murdered King Laurence, but you aren't one to cry over spilt milk, and trying her for murder will make a filthy row. Then one day Charles says, 'Oh, by the by, I've divorced my cousin Amaryllis from her husband, and I think I'll marry her tomorrow—so our child will be legitimate, you understand. Wear your best for the wedding.' You, Gorboduc Briskett, are now in a terrible mess."

"How so?" Felix said.

Lord Antony wheeled around, his eyes lit up like chandeliers. "One. You cannot under any circumstances have Charles produce an heir *now*. You need the last three years of his minority to consolidate your power. I'll even grant that you may sincerely have the best interests of the kingdom somewhere in the general vicinity of what passes for your heart. Two. You know perfectly well that Laurence didn't want Amaryllis Emarthia anywhere near the seat of power, and I suspect you concur with your late sovereign's judgment. And furthermore—let's call it two-and-a-half—you remember your suspicions that she murdered Laurence, and for certain you don't want a regicide on the throne. Three. If Charles has already divorced her from Wilfrid, privately, then your chance of patching things over is gone. You know you won't be able to convince her to hush things up and raise Charles's bastard as an Emarthius. She's a strong-willed woman, and she knows what she wants. Where was I?"

"That was three," Felix said, dry as salt.

"Thank you. Four. *If* Amaryllis Emarthia is pregnant with Charles's child—or is patently willing to claim to the death that she is—then you cannot under any circumstances try her for Laurence's murder, which would otherwise be the ideal way to scotch this unpleasant marriage."

"Why not?" Mehitabel said.

"Two reasons. One is that everyone will believe the murder charges are trumped up to keep Amaryllis from marrying Charles. If you try her, and she's acquitted, she marries Charles, and you're out on your ear—or, more likely, executed yourself. The other reason is that, if you try her, it will come out that she's pregnant with Charles's child. Whether she's convicted or not, it is entirely illegal to kill a prince of the blood, i.e., any child of a king. And you can bet any sum of money you like that Amaryllis Cordelia's dying request would be that Charles recognize her child as his heir. Then, poof, Charles has an heir, and you're right back where you started: he's got the power and you're out on your ear."

"So," Felix said, "you have to erase Amaryllis Cordelia."

"Precisely. But you have to erase her without allowing her to disappear. If she simply vanishes—well, she was not an obscure figure at the courts of Laurence and Charles. People would wonder, and they'd pry, and they'd find out. If you simply smother her and try the normal trick of 'died of fever,' some clever-boots doctor is going to notice she was pregnant—it was so common for members of the house of Cordelius to die, er, unexpectedly that postmortem examinations were a normal part of the proceedings. And there must have been plenty of people around the Mirador who knew exactly what Amaryllis's relative relations were with her husband and her king."

"But," Mehitabel said, "if she was six months pregnant and wearing that dress—"

"We don't know that she was six months pregnant. I don't think she *can* have been. I'd be willing to bet it was more like three or maybe four. The dress was just a means of flaunting her victory." The light died out of his face. "I think they moved very fast. I think she was murdered the same day Charles divorced her from Wilfrid."

"And a new Amaryllis Cordelia took her place," Felix said.

"But who?" Mehitabel said. "And how? How could they carry it off?"

Lord Antony said, "I suspect that's why Wilfrid lost his government post and returned to Diggory Chase. He seems to have been a remarkably obliging man. Although I suppose he had little reason to mourn her."

"And Charles, who was going to marry her?"

"The kindest thing I've ever seen written about Charles—that wasn't intended for public consumption, of course—was that he was a pragmatist. Once Amaryllis was dead, and his potential heir with her, there was no profit for Charles in making a fuss. And he married Jemima well before Amaryllis's alleged death."

"A bribe," Mehitabel said.

"The councillors would have had it in their power to delay Charles's marriage until he turned twenty-one. All things considered, the fact that they didn't suggests that they had reached some kind of agreement with him."

"The whole thing hardly seems credible," Mehitabel said.

"I'm still working through it," Lord Antony said, sitting down again. "Plainly they did it, whether we believe it or not."

"Well, *someone* did it," Mehitabel said.

Lord Antony nodded. "But I still think it's Gorboduc Briskett."

Felix

I was late, but Thamuris greeted me without rancor or any sign of impatience. I told him a little bit about Amaryllis Cordelia, and he was fascinated, remarking wistfully that it was a pity there were no books of Marathine history in Troia.

"Most of it is just as unpleasant as that poor woman's fate, if not more so. I suppose it makes sense, really, that the Mirador has so many ghosts."

"Ghosts?"

"Oh, it's heresy to admit it, although they'd probably just call me mad. Again."

"You've seen actual ghosts?" he persisted.

"Assuming they *were* more than elaborate hallucinations, yes. And I've seen ghouls. I was sane, then. Why? Does Troian thaumaturgy deny the agency of the dead as Cabaline thaumaturgy does?"

"Does it?"

"Very much so."

"No wonder your ancestors are angry," he said somberly.

"I beg your pardon?"

"Your ancestors. They cannot rest, and that's bad enough. But it's even worse to be denied."

"You realize I have no idea what you're talking about." It was not an admission I made easily, but I trusted Thamuris not to use it against me.

For his part, he seemed merely puzzled. "You do not venerate your ancestors? At all?"

"I don't *know* my ancestors," I said, but he waved it aside.

"Not ancestors of the blood. Ancestors of the spirit. Like your Cabal."

"I beg your pardon?" I said again, helplessly.

"Are they not . . . I thought they were your Tetrarchs."

"I thought your Tetrarchs were gods."

"Gods?" He was shocked enough that I realized the suggestion was blasphemous.

I said hastily, "I didn't know. No one ever said . . ."

"The Tetrarchs are the founders of the four covenants. *Not* gods."

We were both silent for a moment; I was afraid that anything I said would only make matters worse. But finally my curiosity, and the uneasy, never-absent wondering if my katharsis was truly enough to keep Malkar away, drove me to ask, "You don't have ghosts?"

"Only very rarely. If the thanatopsis isn't performed properly."

"Thanatopsis?"

"The . . ." He grimaced, searching for words. "The ceremony. Would you say 'funeral'?"

"Not if it prevents ghosts. How does that work?"

"What do you mean, how does it work?"

"Well, I know how to lay a ghost, but how do you go about *preventing* one?"

"You start by honoring the dead," he snapped.

I was more than taken aback; I was shocked. "Thamuris? What did I say?"

"Nothing. You just . . . Do you approach *everything* as if it was a puzzle box?"

I considered the question. "Most things, I suppose. I wasn't trying to . . . I didn't mean to be callous."

"I know," he said, and managed a smile. "Discussing funerary rites just cuts a little close to the bone."

I was normally careful not to ask how he was, and his dream-avatar did not reflect his physical body unless he was truly ill. I said unhappily, "Are you, er, much worse these days?"

"No, it's not that. I'm doing rather well, really. All things considered. But . . . I can't ever *forget* it, either. And the celebrants at Hakko—I think they'd prefer it if I hurried up and finished dying."

"What they'd prefer is hardly relevant," I said and was rewarded with a better smile. "I didn't think you were still . . . that is . . ."

"They visit if their work happens to take them near the Gardens. They're very conscientious."

"Oh, are they?" I knew what that looked like.

"And they—" His face twisted, and emotion suddenly flared around him; we'd both learned to dampen the Khloïdanikos's more inconvenient effects, but his control had slipped. "They've started bringing their acolytes. I make a wonderful object lesson. And I can't very well protest, can I? I don't *want* anyone else killing themselves the way I—" He choked it off.

I gritted my teeth and patted his shoulder. And I resolved not to bring up the subject of ghosts again.

Mildmay

There was a Curia meeting after court. The Curia's the group of hocuses that tells the Lord Protector what to do. That ain't the right way to put it, of course, but it's enough to get by on. And don't ask me how they decide who gets to sit on the Curia and who don't. Felix was a member, even though I think about half the Curia would rather've taken him up to the battlements and pitched him over. So off we went, but Isaac Garamond caught us in the hall.

Shit, I thought, feeling sick for Gideon. I leaned against the wall to take some of the weight off my leg, and waited.

Mehitabel found me a couple minutes later. "Can you meet me tonight?" she said. "Usual place?"

When they left the suite, I'd seen Lord Antony put his arm around her. She hadn't shaken him off. I'd laid awake the rest of the night trying not to imagine what her and Lord Antony might be doing. I wondered what her voice sounded like when she talked to him, if she kissed him the same way she kissed me. I wondered what she said to him about me. Did she tell him I didn't mean anything to her, the same thing she'd said to me about him?

"What for?"

"I beg your pardon?"

"What *for*?"

She tried to laugh it off. "You have to ask?"

I wasn't laughing. "Yeah, I do. What do you want me for? You can have any man you want, and we both know it. So why the fuck d'you bother with me? Got a taste for freaks?"

"Mildmay, please. Don't—"

"Why not?" And then I said it. I'd been keeping the question back for months, not letting it out into the daylight, but there didn't seem no point no more. "How many other men are you fucking?"

"Mildmay, I—"

"Answer me."

"I don't see what business it is of yours."

I felt something tear loose inside me. I dragged her into a side-alcove and pinned her against the wall. *"Answer me."*

She gave me a glare fit to kill. She was going to tell me the truth, not because I'd frightened her, but because I'd made her mad. "Three or four. I don't keep count."

We'd both known that knowing would only make things worse. I let go of her and stepped back. She fussed with her sleeves, like that was what mattered. I said, "I think we better not see each other again."

Her head came up. She looked horrified. I suppose it might've been real. "What are you talking about? I've never made any secret—"

"I can't bear it no more," I said. "I don't mind the sleeping around so much, but I don't know who you are. I can't trust you, and there ain't no point if we don't trust each other. Good-bye, Mehitabel."

I couldn't look at her no more. I went back to Felix. Him and Mr. Garamond were standing, waiting, watching me.

"What's the matter, Messire Foxe?" Mr. Garamond said as I came up to them. "Crossed in love?"

Kethe. Does it show? "Nothing," I said. And I was glad I didn't have to try and smile at him.

"I'll see you later, Isaac," Felix said. "Come on, then, Mildmay, if you're done with your light of love."

I swallowed hard and went after him.

Mehitabel

First things first, I scolded myself fiercely. You *will not* panic. But controlling my panic felt like trying to kill a fast-moving snake with a shovel. Mildmay had always seen me more clearly than I wanted, but I hadn't realized just how *much* he saw. I felt horribly naked now, knowing that all this time he'd been aware that I was acting, even if he didn't know exactly how to articulate his awareness.

It could be worse, I said to myself and then had to stop to think of a scenario to prove it. But it *could* have been worse. Mildmay could see I was acting, but even his eyes weren't sharp enough to see behind the façade. And he wouldn't push me. That was the part he hadn't said, although I could fill it in for myself: he had reached the point where he had either to demand the truth from me or to leave, and he had left. I wondered, a little bleakly, whether that was because he knew he couldn't make me tell him, or because he thought he could. Either way, he'd chosen to respect my boundaries and withdraw from the battle. I was grateful to him for that, as my instinctual panic began to ebb. Grateful that he was shy, taciturn. That coercion wasn't in his nature. That he didn't want to know.

If I was honest with myself—and I might as well be, since I certainly couldn't be honest with anybody else—I could admit that it hurt, too. Particularly my pride. I couldn't remember the last time I'd had a man walk out on me. And it *would* be stubborn, silent Mildmay who had the balls to do it.

I would miss him. I didn't love him—not the way he'd wanted me to—but he'd been a delight to listen to, once you got him started, and a virgin's wet dream in bed. And I'd become fond of him.

"Oh, God *damn*," I said and pinched the bridge of my nose.

"Are you all right?"

I nearly had a coronary on the spot, not just because I hadn't known anyone was there, but because I recognized the voice, and I didn't need to meet Lord Stephen Teverius's slate-gray eyes to place it, either.

I'd never been this close to Lord Stephen before; he wasn't the sort to flirt with actresses. His bulk was impressive—more muscle and bone than fat—but it was his gaze that went through me like a skewer and made me feel oddly breathless. Like a basilisk, I thought, too dazed at that moment to know whether it was a sensible comparison or not, and then pulled myself together by main force, faked a smile, dropped a curtsy, said, "I am fine, my lord, thank you."

"Did he hurt you?" Lord Stephen said, disregarding what I supposed had been a rather obvious lie.

"No, quite the reverse." And Mildmay *had* upset me, because it came out waspish. And it wasn't what I should have said, anyway. Well, precious little point in doing things by halves, as Gilbert says in *Third Time's the Charm*, between murdering his loathly wife and dispatching her aged and equally loathly mother. I let myself laugh, a little deeper and earthier than I usually considered prudent, and it paid off, for Lord Stephen said with a reluctant twinkle, "I suppose I *was* asking for that."

"I shouldn't conduct the messy termination of my love affairs in public," I said.

"Termination?" His eyebrows went up.

"Oh, very definitely."

"Ah." Something flared in his eyes before he banked it down again. "Then will you have dinner with me this evening?"

And no matter what turmoil I might be in, I'd be dead before I was stupid enough to turn him down.

જ⁊

No sooner was I out of sight of the Hall of the Chimeras' great bronze doors than Vulpes emerged from a cross-corridor, caught my elbow, and dragged me bodily into one of the little parlors this part of the Mirador was infested with.

"We must stop meeting like this," I murmured crossly, disengaging from him.

He ignored it. "What did you do to Messire Foxe? And what were you talking about with the Lord Protector?"

I hadn't seen him at all—but he was a wizard. And Eusebians had spells for that sort of thing.

"Lord Stephen invited me to dine with him tonight," I said, betting—correctly—that that would make Vulpes forget about Mildmay entirely. He thought of a great many things he wanted

me to find out—more when I told him what I'd learned from
Mildmay; I finally shut him up by asking if I should get pen and
paper to make a list, and I escaped shortly thereafter.

I got back to the Velvet Tears as fast as I could, and there
God smiled on me at last: Corinna was in her room, masking
the moth-holes in a velvet suit-coat with embroidery of dragon-
flies. I halted in her doorway, breathing hard; she glanced up,
then her eyes widened. "Powers, Tabby, what's got into you?"

"I have . . . a date this evening," I panted. "With . . . Lord
Stephen."

She stared at me, her mouth dropping open. "You're kidding."

I shook my head helplessly.

"Powers and saints," she said, awed.

I finally had my breath back. "I need a dress."

"Oh, lovey, you sure do. Come here, and let's see what's
what." And she carefully anchored her needle in the lapel of the
suit-coat and stood up to throw open before me the treasures of
the Empyrean and the Merveille.

Mildmay

I watched the things that happened in the Curia meeting that afternoon like I was planning a hit, studying everybody's faces
and voices like if I understood them I could understand the
world. Five minutes after we left the Lesser Coricopat, I
couldn't remember a single damn thing anybody'd said.

"Are you all right?" Felix said as soon as we were clear of the
hocuses.

"Yeah."

"You don't want to talk about it, you mean."

"Well, I don't."

"Suit yourself," and we went off to the Fevrier Archive for
what was left of the afternoon.

Whatever Felix was after, he didn't find it, and dinner that
night was silent like falling down a well. Felix was staring off
into space like he was waiting for some answer to come walking
through the door. Gideon looked like the only reason he wasn't
asking questions was being afraid Felix would answer him. I remembered that I still didn't know what Felix had been doing the
night I showed Mehitabel and Lord Antony the crypt of the

Cordelii—and was she with him now?—and I didn't blame Gideon for not really wanting to know. There's things you can't unknow once you've got a good look at them, and some of them are the kind of thing that kills love dead as stone.

When I asked, Felix let me go without so much as a raised eyebrow. He probably thought I was meeting Mehitabel, and I didn't tell him otherwise.

What I did, because I couldn't stand having nothing to think about but my own stupid self, was go hunt up Hugo Chandler.

I knew where Hugo lived. There was a whole gaggle of musicians living along a kind of half-floor called the Mesmerine. It was in one of the older sections of the Mirador, kind of run-down. Nobody else wanted to live there, so nobody minded if the musicians wanted to practice in the middle of the night.

I knocked on Hugo's door, and after a moment, he opened it.

"Mildmay!"

"Hey, Hugo. Can I come in?"

He blinked at me. "Sure, I guess." He stood aside. I tried not to limp going past him, but I don't even know why I cared. It wasn't like he could tell Ginevra or nothing.

"S-sit down," Hugo said.

"I don't mean to make you nervous," I said. "I just wanted to ask you something."

"No, it's fine. Really. What did you want to ask?"

"Well, I was wondering." Powers, I couldn't think of a way to say it that didn't sound like the stupidest fucking thing in the world. I did sit down—he had a couple chairs, cheap knockoffs of Ervenzian vinework from St. Millefleur. Hugo didn't sit. "You know how when Ginevra died?"

"Yeah."

Well, of course he did, Milly-Fox. Not the sort of thing he was going to forget any more than I was. But I couldn't bail now. "I figure it wouldn't've been worth Vey's while to go hunt her out. Not up in Nill where Austin was. So somebody must've told her."

"Yeah?" He was fidgeting around the room. I'd better make this quick, before I spooked him into a brain-strike or something.

"So I was wondering if you remember anybody asking questions. You know, like they were fishing. Or anybody new around. Or anything like that."

He was shaking his head almost before I'd got the words out.

"Nothing like that. I'm sorry." And then he gave me this funny little sideways look through his eyelashes. "Why're you asking now? It's been—"

"A while," I said, because I didn't want either of us doing the math. "I know. I just . . ." I wasn't going to try to explain to Hugo about Mehitabel, and about what she'd said, and about how it'd kind of been like a kick in the head and made me start thinking again—after working so hard on *not* thinking for so long. "Well, it itches at me. That's all."

"Okay," Hugo said, like he wasn't sure it was.

"I'll clear off," I said and got up. "Thanks, Hugo."

"Good night, Mildmay," Hugo said, and I heard him bolt the door after he'd closed it.

"Boo," I said under my breath at the door and went off home.

Mehitabel

Corinna's eye for fashion was second to none; I left the Velvet Tears that evening certain at least that I was as close to beautiful as I would ever get. She had chosen a severe dress in green-black silk and dressed my hair in the stark lines of the Amadée—both utterly inappropriate to an actress of known immorality and all the more satisfying for that.

The guards at Chevalgate had clearly been told to expect me, and there was a page waiting, a skinny brown child like a sparrow, to guide me to the Lord Protector's private apartments. I followed him through the Mirador as a swan-daughter, tall and grave and pale. Well, sallow, but it would have to do.

The page knocked at the door for me and did not bow himself away until it was answered, by a stout middle-aged man in livery. The butler, assuming the Lord Protector had such a thing.

He showed me into a small sitting room, less lavishly appointed than I had expected; the furniture was well cared for and clearly valuable, but not yet beyond the borders of "old" into "antique." Lord Stephen rose from the depths of a wingback chair to bow over my hand in a way that the court gallants would have considered hopelessly old-fashioned—a good match for his conservative tailoring and the soberly symmetrical curls of his powdered and pigtailed hair.

There was a portrait over the mantel, a slender bronze-skinned woman, very young, with large, dark eyes and smoky-black hair; she was wearing a pale blue dress that suited her far better than the massive crimson and gold court gown of the formal portrait. Gambling that Lord Stephen would be unimpressed by small talk, I asked, "Is that a portrait of your wife, my lord?"

He glanced up at it, as if it had become part of the furniture for him. "Yes. It was painted before our marriage."

Now there, I thought irritably, is a gnomic utterance. Was it a fact? A judgment? A regret? He seemed himself to feel that he hadn't quite said enough, for he added, "It's the only picture of her that does her justice." He paused, thinking, and added, "She was very pretty, but not . . . not robust."

"She couldn't stand up to yards of stiffened brocade," I suggested, and his dark, blocky face was transfigured by a sudden smile. All those soirées, all those mornings in court, and I'd never seen him smile before.

"That's a very good way of putting it. She was like a princess in a fairy tale, but not . . ."

"Did you love her?" I said, deliberately provocative. I wanted to know what I could get away with.

He didn't take offense, seeming to consider the question a perfectly reasonable one. "I don't know. I don't think so, really. I doted on her, and I enjoyed the role of protector—ha! Didn't mean the pun. Sorry. I love her memory, but I'm not sure I'd love *her* now." His mouth quirked. "Easy to love a memory."

I thought, without at all wanting to, of Mildmay and the torch he was still carrying for Ginevra, and I was grateful that the manservant—butler or whatever he was—reappeared just then to announce dinner. I accepted Lord Stephen's arm to proceed into the dining room. Swan-daughter.

Lord Stephen held the chair for me, which I found more disconcerting than anything else. Actresses didn't rate that sort of courtesy from lords, regardless of anyone's intentions toward anyone else. And I didn't know what his intentions were.

Two young men, also in livery, served the soup, and I decided the imaginary Vulpes breathing down my neck could just go twiddle his thumbs in the corner for a minute. I had my own priorities to deal with, and the first had to be getting a handle on what Lord Stephen wanted.

I tried a feint toward the theater, but realized, horrified, several minutes later, that he had me doing all the talking. That wouldn't do. Well, he seemed to favor plain-speaking. I'd have to try again. "It was very kind of you to invite me, my lord," I began, but he cut me off with another of his barking laughs.

"Nothing of the sort. I'm putting the wind up Philip and Vicky."

"I'm sorry, my lord?"

"Beg pardon," he said, waving a roll in a sort of negligent apology. "My sister Victoria and Philip Lemerius. I'm sure you know I'm supposed to be getting married again."

"Yes, my lord."

"Well then," he said.

"I'm sorry, I still don't—"

"No, it's my fault. Shannon and Vicky are always on at me about it. But this is simple enough, really. Vicky and Philip are driving themselves mad looking for eligible girls."

I dared a smile, a wicked twinkle. "So you're hoping to send them into an apoplexy by dining privately with an actress."

"And I wanted to talk to you."

For a moment, I'd thought I understood, but now he was talking a foreign language again. "To me?"

His eyes, gray and unfathomable and suddenly frightening, caught mine. "You seem interesting," he said, and then the footmen came in to clear away the first course, and I couldn't tell what he meant.

5♪

For someone who seemed so simple and direct, Lord Stephen was a nerve-wracking dinner partner. When the footmen had gone again, and I could ask, he pretended not to remember what he'd said, much less what he'd meant by it, and diverted the conversation into other channels: the theater again; my impressions of the court; what I, as a Kekropian, thought about the Bastion and its recent upheavals. I felt like I was walking on an imperfectly frozen pond, under whose thin skin of ice a hungry monster lurked. There was no way to tell from Lord Stephen's manner what he knew or guessed or thought about my connections either to Felix or to the Bastion, but I was morally certain he was fishing for information about one or the other.

It was only after the footmen had wafted in and out one last time, leaving us with two snifters of brandy and a plate of sticky macaroons that I suspected were meant to appeal to my plebeian tastes, that Lord Stephen said, "You're a patient woman, Madame Parr."

"My lord?" I said.

"Shall we take the gloves off?"

"As your lordship wishes." If he'd meant to catch me off guard, he shouldn't have given me a whole dinner to get used to his conversational style.

"You're not telling me everything," he said, contemplating his brandy. "And that's fine. No reason you should. But I asked you to dinner because I wanted to ask you about someone."

"About whom, my lord?"

"Felix Harrowgate."

"What about him?"

"Just tell me what you think of him."

"Beautiful as daylight and knows it. Vain, self-centered, hot-tempered, and a born troublemaker."

Lord Stephen said after a thoughtful pause, "You know, of course, how much I dislike him."

"It's hardly a secret."

"No." His gaze skewered me again. "I would rather you *didn't* tell me what you think I want to hear."

"I don't know what you want."

"I've gone about this all wrong," he said sadly. "Madame Parr, I'm not trying to pry anybody's secrets out of you. I just wanted the opinion of someone without quite so much . . . *baggage*."

"What makes you think I don't have baggage?"

"Well, you do, of course, but my impression was that it was more on the other side."

"It's not that simple."

"Nothing ever is." He contemplated the brandy in his glass. "He worries me, you know."

"Felix? But I thought you—"

I cut myself off, quite deliberately, as if I hadn't meant to be tactless. It made him laugh.

"Hated each other? We do. But—Malkar Gennadion brought him to the Mirador the same year I became Lord Protector. I suspect now that the timing was deliberate. Certainly, there are a number of questions *someone* should have been asking that never got asked."

"What do you mean?"

"Malkar Gennadion," Stephen said with a grimace of distaste. "Brinvillier Strych. If we'd just been paying attention, he wouldn't have been able to worm his way in, wouldn't have been able to get close enough to destroy the Virtu. And my sister wouldn't have had an affair with our grandmother's murderer."

"Um," I said, this time not faking uncertainty.

"Sorry," Stephen said. "It rankles."

"It must," I agreed cautiously.

"Wasn't my point." He took a swallow of brandy. "It's how Malkar always worked, you know. You started off on one thing, and somehow he'd get you going on something else. So you'd ask the question *he* wanted. And you wouldn't ask all the other questions. Like what he *did* to Felix."

"What do you mean?"

"Oh, lots of things," Stephen said grimly. "But does he ever talk about him? About Malkar?"

"No, of course not."

"Why 'of course'?"

"Felix values his privacy far too highly to talk about anything that serious."

Stephen snorted.

"No, it's true," I said. "Of all the things you know about Felix, how many of them really matter? To him, I mean?"

Lord Stephen's expression grew blank and arrested. "Precious few," he said, more to himself than to me.

When his eyes came back to me, something in them had changed, and I knew that the audience, for lack of a better word, was over.

"It's been very kind of you, my lord," I said, rising. He accepted the cue with something suspiciously like a smile, and escorted me to the door, where his butler, alerted by something I had missed, was waiting.

"This was fun," Lord Stephen said as his butler opened the door. "Let's do it again sometime soon." When I looked up at him, I was more than a little alarmed to see that he wasn't being ironic. He meant it.

Mildmay

By the time I got back to the suite, it was all crashing down on me again. There was nobody in the sitting room. I shut the door of my bedroom behind me like it was a magic door in a story that you couldn't open without knowing the right word. I sat on my bed in the dark, staring at nothing, and just waited for time to pass. There wasn't nothing else I could do.

After a while, there was a knock at the door. Felix came in without waiting for an answer. He was wearing his favorite mouse-colored dressing gown and had his hair tied with a faded piece of green ribbon. His eyes were clear again. He was back from wherever his head had been during dinner. Fuck, I thought.

"Mildmay, are you—" He stopped, called witchlights. "Why are you sitting here in the dark? What's wrong?"

He sounded like he really cared. I turned away from him so he wouldn't see how close I was to crying. "Nothing," I said.

"Don't give me that. You were upset earlier, too. Is it something I did?"

I thought of all the times he'd upset me and known it and been glad of it. "No," I said. "It ain't you." I couldn't think of how to put it, so I had to fall back on the way people said things like this in stories. "I've left Mehitabel."

"Left?" he said. "Well, clearly you . . . wait. You mean *left*?"

I took a deep breath, like it would help somehow. "I told her I didn't want to see her again."

There was a long silence. I didn't look at him. Finally, he said, "Why?"

"I had to," I said. "Could you just leave me alone for a while?"

"If it's what you want," he said.

I couldn't bear crying in front of him. I just nodded.

"All right." He stopped in the doorway. "Would you . . . would you prefer to talk to Gideon?"

I was almost choking on the hard lump blocking my chest and throat. "No," I said. "Just leave me alone."

"All right," he said, his voice barely more than a whisper, and closed the door behind him.

And I sat there in the dark and rubbed the water out of my eyes as fast as it gathered and tried to figure out what was wrong with me anyway. I'd gone two indictions without asking Mehitabel how many other guys she had, so what the fuck had got into me that I went and asked her today?

I didn't know. That was the bitchkitty and the Queen of Swords. I didn't fucking know. Just that I hadn't been able to keep it down no more, and it wasn't even that I cared if she was sleeping with other guys—I ain't so stupid I think sex has to mean anything, and most times it don't—it was that she wouldn't even give me a straight answer. Because I knew how careful she ran her life. She knew exactly how many guys there were, and how often she'd fucked each one of 'em, and what she'd said to them when she did. And that didn't bother me, neither. What bothered me was, she didn't want me to know that. She didn't want me to know who she was. Not really. Not down where it counts.

And, I mean, I ain't keen on letting people know my private stuff, but I don't try to pretend to be anything I ain't. That was what it was, I figured. Not that she hid things, and not that she lied. But that she didn't trust me with herself.

I got my clothes off and lay down and wished I could fucking well stop crying. It was a good long while before I got to sleep, and when I did, I fell straight into this nightmare I'd been having on and off for, powers, I don't know, half an indiction at least. In the dream, I'm going again with Cardenio to see Ginevra's body in the morgue underneath the Fishmarket, the cade-skiffs' guildhall, except when we reach the table, her body's gone. I look at Cardenio and I see that he's dead, all blue and bloodless and horrible. He tells me that somebody whose name I can't quite hear has stolen Ginevra's body, and I have to get it back or they'll put me in her place. So I'm searching everywhere but I can't find her, and every time I look back, Master Auberon, Cardenio's master, is a little closer. He's dead, too, and he's holding a very sharp knife. And it was one of those dreams you get sometimes where you know you're dreaming and you can feel where the real world is, but like the old joke says, you can't get there from here. I didn't shake myself free of it until I was actually falling out of bed, a thing that hadn't happened to me since I'd reached my first septad. I sat there on the floor, my bad leg singing its old stupid song at me, and I laughed until I cried.

It was a long time before I could calm down, and that was kind of scary. I'm losing it, I thought. I'm really, really losing it, and I don't know what the fuck to do about it.

Pull yourself together, Milly-Fox, Keeper's voice said in my head, cold and hard, like she got when I was about to fuck up something stupid and simple. It worked like a slap. I knew it wasn't going to work for long—I didn't trust Keeper enough now for her voice to do much—but it lasted at least long enough for me to think, I need to get out of this fucking walk-in tomb.

I found my lucifers and lit one. The clock said it was the last hour of the night. Getting up now wouldn't be a sign of going crazy or nothing. I could go down to the public baths in the Warren—St. Dismas was their patron saint, so of course they were called the Dismal Baths—and maybe soak some of the jitters out. Felix wouldn't be getting up for another two hours. I had plenty of time to get back so he wouldn't know I'd gone. Felix didn't like me using the Dismal Baths, although he wouldn't ever say exactly why. But, then, he hated public baths just on principle because he was so uptight about the scars on his back.

The Dismal Baths were Lower City baths. I thought that was probably one of the reasons Felix didn't like them. They were right on the border between the Arcane and the Warren. The Mortisgate was actually the entrance to the baths from the Warren side, and the guards watched real close about who used the Mortisgate—it was a shitty way to try to sneak in or out of the Mirador. There were other, better ways, if you knew what you were doing. Lots of people came up from the Arcane to use the Dismal, but none of them were stupid enough to try waltzing out the Mortisgate—or, at least, not stupid enough to try twice.

I knew the guys on duty at the Mortisgate—I'd gotten to the point where I knew most of the Protectorate Guard. They didn't much like Felix, but they weren't stupid enough to fuck with him, and they didn't hold him against me. I don't think they liked any of the hocuses much, and they knew all about working for people 'cause you had to, not 'cause it was anything you wanted.

Winn and Josiah gave me a wave, and I waved back and kept moving. I didn't think I could talk to anybody like a normal person, not with that dream still banging around in my head.

At this time of day, it was no surprise to find the changing rooms full of whores. They all looked at me funny, but nobody said nothing. I wished I'd never let Mavortian talk me out of dyeing my hair.

But at least it was safe here. I didn't have to worry about people trying to pick fights or nothing. Nobody did that kind of thing in the Dismal Baths—or St. Veronique's Baths in Pharaoh-light, or the Tunny Street Baths down in Gilgamesh. People wouldn't put up with it. I mean, not only do you not want to worry about being knifed just because you want to wash your hair, you particularly don't want somebody else getting knifed in the same water with you and your soap. Crime in the Lower City ain't exactly organized, but it's organized enough for that. Dunno what the flashies and the bourgeoisie do in their baths—the Caliphate Baths in Verdigris or the St. Nebular Baths in Shatterglass or any of the others—but people in the Lower City just use theirs for bathing in.

I paid a septad-centime for towels, and another three centimes for soap—you could fork over a half-gorgon and get the fancy soaps imported from the south, the ones that smelled like lavender or lemons or roses, but the common soap, the stuff people just called "pig," was good enough for me. I've never been real big on perfumes. Felix wasn't, either. I think perfumes brought back too many memories of Pharaohlight on him. He was such a dandy otherwise—and got such a kick out of twisting the flashies' tails—that I couldn't think of much else that would make sense of him not using ambergris or one of the other fancy flashie perfumes.

The calder at the Dismal Baths was a long, vaulted room with a walkway down the middle and the hot pools on both sides. There was a bench built into each wall. I found a place to put my towels and slid down into the water.

I scrubbed myself with the pig until my skin was red and I'd worn the cake down to a handful of slivers. Then I lay back in the water and floated for a while, but I get nervous when I can't see everybody in the room with me, and I stood up again before long. I climbed out and went to the froy. A two-second plunge was about all I could stand, but I came out with my head feeling a lot clearer and not so much like I was working on four hours of bad sleep. I went back, got my towels, and put myself together to face the day.

When I was coming back through the Mortisgate, Josiah said, "Hey, Mildmay!"

Sunrise, I thought. They were coming off shift. Winn would be going into the Arcane to find that whore he was crazy about. I stopped and waited for Josiah.

"Hey, Josiah," I said when he came up to me. "What's new?"

"Not much," he said. "How 'bout you?"

"You know," I said. "Same old."

He nodded and laughed. We started back up into the Mirador.

"I'm glad to be done for tonight," he said after a while. "It's getting weird."

"Whatcha mean?"

"Oh, I dunno. Just weird. The news is getting out about the Bastion, and people are getting kind of twitchy."

"Scared?"

"Nah, not scared so much. Just, like . . . twitchy."

"Don't blame 'em."

"Me neither, but it gets on your nerves after a while. You hear about Lord Thaddeus?"

"What about Lord Thaddeus?"

"He says it's all a trick," Josiah said, and I saw his sideways look at me, like he wanted to see if I would say so, too. "He says the Bastion don't want peace with us, they just want us to *think* they want peace with us, so we'll do something dumb and they can get in."

That sounded like something Thaddeus would say, all right. "I think Lord Thaddeus thinks too much," I said.

"Yeah, but do you think . . . ?"

"I don't know what to think. But Lord Thaddeus ain't on the Curia."

"That's a fact." He gave me another sideways look. "What does Lord Felix think?"

"You know Felix ain't in no hurry to trust the Bastion," I said. We'd reached Ucopian's Cross by then—where Josiah had to head northeasterly to the guard barracks and I had to tack off northwest to get back to Felix's suite—standing under the dome painted with a fairly hardcore take on the martyrdom of St. Ucopian. Our voices were echoing up and around, and the shadows made Josiah's face look like a bad mask. I didn't like to think what they must've been doing to me.

"Yeah," he said, like he'd needed to hear me say that. "I know." There was a little pause, prickly with things we weren't saying. "Igny says the Tibernians are just about shitting bricks. In case Lord Stephen *does* start signing treaties and stuff."

"Worried he'll find a way to give 'em the boot."

"Yeah. Igny says that Mr. Clef has a tongue on him it's an honor to listen to. Him and that hocus going at it hammer and tongs, up one side and down the other."

"Hocus's a nasty piece of work."

"Sorry?"

I said it again.

"Yeah. Seems like he wants us to be all grateful and shit, and it sure is getting up his nose that we ain't. Igny says Mr. Clef says they got to find a way to make friends proper-like or Lord Stephen'll throw 'em over for the Kekropians."

"Powers. He ain't a gal looking for a dance partner."

Josiah laughed. "Well, he got people want to dance with him, that's for sure." We heard a clock strike, somewhere off in the dark, and he sighed. "Better be going."

"Yeah, me too. See you 'round."

"Later," he said and headed away at a brisk march, his chain mail jingling and his boot heels smacking sharply against the flagstones. He turned a corner and was gone, swallowed by the Mirador.

ↄ৯

"Where have you been?" Felix said the instant the door opened.

It was a good half hour before he normally got up, and I was so startled I said, "How the fuck did you know I was gone?"

He shrugged, sort of embarrassed and sort of impatient, and said, "I woke up, and you weren't there. Where did you go?"

"Down to the Dismal."

"The . . ." He looked for a second like he'd swallowed a spider, but he recovered fast. "You know I don't like you going there."

"Yeah, you've said so often enough. But I didn't drown nobody or nothing."

"*Any*body or *any*thing," he said. "And I didn't imagine you had."

"Then what's the problem?"

"The Dismal Baths are not a nice place."

I couldn't help it. I burst out laughing. "What? You think I can't take care of myself?"

"Look, I don't like you going there, all right?"

"You gonna forbid me?"

"I will if I have to." He meant it. I could see that in the way his face reddened and he wouldn't quite meet my eyes. When he was bluffing, he'd look me straight in the eyes and not so much as turn a hair. He hated using the binding-by-forms like that. He said it made him feel sick. Which mostly was fine by me.

But this was just weird. "I don't see what you got against the Dismal."

"Do I have to give you reasons for everything I do?"

"But this ain't something *you* do. I ain't making *you* go down there, so what does it matter if I go every once in a while?"

"I don't want you to."

"Powers, I done figured that part out. I just don't understand *why*."

He caught my eyes. "Don't go down there. And don't *argue* about it." Commands, both of them. Whatever it was that had got him, it had him by the short hairs.

"You're the boss," I said, and I didn't care if I sounded sullen.

He looked at me for a moment, like there was something he wanted to say—but he never apologized for nothing. He went back into his and Gideon's bedroom to start getting ready for court.

And I stood there with that fucking dream still like wet shiny paint in my head, and I started to wonder if maybe I needed to go talk to Keeper after all.

Chapter 5

Mehitabel

I thought about my mother a lot that night, as I lay in the bed Mildmay and I had occasionally shared and tried not to think about him, not to think about Vulpes, and above all else not to let my memories of Hallam overwhelm me. Her name had been Dorothea. She had been from Skaar, the daughter of a carnival sword-swallower, and she'd had broad, flat cheekbones that had given her face the perfect, watchful stillness of a mask. She had been breathtakingly beautiful. She'd always said she lost her virginity to a snake-handler when she was thirteen.

She had been fifteen when the Zamyatin-Parr troupe came through the village of Tumbril, where her carnival was playing. She had helped her father, a drunken gambler whom she hated, with his act since she was old enough to walk, and since her body had matured, she'd had an additional act of her own as a dancer. When I was a little girl, she'd danced sometimes before the troupe performed, if Gran'père Mato thought the crowd needed "softening up," and I remembered the amazement with which I had watched her, knowing that this was my mama. My father, Ephesus Parr, had gone to the carnival in Tumbril, seen my mother dance, and fallen instantly in love. Or so the story went.

I did in fact believe that my father had loved my mother madly; she died in childbirth when I was twelve, and my father might as well have died with her for all the interest he showed in life after that. His children—me, my sister Elisabeth, and our little brother Damian—became scarcely more than ghostly shadows to him, things that hurt him to think about because they reminded him of Dorothea. I'd remember all my life the night I'd finally gone to him and said I didn't like the way Uncle René was staring at me. Even then, Uncle René had gone considerably beyond staring, but I hadn't wanted to tell my father that. I wondered sometimes, as an adult, whether if I'd told him everything, he might have responded differently, but I couldn't have done it. I was only fifteen, and Uncle René terrified me. And my father had looked at me as if I had no right to remind him of my mother if I wasn't going to be her and said, "Tabby, don't make up stories."

I'd run away that night, knowing that if my father wouldn't believe me, no one would, and the only thing I regretted was that I'd left Libbie and Damian on their own.

So, certainly, Ephesus Parr had loved Dorothea Stillman Parr, but I'd never been sure what she felt for him. She had been a very catlike person, affectionate when she wanted to be but entirely self-sufficient; I'd been old enough when she died to understand that she never allowed anyone to touch her very deeply.

And if I'd learned that lesson from her properly, I wouldn't be in the bind I was in now.

I knew for a fact she had been unfaithful to my father, that she'd had lovers in every town we toured regularly; it had been an open secret in the troupe that Damian was the son of a bank clerk in Iver, and it was anybody's guess who had fathered the poor little girl that died with her.

Gran'père Mato had hated her. "Whore," he called her, and worse things, and my father went red in the face and shouted and raved, and my mother just sat and smiled her tiny, secret smile, and went her own way. She'd left pain and destruction in her wake, but she'd taught me how to be what I was. My Aven in *Berinth the King* was almost entirely my memories of my mother; any situation that required brass-faced flaunting called her up in me, and I needed that now.

I took up my usual position in the Hall of the Chimeras, conspicuous but not encroaching upon the nobles' space, and heard the susurration of rumors spreading out around me; for a moment, purely as my mother's daughter, I reveled in it. People would come to see *Edith Pelpheria* just for the scandal, and that was absolutely fine with me.

When Lord Stephen came in, I felt his single glance like a fire. And then his siblings' attention: Lady Victoria's cool hostility and Lord Shannon's bright blue curiosity. I wondered what, if anything, Lord Stephen had told them.

And then the wizards came in, and I forgot about the Teverii. The other reason I'd been determined to attend court before returning to the Empyrean was that it was never going to get easier to look Mildmay in the face. Best to get that first, worst confrontation over with before I could develop the habit of avoiding him. For a flashing, craven moment, I wanted to step backwards into the crowd and escape Mildmay's cold green eyes. I needn't have worried; he didn't so much as glance at me as they passed, although I knew from the rigid way he held himself that he knew I was there.

I was taken aback by the venomous glare Felix gave me, there and gone like a flash of lightning. I hadn't expected that, and I felt absurdly like cornering him and saying, *He* ditched *me*, you asshole. But I knew that wasn't true in the strictest sense of the word, and also, inescapably, that I had hurt Mildmay far worse than he had hurt me.

And then they were past, and I made a shaken mental note to avoid being alone with Felix Harrowgate for a while. And I wondered, uncomfortably, just how hard Mildmay was taking it.

He ditched *me*! a little interior voice protested again. But that wasn't the issue, and I knew it. I played swan-daughter all through court, using that to keep myself calm, centered, not thinking about the thousand and one things that suddenly seemed too dangerous to contemplate. As I was leaving the Hall of the Chimeras, a page panted up to me, presented a note with a nervous little bow, and pelted off. I stopped and read it where I stood, letting the courtiers eddy around me. It was an invitation to lunch from Shannon Teverius.

Mildmay

The Mirador called today Samedy. It was Felix's other day to get out from under the committee meetings and shit and go do what he wanted. Usually, he went poking around in one of the libraries. Today, I didn't know what he was planning to do—something with Edgar and Fleur, and that could mean anything—but a blind man could've seen he didn't want me around.

"It's okay," I said to his nervous, sort of embarrassed look. "Really. I just need to talk to you for a second."

"Talk away, darling," he said, lordly and bored and loud enough for Fleur and Edgar to hear. I made him follow me far-

ther down the corridor before I told him what Josiah had said
about what Thaddeus was saying. I didn't know if Felix and
Edgar had a thing going, but I didn't have to climb in bed with
them if they did—especially when I was only half sure I wanted
to tell Felix this anyway. But even pissed at him like I was, there
was this little voice in my head saying that he needed to know,
that it didn't matter what we thought of each other right now,
that letting him go on not knowing about what Thaddeus was
saying was just plain dumb. Thaddeus might not be on the Curia himself, but I knew he was pretty thick with Lady Agnes,
and it's purely amazing how much trouble one asshole can
cause if he's got his heart set on it.

"I'm not surprised," Felix said when I was done. "Thaddeus
really is a little unbalanced on the subject of the Bastion. I'll ask
around and see if it's anything more serious than that."

It was a dismissal—take yourself off now, kid—and that was
fair enough.

"See you later," I said.

"Are you all right? Really?" I wasn't sure whether he meant
about our argument this morning or Mehitabel, but I wasn't talking to him either way.

"Yeah, I'm fine. Go on and have a good time."

He gave me a look. I thought for a moment we were going to
get in another fight right there in the middle of the corridor with
Edgar and Fleur watching. But then he decided I wasn't worth
it. He turned on his heel and went back down the hall. Soon as I
was sure he wasn't going to change his mind, I limped off fast
as I could in the opposite direction.

Mehitabel

It was not, of course, an *invitation* so much as a *command*. I
would be cutting it fine to get back to the Empyrean before the
audition for our new ingenue started, but I could hardly tell the
Lord Protector's brother that I was too busy for him. I presented
myself at his door precisely at noon and was admitted by a
manservant very nearly as handsome as his master, although his
brilliant dark eyes and olive-bronze complexion spoke of Grasslander blood rather than Monspulchran. Lord Stephen's butler
had had "old family retainer" written all over him; after two years
of Mildmay's quiet tutelage, I could easily identify this one as

"Lower City boy on his way up." I wondered if it was luck that had gotten him this far or if he'd made his own. For a young man as beautiful as this one, manufacturing luck wouldn't have been hard.

Lord Shannon was waiting for me in a pleasant sitting room, made even more pleasant by one of the Mirador's rare interior windows. The view, of course, was only of another blind wall, but it was still real sunlight beyond the leaded glass. Lord Shannon, disconcertingly beautiful, rose to meet me and shook hands. "I have admired you from a distance for a very long time, Madame Parr. It is truly delightful to have this chance to meet you."

"Your invitation was most kind, my lord," I said with a cautious half-curtsy.

He looked at me quizzically for a moment, and then said, "The pleasure is all mine," and began talking lightly, but with evident devotion, about the theater. I followed his lead, and the conversation continued over lunch: an exquisite omelette and accompanying dry white wine. Lord Shannon didn't do a very good job of hiding his anxiety, but he didn't let the conversation falter.

It was only as the plates were cleared away that he said, twisting a napkin nervously in his elegant hands, "What did you think of my brother, Madame Parr?"

"He was a charming host, my lord," I said, not quite certain what Lord Stephen would want me to say.

"Do you . . . *like* him?"

Clumsy. I remembered Felix remarking once that Shannon had no head for intrigue. "I have only met him the once, my lord."

"Ah." He was manifestly unhappy, and I thought, Victoria put him up to this.

I smiled at him brilliantly and said, "Are you looking forward to your brother finding a new bride?"

I expected a charming and platitudinous lie; I was surprised when he paused to consider his answer, even more surprised when the answer he gave was blunt and unvarnished truth. "I think his methods are misguided—not to mention barbaric—but I hope it works. Stephen needs an heir."

"You don't wish to be Lord Protector?"

"Great powers, no! I'd rather be walled up in a church like an anchorite."

I was startled all over again because he clearly meant it.

There was a pause; he seemed to be girding himself to try again, and I was quite grateful when his manservant came in with a message from Arden Anastasius. I leapt at the excuse, thanked him profusely, and made my escape. If I caught a hansom in the Plaza, I'd be on time for the audition at the Empyrean.

Mildmay

I got as far as Ucopian's Cross before I figured out just how much Felix had fucked me over. And then I stood there and cussed for a couple minutes before I could think straight again.

See, I'd had a plan. Go down in the Arcane and pay somebody enough that they'd forget they hated me for an hour. Get 'em to take a message to the Stag and Candles telling Keeper to meet me in the Iron Chapel at the septad-night. But Felix had put paid to that.

Don't go down there, he'd said, and he hadn't just meant the Dismal Baths. He'd meant the whole Arcane. Not the Lower City, mind. Just the motherfucking Arcane and how the fuck did he think I was supposed to live in the motherfucking Mirador if I couldn't get *out* of it when I needed?

I cussed some more, and then I turned around and went back to Felix's suite. But I wasn't beat yet, not by a long shot. If Felix didn't want me to go to the Arcane, fine, but I'd be fucked blind if he was going to keep me out of the Lower City altogether.

Gideon wasn't there, and I was fine with that. Because once he knew something was up, he wouldn't let me leave until he knew what it was. And once he knew what I was doing, he wouldn't let me do it.

I knew where to find what I wanted, which was a damn good thing. I hated being in their bedroom. But Felix had a couple of headscarves—he used 'em when he was working with fire spells because his hair never would stay in a braid—and my hair was the thing that would be a dead giveaway. Sure, the scar and the limp didn't help, but there are a lot more lame guys in the Lower City than there are redheads, and I wasn't planning on letting anybody get a good look at my face. And I couldn't do nothing about the scar anyway.

I was on my way out when I had another idea. Might as well

be hanged for a sheep. I grabbed one of Gideon's coats. Mine were all black, and Felix's, aside from not fitting, were carnival-tent gaudy. Gideon's didn't fit quite right, either—I was broader in the shoulders—but that was okay. Nobody'd look twice at a guy wearing an obviously secondhand coat.

I got some soot from the fireplace to darken my eyebrows and my hairline, took off my waistcoat, shrugged into Gideon's coat, and tied the scarf. I tucked my pigtail up into it and checked the effect in the sitting room mirror. It was okay. The scar was ugly, but I was used to that. At least I didn't look like a redhead. I left the sitting room again, and this time I wasn't coming back until I'd talked to Keeper.

Felix

Edgar's plan for the afternoon was perfectly innocuous: a visit to his tailor. He wanted my advice, and I had no objections. Perhaps getting out of the Mirador would clear my head.

But Fleur's plan was not so innocent. She wanted to talk—more precisely, she wanted *me* to talk—and she had no compunction about taking advantage of a captive audience. She waited until the first flurry was over and Edgar had been taken off to look at fashion plates from Vusantine and Igensbeck, and her opening salvo was quite mild: "How's Gideon?"

"Fine, thank you," I said warily. I knew Fleur and that brightly casual tone, and I remembered her the night of our semi-impromptu soirée for Aias Perrault, talking to Mildmay—or trying to.

"And you?" she said, rather more pointedly. "How are you doing?"

"I'm fine, too, thank you for asking," I said and gritted my teeth in a smile.

"Your work going well?"

"Perfectly fine. What next, Fleur? I don't have an aged mother you can ask after, and you like to pretend my brother doesn't exist—except when you're pumping him for information, of course."

"Felix!" But she kept her voice low, mindful of the tailor's assistants, hovering gracefully not quite in earshot.

"What is it you want to know? Why don't you spare us all a good deal of tedium, and just ask?"

She laughed. "You never change, do you? Tact is for the weak of heart."

"And what is it you were going to be tactful about?"

"We're getting a little worried about you, you know," she said, and I wondered, with a shudder I was careful to hide, if there were genuinely more people than Fleur in that *we*. "You've been awfully short tempered lately, even for you. And you've been . . ."

"What?" Whoring in the Arcane? Practicing heresy?

"Drinking," she said in a hushed voice.

I truly didn't intend to laugh—although it was the best response I could have made. At least I didn't have to try to stop myself. "Oh horrors!" I said finally, fighting my giggles back under control. "Next thing you know, I'll be going down to Dragonteeth to pick up boys."

"I'm serious," Fleur said forcefully. "I'm worried about you. I'd like to help."

"You'd like to have me pour my heart out to you, you mean," I said, and would have gone on to tell her just how unlikely such an event was except that Edgar called me over to talk about imported lace.

When I came back, Fleur picked up right where she'd left off. "Felix, it's not a crime to let someone help you."

"You're assuming there's something to help with, Fleur. So far as I know, I haven't agreed to your starting premise."

"Oh please. I've known you long enough to see there's something wrong. And if you recall, two years ago you were angry with me because I *hadn't* tried to help. You can't have it both ways."

"The situations are not the same," I said through my teeth.

"You want me to wait until they are?"

"Malkar's dead." I caught myself just before my voice lifted into a shriek. Mustn't scare the nice bourgeois young men who are trying to pretend they aren't anxiously watching this little contretemps. "That is to say, *that* situation will not be recurring. Thank you *very* much."

Her eyes had gone wide. "Oh, Felix. I thought you were over him."

This time, I choked back my laughter. It would have been as bitter as the dregs of long-abandoned tea. No, I wasn't "over" Malkar, the same way one could never be "over" having a limb severed. "That," I said carefully, evenly, "is neither here nor there. The point is that Malkar isn't going to waltz in and break my mind like a twig. If I *needed* help, I would ask for it."

Mildmay wouldn't have said a word, just let the silence sit and fester until I admitted I was lying. Fleur eyed me uncertainly, but she didn't honestly want to start a fight in the front room of Edgar's tailor any more than I did. "All right," she said and gave me a rather weak smile. "But remember you said that."

"Yes, Fleur," I said—and did not roll my eyes. But I moved with alacrity when Edgar called my name again.

Mehitabel

Five young women showed up to Jean-Soleil's audition, which was five more than I'd expected; the pool of literate women in Mélusine couldn't be very large. Corinna was unusual, and how she'd learned to read, I had no idea. Most literate women were gentlewomen, and generally they considered actresses no better than prostitutes—certainly not a fit profession for a young woman of good breeding. Susan was the daughter of a butler.

Three of the women standing on the Empyrean's stage, blinking nervously in the light of the lamps, were clearly of Susan's class: dowdy, painfully neat clothing; prim gray gloves; hair ruthlessly pinned into a swollen knot at the back of the head. To my admittedly indifferent eye, the three of them were as alike as peas in a pod. One of the others was of the demimonde, whether she'd clawed her way up to it or been forced down. Her clothes were shabby, but they'd been remade for this year's fashions by someone who knew what they were doing. She was insipidly pretty; like Susan, she put belladonna in her eyes.

The fifth was dressed like the others, but the way she stood on the stage couldn't have been more different. Graceful, poised, utterly, artfully unselfconscious. She reminded me strongly of Lord Shannon, and a little of Mildmay. I wondered where she was from and what her voice was like.

Jean-Soleil, dressed in his impresarial best, came down the aisle. All five women's gazes locked on him. He stopped just in front of the fifth row of seats, where all of us were sitting, and said, pleasantly but letting his voice out to show them how it was done, "Good afternoon. Welcome to the Empyrean. We

hope that one of you will prove worthy of a place in our troupe.
I am Jean-Soleil Aubert. Will you step forward one at a time,
starting from stage left—" He pointed at one of the drab mice
to show them which side that was. "And tell us your name." He
sat down in the empty seat Drin and Jabez had left between
them, folded his hands over his ample stomach, and beamed
impartially at the women on the stage.

The first woman stepped forward and announced her name to
be Henriette Tucker. The second, the demimondaine, wanted to
be called Nuée Duskrose—she might as well have carried a sign:
NOT MY REAL NAME. The third and fourth women were
completely inaudible; after their third attempts, each had failed
to carry to us, and Jean-Soleil dismissed them. The fifth woman,
the one who didn't match, stepped forward insouciantly, and
said, "My name's Gordeny Fisher."

Two things were immediately apparent. One was the exquisite quality of her voice, which was warm and dark and pure as
a bell and effortlessly carrying; the second was the appalling
commonness of her accent.

There was a moment of silence, at once appreciative and
taken-aback, and Jean-Soleil said, "Miss Fisher, you know that
won't do."

"Yeah," she said, unabashed. "I figured I could learn better,
with somebody to teach me."

"Mayhap," Jean-Soleil said, his own peculiarly affected way
of saying, *We'll see about that later.* "Miss Tucker, Miss
Duskrose, Miss Fisher, let us see what you can do."

He produced pages of scripts from *Edith Pelpheria*; I was in-
expressibly relieved to observe that Gordeny Fisher really was
literate. Despite her accent, she read better and more naturally
than either Henriette Tucker, who stumbled over words and got
tripped up in the scansion and ended up tongue-tied and mortified before she'd even gotten through the scene, or Nuée
Duskrose, who had mistaken *shouting* for *acting* and was all over
Drin like a wet sheet. Gordeny Fisher watched Drin carefully and
emulated him. She understood how to use the long, limber line of
her back, and her long-fingered, graceful hands.

"We must confer," Jean-Soleil said grandly to the three of
them, as he'd said to me when I'd stood alone on that stage.
Drin, Corinna, Jabez, Levry, and I followed him back and down,
into the largest rehearsal room.

"Well?" Jean-Soleil said.

"Gordeny Fisher," I said at once. Corinna, beside me, nodded emphatically.

"I agree," Jabez said, and Levry seconded him as always.

We all looked at Drin. He was an actor, so he neither dropped his eyes nor fidgeted, but his expression was obstinate. "Oh I agree she's the best of the three, but I'm not sure we want her."

"What's *that* supposed to mean?" Corinna said.

"Well, we don't know anything about her, do we?" Drin said. "Even if you ask, she'll only lie, and the saints only know what she might have done, or what might come find her."

"She doesn't look like a woman on the run to me," I said.

"I'll warn her to mind her manners," Corinna said, angry and sarcastic both at once.

"*Gentle* persons," Jean-Soleil said warningly, and both Corinna and Drin looked abashedly away. Jean-Soleil sighed heavily enough to disturb his mustaches and asked Drin, "Are your objections insurmountable?"

There was a pause while Drin thought it over. I had to do him the justice of recognizing that he *was* thinking, that something about Gordeny Fisher honestly upset him, even though I couldn't imagine what it was. Finally he said, "No," and then his face opened up in a radiant grin. "And I'd rather have her than whatsherface Duskrose any day."

"At least you've got your priorities straight," Corinna said.

"Let's go get this over with," Jean-Soleil said and got up.

Mildmay

I got down to Britomart just fine. I took a hansom part of the way, down to the south end of Havelock, just because I could. Whatever else you could say about him, Felix was never stingy, and he got a damn generous stipend as a member of the Curia.

I paid the hansom off at the Tibernine Post and walked through Gilgamesh and Britomart, trying to remember to keep my head down and not stare at the Lower City going about its business. It wasn't easy. But I got to the Stag and Candles without anybody catching on. It didn't open for business until sundown, but the door was unlocked, and I went in.

Byron Rosemary recognized me straight off. He was like

that—a little, thin-faced, bucktoothed guy you wouldn't look at twice—and then you find out how sharp he is and how he never has forgotten a face, and you start to think back over everything you said when you thought he wasn't listening. It's an awful feeling.

"You," he said and went back to polishing his bar.

"Yeah," I said.

"Whatcha want?" He didn't give a shit, but I didn't expect him to.

"Hob around?"

"Hob's most always around here someplace. HOB!"

Hob had been a skinny little kid, around about a septad and four, when I left Keeper. Now he was nearly Felix's height but still skinny, all elbows and knees. He recognized me, too. All of the little kids had gone in mortal terror of me, and if you think that's a fine feeling, I'm here to tell you it ain't.

"Oh shit," he said.

"Nice to see you, too, Hob," I said. "Know where to find Keeper?"

"Oh shit. Mildmay, you don't wanna—"

"Man knows his own mind, Hob," Byron Rosemary said. "His problem, not yours. Go on."

"Oh *shit*," Hob said a third time and went.

Byron Rosemary gave me a look. It said pretty clear how he didn't care what I'd done and he didn't have to like me, but if I was going to sit in his bar, I'd damn well better buy a drink. I'd seen him turn that look on Keeper I don't know how many times. He didn't like her neither.

"Bourbon and water," I said and ponied up. It was Felix's drink, and I felt like I could use the moral support.

Byron Rosemary poured it out without comment and went back to polishing his fucking bar. I sat and drank and tried not to think about anything.

But he kept looking at me, and finally he said, "Nice hair."

I put my hand up. Sure enough, the scarf had slipped. I jerked it back into place. "Fuck you, too, Byron."

He wasn't bothered. "It natural?"

"Would it be this color if it wasn't?"

"Huh." And he was giving me this weird look.

"*What*, for fuck's sake?"

"Nothing. It's just, we always figured, you and Kolkhis . . ."

"What about me and Kolkhis?"

"We always figured you were her kid brother."

Powers and saints, I damn near drowned in that bourbon. Sat there for nearly half a minute, coughing like I'd never tasted hard liquor before. "Well, that's a real fucking interesting notion, Byron."

He shrugged. He still wasn't bothered. "Y'all got that same corpse-color skin. And *we* didn't know you dyed your hair."

Kethe. I could even see where it made sense, but fuck me sideways, what was I doing wrong that everybody thought I was committing incest once a decad and all night during the Trials?

"Well, I ain't. Related to her."

"I can see that," Byron said, dry as fucking dust, and we didn't say nothing more to each other until Hob came back, in about as much hurry as he'd left. I figured he must have run both ways. He stood, leaning on the bar and panting for breath, goggling at me like a fish in a tank.

"Well?" I said.

"She says you come this far, so you might as well come the rest of the way."

Of course she does, I thought. If there were strings Keeper could pull, you could bet on her making you dance. "Thanks, Hob," I said. "I know how to find her."

"She says . . ."

"Yeah?"

"She says I should come with you. In case of . . . trouble."

Byron Rosemary snorted. Felix would've said, How kind of her, with a smile that would've turned Hob red up to the roots of his hair. I knocked back the last of my bourbon and followed Hob out of the Stag and Candles.

We walked through Britomart without talking to each other. He looked at me once or twice like he wanted to say something, but his nerve must've failed him. I don't suppose I was looking any too friendly.

Keeper was still in that old converted warehouse near the eastern edge of Britomart. Hob led me straight to the corner fitted out as Keeper's private apartment. The kids we met looked at him, then looked at me and faded away. I couldn't read their faces, and I got to admit I didn't try real hard. I was afraid of picking out whoever it was that was sleeping with her now, and I didn't want to look him in the eye.

Hob knocked on Keeper's door. That was one of the first five things you learned when you became one of Keeper's thieves, that you always knocked on her door, no matter how important you thought what you had to say was and no matter how much you thought she liked you. One day, when we'd been lovers for two indictions, I'd walked in without knocking—not on purpose or nothing, I just forgot—and she belted me one hard enough to knock me flat on my ass.

Her voice came floating out, and, powers and saints, I was at my second septad again, and Keeper was the moon and stars and sun. "Is that you, Hob?"

"Yes'm," Hob said.

"Send him in and go away."

"Yes'm." Hob darted a glance at me, opened the door with a shove, and bailed. I wanted to follow him, but I went inside instead.

Keeper was waiting, sitting on that chaise longue me and Sabin had busted our asses dragging out of Queensdock one hot day in the middle of Fructidor. She looked exactly the way I remembered her, tall and skinny and gorgeous, her hair as dark and smooth as the Sim. She liked to dress like a lady when she wasn't on a job, and she was wearing a dress the same color as her eyes. And she was smiling.

"Milly-Fox," she said. "How nice to see you again."

"K-Keeper." I'd meant to call her by her name—it wasn't like I didn't know it or anything—but I couldn't. I wasn't her equal, I wasn't ever going to be her equal, and we both knew it.

She waited a moment, like she thought I was going to manage to say something more, and then said, her voice poison-sweet, "Please, sit down."

I crossed the room to the chair she'd pointed at and sat down, clamping my hands together between my knees because they were starting to shake.

"The limp is new," she said.

"Yeah."

"What happened?"

"The Mirador's curse caught up with me," I said.

She made a little face, like it was rude of me to remind her of that—it being her fault and all—and stood up, all in one movement like water flowing uphill. She floated across the room, the way she did, and shut the door. I heard the bolt shoot home. She came around behind my chair. I realized what she was going to do the second before she did it, and so I didn't flinch when she touched me, dragging her fingers across my neck, tugging away the scarf. My pigtail flopped down my back like a dead vine.

"You quit dyeing your hair," she said.

"No point," I said.

She sat down again and smiled at me. It was a full-force smile from Keeper, but it wasn't a patch on what Felix could do when he put his mind to it, and from watching Felix for two indictions, I'd at least learned how to tell when a smile was meant to turn somebody's knees watery. "Now," she said, "what can I do for you?"

"You know what I want," I said.

"Do I, sweetheart? Suppose you tell me anyway. I'm getting forgetful in my old age."

Powers. Powers and fucking saints. You knew she'd do this, a voice said in my head. Give her what she wants and get it over with. I'd told myself that about Keeper for indictions, up until the day I realized I couldn't stand giving her what she wanted no more, and I didn't like the way the idea had crawled right back up to the top of my mind. But it was still good advice.

"Elvire gave me your message."

"Yes?"

Kethe, I hated her. Hated her and her games—and I hated myself while I was at it for letting her play me. I said through my teeth, "You got some information I want."

"Darling Milly-Fox, no one will ever understand you if you don't at least *try* not to mumble."

Powers and saints preserve me, I flinched. And said like a stupid bleating fuckheaded fool, "Stop it."

Her eyebrows went up. "Stop what?"

I was red as a tomato. I knew it, and there wasn't a fucking thing in the world I could do about it. "Stop treating me like . . ." Like you used to. Like a half-wit dog. "Like a kid."

"Oh, I have *no* intention of treating you like a kid," she said, and I flinched again. Because I knew what she meant.

"I ain't doing that."

"Doing what?" she said and smirked at me. She knew I didn't have the balls to say it out loud. I never had done, not in all the time she'd been fucking me, and not when I left either.

Never put words to what we did in bed. And if I admitted it now, I was afraid she'd make me do it.

And she could make me. I wasn't even trying to kid myself about that. She'd done it before.

Get a grip, I said to myself. Hauled air in, back out again. Said, "Tell me what the fuck you want."

"You still have a mouth like a sewer," she said, like she'd expected better of me.

"You always said I was too stupid to learn." And then I said, slow and deliberate, "Get. To. The. Fucking. Point."

"Very good. That was much clearer." And the bitch smiled at me. "You want information. So do I. You get me what I want, and I'll give you what you want."

"Okay, so what is it you want?"

"On Dixième, Guinevere Dawnlight—you remember Jenny, don't you, Milly-Fox?—was arrested in Laceshroud with a freshly exhumed corpse. I want to know why she was there, who sent her, and who she dug up."

Yeah, I remembered Jenny. She wasn't born with a name like "Guinevere Dawnlight," but you knew that already. She tarted up her name when she joined the Green Dancers, which is one of them stupid packs in Dragonteeth that are about half kids from Havelock and Breadoven. They got funny ideas about what being in a pack means, like Ginevra had funny ideas about what being a cat burglar was all about.

Jenny loved it. Last time I'd seen her—about the time I was working myself up to leave Keeper, as it happens—we'd had this terrible fight, me wanting her to get out and get into one of the real packs if she couldn't do no better for herself, her shouting that I was just envious and mean and couldn't bear for anybody to be happy if I wasn't. There for a month or two I was fighting with everybody I came across, because I knew I was going to leave but I wasn't brave enough to just fucking get it over with. But I never mended my fences with Jenny. I didn't want her using me to lord it over the other kids in her pack, and I knew she would. Jenny always had to be the most important person in any room.

But what the sweet sacred fuck was Jenny, of all people, playing resurrectionist for? Not for the Green Dancers, that was for damn sure.

I actually even kind of sympathized with Keeper for wanting to know what was going on. "And I find out, and you'll tell me who got Ginevra Thomson killed."

"Yes."

"And who rolled over on me?"

"Oh, I'll tell you that now, if you take down your hair."

"What?"

"Take down your hair," she said. "Oh, and wash that ridiculous soot out of your eyebrows."

"You want me to take down my hair?"

"You're slow, Milly-Fox, but you get there eventually."

"*Why*, for fuck's sake?"

Her smile was horrible. "Because otherwise I won't tell you what you want to know."

Give her what she wants and get it the fuck over with. I unbraided my hair, used the washrag she gave me on my eyebrows and hairline. Bared my teeth at her, and I wasn't even pretending I was trying to smile. "Happy now?"

"Good boy," said Keeper. "The young woman went by the unlikely name of Estella Velvet."

"Oh." I didn't mean to make any kind of a noise. It just got out.

"She and another young woman left the next morning on the diligence for St. Millefleur." Ginevra's friend Estella. And her girlfriend, Faith Cowry. Estella must've cut a deal with the Dogs, traded Faith for me. I bet it hadn't cost her so much as a sleepless night.

"Now, before you leave," Keeper said brightly, "I need to introduce you to someone. His name's Septimus Wilder. And, no, don't you touch your hair."

Oh shit. She'd never hit you once if she could hit you twice, and I knew that tone in her voice, too, the one that said as how she had your balls in a vise, and she thought she'd tighten it another notch, just to see what happened.

I figured I could guess who Septimus was, and I'd rather've gone out and jumped in the Sim than meet him, but that wasn't something I got a vote on, so I didn't say nothing—I fucking well knew better—and she got up and stuck her head out to yell at the nearest kid to go tell Septimus to get his ass down here. I sat still and kept my mouth shut, and concentrated on getting my face to where it wasn't going to give nothing away.

'Cause I *knew* Keeper was going to be watching.

Keeper went wandering around the room, and it just about killed me, but I didn't try to track her. It didn't take long before there was a knock on the door.

"Come in," she said, from right behind me, and maybe I should've been expecting her to knot her hand in my hair and drag my head back, but I wasn't, and just as the door opened, she leaned down and kissed me, mean and nasty, and fuck me for a half-wit dog, I just sat there and *took* it.

And then she let me go and went back to her chair, and I couldn't get myself to look away from her. "Mildmay," she said, and she was smirking like a gator, damn her, "this is Septimus. Septimus, this is your . . . predecessor, Mildmay the Fox." And then she just sat back to watch.

Bull's-fucking-eye.

I turned my head like it was made of stone. Septimus Wilder was somewhere toward the end of his third septad. He was Keeper's height and skinny and dark. He reminded me of a racing dog—all that energy and nowhere to put it. And he moved that way, too, sharp and finicky. You wouldn't see a dog with eyes like that, though. I knew right off he had Keeper's sense of humor. I didn't recognize him, but that didn't mean much. Those last couple indictions with Keeper, I hadn't been paying no mind to the little kids, and if he'd kept his head down and his mouth shut, I wouldn't hardly have known he was there.

Yeah, I know. And I'd got the same way—and oh powers and saints, this was no time to realize it, with him glaring murder at me and the taste of her like ashes in my mouth—after Strych. Not noticing nothing. Not doing nothing but what I was told. Not caring about nothing and not even being awake enough to see what I was doing to myself. With Keeper, I'd started to come up out of it once I started to think I was really going to do it, really going to leave—and had that horrible fucking fight with Jenny, too—but it wasn't 'til maybe four or five months after I'd left that I realized how bad I'd been. And I'd sworn I'd never get that way again, too. I'm surprised I hadn't been able to hear Kethe laughing at me.

Septimus Wilder looked me over real good, like he wanted to be sure he could describe me to the Dogs if he got the chance, and then he smiled, all teeth, and said, "Charmed."

I said, "Likewise." Both of us lying like rugs.

"Septimus is going to act as my liaison," Keeper said, and I knew she was hoping to make me ask what that meant.

Sorry, sweetheart, you're shit out of luck. I'd been going to Curia meetings for two indictions. I only wished I could smirk at her the way she'd been smirking at me.

"Okay," I said, like it didn't make no nevermind to me.

And what she did next was Keeper in a nutshell—if I ever started to forget what she was like, all I'd need to do was remember her right then. She didn't get what she wanted from me, so she turned right around and went after Septimus.

"Septimus," she said, sweet as poison, "can use the practice."

He was too dark to show a blush easy, but the way he said, "Keeper!" was just the same as me going tomato-red. And Keeper gave me a look I'd seen her give her friends over and over and over. Her *Isn't he cute when he's flustered?* look, and if I started trying to tell you how much I hated it, we'd be here all night.

I didn't like it no better from this side, neither. I didn't say nothing, and Keeper gave Septimus the eyebrow—and powers, I remembered *that*, too—and he said, trying hard not to let on she'd got him flustered as bad as a virgin in a tarquin bar, "We need to fix a meet."

It hit me then, the trap Keeper'd laid for me and I'd walked right into. Because the last thing in the world I wanted was to talk about the binding-by-forms. With anybody. But especially not in front of her. I said, "Good fucking luck."

"I beg your pardon?"

Keeper said, "I will suggest you *not* adopt Mildmay's vocabulary."

"I'd have to be able to understand him first."

I see why she likes you, I thought. But I didn't say it. They could go on and be snarky at me 'til the end of time. I didn't care.

But Keeper turned it back on me. "If you recall, you have a stake in this matter, too. You'd be wise to be helpful."

She got me on the raw just like she meant to. "You know perfectly fucking well I can't go making arrangements like that."

"No? Why not?"

"You *know*." I knew she did. Because the whole fucking city knew. And because she'd set this up. She knew me, knew just how fucking putrid this was going to be. And the look in her eye said this was what I got for walking out on her.

"Oh!" said Septimus. "You mean the binding-by-forms."

"Yes, the fucking binding-by-forms!"

"Well, you came down here, didn't you?"

He sounded like he honestly didn't understand what the problem was, and I knew I shouldn't hate him more for that.

"I got lucky," I said. "I can't . . ." But I didn't know how to explain it, didn't know the right words to use.

"What Mildmay is trying to say—and so eloquently, sweetheart—is that he is not his own master. Does your brother even know you're here, Milly-Fox?"

"No," I said, and powers, I could hear it myself—she'd got me right back where she wanted me, like I'd never fucking left.

"And I doubt he'd be pleased if he learned, would he? No, don't bother to lie. You do it so badly. And anyway, I've met him."

"You *what*?" And for all she wasn't leaning on it, I knew blackmail when I heard it. For a moment, I thought I was actually going to be sick, but I swallowed hard, and it passed.

"We did business together a couple indictions ago. I'm surprised he didn't mention it."

No, you ain't, you fucking bitch. I don't know how I kept from saying it. My hands were clenched so tight the bones ached. And there was Septimus Wilder with his ears flapping.

It hurt like eating glass, but I talked myself back down. Keeper let me—she always did know exactly when to stop pushing if she wanted any use out of me. I wanted to tell her to go fuck herself, to just get up and walk *out* of there, but I couldn't do it, may Kethe bless my stupid, stupid head.

Finally, I said, "How you getting in?"

"Sorry?" said Septimus.

I repeated myself.

He gave Keeper a kind of funny look. I said, "Oh for fuck's sake. Whatever it is, I know about it already. Talk!"

He startled a little, but he said, "The shrine to St. Holofernes."

"In the Altanueva, yeah. Okay. That's as good a place as any. You be there every night at the septad-night. If I ain't there in half an hour, I ain't coming."

"*Every—*"

"Septimus," Keeper said, and he shut up meek as you please.

"You got what you wanted?" I said to her.

We both knew what I was asking. "For now," she said, and I could still feel her smirk in the back of my neck—still fucking *taste* her in the back of my throat—when I slammed the warehouse door behind me.

Mehitabel

As Jean-Soleil had been expecting, Nuée Duskrose made a dreadful scene. Growing up in an acting troupe, I'd been a connoisseur of hysterics by the age of five; my mama had thrown some very pretty tantrums in her time, and she had been nothing compared to my Norvenan aunt Anna Melissa, of whom even Gran'père Mato went in awe. Nuée Duskrose was, by comparison, a rank amateur. Jean-Soleil dealt with her in a matter of moments and evicted her onto the pavement still shrieking.

At close range, Gordeny Fisher was even more arresting. Although she did not have Susan's stunning beauty, the sulfurous yellow glints in her brown eyes were as disconcerting as the gaze of a half-tamed hawk. The eyes and the voice were what you would remember, and that was enough to start with.

She listened attentively to Jean-Soleil's strictures and promised quite faithfully to abide by them all. When he dismissed us, Corinna said, "Come on, Tabby, let's give Gordeny the grand tour."

"I'm game," I said, "although I warn you now, Gordeny, you're going to spend a week getting lost anyway."

We took her all over the labyrinth of the Empyrean, from the attics to the storage rooms beneath the stage. We showed her Hell and the Firmament, introduced her to Cat and Toad, the two silent boys—lovers or brothers, I'd never been able to determine which—who ran the scenery and lights and did sound effects when we needed them. They practically lived up in the Firmament among the catwalks and pulleys, and Jabez had told me they'd rigged the thunder machine all by themselves. We showed Gordeny Jean-Soleil's office, an oddly shaped wedge chopped out of the space behind the stage. It was actually about halfway up the back wall, and had a spindly stair—almost more of a ladder—that led to it and nowhere else. Jean-Soleil claimed that it was only the fear of someday not being able to get up there that kept him from becoming grossly obese. His office window was a jutting oriel, allowing him to survey his kingdom from above.

We showed Gordeny the rehearsal areas and the dressing rooms, with particular attention to Susan's, which would now be hers. Corinna promised to introduce her to the rest of the staff—the ushers, the house managers, the rest of the crew—and the two of them departed to see if the Velvet Tears had a free room.

I had business in the Mirador.

Vulpes's business, of course. He wanted to know more about Gideon; he wanted to know how the Mirador was reacting to Stephen's marriage plans. No power in the world would have gotten me anywhere near Felix's suite, but Felix was hardly the only person—or even the only wizard—I knew in the Mirador. And truth be told, I didn't want to go back to the Velvet Tears, to a barren room and a narrow bed, to the images that would be waiting for me when I closed my eyes. Anything was better than lying awake in the dark, thinking about Hallam.

I started in the Painted Grotto, where the young nobles and their lovers came to see and be seen. There, the talk was all of younger sisters and cousins, and I noted carefully which names were already being bandied about: the Novadii, the Lemerii, the Valerii. Lionel Verlalius told me that his manservant had told him that the Polydorius suite was being aired out and that that could only mean Lord Ivo Polydorius was bringing his daughter to the market.

Not that Lionel put it like that, of course.

I bore the Painted Grotto as long as I could, but the company seemed to me too much like a pack of coyotes, hiding their interest in a dying buffalo behind their sharp-toothed smiles. And I was not in the mood for fending off delicate insinuations about my own interest in the Teverii. I left sooner than I'd meant to.

It was hard not to imagine Vulpes watching from every shadow, and I had to restrain myself from telling the page who guided me from the Painted Grotto to Simon and Rinaldo's suite to hurry. I am still doing your bidding, lieutenant! Leave me be!

Simon and Rinaldo were at home, as I'd expected. They didn't go out much.

They weren't lovers, although most people thought they

were. They were as comfortable with each other as a long-married couple; being imprisoned together in a small room in the Bastion for a number of years will do that to you. Rinaldo wasn't molly. He said he was merely lazy, and growing old; if there was some darker reason, I didn't know it. Simon, tall, stooped, myopic Simon, was janus—and terribly shy. And also painfully self-conscious about his mutilated hands. Another blight to thank Malkar Gennadion for.

They were pleased to see me. Simon fussed about chairs and drinks, while Rinaldo blinked at me like a magnificently self-satisfied portly old tomcat and said, "To what do we owe the honor?"

It didn't bother him in the slightest that he knew I had an ulterior motive. I smiled and said, "I'm a little unwelcome in the Harrowgate household at the moment."

"Then Mildmay really . . . ?" Simon asked.

"Mildmay dropped me like a dead rat," I said and let my smile twist out of true.

They both made sympathetic noises, and Simon pushed a glass of sherry into my hand. From there, asking them about Stephen's marriage was easy and natural: of course I would want to change the subject.

Their take on the matter was quite different from the Painted Grotto's, for they weren't interested in the question of which lucky girl Stephen was going to choose. Simon said, "Robert looks like he sat on a hornet."

"Robert," Rinaldo said, "was expecting to leech off Stephen for the rest of his unpleasant life. But even the most amiable sheep of a girl is going to object to having her predecessor's brother around."

"Especially *that* brother," Simon said.

"Will he make trouble?" I asked.

"He would if he could."

"Would have already," Simon said.

"Probably did. But even if Stephen would marry him, *he* can't provide an heir."

"At least he's quit bleating about Lord Shannon's claim."

"Shannon said he didn't want to be Lord Protector," I said.

"Of course he doesn't," Rinaldo said. "He may be a feather-brained fop, but he's not a fool."

"Then why would Robert . . . ?"

"Not out of any love for Shannon, I assure you. But that's the solution that allows him to maintain his own status quo. And that, my dear, is the only thing Robert of Hermione has ever or will ever care about."

I asked, because I'd always wanted to know, "Why do he and Felix hate each other so much?"

"Natural antipathy," Simon said with a shrug.

"Robert, like Stephen, does not like gentlemen of Felix's, ah, persuasion," Rinaldo said. "And Felix doesn't have the tact to be ashamed of himself."

Simon added, "He is also, to be fair, monumentally inconvenient."

"How so?"

"He has ideals. And he insists on making the Mirador live up to them."

"Oh," I said, rather blankly. It had never occurred to me to cast Felix as an idealist.

"He does not," Rinaldo said, dry as a sandstorm, "compromise well."

"And he isn't *quiet*. Well, you know how he argues."

"Yes."

"And his influence isn't dependent on anyone's good will," Rinaldo said abruptly, as if he'd only just thought of it himself. "His influence is based entirely on his being himself. Robert is not the only one to find this irksome."

"I'm sure he isn't," I said. And wondered in a back corner of my mind if that was why Vulpes found him so interesting.

"Felix, you see, doesn't need to worry about who Lord Stephen marries. And that must gnaw at Robert's dry little soul like a rat."

"How poetic of you, Simon," Rinaldo said, and Simon laughed and poured him more wine.

Mildmay

Somebody'd told somebody else. It's the way things work in the Lower City, and if I'd had my head screwed on straight I would've been expecting it.

They caught me in Gilgamesh—being careful not to embarrass Keeper by taking me down on her turf. They were all heart, those guys. There were three or four of them—I never did get an exact count—and they were stupid enough to think that just because I was a crip, I was easy pickings. They didn't know I was too fucking mad to see straight.

They weren't expecting the knife, either.

I don't think anybody got killed, but one guy ended up two fingers less than he'd come into the world, and another one went through a shop window when he hadn't meant to. But I *was* a crip, and there were more of them than there was of me. Shit, the details don't matter, do they? We were just to the point where I was either going to have to do something fucking amazing or I was going to go down and they were going to kick me the rest of the way out, when we heard the thump and jingle and shouting of Dogs running toward us. Me and the guys still interested in the fight all froze. We might hate each other's guts, but Dogs were Dogs. Then one of them said, "You got lucky, cocksucker," and they bounced me off a wall and lit out running south.

I couldn't run, but I staggered down an alley, then got my feet sort of under me. I cut across two more streets, and then found a fire escape, and dragged myself up to the roof. From there I could get anywhere I wanted.

Right then, I didn't want nothing except to sit down. So I sat and panted, and about half a heartbeat ahead of when he spoke, I knew somebody was there.

"So that was Mildmay the Fox in action."

Septimus fucking Wilder, as I live and breathe.

"Fuck you," I said.

"Very impressive," he said, and it wasn't a bad imitation of Keeper, if you didn't still hear the real thing in your dreams. "Really something to aspire to."

And I was still so fucking mad I could breathe it.

"All right, fuckhead," I said. "You want it? Let's do it."

I came up hard and fast, and I knew right where he was, because he'd been running his stupid mouth off.

Now, he was good. Don't get me wrong. Keeper knew what she was doing, and he was fast and agile like a spider and he knew how to use his reach. And he hadn't just had a go-round with a bunch of goons, neither. But he'd never been a knife-fighter—never had to do this for real where if you fucked up or blinked wrong, you might find yourself holding your guts in both hands. Or, you know, you might find yourself with one whole half of your face nothing but raw, screaming, sheeting pain, and your own blood fouling your grip on your knife. And I didn't think Keeper'd actually sent him out to kill anybody yet.

It changes how you look at things.

So he was good, but I was mean. I got him down, my knife just nudging the hinge of his jaw and my other hand gripping his balls. Because I was not in a mood to fuck around.

"Now," I said. "You were saying something before I went and interrupted you."

"Nnnnnnn . . ." It wasn't even a word, more like a groan that had gotten some letters tangled in it.

I waited, but he didn't seem to have nothing more to say for himself. "Okay," I said. "I can't hold grudges for shit, so's far as I'm concerned, this is over. D'you wanna go round again?"

This time, it did come out a word, although it sounded like it hurt. "No."

"That's good." I like it when people ain't stupid at me. "I'm gonna let go of you now, but the knife ain't moving yet. Just so you know."

"I ain't gonna try nothing," he said. It was the first thing he'd said didn't sound like Keeper.

"Good plan." I moved my left hand away from him, and he took a deep gasping breath. He'd probably been expecting me to twist, or at least squeeze real hard. Or maybe rip his balls off and make him eat 'em. And I ain't going to lie and say I wasn't tempted. But 'cept for breathing like a bellows, he didn't move, didn't try nothing, like he'd said he wouldn't.

"Did you set 'em on me?" I asked—mostly just curious. And I wanted to know how twisty his mind was.

"No! Powers, I wouldn't—"

"You just didn't feel like helping."

That shut him up. Finally, he said, "Yeah, I wanted . . ."

"You wanted to see me get my ass kicked." I didn't say it nasty or nothing, because, powers and saints, I understood how that went, but I felt him flinch, just a little.

Okay, so at least he could recognize he was a prick.

"I put my knife up," I said. "What're you gonna do?"

"What d'you want me to do?"

"Look. I ain't into mind-games like Keep—like Kolkhis is. As long as you ain't gonna go for me again, I don't give a rat's ass."

"I won't," he said. "I swear. By the Septad Gate and Mélusine's cunt."

I wasn't expecting that, and it hurt a little. Because it'd been something Nikah taught us to say. Before the sangerman got him. And it was just weird to realize that it hadn't died with him. That kids who'd never even known his name were still saying it.

"Okay," I said. "I believe you." I folded my knife back into my boot.

He didn't move for a moment, like he figured it for a trick. But then he was up and gone so fast I didn't think I could've caught him if I'd wanted to. Which I didn't.

I looked up the city at the Mirador. And I guess I was a little light-headed—Kethe knows I ached all over like I'd been rolled downhill in a barrel—because I caught myself thinking, if the Iron Chapel was Mélusine's cunt, then the Mirador had to be her dick.

And somehow that just seemed so perfectly fucking true it was all I could do to keep from bursting into tears right there on that tenement roof in Gilgamesh.

Mehitabel

I left Simon and Rinaldo's rooms well-freighted with tidbits of information Vulpes might find precious. At least I could prove that I was trying, and that was what concerned me. Louis Goliath was a reasonable man, whatever else he might be. He wouldn't punish Hallam simply because the information gathered wasn't the information he wanted.

If indeed it wasn't the information he wanted, and I had no way of determining that. But that wasn't my concern. I'd had my part in this black farce laid out for me very clearly, and I couldn't afford to ad lib bits of business or change my lines to fit a better scansion. My safety and Hallam's safety.

It was lumped up under my breastbone, the fact that we'd been in the Bastion, rescuing people left, right, and center, and I hadn't been able to rescue Hallam. Hadn't even been able to *mention* rescuing Hallam. And I knew it was because we couldn't have, that no matter how lucky we got, nothing would have made it possible for him to survive once ripped free of the spells that chained him. But we'd saved Simon and Rinaldo. Saved Mildmay. And left Hallam there to suffer, to die one cruel inch at a time.

He might live to be a very old man in the Bastion. It wasn't worth anyone's effort to kill him.

"God and the thirteen crimson devils," I said through my teeth, and looked up to find myself in a corridor I didn't know. It was a narrow, twisting hallway, paneled and floored in elaborate interlocking patterns of light and dark wood. False windows flanked each corner, their frames elaborately carved and fretted; looking through one, I discovered a flat painted landscape like nothing I had ever seen—twisted trees and dark, jeering rocks and the gilt sun lying against the pallid sky like a counterfeit coin. I turned away, started walking again, and the Mirador, as was its nature, presented me with an excruciating coincidence.

Mildmay turned the corner.

If I could've retreated, I would have. But it was already too late. His head had come up, and he was staring at me, his eyes hard, over-bright, as unnatural as emeralds. It was the same way he'd looked in the Bastion when he'd nearly killed me—bruises and all.

"Oh for fuck's sake," he said. He stepped around me and kept walking. He was limping badly; his coat was torn. His hair had come out of its usual neat braid and was hanging around his face and shoulders like fire.

"What happened to you?" I said, with the same stupid inevitability as Armet unlocking her husband's closet in *The Seventh Bride*.

He stopped. He didn't turn, but I saw him square his shoulders. "Got into a fight. In Gilgamesh."

"What were you doing *there*?"

He looked over his shoulder, his face hard, unreadable, and more than a little inhuman. "None of your fucking business." And then he turned and left, as if I wasn't there at all.

Part Two

Chapter 6

Mildmay

That night I slept like I'd died. I woke when I normally did, the first hour of the morning, and I lay there for a while, counting up bruises and the sharp way my bad leg was hurting, but that wasn't doing nobody no good. I got up and got dressed and tidied, and it was only the third time I had to step over it that I realized the heap of rags in the middle of the floor was Gideon's coat. Well, what was left of Gideon's coat after the fight. I'd lost Felix's scarf completely.

For a second my breath stopped hard in my throat. Then I grabbed the coat off the floor and fumbled through the pockets, not really praying, just thinking, please, please, please. And it was there, where I remembered shoving it. The black ribbon Mehitabel had given me almost two indictions ago, after Strych. The only thing she'd ever given me.

By that time my hands were shaking so bad I couldn't braid my hair. Fuck, Milly-Fox, it's just a ribbon. And you ain't seeing Mehitabel no more, remember?

But none of that mattered. I sat down on the bed again, my hands clenched on that ribbon like I thought somebody was going to try and take it away from me. There wasn't nothing happening in my head, just this hard, jumbling feeling like big blocks of stone bumping at each other, and my heart was hammering.

And out of all that, this question pushed its way up to the top of my mind: what the fuck had I been *doing* yesterday? Haring off to the Lower City like it was picking buttercups in St. Millefleur, getting within shouting distance of Keeper, doing just what she told me like I was at my second septad again . . . Powers and saints and Kethe's black-hearted mercy, getting in *fights* like I was at my second septad again.

"I must have been out of my fucking mind," I said out loud without meaning to. Then I said, "Fuck," and buried my head in my hands.

Because I knew why I'd done it, and I *was* out of my fucking mind. I'd done it because it beat sitting around thinking about Mehitabel. And it especially beat thinking about the fact that Mehitabel was not the one who'd fucked up here. If I wanted her to trust me, I could've gone about it a better way than calling her by some dead gal's name every time I opened my mouth. I wouldn't've felt like trusting me, either.

But I hadn't wanted to think about that, so I'd thought of something else to do instead. Something really fucking stupid, as it happens. And I hadn't let myself see what I was doing it for, hadn't let the idea get up where I could look at it and how stupid it was and talk myself out of it. I'd just *done* it, like it made sense and was a good idea and didn't have a thing in the world to do with Mehitabel Parr.

"Fuck me for a half-wit dog," I said. But my hands had calmed down. I braided my hair and picked up Gideon's coat and took a deep breath, trying to pretend like yesterday hadn't happened.

It didn't help, but I had to open the door anyway. I can't even tell you how relieved I was when there was nobody there. There was a note on the table, Gideon's handwriting: *HE SAYS MEET HIM IN THE CERULEAN ANTECHAMBER*. It took me a while to figure out "cerulean," but I didn't have to ask who "he" was or what the note really meant, which was, kindly get out before either of us has to look at you. And it was just like Felix to make Gideon write the note.

I was happy to oblige, though. After the scene we'd pitched at each other last night, I didn't want to look at them, neither. I put the coat on the table. I would've liked to leave a note of my own, at least to say, *Sorry about the coat*, but I was afraid if I stayed long enough to do that, one of them might come out of the bedroom. So I left.

I went down to the kitchen. Properly, I guess, I have to say the Fifth Sub-Kitchen, since there are a double septad of kitchens—maybe more than that—scattered through the Mirador: the Great Kitchen, that does the banquets and soirées and all the official stuff, and then the sub-kitchens that cook for the flashies and the hocuses and of course for the servants. I'd been in a septad-worth of 'em, and I liked the Fifth best. It was all warm orangey-red brick, and the ovens kept off the cold. The Mirador was *always* cold. Felix laughed at me about it, but it was true.

It'd taken the servants a while to figure out what to do with me. Most of them were from the Lower City, or had lovers or friends or in-laws in the Lower City, and there was no sense pretending they didn't know what I was. What I'd been. And they weren't sure if I was a servant like them, or if they should treat me like a flashie, or what. I didn't know either, and that didn't help.

But we'd worked things out. I talked like them, not like Felix or Lord Stephen, and I knew too much about how hard they worked to be able to ignore them the way the hocuses and flashies did. Felix got pissed off at me about that, but I couldn't help it. I knew kids who'd entered service, talking their way into a flashie household because it beat turning tricks in alleys, and I couldn't help seeing them in the girls who did our laundry, the guys who carried breakfast trays up and down six flights of stairs without slopping the tea or letting the eggs get cold. And so I couldn't help trying to find ways to make their jobs easier, like going through Felix's coat pockets before giving the week's wash to the laundresses—you wouldn't believe the stuff he shoved in his pockets and forgot about—or warning Maurice, who brought around the breakfast trays, when Felix was in a particularly nasty mood. And after a while the servants decided I was more like them than like Felix, and that I was maybe sort of okay. The kitchen had quit going deathly quiet whenever I walked in, and if I happened to run into one of the maids in the hall, she didn't immediately drop a curtsy to keep from having to look me in the eye. I don't say they were comfortable with me, 'cause they weren't, but they'd more or less decided I wasn't going to bite 'em.

I even got a little chorus of "good mornings" as I came into the kitchen, and Jeanne-Citrine got me tea and a slice of bread and jam without batting an eye. They were all looking sideways at my face, but none of 'em had the balls to ask. Even Geburon, the Fifth Sub-Cook, a huge guy with a scar on his face as ugly as mine, didn't say no more than, "Bring them dishes back when you're done with 'em." But at that time of day he didn't have no time for a heart-to-heart anyways.

I didn't go far—just down to a storeroom—and I ate as

quick as I could. I didn't particularly want to eat at all, but I knew I had to. Keeper—and oh powers, here I go thinking about Keeper again—had been careful about teaching us stuff like that, that even if you didn't think you wanted food sometimes, your body needed it. I hadn't eaten dinner last night, and it was anybody's guess when I might be able to eat again. If Felix was as mad as I thought he was going to be, I'd probably be too upset to eat for most of the day.

Sounds funny, don't it, grown man like me getting all hysterical over a chewing out? And it wasn't that I was scared of Felix and the way he shouted and the things he called me, but he knew how to make me mad. He'd bait me sometimes for fun, because he was bored or just because he thought it was funny, I don't know, and when I'd finally lose my temper and yell at him, he'd just grin and correct my grammar. And I mean, I hated that, but it was okay. But when he was mad himself, like I thought he was going to be today, anything I said he'd turn right back around on me, and he could talk so much better than me that I'd just get madder and madder, and I wouldn't be able to get rid of it with words, and I'd want to hurt him, break his perfect nose or black both his creepy eyes or just get a good handful of his hair and rip it out by the roots. *That* was what scared me.

I had no idea what the binding-by-forms would do if I tried to hurt Felix, but I was betting it wouldn't be anything nice. And more than that, I didn't want to hurt Felix. When he'd been crazy, he'd thought I was his Keeper, who'd left whip scars on his back that he hated for anybody to see, and more than anything else I never wanted that to be true. I *could* hurt him—I never doubted that for a second, no matter what the binding-by-forms did to me afterwards. He wasn't a fighter. And he was . . . not clumsy, exactly, but awkward. Like somebody'd taught him not to be clumsy by belting him one every time he dropped a book or walked into a chair. Like he was frightened of what might happen if he quit watching where his hands and feet went for so much as a second. I could hurt him, and hurt him bad, before he even knew I was thinking about it. But I wasn't going to.

I took my cup and plate to join the already growing stack of washing-up and got out of the kitchen again without bothering nobody or giving them a chance to ask what was going on with me and Felix that I was down in the kitchen half an hour after dawn with my face all black and blue. I could just imagine the rumors that were going to start, but I knew how gossip worked. Anything I said to try and keep them from thinking Felix had beat me up would just make them believe it more.

I went back up into the main halls—what Felix called the surface of the Mirador—and found an empty parlor, one of them little rooms where people can have a private discussion without nobody eavesdropping. There are lots of little rooms like that along the Wooden Hallway and the Pomgarnet Gallery, the two main corridors that lead to the Vielle Roche, the central core of the Mirador where the Hall of the Chimeras is.

I closed the door of the room I'd picked and moved the two chairs to one side. They were School of Jecquardin and would have fetched a pretty price from a broker I knew down in Midwinter. But what I wanted was the floor space. I ached all over, and most particularly in my leg, and if I was going to make it through today without driving Felix absolutely batfuck, I needed to get it stretched out. Felix was never mean about my lameness—never threw it in my face or made nasty jokes about it, the way he would sometimes about my scar—but he had long legs and he walked fast, and he hated having to slow down only a little less than he hated having to wait for me to catch up.

I took off my coat and waistcoat and shoes and did the exercises that Keeper had taught me, and some others that I'd learned in the Gardens of Nephele, working my right thigh especially, trying to get some heat into the muscles where it was needed, trying to get my leg to act like a leg. I couldn't do as much as I liked because I wouldn't make Felix any happier by showing up sweaty for court, but I was able to do enough that I thought I'd be able to fake normal pretty well. It'd have to do. I put myself back together, put the chairs back where they'd been, and took myself off to the Cerulean Antechamber.

The Cerulean Antechamber was one of maybe three-septad-worth of little rooms scattered around the Hall of the Chimeras where the flashies and hocuses could collect before court. They were there to keep people from bunching up in front of the doors, because when they did that the stewards couldn't get the doors open properly and everybody, Felix said, was mortified. So there were these little rooms with swanky names and fancy wallpaper, all of them within earshot of the doors, which always swung open with a crash loud enough to wake the dead.

Felix usually hung out in the Puce Antechamber or the Vermilion, with his particular group of hocus friends or some of the younger flashies, or sometimes in the Cerise when he wanted to get a rise out of somebody. The Cerise was where all the oldest, tightest-assed hocuses twiddled their thumbs. It wasn't 'til I walked in that I remembered who liked the Cerulean.

Simon Barrister looked up from where he was fixing the hang of Rinaldo of Fiora's bulging coat and grunted something that was probably "good morning." Rinaldo looked about like usual—like ten pounds of flour in a five pound sack—and he wheezed out some fancy thing about a lady with rosy fingers and the color of my hair. The lady was a quote from something, Felix had told me, but he either couldn't or wouldn't explain the rest of the joke. I gave them a nod and leaned on the back of another Jecquardin chair to wait for Felix.

"What brings Felix here this morning?" Simon asked when he was done with Rinaldo's coat.

"Dunno," I said.

"I'm sure he has his reasons," Simon said, "even if mere mortals such as myself can't grasp them." He grinned. "I'm even more sure that if it's anything to do with me, I'll hear about it. How are you?"

"Me? Oh, I'm fine."

Rinaldo said, "With your face *those* colors? What happened?"

"Got in a fight. Where's Lady Istrid?"

"Running late," Simon said. "And, before you ask, Winifred has a vile head cold, and Cabot is deep in negotiations with several people in the Carmine Antechamber. You should never try to change the subject to avoid questions. You do it very badly."

"Yeah, well," I said and shrugged.

"I shan't harass you. If Felix wants you harassed, he'll have to do it himself."

"After all," Rinaldo said, "he does such a splendid job."

I didn't know what to say to that.

Simon got me off the hook. He said, "Rinaldo, you look like a bag-pudding."

"I always do," Rinaldo said. "Hephestien says the only way I *won't* look like a bag-pudding is if I wear corsets. I used to, you know."

"You wore corsets?" Simon said, his eyebrows going up.

"When I was young and vain and foolish," Rinaldo said with a shrug that almost undid all the work Simon had put in on the set of his coat. But his face was sad. "Dulcinea used to tease me about them."

"Dulcinea?"

"All this flap over Stephen's marriage makes me think of her," Rinaldo said. "I swore my oaths the same year she married Gareth. There was a time when it seemed as if she might be able to charm Curia and court into bed together."

"By which you do *not* mean—"

"No, of course not, Simon. Control the prurience of your imagination. But we all vied for Lady Dulcinea's favor, wizards and annemer alike, and she had a gift . . ." He was quiet a second, staring off into space, then said, "It is a pity neither of her children inherited it."

I didn't know what to say to that. From the look on his face, neither did Simon. Lady Dulcinea, Lord Stephen and Lady Victoria's mother, had committed suicide when Lord Stephen had had a septad and one. Nobody knew why. She'd slit her wrists in her dressing room an hour and a half before some major function. The story was that the blood had soaked through the carpet and permanently stained the stone floor. I might've believed it if any two people of the double-septad or so I'd heard tell the story had been able to agree on which room it had been.

Rinaldo said, changing the subject about as bald as an egg, "Gideon came to visit us yesterday afternoon."

"Yeah?" I said. So that was where he had gone.

"And Mehitabel in the evening," Simon said.

"Our popularity is becoming quite dizzying."

I knew what Simon was fishing for, and I wasn't going to give it to him. "What did Gideon want?"

"Just to talk to someone who didn't want to argue, I think," Simon said. "He looked tired. Are he and Felix fighting again?"

"You know Felix," I said. "He's got to fight with somebody, and I won't oblige him."

"I wish he would find another hobby," Rinaldo grumbled, and I was actually glad Felix came in then, because that conversation wasn't going to go nowhere good.

Felix's manner was particularly bright and hard, even for Felix in a temper. It was like he was wearing armor made out of diamonds. He gave me one knife-sharp look, and then turned his attention on Simon and Rinaldo, laying himself out to be charming and friendly, showing me, of course, that he was mad specifically at me and not just being cross-grained. Simon gave me a funny look, but him and Rinaldo went along with it.

Lady Istrid came haring in, but she didn't have time to do more than stare at my face before we heard the thundering crash of the doors and it was time to go. Which I was grateful for.

Felix

I would not have wanted Mildmay's company that afternoon, even if we hadn't both been raw-tempered with the memory of last night's argument—even if I hadn't been able to hear him still, snarling, *So what were you getting in bed with Kolkhis for anyway?* I sent him away as soon as court was over, suggested he get some sleep, since he looked dreadful, his eyes bloodshot and his face so colorless where it was not bruised that the scar stood out like the afterimage of lightning.

He didn't even look at me, simply went. I noticed his limp was worse than usual and wished I dared say something. But he wouldn't let me help him—I knew that without making the experiment and getting my head bitten off for my pains—and I did have matters of my own to attend to.

Troia was barely more than a myth on this, the western borders of Kekropia; if I could not get Thamuris to explain a thanatopsis to me, I would not find information about it in the Mirador's libraries. I could not find out how to *prevent* a ghost.

It might not be necessary. It might be too late.

I couldn't tell. Gideon said Malkar was not haunting Mildmay, but Gideon couldn't see ghosts, either, only the "signs" of haunting, whatever exactly those were supposed to be. And I couldn't tell him that I wasn't worried about Mildmay, but about myself. It was unforgivably selfish; even Gideon would find it so.

But I didn't think Malkar was haunting Mildmay, though perhaps it was just my vanity telling me Malkar wouldn't bother with him if I was available. I didn't even truly believe Malkar was haunting me. Not *truly*.

Except sometimes I wondered. And I had no way of finding out.

I had been able to see ghosts once. In the Hospice of St.

Crellifer's, when I was mad. I had seen them in the Mirador, too. Had talked to one. And then the healers in the Gardens of Nephele had mended the damage Malkar had done to my mind, and I didn't see ghosts any longer.

But if I had been able to once, surely I could teach myself to do it again. And not send myself mad in the process. Either that, of course, or it had all been hallucinations, and I was already mad for imagining it had been real.

In which case, I couldn't make things worse by trying, now could I?

I had been thinking about it carefully, and it seemed to me that the best place to experiment would be the crypt of the Cordelii. It was not a place that had any associations with Malkar, and I knew I had seen ghosts there before. And given the recent excursions and what they had found, I thought the chance was excellent that there would be a ghost there who wanted to talk.

Amaryllis Cordelia did not seem like the sort of woman who would choose to suffer in silence.

I had learned to navigate the Mirador by listening to what Ephreal Sand called *manar* in *De Doctrina Labyrinthorum*, the same way Thamuris and I had learned to observe the Khloï-danikos. It was not an infallible method, but it was better than relying on my nonexistent sense of direction. I found the crypt with no more difficulty than was to be expected. Mikkary, that sense of ancient festering fury, of death and despair and madness, permeated the abandoned levels of the Mirador, but in the crypt it was like water in the air. Antony Lemerius's researches had certainly stirred something up.

Determining which of the crypts was Amaryllis Cordelia's was painfully easy. Gideon had mentioned the candles. I called light to them and noted that they did nothing to reduce the sensation of being all but crushed by the darkness in the crypt. That feeling was mikkary and had nothing to do with the available light.

I sat down with my back against the nearest freestanding tomb and contemplated the act of seeing a ghost. Cabaline theory was of no use to me here. What little I did know, picked up from Malkar and from reading heretical books, was rather less slanted toward merely *seeing* ghosts and much more toward bending the dead to one's will. I thought I would do better—in this as in so many other things—*not* to emulate Malkar. And

•

that meant I was essentially reduced to making up the theory as
I went along.

Not an unusual position, but not any the more comfortable
for its familiarity.

As a matter of habit, I did everything I could to avoid thinking about the time I'd spent in St. Crellifer's, but at the moment
those memories were the closest thing I had to guidance. I had
been able to see ghosts then, and if I could remember what it
felt like, maybe I could reproduce the necessary shift.

And maybe I could drive myself mad in the process, too.

That was the mikkary talking, I told myself firmly. I pulled
my knees up against my chest; the marble was cold even
through my coat. Most of what I remembered simply made no
sense: animal-headed monsters, a relentless throbbing, not
quite pressure, not quite sound, like being trapped inside a beat-
ing heart. I had gone days without saying a single word, without
understanding anything that was said to me.

I had been afraid, and I wrapped my arms around my knees,
hugging myself. I was shivering, and I no longer knew whether
it was with remembered fear or present cold.

This wasn't going to work. I was drowning. Even if there
was an answer in that painful chaos, I wasn't going to find it.
Not like this. A convulsive shudder racked me, and I clenched
my teeth against the noise that tried to escape. I didn't want to
hear it.

I pushed to my feet, began to pace. From light to shadow and
back again. Approach this logically. In purely hypothetical
terms, how would one go about seeing ghosts? Where would
one begin?

And I found I knew the answer to that. Openness. Thamuris
called it "surrender," though that was not a word I liked. It had
occurred to me more than once that if one of us had come from
a less strident school—mine denying that the concept of openness had any validity, his privileging it above all else—we might
have had better terminology, better frameworks with which to
understand what we were trying to do. Some guidance as to what
the dangers were, what damage we might do ourselves.

I had tried to talk to Gideon about it. Gideon was terrifyingly
well-read; I had thought if anyone would know where I might
track this idea down, it would be he. But my poor, halting explanation was made worse by my selfish desire to keep the Khloï-

danikos to myself; it was the one thing I had that I did not have to share, not with Mildmay, not with Gideon, not with my foul haunting memories of Malkar. And so I had explained badly and had been unable to distinguish the kind of openness I meant from the Eusebian understanding, which was far closer to the Euryganeic theory Thamuris had been taught. Openness—what the Eusebians called *ereimos*—was a quality in younger wizards which older wizards exploited ruthlessly. One tried to learn to be *anereimos*, closed ("properly bounded in the self" was how Gideon put it), as quickly as one could, so that one could become a predator in turn, instead of remaining prey. There was also some sexual connotation to the word, which Gideon was profoundly unwilling to discuss, but I thought it had to do with why he framed intercourse between two men always and only in terms of one man's submission to the other.

I knew it didn't have to be like that, just as being open did not have to mean being ereimos, being prey, but I didn't know how to explain it. I didn't know how to change the terms of our relationship. And I was afraid. Afraid of giving up control, afraid of letting Gideon see what I truly was. I trusted him not to hurt me, but I couldn't trust him to understand. I couldn't trust him not to leave.

I leaned against the tomb of Leonor Cordelia, bracing myself on my palms. She'd been somebody's sister; I couldn't remember whose. Openness, I said to myself, sternly redirecting my wandering thoughts. You can do that much, anyway.

And I did. I opened myself to the crypt of the Cordelii the same way I'd learned to open myself to the Khloïdanikos. I felt mikkary like spiders along my spine, felt death and grief and the strange iron bitterness of murder unrecognized and unrevenged.

I gave myself a pounding headache, but I did not see any ghosts.

Mildmay

Felix sent me away the moment court was over, and I was glad of it. I had shit I needed to do, and I needed to figure out how I was going to do it without getting my stupid self beaten up again.

Keeper—I mean Kolkhis—Kolkhis wanted to know why

Jenny Dawnlight had gotten herself arrested in Laceshroud with a corpse. And I'd admit if you pushed me that I was curious, too. I mean, it really wasn't Jenny's kind of thing. And more than that, I'd made a bargain with Kolkhis, and if I blew it, not only would I never find out who'd gotten Ginevra killed, it'd be all over the Lower City between one septad-day and the next. And what the Lower City knew, the Mirador would find out sooner or later, and the thought made me want to crawl into a hole and die. So, yeah, the question of what the fuck Jenny thought she was doing needed some answering.

Since I wasn't about to go to the Kennel and ask Jenny herself, I'd have to try and find out some other way. Starting maybe with who'd sent her, because you could've told me it'd all been her idea until you were bright purple, and I wouldn't've believed you. Somebody *sent* her. And it didn't take much thinking to figure that the place to start asking about that somebody was with the resurrectionists.

'Course, as far as I was concerned, it might as well have been the moon. I couldn't go down there. I'd get my ass kicked back to the Mirador so fast my head would still be spinning when Felix took it off my shoulders for me.

And then I thought: no, what I *can't* do is go alone. What point is there in being surrounded by hocuses if you don't make use of 'em?

My first thought was to ask Felix, but that wasn't going to work. I mean, part of it might've—Felix loved mysteries, too—but the other part, the part about going down the city. Felix wouldn't do that for me, and if he knew I was thinking about it, he'd forbid me, just like he'd said. I could only think of a couple hocuses who might help me.

At least I knew where to find them.

Simon answered the door when I knocked. "Mildmay!" He didn't say, *What are you doing here?* but he never had any luck keeping what he was thinking off his face.

"It ain't for Felix," I said, 'cause I figured he'd want to know that right off.

"What isn't—oh, never mind. Come in."

Rinaldo was settled in by the fire with his coat and boots off and his waistcoat unbuttoned. He cracked an eye at me. "*Don't* say you want me to go anywhere, there's a good fellow."

"Nah. Just wanted to ask Simon . . ."

"Just wanted to ask Simon what?" said Simon. "Sit down. Or can't you stay?"

"He's off doing something of his own." I sat down so as to make Simon happy.

"Felix and his little mysteries," Rinaldo grumbled. "And you're no better. What *did* happen to you?"

"I told you. Got in a fight."

"And you don't want to talk about it. Yes, we know."

"It . . . it wasn't Felix, was it?" Simon said anxiously.

I didn't mean to laugh, but powers and saints. Like Felix had the least idea of how to go about doing this kind of damage. "Nah. Some goons down in Gilgamesh."

Rinaldo opened both eyes. "And what, pray tell, were you doing in Gilgamesh?"

This was about where the fight with Felix had started last night. I didn't want to fight with Rinaldo—and Simon, because I wasn't confused about whose side he'd come down on—and I didn't want to lie to them. But I also *really* didn't want to talk about Ginevra. Because for one thing—well, I just didn't want to. But for another, before I could make them understand what Ginevra had to do with getting the shit kicked out of myself in Gilgamesh, I'd have to explain about Keeper—which I also didn't want to do, thanks—and kept-thieves and how the Lower City worked, and it'd be the septad-night before I got anywhere close to talking about Jenny.

So I didn't want to lie, but if I could just leave out some of the middle of the truth . . . I said, "A gal I used to know is in the Kennel."

"I'm sorry," Simon said. "I *can't* have heard you right."

Powers. "The Ebastine. She got picked up in Laceshroud—"

"In *Laceshroud*?" Rinaldo said.

"For digging up a dead guy," I said, more or less over him, and I felt like I deserved a round of applause or something just for getting the whole damn sentence out.

"She was caught exhuming a corpse in the oldest cemetery in Mélusine," Rinaldo said, kind of slow, like he wanted to be sure he understood.

"Yeah."

"You want to help her?" Simon said.

"Sort of. I mean, yeah, but I wanna know what she was doing digging people up. She ain't no resurrectionist."

"A what?" said Rinaldo.

"Resurrectionist. Don't they trade with the Mirador?"

"I don't think I understand," Rinaldo said. "Again, what are resurrectionists?"

"Um," I said. "People that go around digging up dead people."

"Why?" said Simon.

"Well, 'cause people will pay 'em for it."

"What sort of people?"

"Um, well, the necromancers in Scaffelgreen. And there's a market for hair and sometimes people are buried with jewelry and shit like that." You can make a profit off most anything in the Lower City.

"Are they organized?" Simon said. "Like kept-thieves or the assassins' guild?"

"There ain't no assassins' guild. Never has been. But, yeah, the resurrectionists got a kind of system worked out, so they don't go cheating each other or nothing. They even got a kind of guildhall out in Ruthven."

"So why don't you go ask them?"

"Well . . . um . . ."

"What?"

"That's sort of what I need help for."

"What do you mean?"

"I go down there by myself, I won't get nothing. 'Cept another fight. I . . . I ain't exactly popular in the Lower City no more."

"Ah," said Rinaldo. "Because of Felix?"

"Because of a lot of things," I said, and I didn't mean to sound so tired.

"So," Simon said, "where do I fit into this?"

My face went red, but I said it anyway. "The one thing nobody in the Lower City will fuck with is the Mirador's tattoos."

"Oh, then I'll come," Simon said, like it was no big deal.

I couldn't keep from asking, "Are you sure?"

"Oh, yes," Simon said. "It sounds interesting."

"Powers, you're crazier'n I am. But thanks. When d'you want to go?"

"Tomorrow won't do. I've got a committee meeting. What about Mardy afternoon?"

"Fine by me. I'll show up here when Felix is done with me."

And maybe it was dumb, but I felt better. Because I could put off seeing Septimus Wilder again for another couple days.

Mehitabel

It took us a little over four hours that afternoon to read through a play that would take two-and-a-half in performance, not counting intermissions. The language was hard, and Jean-Soleil was visited by occasional spurts of enthusiasm, when he had to stop and try a scene again with a different interpretation.

After the read-through was finally over and Jean-Soleil had bolted off to his office with scribbled-over wax tablets to wrestle out a plan for the play, Gordeny Fisher approached me hesitantly.

"Madame Parr," she said with an awkward bob that wasn't quite a curtsy.

"Don't do that," I said, and remembered to smile at her. "You're Madame Fisher yourself now, you know."

"S'pose I am," she said; her eyes widened with wonder, and for a moment she looked like the street urchin I was sure she had been.

"A lifetime's aspiration achieved?"

"Oh, nothing like that. Just, you know how sometimes you end up places you'd never've thought you wanted to go?"

"Yes."

"I remember coming to a play here once when I was real little, and if you'd told me then I was gonna be one of them fine ladies up there on the stage saying all that poetry, I'd probably've blacked your eye. I was a hellcat."

"What *did* you think you wanted to do?"

"Oh, kids get all sorts of crazy ideas. But I wanted to ask you . . ."

"Yes?" I wasn't going to pursue the evasion.

She made a charming, nervous grimace. "Do you know, have I done something to make Mr. Baillie not like me?"

Drin. "Has he been making himself unpleasant?"

"No," she said, although she clearly wasn't sure of it. "It's mostly the way he looks at me. I mean, maybe I'm imagining things or being too sensitive, but I didn't . . ."

Damn you, Drin. "It's nothing you've done. It's just Drin. He doesn't like change."

"He don't like girls from Queensdock, you mean."

"Doesn't."

"Doesn't," she agreed, but her amber eyes remained steadfastly on my face.

"No, you're right. Drin thinks . . ." Oh dear, how to put it? "He thinks you might have an unsavory past."

She burst out laughing, a warm, full-bodied, infectious laugh as compelling as her speaking voice. "Me? I'm just a docker's kid. Poor but virtuous, that was my parents."

"I didn't say *I* believed it," I said, although my suspicion was that Drin was more right than wrong. Gordeny Fisher would clearly tell lies with the same candid air with which she told the truth. And what *had* she wanted to be when she grew up? "Drin has a fertile imagination."

"Well, if that's the problem, there ain't—I mean, I don't suppose there's anything I can do about it."

"Give him time," I said. "He'll come around."

She thanked me and sauntered off, as nonchalant as an alley cat. I hoped that what I had told her was true, and also that Gordeny Fisher's secrets were not going to turn and bite her.

My own secrets, with their fierce panoply of teeth, were waiting for me in my dressing room. Vulpes was sitting with his feet up on my dressing table, reading my copy of *The Wrong Brother*.

He looked up as I came in; the door closed and bolted behind me, and he said, "What in the name of God did you do to Mildmay Foxe?"

I considered my options for a split second. A little misdirection wouldn't hurt, and I was calm enough that what had been real with Stephen would be playacting with Vulpes. "Nothing," I snarled. "Get out of my chair."

He got up, smirking, and I sat down in front of the mirror and began viciously pulling the pins out of my hair. "What do you want now?"

"What happened to Mildmay Foxe?"

"Somebody beat him up," I said and left the words *you moron* palpable but unspoken.

"Was it Felix?"

The idea was laughable, so I laughed at it. "No."

"How can you be sure?"

"I know both of them," I said, hard and sharp enough to sting.

"I see." Sulky, and that was a real pleasure to hear. He switched topics. "How many wizards do you think will accept the amnesty?"

"Good God, how should I know? Surely you, lieutenant, are in a better position to answer that than I."

In the mirror, I watched him start to pace. "An opinion then, Maselle Cressida. How many do you *think*?"

"I can't imagine what good my opinion will do you, but I don't believe that any of the wizards who have taken the Mirador's vows will return to the Bastion. They don't trust General Parsifal."

"Yes," he said, peevishly. "The busy tongue of Thaddeus de Lalage."

"Don't put it all on Thaddeus," I said. "Eric Ogygios will never trust the Bastion no matter what Gemma promises."

"But at least Eric is rational. What *is* the matter with Lord Thaddeus?"

"I don't know. He hates the Bastion. Many people do, lieutenant."

He waved that away, like the stupidities of lesser beings weren't worth his time. "What of the others? The Eusebians who haven't submitted to those barbaric tattoos?"

"I haven't the faintest idea. I imagine it will depend on the individual wizard."

"What about Gideon Thraxios?"

"You must be out of your mind. What possible reason could Gideon have for returning?"

Vulpes paced crossly; it would probably be quite a coup to get Gideon to return to the Bastion of his own free will. "Have you heard anything else of interest?"

"The Lord Protector's going to hold a soirée on Mercredy," I said. "People are dragging their daughters in from all over the Protectorate."

"Ah, yes, the Lord Protector. Tell me, Maselle Cressida, how was your dinner with his lordship?"

"Very pleasant. Lord Stephen is a charming host."

Vulpes didn't believe me for a second, but it hardly mattered. "What did you learn?"

"He'd like to get along better with Felix."

"Hmmph. What else?"

"I don't think he grieves for his wife any longer. He seems

more amused than anything else by this hunt for a second wife."

There was a pause. "Is that *it*?"

"He's not particularly forthcoming. But he said he would invite me again."

"At least that's something." He muttered something under his breath that was probably blasphemous and took another turn up and down the room.

"You seem edgy, Lieutenant Vulpes. Is something wrong?"

Louis Goliath would have given that question the answer it deserved, and I wouldn't have asked him in the first place. Vulpes said, "Wrong? No, nothing's wrong," and changed the subject. "Are you doing anything tonight, Maselle Cressida?"

"I wasn't."

"Then go up to the Mirador. Talk to your friends. I want to know what people are thinking about the Lord Protector's wedding."

"I can tell you that now," I said, and relayed what I'd learned in the Painted Grotto and from Simon and Rinaldo.

He listened and nodded, but I could see that he was thinking frantically. Racking his brains for some other task to set me, was my guess.

"One of your lovers is a nobleman, isn't he?"

"Antony Lemerius."

"The same Lemerius . . . ?"

"I don't know."

He didn't quite say *Ha!* "Then go find out." And he left hurriedly, as if he didn't want to give me the chance to ask him anything else. I changed into a slightly richer dress, did my hair, and headed doggedly for the Mirador.

The footman who opened the door of the Lemerius apartments seemed distinctly harried; I understood why, sitting in the foyer and listening to the muffled commotion. Antony came out after a few minutes and bowed over my hands with every evidence of delight. I raised my eyebrows expressively in the direction of the ruckus, and he made a pained face. "Father's bringing Enid up from Copal Carnifex."

"Enid?"

"My youngest sister."

"Oh. For the . . . ?"

"Of course," he said bitterly. "Father is slavering at the

prospect of becoming the Lord Protector's in-law. And powers and saints, he's not alone in that." He ushered me through the public rooms to his private sitting room, which an uninformed visitor could have been forgiven for mistaking for one of the Mirador's official libraries. "At least Enid is old enough to handle it. Zelda Polydoria can't have been fifteen for more than a month."

"Polydoria? Isn't that . . ."

"Distant cousins," Antony said, clearing books and tablets and quires of notes off various flat surfaces, including a chair. "Nothing wrong with that. I imagine the real impediment to that match is the prospect of Ivo Polydorius as a father-in-law."

I racked my mind, trying to find a face to put with that name. I failed, although I remembered Lionel Verlalius mentioning him. "I haven't met him, have I?"

"I wouldn't think so. He's been living in seclusion for years and years. Had a big falling-out with Lord Gareth. There's bad blood in the Polydorii, and it seems to have all come out in the dynastic line, more's the pity. Nicoletta Milensia said she'd rather kill herself than marry Ivo, but in the end she didn't have the nerve. Their children take after her, and people still argue over whether that's unfortunate or not. But that sort of gossip"—he straightened up, having unearthed enough furniture that we could both sit down—"isn't fit conversation."

"Did you have a better topic in mind?" I asked, taking a seat.

"Have you dined? Would you care to join me?" He sounded almost embarrassingly hopeful.

I hadn't even had to hint. "I'd like that very much."

"Excellent. Just a moment."

He stepped out. I occupied myself by trying to make sense of his notes; between the illegibility of his handwriting and my own ignorance of Marathine history, it was doomed to failure, but it was an amusing pastime. When he returned, he was neither surprised nor offended, but said, "I've been thinking about the date of Amaryllis Cordelia's alleged death: 11 Floréal 14.6.2, the date on both tombs."

"And when do you think she really died?"

"Late 14.5.7—Wilfrid lost his post sometime in Fructidor and was back at Diggory Chase to celebrate the Trials of Heth-Eskaladen by the end of that month. Between her real and her alleged death—that's only two indictions, and what I was wondering was, what if there was no second Amaryllis Cordelia at all? Wilfrid returns to Diggory Chase in Fructidor of 14.5.7 and writes a letter to the Mirador at the end of Floréal two indictions later saying his beloved wife Amaryllis has died in childbirth and the child along with her, examined by our good doctor Grizzleguts and so on and so forth. Diggory Chase was out in the middle of nowhere in those days, and no one was going to check the facts."

"They would have had to buy off the entire house of Emarthius," I objected.

"No, actually. Diggory Chase was a small secondary residence. The dynastic line of the Emarthii was living at a place called Heligar. I found the records. Diggory Chase was given to Wilfrid on his marriage by his father. He and Amaryllis never went there, since she'd pulled strings to get him a post at the Mirador. The only people who had to be in the know were Wilfrid Emarthius's liveried servants, and probably not many of them. I imagine one could have lived reasonably well at Diggory Chase for two years with only four servants: a valet, a housekeeper, a cook, and a groom. If one retires there in seclusion, having been disgraced by one's wife, no one will be surprised at one's failure to throw parties or invite guests."

"It still seems unlikely."

"Ah," said Antony, and I realized I'd fed him the straight line he'd wanted, "but consider the career of Wilfrid Emarthius after his wife's alleged death on 11 Floréal 14.6.2. Six months later, still dressed in mourning, he receives an even better post in the Mirador than the one he'd lost. Diggory Chase starts expanding like a mushroom—I suppose Wilfrid must have discovered he liked it. In 14.6.4 he marries again, this time to a daughter of the dynastic line of the Milensii—they've fallen on hard times, but in Wilfrid's day Genevieve Milensia was a better match than Amaryllis Cordelia. Although Wilfrid himself is a member of a cadet branch, in 14.7.4, the year after Charles dies, he buys out the dynastic line of the Emarthii."

"I'm sorry. What?"

"It was never a common practice—and it was abolished at the Wizards' Coup—but Wilfrid was neither the first nor the last to manage it. If a cadet line of a noble house became substantially wealthier and more influential than the dynastic line, it could petition the king to have the dynastic privilege transferred to it."

"Bolstered by a generous donation to the royal treasury, no doubt."

"Exactly. Wilfrid died rich and happy and surrounded by grandsons at the age of eighty-one. I haven't traced it, but I think the current House-holder is descended directly from him."

"He was bought."

"Yes. Wilfrid Emarthius was paid exceedingly well to live in obscurity for two years and to add verisimilitude to their lie—which, as you pointed out, is otherwise pretty thin. I don't know if the fake tomb at Diggory Chase was his idea, but it was a nice touch."

"But we're still left with the question we started with," I said after a while. "Who put up that inscription in the crypt?"

"I don't know," Antony said. He looked at his hands as if they did not please him, and then back at me. "I just don't know."

Mildmay

I came bolt awake sometime in the middle of the night feeling like some bastard with a grudge had driven an icepick through my right thigh and was twisting it around. I could hear myself panting for breath like a beaten dog. I reached down and there was nothing but rock from my knee halfway up my thigh. I couldn't even twitch, just lay there, my fingers digging at my leg. I'd had cramps before, but nothing like this, nothing so bad I couldn't even curse it.

Suddenly there was light, a flurry of Felix's little green witchlights. I shut my eyes. The light seemed to make my leg worse.

"Mildmay? Are you—no, clearly not." He was standing by the bed. His fingers touched my thigh, prodding gently. "Here," he said. He shifted my hands and began to knead at the red-hot agony in my leg. I kept my eyes shut.

He worked at my leg for a long time. His hands were strong. I could feel where some of his fingers didn't bend quite right anymore—they'd been broken before I met him and had healed a little funny—but he knew what he was doing. After a while, I was able to breathe again. A little after that, he pushed my leg into straightening.

"Better?"

"Yeah. Thanks."

"What brought it on?"

"Dunno. Most likely the fight I got into yesterday."

"And what was that fight about?"

"I was in the wrong place at the wrong time wearing the wrong fucking face."

"That's straightforward enough, I suppose, although dreadfully nonspecific."

"The only specific thing there was me. Most anybody in the Lower City would have been glad to do what those guys were trying."

"There's one of my questions answered, then. Shall we try for another?"

"Powers, Felix, it's the middle of the fucking *night*!"

"The best time for talking. You should get up and walk around some anyway."

I scrambled out of bed. He had to catch me when my leg buckled.

"Steady, little brother," he said, and I knew he was laughing at me. "The sitting room isn't going anywhere." He helped me out of the bedroom and then dropped into his favorite chair while I began lurching around the room, leaning on the walls and furniture to keep me upright. Three of his witchlights circled around me like tiny dancers. It hurt like fuck, but I kept walking.

"You know," Felix said after a while, "I thought you were smarter than to go anywhere near that woman."

"I made a mistake," I said. Carefully. I didn't want a repeat of last night, when he'd asked me why in the world I'd ever fucked Keeper, and I'd asked him why in the world he'd fucked Shannon Teverius. And it had only gotten uglier from there. I'd said things about Gideon I was going to have to apologize for just as soon as I got up the nerve.

"Yes," he said.

We were silent a while longer while I walked and he watched me. Then he said, all of a sudden, "Do you really not remember anything about Malkar at all?"

I went hot, then cold. "I really don't," I said, as calm as I could, and made myself keep moving.

"That's not . . . healthy," he said, and I wasn't about to look at him.

"My business, ain't it?"

"You don't get—" He cut himself off. I heard the breath he took. "Mildmay. I'm not trying to attack you. Or hurt you. I . . . I'm *worried* about you."

Just when I thought I could deal with him, when I thought I'd finally learned not to mind the things he said to me, he'd do something like this. He'd come out from behind his wicked, spiked armor and say something that showed me he *did* care. And I fell for it every single time.

"Look," I said finally. "I appreciate it. But it don't *change* nothing. It's not like you could make me remember it."

"I could," he said, very quietly.

"Binding-by-forms don't work that way," I said, and the words came out too quick and jumbled, but he understood me anyway.

"Not the obligation d'âme. Or, rather, not it alone. But I could make you remember."

I swallowed hard, trying not to panic. Or at least not to let him see me panic. "You gonna?"

"No," he said promptly, and the thing crunching my chest together eased up a little and let me breathe. "But I wanted you to know . . ." His rings flashed in the witchlights as he wrung his hands. "I wanted you to know that if you *wanted* me to, I could help."

"I ain't the one thinks there's something wrong."

"Then you're lying to yourself."

"Oh, and of course you know better."

"I'm not the only one worried about you."

That wasn't no nice feeling. "Well, if I want help, I'll remember you said that."

"Mildmay—"

"What?"

"Nothing." He stood up. "We both need to get some sleep or we'll be worthless in the morning. Is your leg better?"

"Yeah." I started back for my room. He was letting me go, and I was glad, but I couldn't leave it alone. I'm stupid like that. "You sure it was nothing?"

He hesitated at the door of his own room. I wondered if Gideon was lying awake waiting for him. I thought he wasn't going to say anything, and then it just kind of bolted out of his mouth: "Please don't think of me as your enemy."

"I don't," I said, and I didn't do a very good job of hiding how startled I was, either.

He looked away, and I knew he was blushing up to his hairline. "Then you . . . I didn't . . . well, that's good then," and he all but dove into his room. The door was shut behind him before I'd managed to drag my jaw up off the floor, and I picked my way back to bed in the dark.

Chapter 7

Mildmay

In the morning, it felt like my right thigh bone had been replaced with a jagged piece of glass. And let's not even talk about my knee. My leg always dragged a little, even on my best days, but that Quatrième it wasn't like a leg at all, but a ball-and-chain or something. I told myself to be grateful for small favors—it was at least able to hold me up. Sort of.

Both Felix and Gideon were in the sitting room. My first step away from the support of the door damn near ended with me flat on my face, and I heard Gideon's breath catch. Felix started to get up, but I said, "Don't," between my teeth, and he sat back down. I lurched across to the table, where I could lean on one of the chairs. I got my hands on the chair back, and my fingers dug in like they thought somebody was going to try and take it away from me.

"You look dreadful," Felix said, trying to sound like he was talking about the weather. "Are you going to be able to stand all through court?"

"No," I said, the truth getting out before I had a chance to snatch it back. "I mean, maybe, if I can—"

"Gideon says you should be in bed," Felix said.

"Be better if I keep moving."

"Well, a fine picture you're going to make dragging that chair everywhere you go."

I said back the same way, "Oh fuck off, would you?" And he actually gave me about a quarter of a grin.

He looked over at Gideon, listening. "Gideon says that although he's not keen on helping you kill yourself, it occurs to him that we might ask Rinaldo if you could borrow a walking stick. Would that work?"

Powers and saints. Right back to the Gardens of Nephele

and hobbling in circles in the Three Serenities Garden. But better that than stuck in bed. "Yeah," I said. "Anything up to Rinaldo's weight should do me just fine." Some days Rinaldo could heave his bulk around on his own, but some days he couldn't. Rheumatics, he said.

"We'll send Rollo with a note," Felix said, making a long arm for the inkstand on the other side of the table. "Now sit down before you pass out on the floor."

"Yessir," I said, but I couldn't even make it snarky.

While Felix wrote his note, I sat and made my breathing even out, and then I looked up at Gideon and said, "Sorry."

His eyebrows went up.

"For the things I said." I could feel myself going as red as a tomato. "You know. On Deuxième."

He shook his head and made a kind of gentle pushing-away gesture, like he was saying it didn't matter.

"I kind of think it does matter." I wished like fuck Felix wasn't sitting there, but I couldn't put it off no longer. "And I'm sorry."

Gideon looked at me a moment, and then he smiled, warm as sunlight, and poured me a cup of tea. Which I figured meant I was forgiven.

If Rollo minded playing messenger boy, he didn't show it, and he was back fast enough that we weren't even running later than usual. The stick he brought was almost as thick around as Gideon's wrist, made of some wood I didn't know, knotty and dark, the color of really strong tea. The foot was iron-shod, and the grip was carved with a smiling animal's head—a dog or a bear or something, broad and ugly, but friendly, too.

There was a note. Felix ran an eye down it, more or less on our way out the door. "Rinaldo says it was imported from Imar Elchevar, though he suspects it was made even farther south. The beast is Jashuki, an Imaran guardian spirit. He says you should consider the cane a gift."

"Nice of him."

He gave me a funny look. "Rinaldo isn't about to forget . . ." And then I could see him decide to drop it. "Oh never mind. Come on."

Whatever he'd been going to say, I didn't want to know about it. I just followed him and let Jashuki hold me up.

Mehitabel

When I reached the Empyrean that morning, around ten o'clock, there was a letter waiting in my pigeonhole. I reflexively recognized both paper and wax as the highest-possible quality, and then identified the seal: the tower and sunburst of the Teverii. The letter was addressed to me in a jagged masculine scrawl that would have shamed any secretary in Marathat into ritual suicide.

I broke the seal. Looked first at the signature. *Stephen Teverius*. Then read the letter, which was an invitation to dinner. He would send a page at noon for my reply.

It was nice of him, I supposed, to pretend there was any doubt about my answer.

ॐ

Inevitably, hard on the heels of Stephen's panting but intrigued page came Vulpes.

"Quite a coup, Cressida," he said when we were immured in my dressing room. "My sources in the Mirador say this is the first time he's dined twice with any woman but his sister since his wife died."

"He's just trying to annoy the people who want to find him a wife," I said.

"Lover of the Lord Protector is nothing to scoff at."

"No, lieutenant."

"But that's your lookout, Cressida my dear," he said with a peculiar kind of gaiety. "All I care about is how much information you can get out of him."

"What *kind* of information?"

He raised his eyebrows at me.

"I'm serious. What topics are you interested in? His childhood illnesses or his foreign policy?"

"I'm interested in what the Lord Protector really thinks about wizards, especially the various, er, factions of current and former Eusebians. I am interested in his relations with his family and particularly with Robert of Hermione. I am interested in what his real opinion of the Bastion is, and if he believes General Parsifal's offer. I am interested in how he envisages the Mirador's future. And I want to know more about what he thinks about Felix Harrowgate. Messire Harrowgate is very important to the structure of the Mirador's magic, and it is well known that he does not get along with the Lord Protector. I find the discontinuity . . . provocative."

Of course you do, I thought. Anyone wanting to cause trouble in the Mirador should be fascinated by Felix. But if Vulpes didn't think I was smart enough to figure that out on my own, that was just fine. "All right," I said. "I'll do what I can."

"There's no great hurry," he said—a thing Louis Goliath would never have admitted to any of his spies. "All we're doing now is collecting information."

He left then, and I sat alone for a long time with the implications of his statement. Sat and pondered until Jean-Soleil came pounding on my door to ask, had I died or could we, for the love of all the saints and powers, please start rehearsal? I went out, but I was still wondering: if all we were doing *now* was collecting information, what exactly was it that we were going to be doing *later*?

Mildmay

Felix said under his breath, just before it was our turn through the big bronze doors, "Don't forget it's Lundy."

Which of course I had.

Lundy was Felix's day to teach, which had turned out in a funny way to be almost the most important thing in his schedule. He'd joke about bailing on Curia meetings, although he never did, but he didn't miss Lundy afternoons. Except for last Lundy, when Lord Stephen got in the way.

I'd just about swallowed my teeth, back at the beginning of winter, when Lord Blaise came and asked Felix if he wanted to teach. There'd been a funny kind of silence, and then Felix had said, "I won't take apprentices." His eyes were glass-hard, and I knew he was thinking about Strych.

"You needn't if you don't want to," Lord Blaise said. He was in his tenth septad, a nice old man with long white mustaches. "We have many young wizards who aren't ready for an apprenticeship, and they are my principal concern."

"What is it that you want?" Felix said.

"I am trying to find six or seven wizards who would take an afternoon a week to talk to these students, to help prepare them to *become* someone's apprentice. I naturally had hoped that the wizards who came to teach might be willing to take on the students as they became ready, but if you don't wish it, I respect that. I will make it clear to them that you are not to be asked."

I didn't think they'd be brave enough to ask anyway, but I kept that to myself.

Felix had asked for a day to think about it, but he'd agreed. I remembered now what he'd said about Iosephinus Pompey, who'd taught him, and wondered if that had anything to do with it. And it'd turned out, after a couple decads for him to find his range, that he was a better teacher than anybody, including him and Lord Blaise, had expected.

The kids were scared of him, but I think they liked him, too. There were ten of them, four girls and six guys, and they were kids from the Lower City and the bourgeois districts in the west and from the outlying villages—kids who were lucky if they'd made it through grammar school. Which is more education than I got, but it ain't much if you're setting out to be a hocus.

Felix said Lord Blaise was right to be worried about them, that the system in the Mirador favored kids from rich families or noble families, or kids who'd made a long journey. Kids who came from Monspulchra or farther west, or who came up from the islands—those kids got all kinds of attention, lots of hocuses looking out for them and helping them. It was the local kids that nobody paid much mind to. A lot of them never got their rings and tattoos, just dropped out to go back down the city and learn from the hocuses in Candlewick Mews and Sunslave. And I knew if they learned from the wrong people down there, they'd probably get hunted to death by the same hocuses in the Mirador who hadn't bothered to help them in the first place. But I didn't say that, either. After the fight me and Felix had had in Nivôse, we didn't talk about the witch-hunts no more.

I went with him when he taught. I'd tried suggesting maybe that wasn't necessary, but he said, "No, if they're going to be wizards in the Mirador, they're going to have to get used to you sooner or later. You can just sit in the back, and no one will mind."

Well, that was a lie. The kids weren't mean or nothing—or at least they weren't stupid enough to lip off to Felix Harrowgate— but they knew I was there, and I'd catch them glancing back at me every so often when they thought neither me nor Felix would notice. But that did get better as time went on. Felix ignored me completely while he was teaching, and I think that helped. And I didn't mind sitting back there and watching. Got some thinking done when I needed to. Learned a little bit about magic, some afternoons, although mostly the sort of stuff that made me glad I was annemer.

That afternoon, I got myself as comfortable as I could—which wasn't very, if anybody was wondering—and tried to put my mind to work on Jenny Dawnlight and her corpse in Laceshroud.

It wouldn't stick.

I kept getting hung up on something Felix had said two nights ago. Well, not just one thing. Between us we'd pretty much said everything and then some and most particularly the things we shouldn't've. But he'd been shouting about how come I'd had to go down to Britomart in the first place and Kolkhis didn't seem to have to get into the Mirador when she wanted to talk to people, and he'd said something about "your little musician friend." I'd gone after it, because even as fucking mad as I was, I knew I had to keep him away from what I'd gone to talk to Keeper *about*. And it turned out that Cardenio'd come to see him when Strych got me, and he'd gotten in because Keeper sent him to Hugo.

And powers and saints, that didn't make no fucking sense. I mean, at the time, I'd been screaming at Felix about Cardenio and him not telling me, and he'd been screaming back about how I wouldn't listen to anything he said anyway if it was about Strych and how was he supposed to know this was different, and anyway I'd kind of lost track of Hugo.

But now—what the fuck did Hugo have to do with Keeper? It occurred to me that maybe me showing up on his doorstep had made him twitchy for some other reason than just, well, me. If Keeper had some kind of hold over him . . . that was nasty shit, and no mistake. And it made me nervous, because it would be just like Keeper to get me all focused on Septimus Wilder while my real problem was Hugo Chandler sneaking up behind me. Or, not Hugo himself, because he wouldn't have the guts, but whatever it was he'd been all twitchy about.

And that wasn't no nice thought.

Your own stupid fault, Milly-Fox. Traipsing down to Britomart like that. And all for what? A dead girl. She ain't gonna get no less dead just for you finding out who got her killed. It's too fucking late for that. It was too fucking late for that before you even knew she was dead. It was *too fucking late* for that the moment you let her walk out without—

I dropped my cane.

Felix said, "A little louder next time, Mildmay, if you please. You almost woke up Calvert."

The kids laughed, Calvert with them, though kind of sheepishly. He was a soft, clumsy boy, a shopkeeper's son from Dimcreed, and he had a crush on Felix so heavy I could feel it clear across the room. Felix didn't like him—Calvert *did* sleep in class, sometimes, and it made me wonder what he was doing with his nights—and though Felix did his best not to pick on Calvert, he didn't always succeed.

"Sorry," I said. Felix waved a hand—*no big deal*—and went on with whatever he was saying. Something about the history of the Mirador's magic. I set myself to listen to it, and listen hard. It was better than thinking.

୪୬

"What was the *matter* with you?" Felix said when he'd got free of the kids.

"Just clumsy," I said.

"Yes, but you *aren't*. Clumsy, I mean. Is your leg cramping again?"

"No," I said. "I just ain't used to having a cane to fiddle with, okay?"

"All right," he said, but I could tell he didn't believe me.

It was about the tenth hour of the day. The reason Felix always gave people when they asked why he'd fallen in with Lord Blaise's nutcase idea was that it gave him half an afternoon free. He said now, letting me off the hook, "I'm going off to the Fevrier Archive, but I know you'll be bored to tears. If you want to go back to the suite and sleep, I don't mind."

"Thanks," I said, although I wasn't going to be alone with my thoughts if I could help it. "See you for dinner?"

"Of course," he said. As he walked off, his stride lengthened, since he didn't have to let me keep up with him.

I waited a second—you could never count on Felix not to change his mind—and then headed off in a different direction, toward the Protectorate Guard's barracks. Because I *did* want to know if Hugo was wandering down the city these days, and the Guard would know.

They put a guard on duty at their barracks, one of the guys too old and crippled for regular duty. He had a chair, along of having only one leg, and his sword was down on the floor, but you'd have to be awful dumb to think that made him an easy target. Him and the guy on night shift, who was three septads younger but only had one arm, were the toughest bastards I'd ever met. I wasn't real sure they were necessary—I mean, who'd be nuts enough to attack the Guard in the middle of the fucking Mirador?—but I was sure that if they ever *were* necessary, the guys they were up against were going to be sorry.

The day guy's name was Lemuel. The night guy was Bruno. They were both glad to shoot the shit with me if I happened to stop by. Lemuel was about the only person in the Mirador who'd actually asked me, point-blank and face-to-face, what this binding-by-forms crap was. I'd told him as best I could, going light on the magic shit and leaving out how I felt about Felix, and after that the guards had gotten friendlier. They were used to the idea of being bodyguards to hocuses.

So Lemuel said, "Hey, Mildmay. What happened to your face?"

"Hey, Lemuel," I said. "Got in a fight. Josiah around?"

"He might be. Whatcha want him for?"

"Gossip."

"Well, if *that*'s what you want, why don't you go on in? If'n you don't find Josiah, there'll be somebody else to make you happy." He snorted. "Those boys gossip like a bunch of damn old maids."

"Thanks, Lemuel." I limped into the barracks. I felt conspicuous as hell leaning on my stick and with my left eye like a rainbow, but I didn't exactly have a lot of other choices lined up.

Four guys near the door, playing Long Tiffany, invited me to join the game. I told 'em, thanks, but I had better uses for my money.

"What're *you* doing here?" said another man, who was polishing his boots on the other side of the room. "Running errands for that molly hocus whore of yours?"

I looked at him. His name was Thibaud, and I already knew he didn't like me. He'd been in charge of the guys assigned to figure out Cerberus Cresset's murder, and he was still pissed at not having caught me—and even more pissed at the fact that now he knew who I was he couldn't do nothing about it. There was a whole group of guys who hated me and Felix both—one of 'em, Esmond, hated Felix nearly as much as Robert did, but nobody would tell me why.

"Ain't none of your business if I am," I said.

"Thibaud, would you give it a rest?" said the oldest of the card players, a guy named Cleo who would have made two of anybody in the room. "Whatcha after, Fox?"

"Who ya gonna murder this time?" said one of Thibaud's friends.

"You if you don't shut up." I said to Cleo, "I was just looking for Josiah."

"Has Jo caught Lord Felix's fancy now?" Thibaud again.

"Powers, Thibaud, will you shut your fucking trap?" Cleo said. He bellowed, "Hey, Jo, guy here for you!"

"I don't see why you're getting on my case, Cleo," Thibaud said, going all injured. "I ain't murdered nobody, and I ain't catching flies for no moll, neither."

"Well, very fucking good for you," Cleo said. "All I'm looking for is some peace, and I can't get that with you running your mouth. *Jo!* Move your ass, would you?"

Josiah came through the door at the back of the room, just as Thibaud said, "I ain't the one came walking in here like he owns the place."

"Shut up, Thibaud," Josiah said on his way past. "C'mon, Mildmay. We can go to the Pav."

The Pav's practically in earshot of the barracks. It's a big open room with this kind of lacy stonework like an indoor gazebo or something. It's supposed to be haunted so nobody uses it much.

"You okay?" Josiah said when we'd got settled. "I mean, your face and all, and I ain't seen you with a cane before."

"Yeah, I'm fine," I said, although it felt like a lie.

"I'm sorry about Thibaud."

"It ain't your fault he's an asshole."

"Yeah, but—"

"I don't got to be friends with everybody in the Mirador."

"Thibaud's just mad 'cause you beat him," Josiah said. "He thought he was gonna make it to captain on the strength of finding the guy who waxed Lord Cerberus. But he didn't find you, and he didn't get promoted. That's what's up *his* ass."

"Powers, I'm sorry I got in the way of his career," I said, and we both laughed. Neither of us said nothing about Felix. "Josiah, do you know anything about Hugo Chandler?"

"The molly musician, right? The one that looks like a rabbit?"

It occurred to me for a second how awful it would be to go through life where the first thing anybody remembered about you was that you looked like a rabbit. "Yeah."

"What about him?"

"I dunno. Anything. Who's he hang out with? What's he do with his spare time? Does he leave the Mirador?"

"He crossed you about something?"

"Nah." I thought for a moment about what it was okay to tell Josiah. "I used to know him, in Dragonteeth. I'm worried about him is all, if he's, you know, getting along okay."

"You could ask him," Josiah said.

"He wouldn't tell me."

"Oh, like that, is it? He don't get in trouble, I can tell you that much. We gotta go 'round to the Mesmerine couple times a dec—I mean, about once a week—but it ain't never about Mr. Chandler. I think he's got a pretty steady thing going with one of the other musicians, so he ain't out getting drunk or chasing the serving girls or nothing like that. He's got family in Dragonteeth, but I don't think he even goes out to see 'em—just sends 'em money."

The Protectorate Guard knows just about everything that happens in the Mirador. They have to. It's part of their job. If Josiah said Hugo wasn't leaving the Mirador, he wasn't, because the one thing I was sure of was a rabbit like Hugo wasn't ducking down into the Arcane to get past the gates.

"And nobody's got a down on him?" I said. "None of the flashies?"

"I don't think nobody's *noticed* him. And the flashies that like music all like him just fine."

"Well, that's good to hear. Who's his musician?"

"Boy from Skaar. Name of Axel. Tall, skinny, blond. He's pretty new. He ain't got in trouble, neither, so that's about all I know, but Chilver says he's too pretty for his own good."

"Well, I ain't trying to get his complete life story out of you. Just wondered."

"So long as you ain't gonna go causing trouble where there ain't none, you can wonder all you like."

"Nah, I don't want Hugo in trouble. I just wanted to be sure he *wasn't* in trouble."

"Not with us," Josiah said.

Mehitabel

Corinna and I raided the costumes again, and came up with a dark brown dress, patterned all over in a design of vines and leaves that looked black unless the light caught it at a particular angle, when it showed up a sort of rich puce color. "It suits you," Corinna said, and I saw the truth of that in the eyes of the guards at Chevalgate, and the eyes of the pudgy blotch-faced page who led me to Lord Stephen's apartments.

Lord Stephen rose when I entered his sitting room and, after a moment's contemplation, said, "You are exquisite."

I wished I could fake a blush.

I asked him early on, over the soup, about his family, some inanity about had they been close as children.

"Vicky and I were very close. After our mother died, we . . ." He made a circling gesture with his wineglass, as if to entrap an escaping word. "We had no one else."

"You must have been very lonely."

"No. We had our own private world. We didn't *need* anyone else. I don't remember being lonely until Vicky started learning magic. I couldn't follow her there."

"Do you blame her?"

"For being a wizard?" He snorted. "Powers, no. Vicky wanted children." He looked across at my expression, which I would have made blankly puzzled even if I'd known what he was talking about. "Oh, sorry. You won't know about my cousin Cornell."

"Your cousin Cornell?"

"My grandmother had two sons. My uncle Denis was the older. And a wizard. So he couldn't inherit the Protectorship." He raised his eyebrows at me, and I nodded. "But he got married— nice woman, cadet branch of the Severnii—and had an annemer son."

"Oh," I said. "Your cousin Cornell. I can see where this is going."

He gave me a grimace. "When my father died, Cornell

started making noise about his right to the Protectorship. And some people listened, and they agitated and made a fuss, and things got ugly. 'Til Cornell was found in the Sim with his throat cut."

"That's where I thought we'd end up," I said grimly. Few if any stories in Marathine history had happy endings.

"It was eight years ago," Stephen said. "We still don't know who did it. Vicky says she's not going to have children just to have them murdered for being politically inconvenient. I don't blame her, but it makes her hard to work with sometimes."

"Is it normal for a Lord Protector's siblings to be, er, so high in the government?"

His eyes skewered me for a moment, but he chose not to ask why I wanted to know. "It depends," he said. "Some are, some aren't. I had to . . . show trust in Vicky and Shannon."

"Because of Gloria Aestia?"

"Yes. We had to pull together, as Teverii. But I'd always wanted Vicky beside me."

"Not Shannon?"

"Shannon and I . . ." He shrugged. "We're brothers, but we aren't what you'd call good friends."

Stephen was well known not to like molls especially, and I wondered now how much of that was spillage from what was clearly a difficult relationship with his brother. Then I wondered how much of his dislike of Felix was because of Shannon. But before I could ask, Stephen smiled suddenly. "Powers. Horrible manners, boring on about my family. Here, you pick the topic."

I could hardly tell him that his family was exactly what Vulpes wanted to hear about. Instead, I said, "Do you believe the envoy from the Bastion?"

"Believe how?"

"Well, you—I mean, the Mirador and the Bastion have been enemies for centuries. Do you really believe they want peace?"

"Funny question from a Kekropian." He thought for a moment, choosing his words. "Yes, I think they must be tired of war. The saints know *I* am. I don't *trust* them, but I believe them."

A subtle paradox, especially from someone who seemed so bluntly straightforward. I asked, "How much do people here re-

ally know about the Bastion? Is it just a myth to frighten children, as the Mirador is in the Empire?"

"When Vicky and I were little, our nurse told us that the bad
wizards from the Bastion would carry us off if we didn't behave. And the defectors always tell the most frightful stories."

"Yes," I said. "We were terrified of it as kids—my grandfather threatened to tithe us when we'd been bad."

"We?" said Stephen with an interrogative eyebrow.

You have to give if you want to take; I told him about Libbie
and Damian, about my cousins Sasha and Eve and Quintus and
the twins, Phineas and Geraint. I realized in the middle of one
anecdote that Stephen was genuinely interested—he couldn't
be faking that expression—and with a sudden lightening of my
entire spirit, told him the truly disgraceful story of what happened the time Uncle Kirby and Gran'père Mato got drunk in
Semiramis. He roared with laughter, and for the first time in
years I was able to remember things about my childhood besides
my mother and Uncle René.

Again, Stephen waited until we'd been left with the hard
liquor and sticky desserts to bring out his true purposes. "I am
minded," he said, "to take a lover."

"Are you indeed?"

That got me a quirk of a grin. "I learn from my mistakes. I
didn't have lovers when I was married to Emily, and that gave
her far too much power. Not over me necessarily, but in the
court. My father made the opposite mistake—taking a lover after my mother died—and that landed us with Gloria."

"You have thought about this a good deal."

"Yes."

"But why me?"

"Don't be disingenuous."

That stung. "You've never shown the slightest interest in me
before."

"Because I wasn't getting married," he said patiently. "And
you were . . . occupied."

"I have other lovers."

"You won't," he said, face and voice suddenly hard. "He was
the only one you cared about, and I will not share you."

"You're awfully possessive for a man who hasn't heard the
word 'yes' yet," I said, both because I was irritated and be-

cause I needed to push this situation, find out what its limits were.

"Character flaw," Stephen said. "If you turn me down, I won't hold it against you. But if you accept, it will be exclusive until we tire of each other. I won't hold you against your will, either."

"I am relieved to hear it."

"I'm jealous by nature," he said. "Made more jealous by training. I'm not going to apologize for it, but I am *telling* you. I don't like making uninformed decisions myself, and there's no reason you should have to make them either."

"Do you even *like* me?"

It was a ridiculous, childish question, but Stephen's cold-bloodedness was unnerving me. That in itself was ridiculous, and I knew it, since I'd approached all of my affairs since Hallam with the same rigorous, dispassionate logic, but, no, I did *not* like being on the receiving end.

"Mehitabel." He smiled. "If I didn't want you in my bed, for company as much as for anything else, I'd hardly have gone this far. You aren't an ideal choice by any means."

"Being Kekropian."

"And an actress. And damnably intelligent. Which I prefer, but it makes things more difficult."

"Thank you," I said.

Stephen, unlike Vulpes, wasn't worried over possible irony. "It's up to you."

"If I say yes, I imagine it will be quite official?"

"Oh, yes. There's a suite that belongs to the Lord—or Lady—Protector's lover. It'll be yours."

"You won't want me to give up the Empyrean." I said it flatly, because I wasn't asking.

"Of course not. Just your . . ." He was searching for a word, brows drawn down, and I knew suddenly what word he wanted. *Boy-toys.* Mildmay's word. I wondered, not comfortably, how long Stephen had been watching and how long his jealousy had been festering.

"Quite," I said. "I need some time to think."

"I wouldn't have expected you to answer right away. We—meaning the Mirador—will be holding a soirée on Mercredy. I'll send you an invitation tomorrow. Yes to one is yes to both. Will that do?"

It wasn't much time, but it wasn't the sort of decision that was going to get easier for long contemplation. "Yes," I said. "It'll do."

Felix

I couldn't talk to Thamuris about ghosts. But there was another side to the problem, and maybe the Troian approach to the dead would help here. Because none of the Marathine approaches I knew of were any better than useless. Most of them were worse.

I had worked out what I wanted to say to him about Malkar and what I most emphatically did not. I said, "I have . . . a kind of relic of a powerful blood-wizard, and I need to put it somewhere. But I need it to be safe, and I have to find a way to nullify it thaumaturgically."

"A relic?" Thamuris was frowning. "What sort of relic does a blood-wizard leave? And is a blood-wizard what it sounds like?"

"Yes. And just exactly as vile as you imagine, too. And the, um, the jewels from his rings." Some schools of Troian wizards still used rings; although the diviners of the Euryganeic Covenant were not among them, Thamuris did at least understand the theory.

"And is there a reason you haven't destroyed them?"

"He had these rings for a very long time." As long as I'd known him, anyway. "And the consistent use of architectural thaumaturgy does some very strange things to gemstones."

"Define 'strange,' please."

Damn him for asking cogent questions. I ran imaginary fingers through imaginary hair. "They would be very difficult to destroy, and they would . . . well, think of it as staining the place where it was done." Somewhere in the depths of the Mirador there was a bricked-up room in which Porphyria Levant's emeralds had been destroyed. I had never sought it out, but I knew I had been close to it more than once. I had felt the stain of their magic, their mikkary, like the taste of burning metal in the air. It would disperse, given time, but no one knew how much time, and the Curia seemed determined to remain ignorant, as if refusal to acknowledge the problem could cause it to go away. All I could do, having argued myself hoarse on the subject until Giancarlo forbade me to mention it again, was not add to the problem. And thus I could no more destroy Malkar's rubies than I could simply dispose of them. The mere thought of throwing them in the Sim made me feel as if my blood had been replaced by the river's dark water.

"Ah," said Thamuris. "You don't want to talk about who they belonged to or how you got them, do you?"

"No," I said, faster and harder than I'd meant to, and Thamuris controlled himself just short of recoiling.

"I wouldn't tell anyone," he said, and just as he had seen my semipanicked revulsion, I saw his hurt around him.

I shut my eyes, willing meaning into the gesture, using it to reassert my control over myself, both my construct-self and my own unruly emotions. It took me longer than it should have, long enough that when I opened my construct-eyes again, Thamuris was staring at me worriedly.

"Are you all right?"

"Yes," I said carefully, crisply.

"I'm sorry," he said. "I shouldn't have pried."

It was tempting to agree with that, too, but I said, "The important thing is to find a safe place to put these rubies. I want to be rid of them."

"I can imagine. Are they powerful?"

"Not in their own right. They're thaumaturgically charged, but it's nothing as strong as a curse. It's the synergistic effect with the Mirador that worries me."

"Yes. You know, I wonder . . ."

"Yes?" I said, when the pause had stretched to an irritating length.

"Oh—just that I've been wondering about bringing something material across the boundaries of the Khloïdanikos, and—"

"You really think that's possible?"

"I'm *wondering*. I don't think it would work with ordinary objects, but something with a thaumaturgic charge, something that already casts a shadow into the world of the spirit . . . and it seems to me the Khloïdanikos ought to be able to nullify a mild charge such as you describe."

My first impulse was to reject the idea utterly. I wanted to keep Malkar out of the Khloïdanikos, wanted to have one part of my life he could not touch. But then I caught myself. Malkar was dead. He couldn't touch anything. Even the rubies weren't actually imbued with Malkar's spirit, only with the residue of the magic he had worked.

I am giving him too much power, I thought. There was nothing talismanic about the rubies—nor anything talismanic about the Khloïdanikos, for that matter. It did not symbolize my lost innocence. It most certainly did not need me to protect it, and I needed to rein in my vanity if I was imagining it did.

And what Thamuris was suggesting was, in fact, an elegantly simple solution to a problem over which I'd been giving myself headaches for weeks. "And it's not as if it would have to be permanent," I said, feeling much lighter and more cheerful. "If it doesn't work, we can always remove them and try something else."

"Exactly. It would be quite a useful experiment for any number of reasons."

"Including the question of whether it's possible at all."

"Yes. Quite."

I considered the problem.

"It wouldn't be difficult to create a construct-token," I said and then broke off, my breath catching in my throat as the answer clicked into place like the tumblers of a lock.

"Felix?"

I shook my head sharply, as if that might clear it or settle it. "Nothing. I think I know how to do it."

"Just like that?" He didn't sound disbelieving, merely a little uneasy.

"It . . ." I made a futile shaping gesture with both hands. "It fits with something I've been working on. Working with. A way to link thaumaturgic architecture and architectural thaumaturgy. Anyway, I'll have gotten it worked out by the next time we meet."

"You sound awfully certain."

I smiled at him, trying not to see Malkar bursting into flames behind my eyes. "I've done it before."

Mildmay

I went to bed early that night. Felix let me go, but later, a couple hours after I'd heard him and Gideon go into their room, my door opened and he came in, crowned with witchlights.

"You're awake," he said. He stopped maybe a foot inside the door.

"You ain't asking," I said and sat up.

"Are you all right?"

"Sure, I'm fine."

"I don't suppose it *is* any of my business."

That sat there for a minute, since I didn't know what to say.

"Something's eating at you," he said. "If I promise not to lose my temper and not to say anything cruel, will you tell me what it is?"

"It ain't Strych."

"It doesn't have to be," he said, calm and almost gentle, and that gave me the nerve to say it.

"I've been thinking a lot. About Ginevra."

"Ginevra. She still haunts you." He wasn't asking that time, either.

"Yeah, I guess."

There was another long pause. I couldn't read his face. Then he heaved a sigh and said, "May I sit down?"

"Sure," I said and made room for him on the bed. He sat beside me and looked the candle into flame. He said, "I have always been afflicted with what Gideon calls true-dreaming. The longer the binding-by-forms has been in place, the more that 'true-dreaming' has included awareness of your dreams. I've fought it and fought it. I was afraid it would backlash, and you would start having *my* nightmares. But I can't block it out completely. I didn't want to tell you—I knew how much you'd hate it—but, frankly, I don't think it's going to go away."

"Fucking marvelous." I'd heard—sort of, anyway—his dreams at first, but that had gone after Strych. I'd just been glad.

"You dream about her a lot."

"Yeah."

He looked at me for a moment, then looked away and said, "When I was eleven, I lost everyone I cared about. The person I loved best in all the world died in my arms. I've told you about her."

"Joline." He'd said I reminded him of her.

"Lorenzo—the owner of the Shining Tiger, the brothel where . . . Lorenzo found me in the aftermath. By the time I had recovered from the initial shock, I . . ." He stopped completely.

I remembered the first time he'd told me about this, in the Gardens of Nephele. I remembered the black cloud I'd been in, and how it had been all I could do just to listen to his light voice and pay enough attention that the words made sense. I remembered him making some half-joke about prostitution and moving on, like it wasn't no big deal. And, powers, I'd been so fucked up myself, I hadn't even wondered about it.

He looked at me. I wanted to say something, but I didn't know if he wanted me to. I stayed silent. He said, "It was years before I was able to grieve. Partly, that was because there was always some new and hideous thing to deal with, and partly because Lorenzo didn't waste any time introducing me to phoenix. Phoenix really is splendid, you know. You put the things you don't want to deal with in a drawer and phoenix closes the drawer for you. But I had dreams."

He stopped again. This time he seemed to want me to say something. "I'm sorry," I said, "but I don't see what you're getting at."

"I'm saying that . . . your dreams . . . it's like you're snagged on something. And I wondered . . . if I could help you find it, maybe?" He gave me a look, a funny one, sort of shy and sideways, and I don't know how, but all at once the words were just there, and I said them.

"It's my fault she died. I didn't tell her." There it was, the thing I'd been trying not to think since I'd dropped my cane in the Grenouille Salon. I took a deep, painful breath and buried my face in my hands.

"Didn't tell her *what*?"

"Ginevra didn't understand about Vey," I said. "We never talked about it, but I think she thought Vey would forget or something—you know, after a while it would be okay again. And, powers, I don't know, but I guess my reputation was still enough that it wasn't worth Vey's while to come after me."

"But when Ginevra left you, she lost that protection."

"Yeah. I didn't think she'd leave, so I never sat her down and *made* her understand. She wasn't stupid—you got to understand, Felix, she wasn't *stupid*—but she was . . . she wouldn't believe something unless she'd seen it for herself."

"But you said someone gave information to Vey."

"Yeah."

"So I really *don't* see how it can be your fault."

"Don't you get it? Out of that whole fucking tangle, I was the only guy who knew the stakes. And I didn't tell Ginevra. I never tell people things. That's my whole fucking problem."

"It *is* a persistent motif."

My glare must have been just this side of murder. He said quickly, "I didn't mean to be flip—remember, I promised I wouldn't say anything cruel. But you *don't* tell people things. Only stories."

"I don't like talking," I said and looked at my hands.

"I know that." We were quiet for a while. Then he said, "I've probably got things all wrong, but can I ask a question? I promise I don't mean it to be cruel or glib."

"Go ahead." My head was too heavy to lift.

"Did Ginevra ever *ask* you?"

"What?"

"Did she ever *ask* you about Vey? Did she ever say, 'Tell me about that woman who tried to kill us both'?"

I was staring at him now. "No. I mean—I *did* tell her, but not much. And she . . . she asked about what Vey had been trying to do, but she didn't ask about *Vey*. I don't think she wanted to know."

"Then she is at least as responsible for her death as you are. If someone wants to be blind, Mildmay, you can't make them see." There was a pause where I probably should've said something. He stood up. "I think I've done enough pontificating for one night. Unless . . . do you want me to stay?"

"I . . . no, I need to think." But I wanted to give him something, because he'd cared enough to help, and he hadn't been mean. "I think you said something important, but I gotta work it through."

"I understand." He went to the door, then stopped. "You know," he said. "You know, if you ever want me to ward your dreams, I will. I won't even ask any questions."

"Thanks," I said. "I'll remember."

"Good night, then."

"Yeah, good night."

He went out and shut the door. I was left staring at it, like it could tell me something important. I'd've liked to get up—to leave the suite and go walk around the Mirador while everything settled inside my head—but even with my new stick, I didn't think that was a smart idea.

If someone wants to be blind, you can't make them see.

That was Ginevra all right. It was a lot more *her* than her looks and her figure, which was all anybody, including me, had ever seemed to care about. She hadn't been stupid, but if Ginevra didn't want to see a thing, then that thing just plain was not there. Ever.

I remembered the one time I'd tried to tell her about my childhood, about growing up a kept-thief. She'd asked one day in Thermidor, and I'd known she'd been thrill-seeking, but I'd been mad in love, and I'd tried. I'd really tried to tell her the truth. She'd believed all the things I told her, but I remembered now the way her attention had skipped past the things I'd tried to say about Keeper and about the other kids. She wanted the stuff that sounded romantic to her, that fit in with her ideas about herself and about me and about what I was doing in the great romantic story of Ginevra Thomson.

How had that conversation ended? I racked my memory, staring at the damn door like I'd find the answers there, and finally remembered. I'd lied. I'd been desperate to distract her before she pissed me off and I told her what it was like to strangle somebody and feel their clawing, heaving body become nothing but a dead, stupid sack of meat against you, and so I'd started this huge, elaborate lie about Keeper sending me to steal the great Black Crown of the House of Tamerinsius. It took Ginevra a while to realize I was lying. By the time she did, the story was rolling, and it did its job. When I'd finished—well, actually, a little before the story was really over—we'd made love. It had been good, and by the time we were done, I'd managed to forget how Ginevra had made me feel.

She never listened to you, Milly-Fox, a voice said.

That ain't true! I twisted around and slammed my fist into the pillow, like it was the one saying stuff I didn't want to hear.

She never listened to you. She liked being the lover of Mildmay the Fox, the greatest cat burglar in the Lower City, but she wasn't interested in *you*, you poor, stupid son of a bitch. She was as blind to who *you* are as she was blind to Vey.

I hadn't told her, but odds were she wouldn't have listened if I'd tried.

Whatever she'd loved, it hadn't been me.

Chapter 8

Mildmay

The morning was actually going pretty good for once. I hadn't slept much, but I wasn't no ray of sunshine anyway, and Felix and Gideon seemed to have mended their fences, from what I could tell. I'd thought sometimes that it was Gideon's special curse that he couldn't stay mad at Felix. No matter what Felix did, they never stayed on the outs for long. And maybe Felix *hadn't* done anything with Mr. Garamond. I didn't know and wasn't asking.

So, no fights, nobody running late—we even sat down for breakfast together, which we managed maybe about twice a month. Felix was buttering a biscuit and telling us the latest rumors about Lady Mirabel Valeria and her lover—this gal was supposed to have climbed out a convent window to be with Lady Mirabel—when there was a knock at the door.

"Expecting someone?" Felix said to me.

"Nope," I said.

Him and Gideon shrugged at each other, and he said, "Come in."

It was Rollo, and he was unhappy.

"My lord," he said, "I beg your pardon, for it is no doing of mine, but there is a person who insists on seeing you. He says if you will not see him, he will have no choice save to go to the Lord Protector."

"What sort of a person?" Felix said.

Rollo all but wrung his hands. "A *City Guard*, my lord." Rollo was from Archwolf, and in Archwolf they didn't call 'em Dogs. Though the way Rollo said "City Guard," it meant about the same.

"Did he say what he wanted to see me about?"

"No, my lord. He said it was not my business."

"Well, we certainly don't want him bothering Lord Stephen at this time of day," Felix said. "Show him in."

"*Thank* you, my lord," Rollo said and whisked himself out.

"Are you sure you aren't expecting anyone?" Felix asked me.

"Maybe I ain't surprised he's here," I said, thinking about the goon who went through the window and the goon who was missing a couple of fingers and Kethe knows what all I might've done to the rest of 'em.

"Indeed," Felix said.

The door opened again, and Rollo—showing with every line of his body that he completely disowned the guy and this wasn't none of it *his* fault—showed the Dog in.

The Dog was somewhere around his sixth septad, square-built and big. He was running to fat now, but I was willing to bet he must have been quite something when he was young. His eyes were brown, small, and sharp like needles.

He bowed sort of generally, said, "My lord," and waited. His little bright eyes went from me to Felix to Gideon.

"I am Felix Harrowgate," Felix said. "I am afraid you have the advantage of me."

"My lord," the Dog said again, with a deeper bow this time, aimed directly at Felix. "I'm Sergeant Abelard Morny of the City Guard."

"Sergeant," Felix said with a little nod in return. "What can I do for you?"

"As to that, my lord, I'm not rightly sure." He rocked back on his heels a little. "See, there was a fight down in Gilgamesh the other night, and a boy ended up in the Hospice of St. Latimer. Nasty deep cuts—he got thrown through a window. *He* says"—and the bright little eyes darted from Felix to me and back to Felix—"that his assailant was a redheaded man with a scar on his face—a thing there aren't too many of in this city."

"True," said Felix. He didn't look at me. "What is your point?"

"Well, I'm curious, my lord, about how that boy ended up going through a window, and I was wondering if anybody in this room could tell me anything about it."

Sergeant Morny had done his homework. He knew about the binding-by-forms, about how he wasn't supposed to talk to me without being invited. He knew it, and he'd worked his way around it as slick as you please.

"Will you excuse me one moment, please?" Felix said, rising.

"Of course, my lord." Sergeant Morny's little dark eyes were twinkling, and I could feel him watching me limp as I followed Felix into his and Gideon's bedroom.

Felix shut the door. I was proud of him for not slamming it because I could see how bad he wanted to. Then he gave me a nervous little sidelong look. "Did you really throw someone through a window?"

"It ain't the way it sounds," I said, and I wondered if he'd believe me.

Whether he did or not, he let it go. "We don't have many choices. We either show him the door, or we let him talk to you."

"I think he meant it when he said he'd go to Lord Stephen."

"I do, too. So we show him the door, he goes to Lord Stephen, and I get ordered to cooperate. The only advantage I see is that it would buy a little time."

"It don't matter," I said. "I ain't gonna lie to him. I mean, there ain't no point. But there ain't time for it before court."

"*Isn't*, not *ain't*," said Felix. He stood a moment, his eyes blank and inward-looking, then opened the door and strode back into the sitting room. Sergeant Morny and Gideon hadn't moved an inch, both looking like the taxidermists had been at them.

"Sergeant," said Felix, "we will be enchanted to assist you with your inquiries, but I wonder if you would be so kind as to make an appointment for this afternoon. Court convenes in rather less than an hour."

"That's very kind of you, my lord," Sergeant Morny said, "and more than I expected. I'll come back around the eighth hour of the day, then?"

"Splendid," said Felix and got him out the door with one of his five-alarm smiles.

Mehitabel

I wasn't surprised when my dreams that night were horrid. They evaporated as I woke, leaving only the foul aftertaste of worry and an image, unpleasantly vivid, of Hallam crouching over a dead cat and weeping like a child.

"I can't change what happened," I said, and the sound of my own voice brought me fully awake.

I had just finished buttoning my dress when Corinna tapped on my door. She handed me a cup of tea and said, "So?"

"So what?"

"So! The Lord Protector, dummy! For the *second* time! How'd it go?"

I took a sip of tea. "He made me an offer."

Corinna froze halfway down into the chair. "He what?"

"He made me an offer."

Corinna settled back in the chair, her improbably blonde hair and green calico robe combining to make her look like an opulently overblown yellow rose. "You're not going to stop *there*, are you?"

I hesitated, but Corinna knew the Mirador, had years of experience navigating in and out of the beds of lords and wizards and servants. So I told her what Stephen had said. She listened intently, and when I was done, said, "He's serious then."

"He certainly seems to be."

"The Teverii," she said with a grimace, "are not known for their sense of humor. What are you going to say?"

"Yes," I said and shrugged. "What else *can* I say?"

"This may be a little higher than you want to fly, lovey."

Not with Vulpes watching from the ground, I thought. I told her a different truth: "I'm tired of scrabbling."

"Top of the heap once and for all?"

"Something like that. But let's not talk about me. Any luck with Lord Ignace?"

"He sent me a poem. It's really bad."

"They always are."

"He's a sweet boy. I just wish I wasn't old enough to be his mother."

"You aren't."

Corinna sighed, then shook it off. "Drin's going to be sick as a horse, you know."

"That's Drin's problem," I said. I finished my tea, set the cup down, and picked up my comb. It was time to gird myself for the day. I was in front of the mirror before Corinna's silence registered on me. I turned to look at her. Her face was unexpectedly serious, almost sad.

She said, "What about Mildmay?"

"What *about* Mildmay?" I turned back to the mirror.

"Is it really over, then?"

"Corinna, it couldn't be more over if we'd given it a funeral."

"Just like that?"

I began unbraiding my hair. "Please don't start a melodrama over it."

"You seemed so happy," she said wistfully.

"I'm not sure I've ever seen Mildmay really happy."

"How about you?"

"Me? Do I seem unhappy to you?"

"I'm sure I wouldn't know. But, I mean, you came here because of him . . ."

"I came here *with* him. That's quite different. And my God, there's more to my life here than Mildmay Foxe."

"Of course there is. But do you really not miss him at all?"

"How could I not miss him? But that's not the same thing as loving him. You know that."

"Powers," Corinna said with a grin. "You wouldn't believe how long I spent *not* getting rid of Osram Lelius, who was dull as ditchwater and a pig to boot, just because he was familiar and that was more comfortable than change."

"Speaking of things that don't make sense," I said, both to change the subject and because I wanted to know, "what in the world is the matter with Drin?"

"Speaking of pigs, you mean?"

"All right. Fair enough. But what's gotten into him about Gordeny?"

"Drin's from Breadoven," Corinna said with a shrug.

"So?"

"So he thinks everyone from the Lower City—and that *doesn't* include Breadoven on Drin's map—must be some kind of hardened criminal. Don't you remember . . . oh. No, you weren't here then."

"What?"

"The second principal we had before Bartholmew was a boy named Camillo Dean. He was from Lyonesse. Drin never let up on him. Every time he misplaced something, he was sure Camillo had stolen it. It's just the way he is, and I've told Gordeny not to mind him."

"He's such a pain."

"It's his gift."

"Every troupe has one," I agreed, sliding my last hairpin into place. "Now go on and take yourself off to get dressed. Things to do today, you know."

"Give me a yell when you're ready to go."

"Sure thing," I said, and she collected the tea cups and went.

Mildmay

After court, Felix said, "You'll have to go talk to this tiresome sergeant on your own. I can't wiggle out of my afternoon's agenda."

I went hollow. "But I can't—"

"You said you weren't going to lie to him. You certainly don't need me to hold your hand while you tell him the truth. And Gideon will be there."

"But—"

"He seems a perfectly nice and innocuous sergeant. I doubt he'll bite you." But his eyes were worried.

"Can't you put him off again?"

"He's got the trump card. Stephen will *not* find this amusing. And I don't want him—the sergeant, I mean—to get the idea I'm toying with him. Go on, Mildmay. It'll be fine." He walked off before I could think of something else to say that might convince him.

What could I do? I went back to the suite.

Sergeant Morny hadn't shown up yet, but Gideon was there, looking extremely well-dressed and well-groomed, which I figured to mean he didn't like this no better than I did. He was wearing his best brown coat, and he'd tied his hair back with a wide brown ribbon. He looked absolutely respectable, and the thought got across my mind before I could stop it, that I wished his tongue hadn't been cut out so *he* could talk to the sergeant instead of me. Nice, Milly-Fox. Real fucking classy.

"Hey," I said and sat down.

He nodded back, and we waited together. I used the time to rebraid my hair, pretending hard that if I looked like a cit, the Dogs would treat me like one. Gideon got up and came around behind me and retied the ribbon. He went back to his seat and smiled at me in a way that said he knew as well as I did that we were being stupid.

By the sitting room clock, it was ten minutes past the hour when somebody knocked on the door. I said, "Come in," because there was nobody else to say it. Rollo repeated his morning's performance, but this time the sergeant had somebody with him, a skinny little rat of a guy who screamed *DOG* all over himself the same way the sergeant did. I can't tell you what it was exactly, but anybody who's lived in the Lower City for any amount of time has a good nose for Dog.

Sergeant Morny looked around. He seemed surprised not to see Felix anywhere. The little rat of a constable was trying to look everywhere at once, like he thought I had five more of me hiding in the corners.

There was a pause while Morny rearranged his thinking. He said, "So I'm guessing I can talk to you."

"Yeah," I said. "Mr. Thraxios is just gonna watch."

"That'll do nicely," he said. "This is Constable Waterman."

He was Constable Waterman the same way I was Mr. Foxe, but it was none of my business. The rat bobbed his head and tried to look as polite as Morny, but he wasn't set up for it.

"All right," I said. "What d'you want to know?" I felt like I was asking some guy to knife me, yeah, right here in the stomach.

"The boy you threw through that window is named Jadis," Morny said. "He's got two septads and two. Now, I don't think much of his truthfulness, but there's no denying he went through that window, and not of his own accord." He smiled at me. It didn't make me feel better. "I want to know why."

"'Cause I didn't have nowhere else to put him," I said.

"Don't you give the sergeant none of your lip!" said the constable. He had a great big bullfrog voice in his little ratty body.

Morny said, like neither of us had spoken, "His lordship said as how you'd be happy to help."

There was his trump card, like Felix had said, the threat that he didn't need to say out loud—if I didn't cooperate, he'd go to His *other* Lordship, and at that point, both Lord Stephen *and* Felix would be pissed at me.

I glanced at Gideon—I don't know why—and said, "Okay. I was in Gilgamesh, and these three or four guys decided they didn't like my face. Things got ugly. This Jadis kid went through the window. I didn't mean to put him there."

"Hmmph," said Morny, not like he didn't believe me or anything, just to show that he'd heard me. Constable Waterman made painstaking notes on a little tablet. "Jadis says you attacked him unprovoked."

"Why the fuck would I do that?"

Morny and Waterman both looked at me like I ought to know better than to ask that question. I suppose I did, but it made me mad anyway.

"You seen me walk, sergeant," I said. "Sure, I was hot once, but I'm a crip now, and I ain't *that* dumb." And then I shut my mouth and sat there, hating myself and hating Morny and Waterman and hating Gideon—me for saying what was no more than the truth, and them for hearing it.

Morny said, "I have to admit, I couldn't see a reason why Mildmay the Fox would be bothering with that boy either. And looking at you, I have a hard time believing that our friend Jadis could have done all that damage by himself. Does the rest of you match your face?"

"You wanna see?" I said.

"Evidence would be helpful," Morny said. "Looks good in the report and all."

"Felix said cooperate, so watch me fucking cooperate." I stood up, shrugged out of my coat, unbuttoned my waistcoat, pulled off my cravat, unbuttoned my shirt and took it off. The bruises on my chest and belly and back were in their full rainbow glory, and it was worth it to see Waterman's face when he realized I couldn't possibly be lying. I didn't look at Gideon.

"Thank you," said Morny, still perfectly polite. "I don't suppose you got a good look at any of the others?"

"One of 'em's missing a couple fingers as of Deuxième," I said. I put my shirt back on, but it didn't seem worth bothering with the rest of it. "But I didn't see any of 'em so as to recognize 'em again." I'd been too fucking mad, but I wasn't going to tell Morny that.

"Do you think they were part of a pack?"

That was exactly what I thought, but I shrugged. "No reason they'd have to be. Is your Jadis a pack-rat?"

"He'd like to be," Waterman said, in his ridiculous deep voice.

"Now, constable," Morny said. "We don't know. It ain—it isn't like they come and give us full rosters, now is it?"

"I was never a pack-rat," I said. "I wouldn't know."

"Hmmph," Morny said again.

And then I thought of something I actually wanted to know, "Hey, I heard y'all're holding a gal named Jenny Dawnlight. That true?"

Morny's eyebrows went up, and he traded a look with Waterman. But he said, "Charges of grave-robbing. Yes."

"Why ain't you let her go?" Because, I mean, grave-robbing ain't a nice thing, but it ain't hardly the worst kind of crime the Dogs get handed.

"Because the silly bitch won't talk," Waterman said and then shriveled up under the glare Morny gave him.

The sergeant sighed. "It's true, anyway. She won't say why she was there, and she won't say who the corpse is or why she was digging him out of the oldest part of the oldest cemetery in the city. And, well, it makes us twitchy, as I'm sure you can understand."

"Yeah," I said. I could get behind that.

"Are you a friend of Miss Dawnlight's?" Morny said, almost like he was hoping I was and maybe could explain her to him.

"I used to know her," I said and shrugged.

Morny gave me the hairy eyeball, but I wasn't telling him nothing I didn't have to. And anyway, what he'd wanted me for was whatever trap they were rigging for that Jadis-kid. Who I would almost have been sorry for except for the part where I wasn't and wasn't going to be.

Morny was polite, though. He thanked me for my time before him and Waterman left.

And then it was just me and Gideon, and Gideon was giving me this bright-eyed *I'll get it out of you if I have to ask Felix* look, and fuck, I had to kill *that* before it spread.

I knew right how to do it though. Said, "Hey, you want to come visit the resurrectionists' guildhall with me and Simon?"

And it worked. Like fucking magic.

Mehitabel

I was getting used to finding letters from the Lord Protector in my pigeonhole. Gordeny had escaped from Jean-Soleil's hectoring voice and spotted the new one first, and she was loitering obtrusively when Corinna and I came out.

"You have a letter," she said.

"Mmm," I said. "So I do." I took it and tucked it into my skirt pocket.

Gordeny and Corinna looked at me imploringly, and I laughed. "I'm not going to stage a public reading."

"A public reading of what?" Drin said behind me; he was much too close, and I knew he was within a single inch of encouragement of putting his hands on my shoulders or my waist. I stepped away from him and turned so that I could see him.

Corinna said, "Mehitabel's getting letters from the Lord Protector."

I watched his face shift as he took that in.

"The Lord Protector, eh?" he said, trying to sound like he didn't care. "I wish you much joy of him, Tabby." He stalked off, the living image of Morthenar in *Brannell Heath*.

"And that does for His Lordship," Corinna said under her breath.

"Corinna," I said, "I will thank you *not* to chase off my beaux unless I ask you to."

"What on earth do you want Drin on your string for?"

"I don't. It's the principle of the thing." We grinned at each other. "Now, if you'll excuse me, I have a letter to read."

As soon as I was out of sight, I let the mantle of vivacity drop. I knew what this letter was, knew what my answer to it had to be, and there was no joy in it, no triumph. Just the memory of Hallam weeping in a dream. I resented the knowledge that I would, in fact, do anything to protect him. How trite, how banal. How utterly fucking useless. But hate myself though I might, I couldn't change it. If there was anything I could do that would keep him from pain, I'd do it. I'd slept with worse men than Lord Stephen Teverius, that was for sure.

I closed my dressing room door behind me, passionately grateful that for once Vulpes was not waiting for me. The letter was exactly what I thought it was: an invitation to the soirée on Mercredy and a further invitation to "a private dinner party that same evening at six o'clock," with arrangements carefully provided to ensure Stephen's receipt of my reply.

And the unwritten message was just as clear. If I accepted, he would be moving his plans forward, presenting me to all and sundry ("sundry" in this case most definitely being Lady Victoria) as his new lover.

If I accepted? I snorted. The conditional wasn't fooling

anyone. "All right," I said to my somber, sallow reflection in the mirror. "I guess I'm going to a party."

Felix

In truth I was glad, however guiltily, that Mildmay would not be at my heels this afternoon. The delegation from Vusantine neither liked nor trusted me, and Mildmay did not help matters by staring the secretaries out of countenance, as he invariably did.

It irritated me greatly that I still had to placate the Tiberni-ans, nearly two full years after I had mended the Virtu. But we needed the Coeurterre's help in rebuilding the thaumaturgy that had been broken along with the Virtu, and in Malkar's subsequent attack; I had also been informed, in plain terms, that if I alienated the High King's Treasury, Stephen would have me sold into slavery in the Imari to make up the loss. Thus, twice a month Giancarlo and I met with the Tibernian envoys and described to them the progress being made both here in Mélusine and in the tower of Hermione so that Mortimer Clef, the senior envoy, could in his turn write a report for the High King's ministers in Vusantine. I reminded myself, also twice a month, that this was preferable to the original arrangement, which had the envoys attending Curia meetings. That scheme had proved untenable very quickly.

Clef said very little; he was annemer, and although he had a remarkable grasp of thaumaturgic theory, having served as the liaison between the High King and the Seigneur de la Coeurterre for over twenty years, he was quiet by nature, preferring rather to observe than to perform. When he asked a question, it was almost always of Giancarlo, who had been saddled with the logistical nightmare of herding wizards in three different cities.

The secretaries were dutiful and silent.

Which left, center stage, myself and Arsène L'Hiver.

I could not help thinking of it as a stage play, partly because the location chosen for these meetings was the Allegoria, where—some two hundred and fifty years ago—Violet Novadia had repudiated her husband. Mildmay had told me that story, and it had impressed itself indelibly into my mind. It appealed to my sense of the dramatic almost as much as L'Hiver did.

L'Hiver hated me. He had hated me before he laid eyes on me, considering ganymedes such as myself to be not merely perverse, but also repulsive—disgusting, like a carrion-fed rat. He couldn't look at me without his lip curling. Unfortunately, he was the Coeurterre's nonpareil on the subject of thaumaturgic architecture; we had no choice but to deal with him.

I had expected Giancarlo to do the sensible thing and ban me from his meetings with the Tibernians. After all, he had no great opinion of me. But he had refused, categorically and irately, to do any such thing. "The Coeurterre does not own us," he had said, glaring at me as if daring me to argue. "And if Arsène L'Hiver is their expert, you are ours."

"I've made no study of—"

"You mended the Virtu. That *makes* you our expert. Don't argue with me, Felix. Save it for L'Hiver."

"Yes, my lord," I had said meekly and made him smother a laugh in an unconvincing cough.

Some days these meetings went smoothly. Giancarlo and I explained what we had been doing, L'Hiver made some remarks from the Coeurterre's perspective, Mortimer Clef asked an occasional question. I refrained, every time, from saying that, since Cabaline and Coeurterrene wizards were working together in Hermione on a daily and doubtless first-name basis, there was really no point to this grave little diplomatic gavotte.

Today was not one of those days. L'Hiver snarled at me before I was even through the door, "You're late." Since on his more amiable days he ignored me entirely, this was a bad sign; I glanced past him at Giancarlo, whose face was bleak. Beside him, Clef looked troubled, and the three secretaries were trying to become invisible. Worse and worse, and it was clear there would be no help forthcoming.

"Perhaps my pocket watch is slow," I said, making no move to consult it.

Clef and Giancarlo had done this before, on days when L'Hiver was ripe for murder. Turning me loose like a mastiff in a bear-baiting pit, and there was another reason I was glad Mildmay wasn't with me: I didn't enjoy having him watch me provoke L'Hiver. I was good at it—and I could hardly fault Giancarlo for exploiting a talent I had so often used, to deleterious effect, in Curia meetings—and on my worse days I quite relished it, privately timing the onset of the tic in his right eyelid.

But it made me sick with myself, the same way I'd been sick with myself for taking that stupid bet of Edgar's. I wasn't even sure which of the three secretaries it had been. They all avoided my eyes now with the same shamed alarm, and at the time I had been drunk. More drunk than I should have let myself become.

Or, possibly, not quite drunk enough.

And L'Hiver rose, perfectly predictably, to the bait. "Oh, it's all of a piece. Careless, undisciplined"—depraved, said the sneer on his face—"evading responsibilities whenever—"

"I do *not* evade my responsibilities!" I said, and then hoped L'Hiver couldn't recognize honest outrage when he heard it.

"No? Then why, pray tell, did I not find out until today—and from one of my own wizards—about the fantôme in the Hermione tower?"

"There is no fantôme in the Hermione tower. It was dispersed three years ago."

Now that L'Hiver's fire had been drawn, Giancarlo and Clef were proceeding as they usually did: using me as a stalking horse and getting the work of the meeting done via notes passed between the secretaries. I tried not to wonder if they'd arranged it between them before they even appointed these ridiculous meetings—if what Clef had *really* needed was a safe outlet for L'Hiver's poison. Certainly, I was never chastised for fighting with L'Hiver—no mention was made of Imari slavers—although the single time I'd been a little short with Clef, I'd gotten one of Giancarlo's most impressive scowls.

I tried not to wonder if the entire Curia saw me as a badly-trained bear-baiting dog. I tried desperately not to wonder if they didn't have the right of it.

"By a bunch of Cabalines—and if they knew anything about repolarizing the leys, I'll eat my boots." The look L'Hiver gave me felt like it was scouring the flesh off my bones. "Did it not occur to you it might be important?"

"I had forgotten about it," I said, my voice gone dull, as colorless as any of the secretaries.

"Forgotten?" L'Hiver howled. "How, for the sake of all the powers, could you possibly *forget* about a fantôme?"

All too easily, my lord, if you want not to think about it badly enough.

I had to pull myself together. Giancarlo had noticed my inadvertent retreat, even if L'Hiver hadn't.

I clasped my hands behind my back, where I could drive the rings on my left hand into my right palm without anyone seeing, and said, in a much better approximation of my natural tone, "As I'm sure you're aware, Arsène, I was not thaumaturgically competent when I was in Hermione. I was in fact, in technical terms, not even a Cabaline, and I wasn't reinstated until nearly a year later. So I apologize for the oversight, but I will not be your whipping boy for it." I did not give him the opportunity to respond to that, but said, "Now tell me, what is it that needs to be done? You said something about ley energy."

It rocked him, almost physically, and it was a moment before he said, grinding the words between his teeth as if they were my flesh: "Adrien has dealt with the problem. He wrote merely for my information."

"How very kind of Adrien," I murmured, then said brightly, knowing exactly the effect it would have, "Then you've made this tremendous and unseemly fuss over nothing at all?"

I was not disappointed; L'Hiver exploded: "A nexus of noirant power such as a fantôme is *not* nothing, and you should not speak so dismissively of matters you patently do not understand!"

"This must be Coeurterrene theory. What, exactly, is 'noirant power'?" I let him hear the disdainful quotation marks in my voice, and that was all it took.

I understood perhaps half of the ensuing lecture. The Coeurterre did not practice necromancy, but—signally unlike the Mirador in this regard—they had built their theories to accommodate it. They envisioned magic as water, flowing along channels they called leys, and its flow could be either "noirant" or "clairant," dark or light. They also believed that each wizard was naturally better suited to working with one or the other type of power, and much of the Coeurterre's institutional energies were devoted to trying to maintain a balance between them. One reason the Coeurterre, normally as territorial as a cat—or a wizard—had been so willing to help the Mirador in the wake of our disaster was that in their thinking the Virtu was remarkable for weaving noirant and clairant power together.

L'Hiver's explanation of why it was foolish to think of a fantôme simply as a spirit of the malevolent dead, I did not follow at all, but I did grasp the Coeurterrene belief that summoning a fantôme would change the "polarity" of the architectural thaumaturgy—such as the tower in Hermione—that was used. "Now that I consider the matter," L'Hiver said, "it is no more than reasonable that you would not have noticed. You are a noirant wizard if ever I've seen one."

"I shall choose," I said, baring my teeth back at him, "to take that as a compliment."

"I've often thought," Giancarlo said, "that you would have been magnificent in the days of the great court necromancers."

It was a signal: he and Clef had finished their work. And Clef confirmed it by saying mildly, "Noirant and clairant aren't value judgments, Lord Felix. Simply descriptions."

"Noirant power is a good deal more dangerous if not properly controlled," L'Hiver said.

"And that is why it is a good thing that Adrien observed and cleared the fantôme's residue," Clef said, not budging an inch. "If you are interested, my lord, I imagine there must be a copy of Ynge's *Influence of the Moon on the Energy of Souls* somewhere in the Mirador."

"Thank you," I said. "I shall look for it." It would be comforting to reduce my memories of the fantôme to the cool precision of Coeurterrene diagrams. And—I lost L'Hiver's parting barb entirely in scribbling down the reference Clef had given me—another way of looking at the matter might also help with my niggling uncertainty about the success of the katharsis I had performed.

It would be a great blessing to be *certain*. And maybe Ynge's book could help me find that.

Mildmay

Simon and Rinaldo were both waiting when I showed up with Gideon.

"You coming?" I said to Rinaldo.

He laughed. "Even if you could fit me into any cab in this city, you certainly couldn't get me out again. No, I am going to wait here and demand full details upon your return. That, I think, is my function in this little adventure."

"You sure you want to do this?" I asked Simon.

Simon said, "I've always wanted to visit the Lower City."

I was opening my mouth to say something, Kethe knows what, when Simon shoved his hands in his pockets, and I shut up. Simon might not know the first thing about the Lower City, but he'd been in worse shit than anything we were likely to find today. So I just said, "It ain't pretty," and stood aside for him and Gideon. I wasn't comfortable walking with a hocus at my back. I liked having 'em where I could see 'em.

We went out Livergate, across the Plaza del' Archimago, and Simon flagged down a fiacre. All it took was the rings on his hand, and the cabbie just about turned his horses upside down jerking them to a stop. We climbed in, and the cabbie said through the trap, "Where to, my lord?"

Simon looked at me.

I kept my mouth from twitching into a grin and said, "Ruthven. Corner of Knackers Lane and Dimity."

"*Ruthven?*" said the cabbie. "My lord, I don't—"

"Ruthven is where we want to go," Simon said and shut the trap.

"You'll have to bribe him to wait," I said.

"Really?"

"Oh, yeah. Cab drivers don't like the Lower City."

"Then I'll bribe him. How much, do you think?"

I looked around at the fiacre's shabby upholstery and splintered panels. "A gorgon oughta do it."

"That certainly won't break the bank."

The streets weren't paved no better than I remembered, and I think the cabbie was hitting the potholes hard on purpose. We jostled and jounced. Simon and Gideon got thrown against each other a time or two. I had the back-facing side all to myself, along of my leg and my cane. By the time he pulled up, we were ready to get out. Simon went up to talk to him about staying, and what was in it for him. Me and Gideon stood and looked around.

Ruthven ain't as bad as Queensdock or Simside, but it ain't a nice part of town. We were surrounded by crumbly brick tenements, and you didn't have to see anybody in the windows to know you were being watched. There was a group of guys hanging out on a stoop. The local muscle, and if I'd been here on a normal sort of job, I'd've gone over to them and had a word. Little power like this, you want to let it know it don't want to fuck with you. But I wasn't here on a normal job, and they weren't watching me anyways. They were watching Simon, and I saw it when they figured out for sure he was a hocus. It wasn't

anything big, but everybody shifted a little, so that they were all
leaning away from Simon and Gideon and me. They wouldn't
bug us.

Simon came back and said, "I think he'll wait, but he's not
happy about it."

"Nobody'll bother him," I said. "They've got you pegged."

Simon glanced over. One of them made the sign against
hexes, down by his side where he thought Simon wouldn't notice.

"So they do," Simon said with a sigh. "All right. Where are we
going?"

"There," I said and pointed.

There wasn't much to tell the resurrectionists' building apart
from the others. It was made of the same kind of brick and had
the same sort of dismal look about it. It was lower and wider, and
if you knew what you were looking at, you knew it had started
out as a church, a poor stepchild cousin of churches like St. Kirban in Havelock and St. Rose in Candlewick Mews. I glanced at
the cornerstone as we went past. The little lantern carved on it
showed it'd been dedicated to St. Lemoyne Harkness, and I
made up my mind right then that that was a good omen. St.
Lemoyne Harkness was the patron saint of dark places and con-
fusion, and you couldn't've described better how I was feeling if
you'd written a book.

The huge front doors were unlocked, just like this was still a
real church. In the vestibule, Simon came up short and said,
"I'm sure there's all sorts of protocol involved here that I don't
know about. What should we do?"

"Well, let me do the talking."

"Oh quite."

"I know you don't like to, but if you could leave your hands
out where they can see 'em—we don't want anybody forgetting
you're a hocus." It was a little more complicated than that, but I
didn't want to get into the details with Simon about why people
in the Lower City didn't like hocuses from the Mirador who
looked like they were trying to pretend they were something
else.

Simon made a face. "All right. I agreed to help."

"Other'n that, just stick close, both of you. Nobody wants
anything, um, unfortunate to happen, but they're gonna be nervous, and nervous people do stupid things."

"All right. Ready, Gideon?"

Gideon nodded. His clerky, choirboy face was as hard to read as ever, but his eyes were bright. He looked better than I could remember him looking in a long time, and I wondered if maybe he hated the Mirador as much as I did.

"Okay," I said and opened the inner door.

The resurrectionists had remodeled pretty extensively inside. The huge openness of the nave was gone, except for a narrow corridor that went straight up for three stories. It was like being stuck in a crack. The rest of it they'd partitioned off with a hodgepodge of stuff: bricks, boards, stone columns from somebody else's church. The doors looked like they'd tried to get one from every district in the city and had mostly succeeded. There was nobody in the hallway at all.

"Now what?" Simon whispered.

"We knock," I said. I picked a door, a good big mahogany one that had probably come off one of the abandoned townhouses in Lyonesse, and used the knocker. It echoed like a thunderclap. Simon winced.

"They know we're here anyway," I said. "They ain't stupid. There was a guy watching from the roof when we got out of the fiacre."

Both of them gave me a weird look, but it wasn't my fault if they'd never learned to be nervous about what was over their heads.

I could feel the resurrectionists watching. There were probably a double-septad of spyholes in their makeshift walls. More so than most guilds, they had reason to be twitchy about unexpected visitors. And I could feel them thinking, trying to figure out what to do with us. They knew who I was, and they knew Simon was from the Mirador, and they probably didn't have a clue about Gideon at all.

But they also knew that if we'd come this far, they couldn't outwait us. You come down to Ruthven from the Mirador, you ain't gonna get bored and go away. They waited long enough to let me know they weren't happy about it, and then the door I'd knocked on swung open. The guy behind it looked like some of his own merchandise, he was that thin and his eyes that far back in their sockets. I was glad he was wearing a knitted cap, because I didn't want to know if the rest of his head was as skull-like as his face.

"Yeah?" he said.

"I wanna talk to somebody knows about Laceshroud," I said.

It threw him. Dunno what they'd been expecting—probably to find out that the Mirador was either coming down on necromancy like a ton of bricks or taking it up as a hobby—but for sure I was asking about the wrong end of the business. *"Laceshroud?"*

"Yeah. Whoever knows the most about it."

"Just a minute." He shut the door.

"We wait," I said to Simon's raised eyebrows. Gideon was still looking around like a squirrel in a roomful of nuts.

We didn't have to wait as long this time. I guessed they were hoping now that if they hurried up and humored us, we'd go away quicker. So the door opened again. This time, it was a little balding man with a round face. He bobbed his head nervously, and said, "Your lordships wished to speak to somebody about Laceshroud?"

"I ain't a lordship," I said, "but yeah, that's what we want. Are you the guy to talk to?"

He wanted to say no and bolt. "I . . . I guess so."

"Then let's go somewhere we can sit down," Simon said and smiled when the little man's eyes jerked to him.

"All . . . all right. If your lordships would come this way?"

As we followed him, I said in an undertone to Simon, "I thought I said let me do the talking."

"Sorry, but did *you* want to stand out there all day?"

Not much, but I also wasn't sure we wanted to get caught back here in the resurrectionists' maze. We all knew they didn't want to tangle with the Mirador, but like I said before, people can do some downright stupid things when they're frightened. And if the little man with us was a good example, the resurrectionists were scared shitless.

But we hadn't gone more than a couple of turns before he stopped and opened a door, this one an old iron grille that somebody'd backed with a green brocade curtain. "Here," he said and stood aside. Simon and Gideon went in, but I stopped and waited.

"Oh!" he said, going red. "I wasn't going to . . . you couldn't think . . ."

"I ain't thinking nothing," I said. "Go on in."

He went, and I followed him, closing the door after me.

It was a neat, small room, with one of the old stained glass windows for light. They'd only bricked up half of it, so you could see St. Lemoyne Harkness's head and two crows over him in the weak blue sky. There was a table with four chairs, and some bookcases along the wall opposite the door, and that was it for furniture. We all sat down, and the little man looked around the table.

"I don't know what your lordships are after," he said. "I'm not really a resurrectionist—I haven't been out on a job since I reached my third septad—"

"What d'you do?" I asked.

"Well, I don't know. I guess you'd call me a bookkeeper. I mean, I keep track of our finances and our membership and all the rest of it."

"And you know more about Laceshroud than anybody else?" Simon said. The little man went the color of whey, and I kicked Simon under the table.

"Y-yes, my lord, I guess I do. You see, I'm *interested*."

"Interested in what?" I said.

"Well, in history, I guess. I like knowing who all the people are and why they're buried there. I know a lot about the Boneprince, too, but that's not what you're interested in?"

"Not right now," I said, although all at once I was itching with questions. "We're trying to find out something kind of particular."

"I'll do my best," he said.

"It's like this," I said. "A girl got picked up in Laceshroud last decad for digging up a body. I want to know what she was doing."

"A girl in Laceshroud?" He was frowning, like that hit a nerve. "We don't have many women, and none of them has anything to do with Laceshroud."

"So she ain't a resurrectionist?"

"What's her name?"

"Guinevere Dawnlight."

"No," he said at once, and I could see that he knew what he was talking about.

"So if she wasn't a resurrectionist, what was she doing there?"

"Who did she exhume?"

"Dunno. That's the problem. She won't talk, and the Dogs can't figure it out."

"Dogs," he said with a sniff. "I could write a book on what the Dogs don't know about Laceshroud. Two books."

"Is there any way to figure out who he was?"

The little man thought. We'd got through his fear into his pride, and as long as Simon could keep his big mouth shut, I thought we were okay.

"I'm guessing there wasn't any identification on the body?"

"Not that I know about," I said.

"Hmmm. Well, there's only one thing I can think of, and that's for us to go there."

"Go there?"

"Unless you know where he was buried?"

"The Dogs said the oldest part of the cemetery, but I don't s'pose that's much help."

"I can think of five different areas that might be called 'the oldest part of the cemetery,' so no, not much." He looked from me to Simon to Gideon and back to me. "I really will be happy to go to Laceshroud with you."

I realized I was looking at Simon, too. "I don't see any reason why we shouldn't," he said to me.

"No, I guess not. Okay. We got a fiacre waiting outside."

The little man caught the joke. His eyes crinkled into a smile, and he said, "Just a minute while I get my coat."

Felix

There was no guarantee the Ynge would be of any use, even if I could find it. And I could not allow myself to forget, in my purely theoretical panic about a ghost of whose existence I had no proof of any kind, that I had another problem, an actual problem: ten greasy smoke-dark rubies in a wash-leather bag. I retreated to the Archive of Cinders, repressing with difficulty the desire to barricade the door. No one would look for me here; no one was likely to come here in pursuit of their own research, for the books in the Archive of Cinders were of interest far more for who had owned them than for anything intrinsic to themselves. Vey Coruscant's books were here—the harmless ones, anyway, and if anyone had noticed that de Charon's *Principia Caeli* was missing, they at least hadn't said anything about it to me. Vey Coruscant's books, Susanna Parmenter's books, the books of the annemer heresiarch Arcadian Holter, who had preached that all people could be wizards if they would fast and abjure sex and meditate upon seven sacred symbols, the names of which escaped me at the moment.

There was only one table in the Archive of Cinders, and only one rather rickety chair. I moved a stack of books from the table to the floor, sat down, and took the Sibylline's box out of my pocket.

The catch was hidden, but I knew the secret to it.

I shuffled the cards; I had to concentrate, unlike Mavortian von Heber, whose cards these had been. But some of my finger joints were stiff, and I had never been graceful.

I did not use the Sibylline for divination as Mavortian had, although he had taught me how. Or, rather, I used it for divination, but of a wildly different sort.

I shuffled the cards to rouse them, to get their power flowing, dark and clear and strangely rich. Noirant, I supposed the Coeurterre would call it. Then I sorted out the twenty-one trumps and the four Sibyls; the lesser cards, I had found, were not as responsive outside of the formal nine-card spread. I might proceed to that eventually, but I preferred to start with something simpler.

I shuffled the trumps and Sibyls and laid them out in five rows of five to choose a card to represent Malkar's rubies. What I had realized in the Khloïdanikos was that the Sibylline offered a way, not merely to connect the world of matter and the world of spirit, for any act of magic did that, but to forge links between them, to invest enough meaning in a symbolic representation of a material object that the object could be consumed by the symbol.

At least, I hoped so.

The Khloïdanikos was clearly the Unreal City; even the shifting water-like instability of the card's allegiances, with the Spire on one side and the Dead Tree on the other, suited the Khloïdanikos with its Omphalos which was not like the Omphalos of the waking Gardens and which made both Thamuris and me uneasy. And the world of matter was the Rock, solid, unyielding, inescapably *present*. But choosing a semeion—to borrow a term from what little Thamuris had told me of Troian divination—for the rubies was fraught and deeply unsettling.

Death was the most obvious and immediate choice: they were the remnant of someone dead, someone whose death I had caused, someone who had carried death in his train. But I was unwilling to reinforce that particular piece of symbolism; the rubies carried too much death already. I looked instead for something more neutral, something that would capture what the rubies were rather than who they had belonged to, and settled on the Beehive, the Parliament of Bees, signifying balance and cooperation, many things working toward the same goal. Like the fingers of a hand, Mavortian had said. Like the rubies in the rings that would have adorned those fingers.

I left the Parliament of Bees face up on the table, collected the other cards, shuffled them again. When their power was clear, I cut the deck and dealt three cards in a row beneath the Parliament of Bees.

Death, the Dog, the Prison.

I stared at the cards blankly. Death made sense—too much sense—but the Dog and the Prison? The Dog was loyalty, also the semeion of an animal, or of a person's animal nature . . . I thought of the Two-Headed Beast and shuddered with self-loathing. The Prison was confinement, bad choices, dead ends. Also the need for solitude. The Sibylline, by its nature, invited a multiplicity of meanings.

But even if the Dog and the Prison were pointing to my own dark beast, what had that to do with the rubies? Or even with Malkar?

I collected the cards again, leaving the Parliament of Bees where it was, shuffled, cut, laid them out.

Death, the Dog, the Prison.

The Parliament of Bees led to Death, which meant at least that I'd aligned the symbols correctly; I might not *want* Malkar in my reading, but I couldn't deny he belonged there. But Death leading to the Dog and the Prison . . . it made no sense.

"What in the world is the Dog supposed to mean?" I said under my breath. Loyalty to Malkar was not an option, and I didn't care who was suggesting it.

I stared at the Dog: an enormous black creature, more bear or wolf than any dog I'd ever seen. It bulked across the face of its card, eyes red and mournful, clearly as loyal as it was savage.

No, it was nothing to do with Malkar. But it was linked to him somehow. Loyalty . . . savagery . . .

The answer came to me in a wave of cold nausea, and my

hands clenched painfully. Mildmay. Of course Mildmay was the Dog, my savage, loyal shadow, dismissed as a near animal by those of my friends who even noticed him at all.

And if that was true, then the Prison needed no explanation. I knew Mildmay was trapped.

Death, the Dog, the Prison.

Malkar had trapped him, had hurt him. Hurt him terribly, so terribly that he could not—or would not—remember what had been done. But I could guess. I could guess all too easily. I had been Malkar's . . . *plaything* for six years, bound by the obligation de sang; I knew his full repertoire. I remembered the tearing, sparking pain as Malkar forced the spurred gag between my teeth.

Remembered being bent backwards over a splintery table, Malkar's hand knotted in my hair, his other hand lashing my chest and stomach with a riding crop, his curses and my screams jangling in my ears.

I don't know what I've done, but he pushes me down onto the worn flagstones, bruising my knees. One forearm presses against my throat, holding me upright, and he croons in my ear, the bulk and heat of him all down my back, "Be very still, my darling, or this bauble will tear through you like paper." He shows it to me, cold black iron, shaped with terrible mocking realism. I can't move. Paralyzed with shame, with terror, my breath whining in my throat, the burning cold of the thing as Malkar works it into me.

He leaves me there, unable to move, unable to breathe, blind with tears I dare not wipe away.

And when he returns . . .

I shoved back, almost tipping the chair over, and then sat, my elbows on my knees and my hands tangled in my hair, swallowing hard, until my breathing was steady again and I no longer tasted Malkar in the back of my throat. Gideon had wanted to know why I hadn't made Mildmay talk to me about Malkar, and I'd told him it was because I was afraid he wouldn't answer me. And that was true, but it wasn't the whole truth. I was even more afraid that he *would*.

"I am a coward," I said aloud. "I admit it, all right?"

I drew my chair back close to the table, gathered the cards, shuffled, cut, dealt.

And this time, as if they'd proved their point, they were different.

Mehitabel

Vulpes appeared again that afternoon, like a malevolent spirit in a story, and fidgeted around my dressing room while I told him about Lord Stephen's offer. He pulled himself together to act pleased about it, but I could tell his mind was on something else. So when I'd finished my report, I sat and waited, watching him fidget. He didn't look quite as self-confident as he had the first time I'd seen him. I was glad of it.

He had something he wanted to ask me, I could see that much, but he either wasn't sure how I'd take it, or he didn't want to admit to me that he had a problem. I kept expecting him to leave, and he kept looking at the door like he wanted to—but he didn't. Whatever this problem was, it was serious.

Finally, he burst out, "How well do you know Felix Harrowgate?"

"Well enough for my purposes. Why?" He became suddenly and uncommonly interested in the toes of his shoes, and I thought I knew. "Does Louis want you to seduce him?"

Vulpes glanced at me, looked away, and then looked back defiantly. "Yes," he said, and we were no longer master and servant, but two servants of the same master.

"And have you?"

"Yes," he said, and then added in a lower voice, "Once."

"What do you think of him?"

"That's what I was going to ask you. I mean, you've known him a long time." And the look he gave me was a pointed reminder that he could double-check anything I told him.

"Three years isn't all that long," I said. "And I've never been to bed with him. He doesn't go for women."

"At all?"

"As far as I know." I remembered an old piece of gossip. "There's a story that Roseanna Aemoria tried to surprise him once by waiting for him in his bed, stark naked. He marched her out into the hall and locked his door with her on the wrong side."

"Do you think it's true?"

"I know for a fact she hates him."

"Do you think he did it just to be cruel?"

"I think she made him mad. He has a filthy temper, you know."

"Yes," he said. No one in the Mirador could avoid knowing that. I thought that a more useful index of Felix's character was his social cruelty, the enjoyment he got out of making other people uncomfortable. He did it to Mildmay all the time. But Vulpes was going to have to work that one out for himself.

"What's got you tied up in knots?" I said, turning the focus back on him. "Has something gone wrong?"

"I don't know. That's the problem." He paused for a moment, on the brink of telling me, *Never mind, I'll deal with it myself*, and then simply blurted the whole thing out. The initial seduction had apparently gone just as planned. They flirted; one thing led to another; they ended up in Vulpes's bedroom, in the dark, with their clothes off. And then, the next day, when Vulpes was all prepared to go on to the next step in Louis Goliath's program, suddenly they were back at square one. Felix watched him flirt with a tolerantly amused eye—"the same way he watches Dominic Jocelyn," Vulpes said bitterly—but wouldn't really flirt back. Vulpes had finally got him aside and tried to ask, and Felix stonewalled him. Vulpes didn't go into details, but I could imagine the scene without any help; I'd seen Felix do things like that often enough to know what the expression on his face would be and how his voice would sound. Vulpes hadn't been able to get a straight answer out of him. Felix had been perfectly friendly first to last, a fact which only seemed to aggravate Vulpes further.

When he was done, he looked at me hopefully, as if I could give him the key to Felix's code. Which I couldn't, and wouldn't have if I could. But I still needed to show willing. I said, "Did you know that Felix started out as a prostitute in Pharaohlight?"

He hadn't known. His whole face sagged. I was surprised, since it was a fact that got bandied about in the Mirador quite a bit, especially by the people who wished Felix would go back to Pharaohlight and quit bothering them. But I supposed it wasn't the sort of thing that would immediately get offered up to a defector from the Bastion.

"He has a rather . . . casual attitude toward sex," I said.

"Oh God, you're joking."

"No, I'm sorry, it's perfectly true."

His face worked for a moment; then he said, "Thank you for the information, Mehitabel. I've got to go." He left, quite rapidly. It was only some time later, in the middle of a heated discussion with Corinna about what one ought to wear as the guest of the Lord Protector, that I realized he'd forgotten to call me Cressida.

Mildmay

The little resurrectionist's name was George Tuillery. Simon asked a question as we got in the fiacre and got him launched on the subject of Laceshroud, saving me from having to talk and Mr. Tuillery from his own nerves. Nobody knew exactly when the cemetery had been founded, although there were references to it as far back as the reign of Maxim Thestonarius, the second Thestonarian king, who'd ruled almost twenty-five Great Septads ago. Mr. Tuillery told us about the catacombs beneath the little church of St. Osprey, where skeletons had labeled pigeon-holes, and about the ghosts that were supposed to haunt the cemetery gates. Then he told us about the funeral of Paul Raphenius, and that lasted us all the way to the cemetery itself.

"It didn't used to be in the middle of the city, of course," Mr. Tuillery said as he got out of the fiacre. The cabbie wasn't no happier about Gilgamesh and a cemetery than he'd been about Ruthven and a guildhall, so Simon was up in front arguing with him again. "But cities grow if you let 'em, even cities of the dead. I read a book about a city in the south where it floods every year, so they have to build all the tombs above ground, the city on one side of the river and the cemetery on the other, so you can't hardly tell which is which."

When Simon came back, he gave Gideon a funny look and said to me, "Gideon says the Necropolis of Nimuë."

"Thanks," I said to Gideon.

Mr. Tuillery had gone up ahead to look at the gates, and we joined him. They were locked, of course—Boneprince is the only cemetery in the city that don't keep its gates locked—but Mr. Tuillery said, "I took the liberty of borrowing the correct, um, tools from a friend, but I'm afraid I haven't the foggiest how to use them."

He knew who I was, all right, or one of the other resurrectionists had told him. "Hand 'em here," I said. The other three clumped around in front of me in a kind of nonchalant way that would have had any Dog worth his salt licking his chops. Kethe, spare me from flats. But this wasn't either the time or the place for a lesson in how not to look like you're doing something illegal, so I just hurried. That lock had been picked so many times that it wasn't no bother, not stiff or dirty or nothing like that. And lock picking is more about whether or not you understand what the lock's doing and what you want it to do. I wouldn't have backed myself to do an in-and-out, not with a crippled leg and not going on three indictions out of practice, but the lock clicked open for me in only about twice the time it would take a good crack-man like Sempronias Teach. I pulled the right-hand gate a little ways open, and we slid in.

I could remember once—I guess I was maybe at my first septad, maybe a little older—coming here with Keeper to see a funeral. I don't know anymore whose it was, if I ever did, but I remember the way she had us kids, the five of us she brought, line up along the fence, and the way she said that we weren't to move and we weren't to make noise. I guess she picked us 'cause we were the five most frightened of her. None of us even dreamed of not doing what she wanted, and we stood there, shivering a little in the cold, and watched all the people in black, the way they were standing around one of the graves, the way the priest's movements made little ripples in the big pool of black bodies, the way every so often, somebody'd turn a pale blotch of a face in our direction. But nobody came over to ask what we wanted, and nobody sent for the cemetery guard to do the same. Probably they were afraid Keeper would tell them. When the priest was done, we stood and watched him leave, and then we stood and watched all the people in black leave and try to pretend they couldn't see us, and then we stood and watched the sextons fill in the grave. Keeper stood watching, too, and I think she'd forgotten about us. I think she was crying, but we argued about that for decads among ourselves, me and Christobel saying we were sure she'd been crying, and Devie and Jean-Souris and Nero saying Keeper *couldn't* cry, that she was a witch like in the stories Nikah told. So I don't know about that, any more than I know who the stiff was or what Keeper was trying to prove. Or to who.

But I was a little prepared for Laceshroud. It ain't just the oldest cemetery in the city. Even though it's in Gilgamesh, it's the rich people's cemetery. Poor people don't get buried there. They get stuck in Tammas Yard, down in Scaffelgreen, or in the Ivorene outside the city walls. People living in Gilgamesh are always the first to know when somebody important dies, because the Dogs come down and bust heads.

There's a lot of marble in Laceshroud, a lot of granite. During the Protectorates of Malory and Helen there was this craze for obsidian, so there's a lot of that around, too. The granite's mostly in slabs and the obsidian mostly in these tall skinny sort of towers. The marble's in statues, some of 'em representing the stiff—though I don't know why, since flashies can read—most showing Phi-Kethetin's daughter, Phi-Lazary, since she's supposed to be merciful and loving and sympathetic to the needs of dead folk, being dead herself. We followed Mr. Tuillery up one tidy little gravel path and down the next, me and Simon and Gideon kind of in a clump and Mr. Tuillery trotting ahead like a hunting dog, yipping and muttering to himself.

He tried a couple different places before he hit pay dirt, a place where somebody'd clearly been digging and somebody else had clearly not been at much trouble to fix things up. It was down in the southwest corner of the cemetery, near the iron fence, and the grave markers down here were a lot tamer and low-key than the ones around the gates.

"Well, she certainly wasn't after anybody *important*," Mr. Tuillery said with a sniff, like he'd've liked her better if she had been. "This is the servants' quarter."

"The what?" I said.

He shrugged. He didn't like it neither, but it was how things were. "Faithful servants, devoted retainers. If you were *very* good, your employer might have you buried here, near him."

"Were? Isn't it done anymore?" Simon said.

"Not very much. Although . . ." Mr. Tuillery checked a new-looking granite block. "This poor fellow was only buried an indiction and a half ago, so the custom's got life in it yet, so to speak."

"What about the guy Jenny was after?"

Mr. Tuillery looked at the block at the head of the disturbed piece of ground. He made little tut-tutting noises. "Dear me, I see why the City Guard are distressed."

"Well?" I said, since he didn't seem like he was going to go on by himself.

"This grave belongs to a woman named Ismene Culpepper, and she died, oh, about ten Great Septads ago."

"Well, that don't make no sense at all."

"No," Mr. Tuillery said thoughtfully. "I think I see what happened. I had been wondering how your friend had managed with the coffin."

"Well?"

"It's hard to get buried in Laceshroud anymore. There's not much room left, and most of it belongs to the nobles and the burghers. So if there are reasons you've got to bury somebody here—and there can be—you, um, borrow somebody else's grave."

"What sorts of reasons?" Simon asked before I could say anything, though I ain't sure what I would've said.

"Oh, well," Mr. Tuillery shifted from foot to foot, "I imagine your lordship would know more about that sort of thing than I do."

"I thought as much," Simon said.

"So how do we figure out who this guy was?" I said.

"He was a servant somebody wanted buried in Laceshroud who didn't have access to a plot," Mr. Tuillery said. He spread his hands in a sort of shrug, like that was the best he could do. He was looking nervous again, but this time I didn't think it was about me or Simon. And then I thought about the sort of person who would want or need to break into Laceshroud to bury a body, and I could see his point.

"Thanks, Mr. Tuillery," I said, letting him off the hook, and he sagged a little with relief. "So, my friend not being a resurrectionist, what would she want with this guy?"

"Is your friend perhaps a necromancer?"

"Jenny? Not hardly. Is there any way to find out if a necromancer might've hired her?"

"We don't have anything to do with the necromancers," Mr. Tuillery said. That was a lie, and we both knew it, but I also knew what he meant. The resurrectionists ain't crazy. They try hard not to know anything more about the necromancers than what bits of corpse they'll pay most for.

"There are other ways to find out," Simon said. I wasn't sure if he was talking to Mr. Tuillery or me.

"Yeah," I said. "Thanks, Mr. Tuillery, you been a lot of help."

"You're welcome," he said.

At the gates, Mr. Tuillery refused to let us take him back to
Ruthven. "My sister lives in Gilgamesh," he said, "and I haven't
seen her in a long time." I thought he was lying, but I couldn't
say so, and the last we saw of him he was walking south along
the fence of Laceshroud, almost trotting, like he was afraid
we'd call him back.

Mehitabel

It was Cinquième; Jean-Soleil brooded like the wrath of God
over a rehearsal of *Edith Pelpheria*, then asked me to come talk
to him in his office.

I knew he wasn't firing me, so I settled myself and gave him
a brightly inquiring look, an ingenue's look.

Jean-Soleil sank into his own chair and said, "I'm wondering if you'd do me a favor, Belle."

"What kind of favor?" I said.

"It's the new boy. Bartholmew's replacement."

I remembered he had told me not to worry about the second
principal. "What about him?"

"It's like this. I expect you know there's a boy's choir over in
Shatterglass?"

"I've heard it mentioned, I think. The prior of St. Kemplegate runs it, doesn't he?"

"Exactly. It's a school as well, the idea being that the boys
St. Kemplegate trains will go on to the Academy, or go to Er-
venzia to sing opera, or something like that, and make their en-
trée into the polite world."

"Right. So?"

"It doesn't work all the time, now does it? There are boys
who don't want to go on, which happens with any kind of training," and I knew he was thinking of his own children, none of
whom showed the slightest desire to follow in his footsteps, "and
there are boys who don't have the money to go on. And then
there are the boys whose voices lose their beauty when they become men."

"Which is why the Ervenze practice castration."

"Well, yes. I don't think St. Kemplegate has gotten that desperate yet. And by the time their voices change, most of their
boys have been trained in some other musical instrument, or
have found an aptitude for something else, or the like."

"But not all of them?"

"No," Jean-Soleil said, his mobile, habitually cheerful face for once still and rather sad. "Not all of them." He shook it off and went on. "I don't believe the prior actually likes me very much, but he recognizes that the Empyrean and the Cockatrice are places where boys like that can go. We have an arrangement of mutual convenience. When I need a young actor, I send a letter to the prior, and if he's got some boy he thinks will suit, he sends him over. Jermyn does the same. Mostly they don't stay more than a season before some other thing opens up that's more to their liking, but they're always grateful, and they're always perfectly adequate for second principal."

"So you sent a letter to the prior, and he's sending a boy over."

"Yes."

"And?"

Jean-Soleil chewed on the ends of his mustache for a moment. It was a terrible habit—he said it drove his wife to distraction—but he could never seem to break himself of it. "This boy's situation is a bit different."

"Different how?"

"Well," said Jean-Soleil. "Er."

"What? He's got two heads?"

"No. He's the bastard of Lord Philip Lemerius."

"God *damn*," I said, because Jean-Soleil seemed to want some astonishment. "I didn't think that Lord Philip had any baseborn get." From what Antony had told me about his father, Lord Philip wasn't the sort of man even to admit he had animal instincts, much less act on them.

"Only the one," Jean-Soleil said, "and to do him justice, he seems to have tried to do his best by the boy. He got him into St. Kemplegate, after all."

"That was kind of him."

"Yes, and from what the prior says, it was working out splendidly. The boy was radiantly happy, had a marvelous voice, worked hard, was charming, and all the rest of it. And then his voice changed, and his singing voice was gone. The prior says he has a perfectly nice and utterly mediocre baritone."

"Oh dear," I said.

"Yes," Jean-Soleil said. "Apparently he's been moping around St. Kemplegate for most of an indiction. I don't know

that the prior really believes Semper will be happy here, but
he can't think of anything else to try."

"And what do you want from me?"

"He's coming tonight, and I want to give him a chance to get
used to the theater before we pitchfork him in among the
wolves. Would you take him to see *Mardette*? Corinna and
Jabez decided they could use a run-through, you know. Answer
his questions, hold his hand, be gracious and reassuring, and all
that?"

"Of course," I said. There wasn't anything else I could say.

ᔿ

Semper Philipson did not look like a Lemerius. They were
dark, with brilliant eyes. He was tall, not as tall as Felix—
almost no one was—but two or three inches taller than Mildmay. His hair was brown, his eyes hazel, his complexion, like
mine, rather sallow. His beauty was in his bones. If he took after his mother, I could see why Lord Philip had lost his head.

Semper was younger even than I had expected—just barely
seventeen—and shy and nervous. I thought he was also unhappy, but he clearly didn't want to talk about himself. I occupied the time before the play by telling him about the Empyrean
and the troupe and about acting. He listened attentively and politely, but I couldn't hazard a guess whether any of it pleased or
excited him, which made it a relief when the curtain went up on
The Misadventures of Mardette.

They'd opened the same day we hired Gordeny, so this was
the theatrical equivalent of oiling the machinery to keep it in
good working order. Considering the frenetic pace of the thing,
I could see why you'd want to. The play was stylized nonsense.
Mardette (Corinna) climbs into her trousers to escape from the
importunities of a rich, ugly suitor (Jabez), only to fall madly in
love with a handsome young man (Levry), who, thinking she is
a boy, keeps trying to get her interested in her ugly suitor, who,
it turns out, is a moll and only wants to marry Mardette because
he needs an heir. Naturally, he's even more importunate, in an
inept, grotesque, and comical way, toward Mardette-as-boy
than he was toward Mardette-as-girl. And, of course, the handsome young man has been madly in love with Mardette for
months, and he finally tells her so, trying to get her, in her per-
sona as a boy, to leave him alone. She dares him into asking

Mardette to marry him the next time he sees her, races back into her dress, and the play ends happily. Except of course for the ugly, molly suitor, who is left out in the cold.

It was vulgar and hysterically funny, except that every time Mardette repulsed her ugly suitor, I heard Mildmay saying, *Got a taste for freaks?* and every time she came up with a new ploy to captivate the handsome young man, I saw myself going calculatedly through Corinna's treasure trove, looking for a dress that would turn Stephen's head. By the end of the play I hated both Mardette and myself and wanted nothing more than to shut myself in my dressing room and break something.

But the boy was there beside me, looking worried. "Did you not like the play, Madame Parr?"

"Please call me Mehitabel," I said. "Or Tabby, if you'd rather. The play was fine. Did *you* like it?" It registered on me as I asked that his face had changed, that the inward, shuttered look was gone and the hazel eyes were full of light.

"Oh yes," he said. "If I join your troupe, will I get to meet them?"

"Them? Oh! Jabez and Levry and Corinna? You'll be working with them."

"Oh," he said, in a sort of a gasp. "You mean . . . there isn't . . ."

"Isn't what?"

He twisted his hands together, looking unhappy again. "At St. Kemplegate, new boys were in one choir and the good singers were in another. And you didn't get to be in the Astrophiel Choir unless you were even better than that. I thought maybe . . ."

"No, no, there's only one troupe here. We couldn't possibly afford more. Do you like comedy better than tragedy?"

"I don't know," he said. "I've never seen a proper play before." And then he smiled, dazzlingly, and said, "But I want to find out."

Mildmay

Felix hadn't said nothing about me and Gideon having been gone. I wasn't all that sure he'd noticed. He hadn't been in the suite when we got back, and when he did come in, he was distracted and unhappy-looking, and he hadn't said much all evening. And him and Gideon weren't real good with each other, neither. I didn't want to know what was going on in their bedroom when I slipped out and headed for the Altanueva, but I did kind of hope it was something, I don't know, nice.

St. Holofernes was old and harmless and mostly forgotten. His special province was protection against the bites of mice and rats. Three guesses how *he* died. His shrine was in a back-hallway, and it was dark and dusty. Which was kind of sad, but also kind of a relief—if, you know, you wanted to meet somebody there and not have nobody know about it.

The secret door was in the back of the shrine. It looked like just decoration, an arch over the old, chipped-nosed statue of St. Holofernes, except that if you pushed down on the head of the mouse peeking out beside his left sandal, the arch would kind of shudder, and then if you gave it a good shove, it would swing open.

I got there about quarter-past, and Septimus was waiting for me, dressed in what would pass for livery if nobody was paying attention, and looking bored. He faked it pretty well, but it was the wrong idea, and I said so.

"What d'you mean?" He wasn't bothering to sound like Keep—like Kolkhis. Which was just fucking fine with me.

"Think it through." That wasn't one of Keeper's. My friend Zephyr had said it all the time. "You're pretending to be somebody who's s'posed to be in the Mirador. Why would you be *here*?"

He just frowned at me.

I rolled my eyes. "If you're meeting here, it's along of it being somebody you ain't s'posed to talk to. And there's lots of reasons that could be, but the one'll make people leave you alone is if you're waiting for a gal."

"Waiting for a . . . oh!"

"Or a boy, if you go that way," I said, to be fair.

"So you mean, I *should* look anxious."

"At least like you want to see whoever you're waiting for."

"Right." And he gave me a look that said as how that for sure wasn't me.

No skin off my nose. I didn't even know why I was bothering giving him advice. Except I hate seeing things done wrong.

After a moment, he said, "So you showed up this time. You must have something."

"That might be putting it a little strong." I told him about the Dogs and the resurrectionists. He asked me to repeat myself so often I figured he was doing it to piss me off. Or, you know, maybe I was mumbling to piss *him* off. Septimus Wilder was reminding me of a lot of the reasons I hadn't liked myself the last indiction or so I was with Kolkhis.

Finally, he said, "So what you're saying is, you ain't learned nothing."

"Pretty much."

"Powers!" he said like what he really wanted to do was punch me. "And you hiked your high and mighty ass all the way over here to tell me all this fucking nothing because . . . ?"

"Didn't want Kolkhis to think I was blowing her off," I said and watched him trying to decide if I was being snarky or not.

"Yeah, well. S'pose if I got to be here *anyway*."

"Now you've got something to tell her." He didn't wince, but he went sort of frog-faced for a second. Yeah, I hadn't figured she'd change.

"I'll be back when I got something," I said. "Practice waiting for a gal."

And, okay, I was being snarky. And I'll even admit I hoped it would sting. But I wasn't expecting him to go off like a firecracker.

All at once, he was up in my face. "Don't you tell me what to do! You ain't my boss, you ain't nobody's boss, so don't you go giving me orders like you owned the world!"

"Kethe!" I broke his hold on my coat collar, pushed him back a couple steps. My cane hit the floor with a clatter, and I realized, about an inch and a half shy of where it'd be too late, that making any kind of a move was going to end up with me down there, too.

We both froze for a moment, Septimus and me. Then I leaned down real careful to get the cane, and said, "Y'know, you want to watch that temper, or Ke—Kolkhis'll have you so you don't know your ass from next Thermidor." I straightened up, got myself braced. "I remember how that goes."

"You don't know nothing about it," he said, but his sneer had a kind of wobble in it.

Powers and saints. "See you later, then," I said. I'd wasted enough time on pissing contests with Septimus Wilder.

He made a noise, like he'd started to call me back before he remembered he didn't want to talk to me anyway.

I just kept going.

Mehitabel

Before I'd turned Semper back over to Jean-Soleil, I'd promised to take him along to the Engmond's Tor Cheaps, where I was headed the next day to buy an assortment of sudden necessities: ribbons to match the dress Corinna and I had chosen, a fan, perhaps a pair of beaded gloves if I could find a bargain. We'd ended up agreeing to go in the morning, early. Waking up, therefore, at seven o'clock, I decided that I did not want to spend the morning alone with Antony's seventeen-year-old bastard half brother; I dragged Gordeny out of bed and made her come with us. She didn't grumble as much as I had expected, either because she liked the Cheaps, too, or because she'd gotten a good look at Semper waiting for us on the doorstep before she got her mouth open. Semper didn't bat an eye at her accent, and my opinion of him went up.

We took a fiacre because I insisted on it. From their different perspectives, neither Semper nor Gordeny saw anything wrong with walking halfway across the Lower City. Gordeny was from the far south of the city, which even I knew was the roughest part; probably walking through Ruthven and Ramecrow didn't seem dangerous at all to her. Semper, on the other hand, when I asked, said that he had been raised in a village called Moldwarp near Copal Carnifex, the seat of Antony's branch of the Lemerii. Semper had lived in Moldwarp until he was seven; then he had been brought to St. Kemplegate, and he hadn't left it until the previous day.

"Didn't you go out at all?" Gordeny said.

"Of course we went *out*," Semper said. Gordeny was only a year or two older than he, and her strangeness was quickly wearing off. "We weren't cloistered monks. But mostly we didn't go out of Shatterglass, except to visit the Academy or to sing in the Mirador."

"Have you been in the Mirador often?" I asked.

"A few times," he said, with a fairly unconvincing attempt at nonchalance. I wondered if the blush was because of his father or because someone had made a pass at him.

"What's it like?" Gordeny said, her eyes big as saucers.

I let him tell her. I'd be just as happy not to be at center-stage all morning, and it furthermore would be all to the good if Gordeny and Semper, our youngest as well as our newest members, could forge some sort of alliance before Drin saw Semper.

What a professional choirmaster describes disparagingly as "a very nice baritone" translates for ordinary people to a lovely voice. For speaking, at least, I didn't think Semper could be faulted. His voice was deep and clear, and his accent, unlike Gordeny's, unexceptionable. Add to that his exquisite bone structure and the grace I had already observed in his movements . . . if the boy had any acting ability at all, Drin would be complaining about upstaging in a week or less. He'd done it to Bartholmew, and Bartholmew, poor thing, had a face like a fish.

You've got enough trouble without going borrowing, I said to myself, and put it out of my mind. That was easy to do, because Gordeny and Semper were both pestering me to tell them more about the bits of Ramecrow we were seeing through the fiacre's windows. I laughed and reminded them I was Kekropian and knew less than they did.

"But you—" Gordeny began and stopped.

"Yes? I what?"

"Nothing," she said, "only I would have thought somebody going out with Mildmay the Fox would know all about the Lower City."

"Really? Why?"

She thought I was teasing her; I could see it in the look she gave me. "I'm perfectly serious," I said. "Why?"

"You ain't never heard the stories?" Gordeny said.

"Grammar, Gordeny," I said.

"Sorry," she said; unlike Mildmay, she cheerfully went back and corrected herself: "I mean, haven't you heard the stories about him?"

"He doesn't tell stories about himself," I said, thinking of the astonishing range of stories I *had* heard from him and how they were all either purest fiction or at least a century old.

"Oh," said Gordeny. "Well, *I* can tell you stories . . . I mean, if you want."

"Please," I said.

So Gordeny told me Mildmay the Fox stories for half the morning, and they were a series of painful revelations. I'd known he was infamous, but I'd always assumed that was simply for the murder of Cerberus Cresset, which had seemed like enough infamy for any three people. Mildmay had somehow never gotten around to telling me that he had been Mélusine's most feared assassin when he was in his teens. It was hard for me, and only got harder, to match up the Mildmay I knew with the stories Gordeny told. He was one of the calmest, gentlest, most levelheaded people I knew, and one of the least violent; I couldn't imagine him killing three men in three different ways in three different districts of the city in one night. Nobody knew, Gordeny said, if it had been one commission or three.

"Why did he stop?" I said finally. We were standing in a fan shop, waiting while the proprietress fetched a selection of painted fans from Imar Eolyth out of her back room. Semper was across the lane, drooling over chess sets.

"Nobody knows," Gordeny said. "Just one day he wasn't there anymore. I dunno, like he got tired of it or something."

"Or something," I said, and the proprietress came back.

Mildmay

Yet another of Felix's meetings that afternoon. I never tried to keep them straight, except to know which days were the Curia. He was twice as likely to pick fights at Curia meetings as at the others, don't ask me why. But this was one of the safe ones, just a bunch of hocuses sitting around talking about hocus-stuff. I'd come to find it kind of nice, actually, because nobody gave a rat's ass whether I was paying attention or not. In Curia meetings, I never dared relax, but here things were pretty much okay. Felix even put his foot down and got me a chair, so I could sit back against the wall and—as far as the hocuses were concerned—disappear. And that was fine with me.

Rinaldo was a member of whichever committee this was, and after the meeting when Felix was gossiping with Orson and Zoë Meredith, he came over to me and said, "I see you are using my cane."

"Yeah," I said and got up, to be polite. "Thanks."

"Jashuki should serve you well, I think."

"Sorry?"

"The *koh*—the guardian spirit. Jashuki's principal domain is friendship, and his prime attributes are courage and loyalty."

"Oh," I said, and looked at the smiling face on the cane again.

"He's also supposed to ward against poison. The islanders of Imar Esthivel say that this includes the poison of slander."

"Thanks, Rinaldo."

"It's what friends do. Help each other."

I felt myself go red and didn't say nothing.

"Keep using the cane," Rinaldo said. Marthe de Croupier was waving at him across the room, and he had to go. "Exercise your leg. And for the sake of Jashuki, remember you are lame."

That last stung, like he meant it to. I watched him waddle off, my fingers running over Jashuki's smiling face like there was some secret he could tell me if only I knew how to ask.

Chapter 9

Mehitabel

Gordeny and Corinna helped me find the dress I needed: heavy tea-colored velvet, its only adornment the pearl buttons down the back and sleeves. It draped me as if I'd been measured for it. I braided my hair back and caught the mass in a lace snood the same color as the dress. The effect was unexpectedly stunning; I looked austere and regal, like an Ophidian queen stepped down out of her portrait frame.

Stephen's butler actually bowed slightly to me this time, almost involuntarily. He handed me over to a footman, who escorted me into a part of Stephen's apartments I hadn't seen before. This room was much larger than the parlor I'd rated on previous visits, and I guessed it was what Keria Gauthy would have called a drawing room. Stephen, standing before the mantel, under a portrait of a dark, square-faced man who had to be his father, Lord Gareth, turned when the footman announced me.

"Every time you come, I have to think of a new adjective," he said. "Tonight you are magnificent."

"Thank you, my lord," I said and swept a low curtsy.

"You're the first to arrive," he said, another of his tiresomely gnomic statements. Was it supposed to be a fact, a warning, or a commendation? I said, choosing brisk rather than nervous, "Who else is coming?"

"No one's going to denounce you as a scarlet woman," he said, perfectly deadpan, so that I couldn't tell whether he was teasing or reassuring me. I let a little exasperation show.

"Sorry," he said. "My sister and brother, Lord Philip Lemerius and his daughter Lady Enid, and Lord Robert of Hermione." I thought of Semper, laughing with Gordeny over our impromptu lunch of sausages and spiced chick peas. Thought of Antony savagely dissecting court mores. Of all the people I didn't want to meet at Lord Stephen's dinner table, Semper and Antony's father was near the head of the list.

"Lady Victoria Teveria," said the footman.

I turned as Lady Victoria came into the room. "Good evening, Stephen," she said. "Madame Parr." She gave me a small, stiff nod.

Victoria Teveria was the eldest of Gareth Teverius's three children. She was taller than Stephen, and they looked very little like each other, except for the gray eyes. Victoria wasn't beautiful, but a stern regularity of feature made her uncompromisingly handsome. The words "stern," "uncompromising," and "regular" also did well to sum up her character. She was a wizard (she, like most of the female wizards of the Mirador, scorned the feminines that people persisted in trying to make up: *wizardess*, *wizardine*, or even just *wizarde*). Her dress was gray and severe, tailored to the point of resembling a military uniform. She wore the gold wizard's sash as the men did, diagonally from right shoulder to left hip. Her rings were made of sapphire and silver; they looked odd and slightly unearthly against her dark, brooding presence.

It was immediately obvious that she wasn't pleased with Lord Stephen, and the cause of her displeasure wasn't far to seek. Lord Stephen just smiled and listened to us talk—or, more accurately, listened to his sister unfurl her flags and make the first maneuvers in what was clearly going to be a very polite and very bloody war. Happily, before she'd found her range, more guests were announced, this time Lord Philip and Lady Enid, and Lady Victoria deserted me for them with only the barest apology.

Lord Philip—and oh the idiocy of the Mirador's peerage, in which the head of a cadet branch of a middle-rank family had the identical honorific to the Lord Protector—was a dull, pompous, closed-minded man. He looked choleric this evening, and I saw him glaring at me over his daughter's head. You are a remarkably black pot, my lord, I thought. And what *will* you think when you learn of your son's new occupation?

This was the first time I'd seen Lady Enid, though Antony had told me about her; she was his youngest sister, and the only unmarried one. She was a pretty girl, much resembling Antony, but without the dour lines that marked his face. She was properly and becomingly dressed in yellow, tall and slender and straight, with bright dark eyes far warmer than those of either her father or her full brother. Her swan-daughter was more natural than mine, the result of careful training rather than deliberate artifice. And as befitted a young and unmarried lady, she was staying quiet and grave and graceful; even when she laughed at some remark of Stephen's, it was a brief, trilling chuckle, as decorous as a laugh could possibly be.

She took her introduction to me gracefully as well, and I suspected she had been coached. Enid was not, of course, permitted to attend the theater, but she had read *Berinth the King* in the classroom, and if I thought there was genuine wistfulness in her voice when she said, "I would have liked to see you perform Aven," it might only have been my imagination.

It did, however, give me an opening. "I would be very pleased to give a private recital, if you'd like."

She began to smile, but then glanced at her glowering father and schooled her face. She was about to refuse when Stephen said, "I think that's an excellent idea."

For a moment, we all stood frozen in tableau, and at exactly that moment, the butler announced Lord Shannon.

"Good evening," he said. "What's an excellent idea, Stephen?"

"Madame Parr has offered to give a recital for Enid."

Lord Shannon's gentle, rather shallow eyes lit up. "What a lovely idea! Might others of us attend if we wished?"

"I don't see why not," Stephen said. "I'll tell Leveque to speak to you about the arrangements, Mehitabel."

"Thank you, my lord," I said, and as Shannon immediately claimed my attention with a question about the recent crisis at the Empyrean, Lord Philip was able to get Enid away without being openly rude.

The room divided itself into two camps, made even more obvious when Robert of Hermione arrived. He barely bowed over my hand before all but attaching himself to Victoria, and thus the schism was complete: Lord Philip and Lady Victoria with Enid and Robert on one side, myself and Lord Shannon on the other. Stephen, a neutral potentate, stood by the mantel and watched with great, possibly malicious interest.

Noticing my appraising glance, Lord Shannon murmured, "You shall be known by the company you keep."

"Indeed, my lord. And how do you choose to be known, then?"

"Not meaning any disparagement, Madame Parr, but I would rather stand with a wolverine in heat than with Robert."

"Gracious," I said, and he smiled at me, such a dazzling brightness that it was no wonder he had half the young men of the Mirador at his feet. No wonder he'd held Felix's fickle attention for nearly five years.

"I don't imagine the enmity between us is any secret."

"No, my lord," I said demurely, and he laughed.

"Besides which, I'd much rather be talking to you than Philip and Vicky."

"And Lady Enid?"

He shrugged, as graceful as any ballet dancer. "She's an amiable child, and I wish Stephen much joy of her."

"You think it's settled then?"

"Oh, I don't know, but if it isn't her, it'll be another just like her. But at least," he added savagely, "it'll put Robert's nose out of joint."

"We should talk of something else," I said.

"Powers, why? Robert knows I hate him."

My curiosity got the better of me. "Couldn't you influence Stephen, if you hate him so much?"

"It was Emily's dying wish. She made him promise."

"To protect Lord Robert?" I looked across the room: Robert was tall for a man of Marathine blood, his hair still dark and glossy, although he'd developed a definite paunch, and the lines of what must once have been a handsome face were sagging and puffy. He didn't look like a man who needed protection.

Shannon sighed eloquently. "Emily was . . . she was very loyal. And gullible. She believed what Robert told her—and what Robert told her was that he had many enemies in the court who were plotting against him. I understand that it preyed on her mind toward the end. So Stephen promised he would protect Robert against his enemies."

"And he kept his promise."

"Teverii. As stubborn as they are honorable and vice versa. And Stephen has his own blind spots."

The bitterness in his voice prompted me to ask, "Do you not consider yourself a Teverius, my lord?"

"Me?" And bitterness indeed, more than I would have expected from a man like him. "I'm as faithless as my mother. You know that."

I couldn't have been more utterly taken aback if the sofa I was standing next to had turned and savaged me. I was fully aware of my own discomfiture, and even as I scrambled futilely for a rejoinder, I was thinking I ought to give Shannon Teverius some sort of award. It had been years since I'd been caught out like this.

And then he was saying, "I beg your pardon, Madame Parr. That was unfair and uncalled for, and in any event, I believe Stephen wants to take you into dinner."

And indeed there was Stephen looming at my shoulder. "Mehitabel?"

"Me, my lord?" I said inelegantly. God, the next thing I knew, I'd be blushing. "Shouldn't—"

"You accepted my invitation," he said and held out his arm.

I had been even more right than I knew. There was nothing else for it: I took his arm as gracefully as I could and moved as a swan-daughter into the dining room.

Felix

Gideon did not want me to go to the soirée.

I asked him why, struggling to be reasonable, and he merely shrugged and turned away.

"Gideon?"

:Is it not enough that I have asked?:

:Well, frankly, no. And it's not like you to try that sort of manipulation, anyway.: He'd been out of sorts all afternoon, sniping at me with more than his usual, amiable venom, goading me into retort time and again—Mildmay had made his escape almost immediately after dinner— and if he'd planned to manipulate me, he wouldn't have gotten my back up so thoroughly as a start. Something had to be wrong. :What is it?:

:I don't imagine you'll care about my reasons. You never have before.:

"Either talk to me or don't," I said, stalking into the bedroom to choose a coat.

:Is there any use? Really?:

"I don't know," I said with exaggerated patience. "Since you won't tell me what you're talking about, I'm hardly qualified to say."

:Don't be disingenuous.:

:I'm not.: I turned to face him, digging my nails into my palms against the urge to strike him or shout at him. :I'm asking you to stop fencing and tell me what the *matter* is.:

:Isaac Garamond.:

:What?:

He held my gaze. :Or whoever it is you'll go off with this time. But most likely Messire Garamond, since he is your newest toy.:

"Gideon, I—"

:Don't think of him that way? Of course you do. How stupid have I been, Felix, to imagine that you think of me in any *other* way?:

:You know perfectly well I don't—:

:I know no such thing! You've certainly never bothered to be faithful to me.:

:It's not like that.:

:I beg to differ. It is *exactly* like that. If I asked, could you even tell me the names of all the men you've slept with in the past two years?:

"Sleeping isn't an activity I engage in with other men, darling," I said, turning back to the wardrobe and yanking out a coat. "And anyway, you've made it perfectly clear what you will and won't put up with, so—"

:Have I? When? When have I ever refused you anything?:

"The look on your face was more than enough, thank you." And the memory still stung like salt on raw flesh.

:So it's my fault? You're going out . . . .:

"Whoring is the word you're looking for," I said and gave him a hard smile.

:Is it? Isaac Garamond isn't a whore.:

"Is that what this is about? You're jealous of Isaac?"

:Blessed saints, am I *jealous*?: His stare was incredulous as well as infuriated. :I'm forty-five, Felix, and apparently inadequate for your sexual sophistication. Why in the world would I be *jealous*?:

"Because you're being stupid," I said, shrugging into my waistcoat and doing up the buttons. "Whatever I do with . . . with other men, has nothing to do with you."

:*Yes, it does.*:

The ferocity of his tone startled me into looking at him; his eyes were brilliant with anger, his hands clenched—he was more vital and compelling than I'd seen him in months. :You may believe it has nothing to do with me, but you're wrong. I am telling you, as plainly as I can, it has everything to do with me, and I can't stand it any longer.:

"You're awfully dramatic," I said, going to the mirror to tie my cravat. I was careful not to meet my own eyes.

:No, don't think you'll slide out from under by making me embarrassed. You love dramatics, and you know it.:

"So what are you leading up to, anyway?" I said, doing my best to sound unconcerned. "Throwing me over?"

:Not unless you make me.:

"I can't *make* you do anything."

:Liar.:

I hoped he couldn't see my flinch.

:I'm telling you,: he said, :if you want me to stay, *you* have to stay.:

"But—"

:Coming back is not the same as staying, and don't pretend you think it is.:

Luckily, Malkar had drilled me in the proper tying of a cravat until I could do it with my mind three-quarters elsewhere. "What is it you want, Gideon?"

:I want you to stop going to other men's beds. Whatever it is you need, let me do it.:

Oh, you *don't* want that, I thought, and did not smile at my reflection. I turned to get my coat.

:All or nothing, Felix. I won't stand for anything else.:

"I hear you," I said.

:And?:

"Now that I have my orders," I said, keeping my voice mild, "I guess I can decide whether to obey or to mutiny."

:That's not what I meant.:

"No? That's certainly what it sounded like." I shrugged my coat on, checked my reflection again.

:Do you truly not care?:

"Of course I care. But you don't understand—"

:Because you won't let me.: He caught my wrist. :Felix, *please*.:

"All right!" I said and pulled free. "But I'm still going to this damned soirée. I promise, however, that I will not come back to anyone's bed but yours. Will that do?"

He looked at me for a long moment. I wondered, as I always wondered, what it was he saw, what it was he thought he loved. Finally, he said, :The sign of a good compromise. We're both angry. Yes, go. We'll get no use out of each other this evening anyway.:

"How right you are," I said and left, slamming the door vindictively behind me.

Mildmay

Saints and blessed powers, we were late. We were so late I damn near told Felix we'd be better off not going, but he was in the mood to rip somebody's head off, and I didn't feel like it needed to be mine.

His mood was Gideon's fault. I don't know what Gideon's problem was that afternoon, but he was pissed at Felix and he wasn't letting go of it, neither. They were sort of snarling at each other all through dinner, and it only got worse when Maurice came in with the hot water and Felix started getting ready.

I got dressed and rebraided my hair and tried to ignore them. But Felix was starting to answer Gideon out loud, and that was a real bad sign. I said loudly, "I'll be out in the hall when you're ready, Felix," and ducked out the door before he could think to stop me. I hated watching them fight, and if I was in the hall, it might maybe give Felix a way to escape quicker.

A quarter of an hour later I knew that idea wasn't working, but it was still better to be out there *not* listening to them. I said hello to a couple of maids trotting past. Another half-hour went by, just me and Jashuki and the weird people in the tapestries on the walls, and then Maurice came up from the other direction. He stopped when he saw me.

"Don't go in," I said.

"Are they, er . . . ?"

"Yeah."

"Damn," he said.

"You in a hurry?"

He shifted his weight. Maurice had never told me where he was from, and I pretended I didn't know. Guys who get themselves into the Mirador from Gilgamesh don't need a blab-bermouth spoking their wheel. Maurice and Rollo were a matched set—tall, broad-shouldered, dark—and they got along okay. I knew they wanted to get into service in one of the Houses, and to do that you got to get yourself noticed by the flashies—which ain't easy to do if you're stuck valeting a wing of the Mirador that's all hocuses.

"Master Architrave said that he'd have some work for Rollo and me if we could get there by eight-thirty."

"Then go."

"What? I can't—"

"Sure you can. Felix won't yell."

He gave me a look like he thought maybe I was nuts. Maurice and Rollo were both in the cult of Felix big-time, and they thought Felix would be pissed off or heartbroken or something if they weren't perfect, but the truth was Felix wouldn't even notice.

"*If* he asks," I said, "I'll tell him you've got a chance at something better. Honest, Maurice, he won't mind."

"All right," Maurice said and grinned like a kid. "Thanks! I owe you one."

"Yeah, sure. Just go on."

He went. I walked slowly down to the end of the hall and back, trying to pay attention to what my right leg was telling me. If I'd hurt myself bad enough . . . Just thinking about it felt like somebody'd stuck me in a cage and was getting ready to close the door. My bad leg had already cut me off from what I'd thought was my life—cat burglary and the Lower City and all the trouble you could get yourself into and out of if you had two good legs. And my stupid, dragging, aching leg already made the life I had now worse, because Felix never could quite remember that I couldn't walk as fast as him. I thought of the staircases to the Crown of Nails and felt like crying. And if I'd really made my leg worse, it was going to get real quick to where I'd have to tell Felix I couldn't keep up with him. And that would mean either that Felix would have to rearrange his life for his stupid, crippled brother or that he'd go off without me even more often than he did now. I hated the fuck out of both options.

I walked down to the other end of the hall and back, slowly. Then I stood and waited and tried not to think about anything in particular. That was getting harder, too.

Felix came slamming out the door at about the third hour of the night. Like I said, he was pissed. He gave me one look, like he was daring me to say something, but I wasn't that dumb. He sort of snorted and started down the hall. I followed, laying odds with myself about how drunk he was going to get.

The closer we got to the Hall of the Chimeras, the slower he walked, and he finally ducked aside into the Puce Antechamber. I went after him like a dog on a leash.

"Is my coat straight?" he said. He was wearing a deep violet-blue coat over a green and white striped waistcoat. The combination made his gold sash and garnet-and-gold rings stand out like a shout. I was in my usual black—trousers, waistcoat, coat—and a plain white shirt. Felix had kept trying for months to get me to wear ruffles at cuffs and collar, but that idea was nuts, and I'd told him to go put garlands on a pig. He'd been mad at me for days, but he'd quit hinting.

"Your coat's fine," I said, "and you know it."

I thought he was going to say something nasty, and so did he, but then he sighed and said, "Yes. What about my face?"

"You're a little pale, but you ain't blotchy. Nobody'll notice."

"With the crush in there, I'll be beet-red in two minutes," he said, and he faked cheerful pretty well. He gave me the once-over. "You'll do. Come on." I followed him back out of the Puce Antechamber and into the Hall of the Chimeras.

We'd missed all the formal stuff, so the Hall of the Chimeras was just a big clump of people talking and drinking. In an hour, they'd clear the middle of the floor, and there'd be dancing. Felix would probably be drunk enough by then to dance, which he was good at if he wasn't thinking about it. I couldn't dance no more, so I'd sit somewhere out of the way and watch all the pretty ladies and wish I could get a game of Long Tiffany going. It was what usually happened.

Powers, I hate this, I thought, and I was only glad that I wasn't Felix and didn't have to smile. Although, if I'd been Felix, I would've been able to get drunk, because I would've known my boring little brother would get me home okay. I don't like being drunk and never have, but at the Lord Protector's soirées, it always seemed like a better deal than being sober. Being at home in bed would've been better still.

Sure enough, when we got to the bar, there were Maurice

and Rollo behind it. Master Architrave had done them a high-class favor, because that was the one place in the Hall of the Chimeras where they were guaranteed the flashies would notice them. They both looked guilty when they saw Felix, like a pair of foxes with feathers in their mouths, but he just said, "Bourbon please. Two fingers, straight."

"Yes, my lord," Rollo managed. As he handed Felix the glass, Felix said, "I'm glad to see you get liberated from our corridor once in a while," and sauntered off into the crowd. Maurice gave me a weird look, sort of half-panicked and half-grateful. I shrugged back and kept after Felix. I didn't want to lose him until he'd found somebody safe to talk to.

He came up on a knot of hocuses talking about Lord Stephen's marriage. We'd missed the beauty pageant, too, which I figured was at least one good thing I'd gotten out of the evening. Andromachy Sain and Elissa Bullen were just disgusted with the whole thing, and this mousy little lady wizard who was a connection of the Tamerinsii was trying to make them see how wrong they were. Fleur and Edgar and Simon were working out a pool. Edgar didn't even say hello before he wanted to know what Felix thought the odds were of Lord Stephen marrying a Polydoria.

"Thousand to one," Felix said.

"Even a pretty one?" Fleur asked.

"Just like his mother?" Felix said and bared his teeth at Fleur.

"Well, they're all cousins anyway," Simon said.

"It would be bad politics," Felix said.

"And Stephen won't do that," Edgar said. "I agree with Felix, little flower."

"Don't call me that," Fleur said. "You know it gives me hives."

"Who are the other candidates?" Felix asked.

Edgar rattled them off: "There's a Valeria, a Novadia, the youngest Lemeria chit, an Otania—horse-faced—a Severnia, and of course the Polydoria. Those are the only real contenders."

"Apparently, you can scratch the Polydoria," Simon said. "That brings it down to five."

"Poor little thing," Fleur said. "She can't be a day over fifteen."

"Then it's a good thing Stephen isn't going to marry her, isn't it?" Felix said.

Fleur said, "Felix, you're such a blight. Pick your favorite and quit sniping at me."

"Oh, the Lemeria," Felix said. "Stephen's thick as thieves with that pompous twit."

Fleur and Simon would keep him from getting in a fight if it could be done at all. I faded back. He'd get annoyed with me if I stuck around too much longer, said he didn't like me breathing down his neck. Of course, it wasn't like I had anybody else I could go talk to, but I think that was part of what pissed him off.

So I did what I'd been getting damn good at and just moved through the crowd. I tried to stay in sight of Felix's red hair, but otherwise I didn't even care where I went. It didn't matter. The trick was to keep people from noticing me particularly. That had been really hard at first, when everybody acted like I had plague or lice or something, but I'd been trailing around after Felix for quite a while now, and I hadn't bit nobody yet. People were getting good at ignoring me, and I sure as fuck wasn't listening to them, just trying to keep moving so I wouldn't have to think.

Finally, my bad leg aching, I stopped and leaned against King Richard's pedestal. I figured a maybe-fratricide was good company for me. That's where Thaddeus found me.

"Mildmay! There you are!" So he'd been looking for me, and that was worrisome for a start. Him and Felix had been friends once, but they weren't no more, so what the fuck did he want with me?

But it wasn't like he'd tell me if I asked, so I just said, "Evening, Lord Thaddeus," and tried to sound more or less like I meant it.

"I've been wanting to ask you—how is Gideon taking the news from the Bastion?"

Like we were all friends or something. "You mean General Mercator croaking?"

"And the promise of amnesty."

He hadn't even looked disapproving at my language the way hocuses always did. He wanted something. I said, careful-like, "Well, he ain't in no hurry to go back."

"No, I'm certain he's not." He tried again. "What has he said about it?"

"Nothing to me."

"But surely you've heard him and Felix discussing it." Bright, bright eyes, like a buzzard waiting for a coyote to die.

"They don't do most of their talking out loud." Which was only sort of true, but it'd do for Thaddeus.

He gave me a look, like he was wondering if I was really that stupid or if I was blocking him on purpose. You go on and wonder, asshole, I thought. I could play this game all night if I had to.

One thing you could say about Thaddeus de Lalage. He wasn't a quitter. He said, quiet and pretending to be casual, "They're all spies, you know."

"Um," I said.

"Eusebian wizards. They can't help it. You shouldn't trust any of those who haven't taken our oaths."

Meaning Gideon, of course, who hadn't taken the Mirador's oaths because Thaddeus had made a ruckus and got half the Curia on his side with it.

Now, I didn't know what Thaddeus's thing with the Bastion was—why he hated 'em so much he couldn't see straight. And I didn't want to know. What I *did* know was about witch-hunts and Keeper teaching us all how to recognize hocuses from the Mirador and what we should do if we saw one. The first thing was to get the fuck out of the way. The second was to run—and when she said run, she meant it—to the nearest hocus we knew and tell 'em to get their head down. Keeper charged for most everything she did in the Lower City, but never for that. And it didn't seem to me like there was enough space between *They're all spies* and *They're all filthy heretics*.

But it also didn't seem like that was a smart thing to say to Thaddeus. So I just nodded and kept my mouth shut.

"Gideon lies like an angel," Thaddeus said, and his hand caught my biceps. Hard. Now, I could've made him let go of me, but that was asking for a whole different kind of trouble, and with Felix in the mood he was in, I didn't think more trouble was what anybody needed. Besides, I knew what the Mirador thought of me. Some days it was like I could feel the smug ghost of Cerberus Cresset padding around behind me, a knife sticking out of his chest and blood all over everything. So I stood there and listened to Thaddeus, knowing he was only talking to me because he didn't dare say this shit to Felix. "It was why Major Goliath valued him so highly. And maybe still does."

He was watching me now, slyly, wanting to see his bolts hit home. Even if I *had* believed him, I wouldn't've given him that, so I just looked back at him. He hadn't actually asked a question, and I wasn't volunteering nothing.

After a moment, he let go of me, almost with a push. "I'm watching," he said, and he was angry, so he must've figured out I was stonewalling after all. "And you can tell him that." He stalked off, as mad as if I'd been insulting his friends instead of the other way 'round.

I reckoned it was a good time to go find Felix. Because suddenly I felt like I really needed just to see him. They were getting ready to start the dancing anyway, and I wanted to be sure my spot on the sidelines would be okay with him. For all that he didn't want me with him, it *really* pissed him off when he couldn't find me. So we went together along the lines of spindly Jecquardin chairs, and I was just about to say, "This one'll do fine," when I realized he wasn't paying attention.

He'd stopped dead in his tracks and was staring at two men arguing a little farther down the line. One was a tallish, heavy-set flashie, with one of them blank well-bred faces that don't mean nothing. I didn't think he could be the one Felix was staring at like a sheep. The other man was clearly one of the fancy hookers who cater to the flashies. If you asked me to explain how it was clear, I don't think I could, but he wasn't a flashie and he wasn't a hocus, and he sure as fuck wasn't an ordinary servant, since the coat he was wearing, mulberry with silver embroidery, cost at least as much as Felix's.

Even at this distance, he looked a little old for a hooker. I was guessing he was Felix's age or better. He was a small guy, no more than five-foot-six, and he looked about as heavy-fleshed as a bird. He'd braided his hair down to the nape and then let it fall to his waist, black as sin. The ribbon tying it was mulberry, too, a couple shades lighter than his coat. His skin was pale, like Kolkhis's, with those cold blue undertones that made her look some mornings like the world's most beautiful corpse. This guy just looked tired. Kolkhis always claimed— and I never had decided if she was joking or not—that her coloring showed she descended from the ancient Emperors of the West.

I was just thinking, Oh come on, Felix, *please* don't know this guy, when the hooker turned away from the flashie, full-face to us. His eye caught Felix's. And then he was staring, just like Felix was.

Felix snapped himself out of it and said, in a perfectly normal, cheerful voice, "Well, I'll be damned. Vincent, is that you?"

The hooker's eyes widened. Then he came toward us. "Felix! Merciful powers, I never imagined I would see you again." He extended his hand. His nails were long and lacquered black, another sign of a high-class hooker.

The two of them shook hands. Then Felix laughed and said, "Damn propriety!" and hugged him. The hooker hugged him back, his eyes bright.

"I thought you were dead," he said to Felix. "I couldn't imagine that you would survive that man."

"I nearly didn't. But what happened to you?"

The hooker sighed, and his shoulders sagged. "It is a very long and boring story and certainly not suitable for a soirée."

"Could you come visit me tomorrow afternoon?"

Shit, I thought. That was his research day, and normally nobody could fuck with that.

The hooker stood and thought it over. "I am in the service of Lord Ivo Polydorius. I would have to ask."

"I could send you a fancy invitation," Felix said, teasing and serious both at the same time, "on my best gilt-edged paper. If I can find it, I'll even seal it with my signet."

The hooker gave him a smile, and for a second he looked way younger. "That would be a great help."

"Done. I'll send Mildmay with it—gracious, my manners! Vincent, this is my brother, Mildmay Foxe. Mildmay, this is Vincent Demabrien. I knew him when we were boys."

"Charmed," said Vincent Demabrien.

"Yeah," I said. Felix kicked my right ankle, hard. "I mean, it's nice to meet you, Mr. Demabrien." We shook hands. I didn't think Mr. Demabrien had missed the byplay, but he didn't say nothing about it. Good manners, anyway.

"I have to get back," he said, with a jerk of his head to where the flashie was standing. "If the invitation arrives before court, I may have time to talk him around."

"Marvelous," Felix said and gave him the full-force, five-alarm smile—not to charm him, but just because he liked him. Felix had never smiled that way at me.

"Honestly," Felix said when Mr. Demabrien was out of ear-shot, "I could get better manners out of a hatrack than I can out of you. Will this chair suit your lordship?"

"Yeah, it's fine."

He swanned off to charm Fleur or Lunette or Andromachy into dancing with him. I sat down and put my head in my hands.

Mehitabel

Perhaps an hour and a half into the dancing, Felix approached me, swept a low, magnificent bow, and said, "Will you dance with me, Madame Parr?"

"I don't know. What's your ulterior motive?"

He laughed. "I want to talk with you. Come on, Tabby, I miss your shining wit."

"My susceptibility to flattery, you mean," I said, and he laughed again. I realized that he wasn't drunk, as I'd initially suspected, simply ebullient. "All right. You win."

Felix was a surprisingly good dancer, as long as you never made the critical error of complimenting him on it. After a moment, I asked, "So how do you come to be on such good terms with Ivo Polydorius's light of love?" That was the question occupying at least half the people in the Hall of the Chimeras; speculation was rampant.

"Don't bother with tact, do you?"

"It'd be wasted on you, sunshine. Come on, spill."

"We were boys together," he said negligently.

Considering what very little I knew of Felix Harrowgate's childhood, that raised more questions than it answered. But he clearly wasn't going to tell me, and in any event I'd just caught sight of Vulpes in the crowd. His spell must have slipped. Got you, you little weasel, I thought, and said, "Felix?"

"In your arms, Tabby."

"Don't look like you're looking, but who's the wizard standing by King Cyprian? The one in the mustard-colored coat?"

"Isaac Garamond," Felix said without looking at all. "Why?"

My heart was suddenly pounding nauseously in my chest. "He's from the Bastion, you know."

"Yes, I'm well aware."

"No. I mean, *from* the Bastion."

"What do you—ah. Should I ask why you know, or why you're telling me?"

"Don't," I said, and I knew he could feel the cold sweat starting on my palms. "Please."

We were silent for several measures before he said thoughtfully, "I'd always imagined you were the type to laugh at a blackmailer."

"It's not me. There's someone . . . someone I love, and I can't . . ."

"You've got considerably heavier cannons than me in your arsenal these days."

"It won't help. I know how Eusebian wizards communicate. And how fast. And it wouldn't take . . ." I wasn't faking my distress, although I was giving into it more than I normally would have.

"You must love this person very much," Felix said.

I couldn't answer that, but said simply, "I can't risk him. Felix, please. I told you because you need to know, but Garamond's only gathering information. Just—be careful what you say to him. And don't tell anyone. *Please*."

"I'm surprised you trusted me enough to tell me," he remarked, that negligent tone again, the one that meant he was hiding pain. "Given my past history."

"I do you the honor of thinking you learn from your mistakes," I said stiffly, matching bleakness for bleakness.

"Thank you," he said, and he sounded like he meant it. Then I felt the sudden increase of tension in all the long bones of his already tense body. "I believe our tête-à-tête, delightful though it has been, is about to be ended. Here comes your swain."

"My . . . oh God, Felix, *must* you?"

He was laughing at me as he released my hands and bowed extravagantly to Stephen. But he mouthed silently, *I promise*, just as he turned away, and even if it was foolish of me, I believed him.

Stephen was in a mood to be possessive; I'd never been danced with so heavily in my life. I wasn't in a mood to put up with it and said, "Surely you don't imagine *Felix* would be poaching on your preserves?"

He snorted. "No, it's only my brother Lord Felix steals."

There was nothing I could say to that; another turn and

Stephen said, "Every damn puppy in the room is making eyes at you."

"They can hardly make anything else," I said reasonably, but that, if anything, seemed to increase his anger. Deliberately, coldly, I imagined telling this glowering bear that I spied for the Bastion because they held the life of the man I loved.

He'd send me to the sanguette. And Louis Goliath would tell Hallam I was dead and watch dispassionately as his grief destroyed whatever was left of him. And nothing in the Bastion would change.

I shook off that future and said tartly, "If you bruise me, my lord, you will be looking for another actress."

That reached him. He said, "Oh—sorry," and his grip eased.

"I accepted your invitation. And your terms along with it." And because the conversation with Felix was still fresh to the point of rawness, I added, "I do have my own kind of honor."

The basilisk eyes caught mine, revealing, as ever, nothing of what Stephen thought. Then he nodded. "I will remember."

We finished the waltz in silence, each alone with our own dragons.

Part Three

Chapter 10

Mildmay

The Polydorius suite was in the Mirador's high-rent district, up there with the Emarthii and the Valerii. The door had their crest carved and gilded on it, a sea serpent all coiled back on itself because the Polydorii claimed descent from the last true king of Cymellune. The gilding looked fresh, and I wondered just how heavily they were all banking on the girl catching Lord Stephen; like Felix said, there wasn't no way she was going to. If there had been an excuse in the world that Felix would have bought, I would've lost the letter, because I didn't want to do this, didn't want it so bad I could taste it, thick and hot in the back of my throat. But nobody particularly cared what I did or didn't want, and Felix had talked at me for half an hour before he'd let me leave, telling me all the things I was supposed to do and all the things I wasn't.

I knocked on the door. It was opened by a liveried servant. I ducked my head a little, the way Felix had told me to, and said, "I have a letter for Lord Ivo Polydorius."

"I beg your pardon?" he said, in the sort of flashie accent that shatters glass.

Fuck. I said it again, slower, and after a second he decided to admit he'd understood me. "Very well," he said.

I handed it over and said, slow and careful, but still mushy, "Lord Felix hopes for a prompt response." It was Felix's phrasing, and I didn't dare change it, because he'd know if I did. Somehow. And it would piss him off, because he was like that.

The servant nodded. I wondered if he'd really understood me or if he just didn't want to stand out here and play charades 'til he did. But the door swung shut and I started away from it, almost wanting to sing with relief, and I figured at least the word "prompt" had probably come out pretty clear, and the rest of it was just sort of padding, anyway.

A voice hissed, behind me, "Mr. Foxe!"

I turned around, way too fast, and had to stagger sideways to keep from falling over. It was Mr. Demabrien, standing in front of a door two doors down from where I had been. He waved me over. He was in a hurry, and as I got closer I could see he was frightened.

"He won't let me come," he said when I was close enough to hear him whisper. "I know he won't, although he hasn't said so yet. But I have a letter for your . . . for Felix." He handed it to me, and I wondered which word it was he'd changed his mind about. "Brother" or "master"?

I stuck the letter in my inside coat pocket, gave him the same sort of nod the servant had given me, and started away. He caught at my sleeve.

Felix is the one who hates being touched, but I didn't want Vincent Demabrien's hand on my arm. I gave him a look, and he jerked back like I'd burned him. "You'll give it to him, won't you?" he asked. "You won't . . ."

"He'll get it," I said. I didn't care if Mr. Demabrien could understand me or not. This time when I walked away he didn't try to stop me.

5ʒ

I didn't give Felix the letter before court because there wasn't time for him to read it, and if he knew about it, he'd just drive me and him crazy by fidgeting while we were supposed to be paying attention. Mehitabel was there, just off the dais, wearing the longest rope of pearls I'd ever seen in my life. I tried not to look at her, but my eyes kept sliding back that way. Let it go, I thought. It turned into a kind of prayer, or something, like the chants that some of the cults use to keep sinful thoughts away. I didn't care if my thoughts were sinful. I just wanted to stop thinking.

I gave Felix the letter the instant we were out of the Hall of the Chimeras. For a wonder, he didn't ask me why I'd waited, and he didn't stop to try and read it right there, although I could tell he wanted to, the way his fingers twitched across the sealing wax.

"He don't think he can come," I said.

"Did he say why?"

"Said his master won't let him."

"He is *not* a slave," Felix said, and I knew I'd hit him on the raw.

"Servants got masters, don't they?"

He pulled himself up short on whatever he'd been going to answer that with, and said, "Let's not fight. Did he give you any reason?"

"Nope." I didn't want him mad at me really, so I said, "He seemed scared."

"Scared?" Felix frowned and quit talking.

We went back to the suite, where there was a letter sealed with the Polydorius crest waiting on the mantelpiece. Felix ripped it open and glared at it. "It does not suit his lordship's pleasure," he said to me and Gideon, "to allow his servants to go gallivanting about the Mirador with persons of questionable morals."

"Um," I said.

"Charming," Felix said. "Let's see what light Vincent's commentary throws on this." He opened Mr. Demabrien's letter and read it, once quickly and then again slower. "Vincent says only that Lord Ivo is jealous and capricious. He says that he will try again when his lordship is in a better humor." He stood for a moment, frowning like a thundercloud, and his hands crumpling and twisting at Lord Ivo's letter. Then he came back to himself and said, "I won't want you this afternoon, Mildmay. Do what you like." He didn't give either of us time to say anything, but was gone almost before the words were out of his mouth.

I shrugged at Gideon. Gideon shrugged back at me. And, well, it'd worked last time, so I said, "Hey, you wanna go to the Lower City with Simon and me?"

And Gideon grinned like a kid.

Mehitabel

"You're *late*, Madame Parr," Jean-Soleil's voice came booming at me from the stage.

I had thought carefully all the way from the Mirador to the Empyrean about how to play this scene, about what I wanted the troupe to know, assume, and conjecture about my arrangement with Stephen. Breezy and self-satisfied, I had decided. A woman who had what she wanted. "Damn. Am I really?"

"I trust you were enjoying yourself, wherever you were."

"Enormously," I said, grinned impudently, and started down the aisle. As a dignified tragedienne, I was supposed to go around the auditorium and make my entrance always from the wings, but even Jean-Soleil wouldn't care about that today. I *was* late. I had promised to be on time for a noon rehearsal, and I'd just heard the bells chime the half hour as I came in through the Paixe Street entrance.

"I'm delighted that you could find time for us in your crowded schedule, madame," Jean-Soleil said, giving me a hand up onto the stage. "I trust we aren't inconveniencing you too greatly?"

"Of course not, messire," I said and swept him a low curtsy.

His mustache twitched, and I knew my new role was working. One less thing to worry about. He turned to the other actors and said, "Now that our Edith has joined us, shall we start from the beginning of Act Two?"

We all shuffled around in our scripts, and I was deeply comforted to feel my normal, daylight life wrapping itself back around me as if I had never been gone.

Mildmay

So the resurrectionists had been interesting, but not, you know, actually very helpful, and I'd been racking my brains—in between getting told off by Rinaldo for being a half-wit dog and avoiding three different fights Felix tried to pick and all the rest of the stuff that made up my life these days—trying to figure out what to do next. Keeper wasn't a patient lady, and if I didn't get her something soon, she was liable to decide it'd be more fun to tell Felix the whole thing. I mean, it wasn't like I was the only goon she could send running around the city. I was just the goon it amused her to play with. Her very own clockwork bear.

And, you know, I probably could've dealt with Felix finding out—he already knew enough bits of it that it wouldn't be the end of the world. I even thought about telling him myself, but I was too afraid he'd forbid me to keep going, and even leaving aside the mystery—and it had its teeth sunk in me pretty good—this was still the only way I could find out who got Ginevra killed. And maybe it was too fucking late, and maybe it wouldn't change how much of it was my fault, and it sure as fuck wouldn't make her love me—but it was the only thing I could do, and the fact that it wasn't enough didn't make a difference.

And the answer had come to me in the middle of the night, the way things do sometimes when you think you're stuck fast and ain't never moving again in this life or any other. So me and Gideon went over to Simon and Rinaldo's suite. When Simon opened the door, I said, "Want to go out?"

"Of course. Where?"

"Havelock. I want to talk to somebody who might maybe still be a friend."

Simon wasn't anywhere near as involved in the running of the Mirador as Felix was. He was ready to go almost before I'd told him what I wanted. He didn't have as bad a time with the cabbie this time 'round. Havelock's pretty respectable. Although I did wonder if the cabbie knew enough to refuse to go to St. Kirban's, which was not only not respectable, but also really unhealthy. Either way, he only grumbled a little about taking us to the Fishmarket. Even people from the Mirador went sometimes, and you didn't have to worry that the cade-skiffs were sizing you up as their next piece of merchandise. They were paid by the Lord Protector himself, whether he knew it or not, and that made them as close to incorruptible as any set of people is likely to get.

Simon paid the cabbie to wait again. I said, "Get your hands out of your pockets." He made a face at me, but he did, and him and Gideon followed me through the colonnade to the Fishmarket's front door. I couldn't remember off the top of my head who put the colonnade up—some flashie with more gorgons than brains who'd lived during the reign of Matthias Cordelius, was all I could get, and that was just from the way the columns, in the Imperial style with the big leaves at the tops, didn't sit right with the building itself. The Fishmarket really did start out as a fish market. They used the Dead Gallery to keep the fish fresh long enough to sell it. Dunno how or why the cade-skiffs got it, back in the day of Cyprian Ophidius, but it still looks like a warehouse and so not very well suited to columns.

The doors had been redone when they put the colonnade in. They were ironbound oak and fucking huge, and if one of 'em fell on you, you'd probably be dead. I didn't have to knock. The right-hand door swung open as we got close, and a tall, dark cade-skiff built like an ox was staring at us. I couldn't read from his face what he thought about us, but I figured it was a good sign he'd opened the door.

I said, "Can I talk to Cardenio?"

"Cardenio?"

"He's still here, ain't he?"

"Yes," he said. "Master Cardenio is here."

Shit. Cardenio is a Master now? And then I thought, Time don't hold still just 'cause you ain't watching, Milly-Fox. Get a grip. "Then can I talk to him?"

"Who should I say wishes to see him?"

I gave him a look, but he was pretending to be stupid.

"Mildmay the Fox," I said. "And these are Lord Simon Barrister and Gideon Thraxios."

"I will see if he is available," the cade-skiff said and shut the door.

"So what weird guild is this?" Simon said.

I reminded myself again that Simon wasn't from Mélusine. "This is the cade-skiffs' guildhall."

"And what are cade-skiffs?" Beside him, I could see Gideon's eyes lighting with interest.

"They're cade-skiffs," I said. "You know."

"No, I don't have the foggiest idea, aside from a guess that they've got something to do with Cade-Cholera and boats."

"Well, there you go."

"What?"

"I mean you got it. Mostly what they do is fish dead people out of the Sim."

"It takes a *guild* for that?"

"They do other stuff, but—"

The door swung open again, silent as death, and I wondered how much oil they went through keeping these monsters in shape. The big cade-skiff said, "Master Cardenio will see you. Follow me."

We followed. I'd been in the Fishmarket, even before I'd had to come identify Ginevra. When you get an assassin job, it generally pays to go eyeball what the cade-skiffs got in the Dead Gallery. I'd saved myself a lot of work a couple of times. Oftentimes people who get one guy mad enough at them to hire them dead, they've got a lot of other people mad at them, too. Sometimes the other people ain't so squeamish. So I knew the big square corridors, the white plaster walls, the flagstoned floor. None of it had changed, and I was in the sort of mood where that was a comfort, even though I knew how stupid it was. The cade-skiffs hadn't done it for me.

Cardenio was waiting for us in the Masters' Hall, which was otherwise just a big room with a long table and a bunch of chairs. The carpet on the floor had been high-quality once, say a Great Septad or two ago, but it was frayed and worn now, with the dye rubbed away in a circuit around the table and a big inkblot right by the door. Cardenio didn't look much different from what I remembered. He was still small and mild, but I would never have thought of calling him a mouse. Something had steadied in him. I thought for a second about the way everybody identified Hugo Chandler as a rabbit first and foremost, and wondered what Cardenio had found that Hugo hadn't.

Then he said, "Hey, Mildmay," just like he always did, and I saw he was still wearing the jade dragon earrings I'd given him.

A big heavy dog jumped off my shoulders, and I said, "Hey, Cardenio. Congratulations on your Mastership. When'd you get it?"

He went a little pink. "Just a few months ago. I'm afraid I ain't what you might call an important person."

"You got time yet," I said.

He went pinker and said, "Will you sit down, you and your . . . friends?"

"Cardenio, this is Simon, and this is Gideon."

Cardenio almost boggled, but he pulled himself together and stuck his hand out. Definitely not a mouse. He shook hands with Simon and with Gideon, and we all sat down around the table. Cardenio said, formally, "What brings you to the guildhall of the cade-skiffs?"

"I need information," I said.

"Information we got. What do you need to know?"

I told him about Jenny, with him listening close and asking me to go back when he hadn't understood something. I was getting pretty good at my spiel, and if I had to tell it many more times, it was going to turn into a story instead of just half a lie. "So if she ain't a resurrectionist," I finished, "I kind of figure she's got to be working for a necromancer, and I was wondering if y'all could tell me which one."

"Why do you want to know?"

Shit. I gave him a glare, and he went pink again, but he didn't back down. "I ain't bringing the Mirador down on anybody."

"Fuck me *sideways*, Cardenio, that ain't what I want."

Simon said, "Should I wait outside?" sounding sort of uncomfortable and guilty, and me and Cardenio fell over each other apologizing to him.

He waved it off. "I promise I won't, er, 'bring the Mirador down on' anyone. I'm mostly doing Mildmay a favor—and your guild fascinates me."

Cardenio perked up. "I could give you a tour. Once I get this thing settled for him. Y'all wait here, okay?"

"Sure," I said, and he went to talk to the other cade-skiffs or whatever it was he had to do. I sat and priced the table and the drapes, just from habit. Gideon and Simon were talking. I knew how that looked.

It took Cardenio a long time. I wondered if he was having to do some fast talking to get anybody else to want to help us. He didn't say nothing about it when he came back, just sat down again and said, "Your friend seems to be working for a necromancer named Augusta Fenris."

"D'you know anything about Mrs. Fenris?"

Cardenio shrugged a little. "For a necromancer, she seems honest and reliable. I mean, she's half-crazy, but they all are. She gets her subjects from the resurrectionists, rather than, um, making them herself. She does divining for us sometimes."

"Does what?" Simon said.

"Identifies bodies. She's pretty good at getting 'em to talk—better than Otto Yarley, for all that he's here twice a decad asking if we need any help."

It sounded like there were a couple-septad worse people Jenny could have fallen in with. "If I wanted to talk to this Fenris lady, how would I go about it?"

"I got her address."

He handed me a raggedy slip of paper and I shoved it in my pocket. "Thanks."

"You're welcome. Anything else I can do for you?"

"No. Mrs. Fenris's name was all I was after."

"Then, if your lordship would like . . . ?"

Simon was delighted and said so, and Cardenio showed us all over the Fishmarket, and answered Simon's questions—and about half of 'em I figured for Gideon's questions. It was nothing I hadn't seen before, of course, but I wasn't bored. I was watching Cardenio, saving up his voice, and the way he smiled, and the way he was happy and loved what he was doing.

When he'd showed us everything the cade-skiffs'll show to outsiders, Cardenio walked with us back to the front door, walking with me this time. He talked about himself, and I knew it was 'cause he didn't want to make me uncomfortable by asking how I was doing. So he told me what his duties as a Master were and how much he liked his job. When we got to the doors, he stopped and looked me in the eye and said, "Are you okay? Really?"

I owed it to him not to lie. I said, "I think I'm getting better."

"That's good," he said. "I mean . . ." And he was blushing, and it was so like old times I wanted to cry.

"Hey," I said. "Nice earrings."

His face lit up. I mean, it was a smile and a half. He said, shyly, "Good luck," and I said, "Thanks," and then I followed Simon and Gideon out to the fiacre. Cardenio stood in the doorway of the Fishmarket, waving, until we were out of sight.

Mehitabel

Isaac Garamond was waiting for me in my dressing room; I didn't even bother wondering anymore how he made his way in and out of the theater. "You must grow here like mold," I said and shut the door behind me.

He said, "Aias Perrault left this morning."

I knew that; most of the court's business had been a tedious ceremonial farewell to Messire Perrault and the small handful of Eusebians who had chosen to return to the Bastion with him. Laurel de Narance and Andromachy Sain had worn matching scowls.

I also knew that Isaac would have seen me in the Hall of the Chimeras that morning—although again I hadn't seen him. He'd slipped up last night, and I wasn't about to tell him so. I folded my arms and waited for him to get to his point.

"My report went with him."

"Messire Perrault works for Louis Goliath?"

"Good God, no! As far as Aias knows, he's carrying a letter from me to Captain Sarpedon. Captain Sarpedon will pass my report on to Major Goliath."

"And what did you report, Lieutenant Vulpes?" I said.

"Precious little. I fear Louis will not be happy with me, even though I promised to hold myself in readiness for a sending." He turned on me with a snarl. "What did you and Felix talk about last night?"

"The Lord Protector's marriage," I lied.

"And what did you and the Lord Protector talk about last night?"

Oh, God, here we go again. I summoned up a half-smirk. "Surely, lieutenant, you do not imagine we wasted our time with *talking*."

He was visibly taken aback; it took him a moment to regroup. "I did not mean to pry into your private affairs, maselle. I merely thought that you might have learned something of interest."

"Not to you, lieutenant," and I did get some small, vicious satisfaction out of watching his embarrassment. I was almost beginning to feel sorry for Isaac Garamond, caught between Felix and Louis. I knew what Louis Goliath's anger was like, and Hallam had told me about sendings, how a powerful wizard could walk in another wizard's dreams. The sendings from his master Octavian d'Armigier had been one of the reasons Hallam had tried to run. When he could no longer tell his own nightmares from Colonel d'Armigier's sendings, his nerve had snapped.

"Well, then, what do you know of Ivo Polydorius?"

"Very little, Lieutenant Vulpes."

He glared at me. "Felix seems to be very familiar with Lord Ivo's protégé."

"Oh, please. The word you want is catamite."

And that flustered him all over again.

"It's common knowledge," I said. I'd heard the story several times—with varying levels of frankness and innuendo—both last night and this morning. "The man's name is Vincent Demabrien. He was a prostitute in the Unicorn's Mirror—it's one of the top-end brothels, about two blocks from here as a matter of fact—and Lord Ivo found him there and, um, bought him."

"*Bought* him? Like a slave?"

"More like than not," I said. Marathines insisted, with great indignation, that there was no slavery in their country, but I couldn't see any difference to speak of between that and the system of contracts and indentures in the Pharaohlight brothels.

"Is that how Felix knows him?"

"I didn't ask," I said quellingly and hid my amusement when it worked. Isaac changed the subject.

"What sort of man is Lord Ivo?"

"I haven't heard anything good about him. He's kept himself and his family sequestered at Arborstell for years and years. He only came back because Lady Zelda is just old enough to be put forward in this marriage nonsense."

"Is that his daughter?"

"Yes. I don't know anything about his wife—if she's here, if she's still alive. I don't *think* she was at the soirée. I'm pretty sure Lionel would have pointed her out to me."

"Why did Lord Ivo leave the court?"

"I don't know. I got lots of conflicting stories about that. Some people were saying he'd quarreled with Lord Gareth, others that his son had bankrupted the family."

"He has a son?"

"Yes. He's here, too. I get the impression Lord Ivo wants him under his eye. His name is Manfred, and he's a friend of Lionel Verlalius's. From what I can tell, he's weak and silly, and Lionel runs with a very expensive crowd."

"Isn't it strange for a nobleman to stay away from the Mirador for so long?"

"There are lots who never come near it, except for the investiture of a new Lord Protector. Many of them don't find the politics worth the expenditure."

"Yes, but if Lord Ivo *was*—"

"Perhaps he and Lord Stephen don't get along."

"Perhaps. But it still seems strange."

"Most things about the Mirador are strange."

"I suppose so," Isaac said, but he still looked dissatisfied as he left.

Mildmay

Simon had things to do, so me and Gideon went back to the suite. Felix wasn't back from wherever he'd gone, and I figured that was okay.

I shut the door. Gideon touched my arm. I looked at him, and he pointed at my leg, and raised his eyebrows.

"It's okay," I said.

He gave me a look, sort of impatient and disgusted, and pointed at my leg again.

"No, really, it's okay. It don't hurt too bad."

He flapped his hand at me, like it wasn't worth arguing about, and pointed me at a chair. I sat down and waited. He sat down across from me and got out his tablet. Wrote a word on it and pushed it across the table.

JENNY?

"You're curious."

He nodded with a sort of apologetic shrug.

"We were kids together. I mean, Keep—Kolkhis ran her like she did me."

He made a *go on* sort of gesture.

"There ain't no more. She started hooking 'bout the time I was getting good at killing people."

He took his tablet back and wrote another word. He pushed it back at me. Now, under *JENNY?* it said: *FRIENDS?* He was good about making the letters regular and not using hard words. It was still a fucking awful way to run a conversation, though.

"Me and Jenny?"

He nodded.

"I dunno. I never liked her much."

He yanked the tablet back and wrote in big letters: *WHY?* And he jabbed with his stylus more or less in the direction of the Lower City.

"Can you explain everything *you* do?"

He shook his head, but the way he kept his eyes on me told me he wasn't letting me off the hook.

I wasn't getting into the whole thing about Ginevra and Keeper with him. And even if I didn't like it, there was another side to the thing. Because I kept thinking about Jenny being in the Kennel, and it wasn't making me happy, neither. So I said, "Maybe 'cause there's so few of us left. I mean, there's Margot, and she hates me, and there's Jean-Tigre, and he don't know me to spit on me no more. Lots of 'em I just lost, and the rest are dead. So it's like I can't just pretend Jenny don't exist, 'cause I remember her when we were little and we worked together."

He nodded. He seemed to understand what I meant.

I'd been meaning to tell him about Thaddeus anyway, and now seemed like a perfect fucking time to distract him away from me. I said, "I mean, that don't work for everybody. You and Thaddeus were kids together, weren't you?"

He nodded, but his face went wary.

"He, um, said some stuff at the soirée."

Gideon fished a piece of paper out of his pocket and pushed it across the table. This one was one of his savers—the things he would've been writing so often it made more sense to just keep 'em—a little square with a big question mark on it.

"Same old. About you being a spy."

Gideon made a face.

"Well, you know, I don't think he really believes it, or he wouldn't be saying it to me. I mean, of all the people he could pick. But he *is* saying it." I looked at him, wishing I had a better idea of what happened in his head. "He don't seem to like you very much."

Gideon thought that was funny. He didn't really laugh anymore—he wouldn't open his mouth—but you knew when he was laughing just the same.

"Felix says Thaddeus helped you get to the Mirador."

Gideon shrugged widely and then nodded.

"You got something on him."

He grinned at me. It was a sharp, nasty grin. Mute or not, Gideon wasn't somebody to fuck with. I had to remind myself of that every so often, because it was easy to be sorry for him and forget just how hard he could bite if somebody pissed him off. Him and Felix were well matched.

"He ain't a spy, is he?"

He shook his head.

"Then it ain't none of my business, I guess," I said. "But if you got a leash on him, you might want to give it a yank."

Gideon waved that away.

"You sure?"

Gideon nodded.

"Then I won't ride you about it. But Thaddeus'll do you a mischief if he can."

Gideon shook his head, and I knew what he meant: *He can't.*

Felix

Finding a copy of Ezrabeth Ynge's *Influence of the Moon on the Energy of Souls* was simplicity itself compared to some of the treasure hunts I'd gone on for Gideon. It had taken me over a month and visits to three different booksellers to replace the copy of Chattan d'Islay's *A Treatise upon Spirit* he'd lost in Aiaia, and I wouldn't have found Edmond Sang's translation of Matthew Nausikaaïos's *Psukhomakhia* at all if I hadn't quite literally fallen over it in the Archive of the Seven Queens. The Ynge only took me the better part of an afternoon.

I found it in the Starlings' Archive, up under the roofs of the Tiamat. The reek of smoke lingered, even three years on, and the carved pillars were blackened, although I saw no signs that the fire itself had reached this far. I had to make a conscious effort not to hold my breath as I scanned the shelves, and when I saw the Ynge, wedged among a collection of almanacs from western Tibernia, I grabbed it and frankly ran—three flights down and two hallways south to the Archive of the Chamberlain, where I could no longer smell old smoke, no longer hear the echoes of Malkar's laughter still dying in my ears.

The *Influence of the Moon on the Energy of Souls* was also smoke damaged, the edges of the pages crumbling to the touch, but the text was undarkened and the binding still held.

I didn't have time to read it properly—Gideon would no doubt imagine I was out propositioning half the Mirador if I was late for dinner—but I skimmed the exordium and flipped through the body of the book, reading the chapter headings and examining Ynge's diagrams. She *was* using "noirant" and "clairant" at least in part to talk about necromancy and the dismantling of its workings; that much I could tell at even a cursory glance, and I took the book with me when I went back to my rooms, stopping along the way to leave Giancarlo a note that the cost of a four hundred twenty-nine page octavo volume published in Ormaut should be deducted from my stipend. The privilege was one I was careful not to abuse, but the state of the Starlings' Archive showed plainly enough that no one would miss any of its books.

Gideon greeted me with a scowl, which lightened quite perceptibly when he saw the book in my hand.

:No,: I said, :I was *not* indulging in an afternoon assignation, with Isaac Garamond or anyone else.:

:I didn't think you were. But I've noticed how careful you're being not to be alone with me since last night.:

:Less than twenty-four hours hardly constitutes evidence of anything,: I said, more sharply than I meant to because he was right.

:Don't forget that I know you,: he said, and I irritated myself immeasurably by blushing.

Dinner was not a comfortable meal, and afterward, Gideon said bluntly, :Let us adjourn to the bedroom.:

I could think of few things I felt less like doing. But I could not say so. It was so rare for Gideon to instigate sex, and after the fight we'd had before the soirée . . . I couldn't reject him.

I put the Ynge aside and followed him into the bedroom.

We undressed in the dark and lay down together. I spun the foreplay out as long as I could; Gideon loved kissing, loved having my tongue in his mouth. I found the sensation more disturbing than erotic, and if I sometimes imagined what it would be like to have his mouth, that warm wet emptiness, engulfing my sex, I never said so. Gideon was not a whore, to make such cruel demands of. But still, I would kiss him for as long as he wanted.

But he was also intensely self-conscious about his desires—embarrassed by them. I had tried, once, to tell him he shouldn't be; he had told me furiously not to patronize him. I had not mentioned the matter again except, of course, when we fought.

So I didn't demur when he pulled away, although I was still not aroused. I moved down the bed. He was only half-hard, but he responded well to my mouth and fingers. My own body remained sluggish; even a calculated, clandestine brutality got no more than a flicker. With the right erotiques, I might have been able to remedy the problem, but I kept no such toys. I had not, I thought bitterly, anticipated the need.

I would not be able to sustain the active role tonight. I drew back, lay down on my stomach beside him, deviating from our usual practice, a series of actions as formal and measured as a ritual, and felt Gideon's surprise, even before he spoke.

:Felix?:

All the words I knew for this were ugly.

I said, :You wanted . . . more. More of me.: I reached, found his hand in the darkness, placed it on my left buttock. Surely that was explicit enough, invitation enough.

But Gideon did not move. After a long, deathly pause, he said, :Why now?:

:What?:

His fingers tightened, very slightly, forbidding me to move. :We've been lovers for two years. Why *now*?:

:You said—:

:*This*,: he said, with a stinging slap to my haunch as he released me, :isn't what I meant, and you know it.:

"You don't want me?"

:That's not the point here.:

"Oh, I don't know," I said, sitting up. "Seeing as how we're *in bed together*, I think whether you want me or not might be very much to the point."

:No, the point is whether *you* want *me*.: I flinched away from his hand cupping my genitals. :You don't, do you?:

"Gideon, it's not—"

:Oh, but it is. *Darling*.:

I snarled back, "Well, forgive me for not finding self-sacrifice arousing."

:What's *that* supposed to mean?:

I got up, called witchlight in a hard glare, dragged on my dressing gown. "It's not like you've taken any particular pains to hide the fact that you'd rather read Coeurterrene theory than come to bed with me.:

:And how am I supposed to feel, sharing you with—Felix! Don't you dare walk out in—:

I slammed the bedroom door open.

On the other side of the sitting room, Mildmay startled so violently that a half-finished layout of the Queen of Tambrin cascaded gracefully to the floor.

"Come on," I said.

He'd already been halfway to his feet, but he froze, staring at me. "Where?"

I bared my teeth at him in a hard, savage smile. "The Crown of Nails. Now."

:Felix!:

I ignored Gideon; Mildmay picked up his cane and said, "You catch the Winter Fever and die, don't blame me."

"Oh, I won't." I called to Gideon, "Don't wait up, darling," and set out into the Mirador. If we happened to meet anyone, that would be their problem.

Mehitabel

I dined with Stephen. Ironically, we were more awkward now than we had been before we'd entered into the formal agreement. I was second-guessing everything in sight, unable to tell what Stephen wanted from me—bright chitchat or compliance with his taciturnity? For his part, he seemed to feel he no longer needed to act as my host; although he responded to my gambits, he made none of his own, and his answers were terse.

Dispirited and uncomfortable, I gave up, and we finished dinner in silence.

He seemed to come awake as he poured brandy, and said, "I told you, I think, that as my lover, you're expected to make your residence in the Mirador."

"I remember."

"At my expense. There's a suite. Tradition, and all that."

"Of course there is."

"Would you like to come look at it? You don't have to stay there, if you don't want to."

"Actually, I would like to see it. I'm curious."

He handed me a brandy snifter and said, "This way, then. Hemminge has the keys."

Hemminge was Stephen's butler; he had a branched candelabra as well as the keys, and he led the way, not back out to the public hallways, but through a side-door into a maze of narrow corridors.

"Where are we?" I said.

"Good question," Stephen said, and to my astonishment, kept talking. "There aren't any maps of this part of the Mirador. We think one of the Cordelius kings must've had them destroyed. Paranoia." He stopped at a T-intersection; Hemminge obediently paused as well. "My father's suite is down that way," Stephen said, gesturing to the right with his snifter, "along with my mother's and Gloria's. The nursery of the Cordelii is somewhere under our feet. I'll take you to see Grendille Moran's suite some other time. I don't like to go there at night."

"Who's Grendille Moran?"

"Come this way," he said, and started walking again. "It isn't far. Grendille Moran was one of the court poisoners. Reigns of Laurence and Charles. She probably poisoned Laurence. And then a few years later, her maid found her decapitated on the floor of her sitting room. Whoever did it took the head with them, but it was found about a week later somewhere unlikely—I can't remember where."

"What a charming story," I said, and got a grin for my irony.

"Mirador's full of 'em," he said. I remembered Mildmay saying something similar. "Here we are."

Hemminge had to wrestle a little with the lock, and the hinges groaned when he pushed the door open.

"No one's been here in years," Stephen said. "Gloria was never here . . . I think the last person to live in this suite must have been my great-great-grandfather's lover. Can't remember her name."

"And no one's been in here since?"

"Well, my great-grandmother, Helen, hated her father's lover—Sophia, that was her name, Sophia Vesperia—and she threw Sophia out when Malory died. She used it as a sitting room for a while. And it gets aired out once a year. Go on in."

The weight of history in the Mirador rarely bothered me, but Stephen's casual familiarity with the doings of a woman who had died more than a century before his own birth was uncomfortable in a way Mildmay's stories never had been. It could be worse, I told myself. He could have picked Grendille Moran's suite. And I walked through the door.

I had more than half expected to hate it, although I wouldn't have said so. But the suite was charming.

All the furniture had been taken out, so there was nothing to observe but the shape of the rooms and the beauties of the parquet floor. The first room was octagonal; the ceiling arched into a miniature vault on which someone had painted a night sky, complete with accurate constellations.

It was a larger suite than Felix's, with a room on each side of the octagonal one, each with another room beyond it, and a third room opposite the door to the hall, exactly the width of the wall. I looked at Stephen. "Closet? Or oubliette?"

"Anything you like it to be," he said. "You can have carte blanche."

"How blanche?"

He raised his eyebrows at me. "I'm friends with Phegenie Brome," I said, "and I've seen what happens when Lord Edmund gives her carte blanche. I don't intend to behave like that, thank you very much."

"I'm glad to hear it," he said.

"You should be. So what do *you* mean by carte blanche?"

"Don't decorate in cloth-of-gold."

"That's it?"

He shrugged a little. "You've got good taste, if your clothes are anything to go by. Use it."

Absurdly, I was flattered.

Mildmay

I knew—I'd learned the hard way—that the only way to do something that scares you is to just go up to it and *do* the fucker. You don't want to pussyfoot around looking for the right angle and the right kind of light and all that other shit. That's just excuses not to do it, and if you give into enough of 'em, sure enough, whatever it is, you ain't gonna be the guy doing it. And mostly that's worse than just going and doing it when you got the chance.

So we're up on the Crown of Nails in the middle of the night, me and Felix, him in nothing but his dressing gown but not even seeming to feel the wind, pacing up and down and kind of growling under his breath, and me just standing there, saying goodbye to my chances of getting over to St. Holofernes tonight, and it hit me that we were never going to get more private than this. And the thing about Felix and his temper was, if you could keep him from turning on you and mauling you half to death, his armor was already down, and *if* you could get through to him, he'd hear what you were trying to say.

So, after a while—dunno, maybe a septad-minute—I said, "Felix?"

"Mildmay."

"Can I, um, talk to you?"

He stopped pacing, looked around in a *what the fuck?* sort of way. Shoved his hair off his face and gave a kind of raspy little laugh. "Well, it's not like I've got anything *better* to do. What is it?"

I took a deep breath, although it didn't seem to do me no good, and said, "I'm worried about you."

He waved it off. "Gideon and I are just having—"

"Not that."

Witchlights are crap for actually seeing anybody by, so I couldn't make out his expression.

"Then what?"

"Well, I mean . . ." And then I thought, fuck this for the Emperor's snotrag, and just came out with it. "You're drinking. And you're fighting—not just with Gideon. And it's ugly. And you ain't talking to me no more. And, well, I'm worried about me, too."

I think it was the last one that brought him up short. He'd've laughed off me worrying about him—and done it in a nasty way so as to be sure I'd never bring it up again—but I threw it back on myself before he could, and that meant he thought before he opened his mouth.

"Why are you worried about yourself?" he said.

"I been pretending—I think maybe we both been pretending—that I ain't lame, not really, I mean, not to matter, but we can't go on pretending that."

I stopped, hoping he'd want to say something there, but he just said, "Go on."

"So I was thinking about that, and then I was sort of thinking about all the *other* things you and me pretend, about how there ain't nothing wrong with me, and there ain't nothing wrong with you, and I thought how maybe we really needed to quit pretending about all of it. And you must think so, too, 'cause you were trying the other night."

I stopped again, but he was just staring at me now, spooky as fuck in the witchlights, like he'd never seen me before.

"We're brothers," I said, like I was wrenching my heart out of my chest. "We should help each other. I don't know if I *can* help you, but I want to try. And . . ." I stopped and took another huge breath, "and I think I need your help, too."

After a long, long silence, he said, "How long have you been working out that little speech?"

I couldn't make out his tone or his expression. "Dunno, exactly."

"You're very eloquent. I hadn't expected it of you."

Why the fuck had I even bothered? How many times do you got to be kicked, Milly-Fox? "Yeah. Funny, ain't it."

"I didn't mean that." He didn't sound amused or defensive—either one would have meant he was lying. He just sounded sad. "I was serious. I hadn't expected you to be able to speak so eloquently. This suggests, I suppose, how little I know you. Do you think we *can* talk to each other, Mildmay? For myself, I fear that we cannot."

"Why not?"

"What common ground do we have? What do we share?"

"The binding-by-forms," I said. It made him flinch.

"That's unnatural," he said. "Forced intimacy means nothing. I ask you again: what do we share?"

"How'm I s'posed to answer that? I mean, no, I ain't like you. I ain't a hocus and I ain't educated or nothing, and I don't understand most of the stuff you talk about with your friends. But is that it? Ain't there nothing but magic and words?"

"Sex," he said tiredly. "It's the only other thing I know. But you don't want that from me."

"No," I said. Because I didn't.

"So what else is there? What alternative do you suggest?"

"*I don't know.* I ain't the smart one. And maybe I am too fucking dumb for any of this to work, but could you just fucking *try*?"

I'd lost him somewhere. The shutters had come down across his face. He said, "I will consider what you've said. We'd better go in."

I followed him, and we didn't say nothing more all the way back.

🜂

My dreams that night were something else. Ginevra and Strych standing together in the Bastion, watching Felix cut lines in my skin. Felix had that awful, fiery look he got on his face when he was working hard magic. And I knew in the dream—the way you do—the magic he was working was going to bring them back to life, and I kept trying to tell him not to, that it wasn't worth it, but no matter what I said or screamed, he didn't seem to hear me, or even know it was me.

I was so glad to wake up I could've cried.

I lay there for a while in the dark, but the thing I can't do when I wake up like that is get back to sleep. I'm always afraid the dream will come back and find me, and I didn't want to dream about Strych no more. Or Ginevra. So I lit the lamp and got up and got dressed and went out into the sitting room.

Felix was sitting there, in his chair by the fire, staring at a spread of the Sibylline he'd laid out on the side table. He didn't look like he'd slept. I startled back, like he was a snake or something, and damn near dropped my cane. He raised his head, but didn't say anything, just sat there and watched me.

"Good morning," I managed to say finally.

"Good morning," he said. No inflection, no smile, no clue what was going on behind his spooky eyes.

"You're up early," I said.

"Yes," he said.

By then I had a hold on myself, enough not to go on babbling like a fool since it was clear he wasn't going to help out none. I sat down in the other armchair, got my foot up on the footstool— it made things some better—and waited. If he wanted to say something to me, he would, and if he was out here looking like leftover death for some other reason, then he wouldn't want to talk to me anyway.

After a long silence, he said, "Do you remember Methony at all?" He was staring into the fire, like he didn't want to look at me.

"No," I said.

"I do, a little. I wonder what she would think of us."

"Prob'ly that we're both wicked sinners. I mean, based on my name."

"Your name?"

"Powers, ain't I told you that? She named me Mild-may-your-sufferings-be-at-the-hands-of-the-wicked. She was in some kind of a cult."

"Methony?"

"Yeah."

"Named you *that*?"

"Yeah. Kolkhis axed it, first thing."

"I can't say that I blame her. Methony must have been out of her mind." He was finally smiling a little, and I was glad to see it.

"Yeah, well. But that's all I know about her, except that we both look like her."

We were quiet for a while until he said, "Do you remember anything about your childhood before your keeper bought you?"

"Not really. I mean, I think I sort of remember the brothel, but it's just colors. I remember sitting on a wooden floor with a toy duck on wheels. But that's it. No people or nothing." I stopped and got some courage together and said, "Do you?"

"A little," he said. "I remember her singing to me. And the other girls liked me, I think. I remember feeling, I don't know, *cherished*, as if everywhere I went, I would be safe." He shook his head. "Madame Poluphemie cherished no one."

We sat there for another while, and he said, I think more to himself than to me, "Those memories get very hard to find. They're so thin and fragile and small, and the other memories are so strong. I'm almost afraid to look at them, as if they might disintegrate under the weight of my gaze or get contaminated by other things. But perhaps that's foolish."

"I dunno," I said.

"Neither do I, more's the pity." He sighed, and then I could see him throwing the mood off, like it was a coat he'd decided didn't suit him. He said, "I'd better go change," and left the room. I sat and waited and wondered if maybe that conversation meant he'd decided he didn't have to fuck me to know me after all.

Mehitabel

Stephen's steward Leveque had a suggestion.

He came in while I was pouring a last cup of tea before taking myself back to the Empyrean. I wasn't attending court. I had told Stephen so, emphatically if not defiantly, and he'd just said, "Powers, I wish I didn't have to."

So I was in his private dining room, wearing a ridiculous trailing lacy wrap over my shift. Stephen had given it to me, almost shyly if you could say that about a man of his temperament; it occurred to me that he'd probably sent Leveque out to buy it.

Leveque was a smallish man, wiry, dark, Mélusinien to his bones. He had the ability I'd noticed in other liveried servants in the Mirador, to make it plain he wanted to talk to you without so much as clearing his throat. Some of my lovers had ignored that with the arrogance of men born to privilege. I set my teacup down and said, "Yes?"

Leveque gave me a nod and said, "His Lordship said as how you'd be needing a maid."

"Yes, I suppose so. Did you have a suggestion?"

He coughed a little, nervously. "Not so much a *suggestion*, miss, as maybe a request?"

Doing Stephen's steward a favor could only benefit me in the long run. "What is it?"

"Well, you see—" Oh, he was uncomfortable. "I have a kind of agreement with one of the brothers at St. Crellifer."

I was irresistibly reminded of Jean-Soleil and the prior of St. Kemplegate. "Go on."

"When Torquil has someone he thinks might be able to cope with service here, he lets me know, and if I've got anything . . . It's worked out so far."

"So you're doing this Brother Torquil a favor," I said cautiously.

He shrugged it off. "It doesn't hurt anything. And they're good workers. Don't want to go back, do they?"

I thought of the little I'd heard about St. Crellifer's, most of it bad. "I can't blame them. And you think Torquil's latest might suit me?"

"She was apprenticed to a modiste, Torquil says."

"And she's not likely to take after me with a cleaver or anything?"

Leveque looked horrified. "Even if Torquil would, miss—which he wouldn't—I would *never*—"

"No, I'm sorry. I shouldn't have said that. If you think she'll do, I've no objections."

"You could meet her first, miss, if you wanted."

"At St. Crellifer's?"

He looked horrified again. "Powers, no. She's waiting outside. If you want."

"Bring her in," I said, since there didn't seem to be much alternative. And I was curious.

Leveque slipped back out through the servants' door, and reappeared in a moment, ushering in a young woman dressed with painfully respectable neatness, tall and without enough flesh on her long-boned frame, but with lovely skin the warm color of bronze and great luminous dark eyes. She didn't look mad, although she didn't meet my eyes, nor, indeed, look any higher than my collarbone.

"This is Lenore Nevillson, Miss Parr."

"Miss," Lenore said, in a frail, half-drowned voice, and

dropped a curtsy. She did it easily, gracefully, and I could see that she would do well answering my door, fetching and carrying, which was all I needed a maid for. Appearances.

"It's fine with me, Leveque," I said. "Honestly."

"Good," said Leveque. "I'll get her on the rolls. When would you like her to start?"

"Tonight," I said. And had to swallow hard against a sudden choking feeling. "I'm moving into the Mirador tonight."

Mildmay

More meetings that afternoon. I wondered sometimes how Felix kept track of them all, but we didn't talk about hocus business. I think he felt like it would be betraying the other hocuses if he told me what he really thought of them. I'd also wondered why he put up with it all, but I thought that afternoon that maybe I knew the answer to that one. I mean, whatever else you could say about the way Felix and the other hocuses got along, they knew what he was worth to them. Now, personally, I thought that was a shitty replacement for being cherished like he'd talked about, but Felix wasn't very smart about stuff like that sometimes. I'd seen that in the Gardens of Nephele, the way he didn't seem to want to see the difference between people liking him for himself and liking him for other reasons. I didn't think that Felix had had a lot of practice at being liked for himself. It wasn't something Strych would have taught him.

Mr. Garamond bounced up again out of nowhere after the committee meeting. They talked for a little bit, and then Felix said, "All *right*, Isaac. Mildmay, we're invited to dinner."

Mr. Garamond looked taken aback, but I could see Felix daring him to say he hadn't meant me.

"You don't want me along," I said.

"Nonsense," Felix said. "Isaac is forever telling me he wants to get to know you better, aren't you, Isaac?"

I didn't like Mr. Garamond, but I wanted all of a sudden to get him aside and tell him not to play Felix's games. You couldn't *ever* win. But Mr. Garamond didn't seem to have picked up on that. He pulled a smile together from somewhere and nodded and said, "I shall be enchanted to have your company, Mr. Foxe."

"That's settled then," Felix said. "Shall we say eight? Splendid. We'll see you then. Come on, Mildmay."

Powers. I'd rather eat soap. I went after him, wondering if even that would be a good enough excuse for Felix. Probably not.

Felix

I had known Gideon would be incandescent with jealousy, and I bore his tirade as long as I could. But finally, I said, "*He invited me to dinner.* What was I supposed to do, tell him my lover won't let me go?" Gideon didn't dignify that with a response, which had been my intention. Anything to get him to shut up.

Mildmay was next, trying to weasel out of accompanying me. I had no intention of going without him—it would serve Isaac right—and was on the verge of warning him that I would invoke the obligation d'âme if I had to when I saw Gideon catch his eye, and Mildmay subsided.

That was how it was, then.

Very well.

I dressed with particular care, collected Mildmay without a glance in Gideon's direction. Mildmay trailed me like my own black thundercloud of disapproval to Isaac's rooms, where he sat wearing the dullest look in his arsenal like a shield. It infuriated me, that he would not even *try*, that he sat there and glowered and gave Isaac no reason to think him any brighter than a dray horse.

Not that I cared what Isaac Garamond thought, but he was one of those men who considered themselves far smarter than anyone around them—far smarter than they actually were—and I wanted, savagely, to see him taken down in his own estimation. His attempts to manipulate me were childish, his attempts to seduce me laughable. I had let him do it, partly out of curiosity, partly because it was such a relief to be able to have sex with—to *fuck*, to use the ugliest word I knew—someone for whom I did not care in the slightest. The martyrs in the Arcane deserved my attention and mindfulness. Isaac Garamond did not. I could be myself with him in a way I never could with Gideon—Gideon, who claimed he did not want to change me, but who would not accept me as I was.

And now, with Mehitabel's information that Isaac was spying—or trying to spy—for the Bastion, I no longer even needed to wonder what it was he wanted, for surely I had never in my life seen a man more inept at seduction, or one who desired

less my company in his bed. I had taken a great, perverse pleasure in submitting to him—*exactly* in the sense Gideon meant—
when he'd clearly expected to have to debase himself for me, an
even greater pleasure in making him *want* me, making him beg,
making him climax. I smiled at him over my wineglass, watched
him lose the thread of his conversation.

And still Mildmay sat there like a block of stone, as if he
couldn't even be bothered to admit I was in the same room with
him.

I could change that, I thought, and let my smile sharpen.

Mildmay

Felix said, out of fucking nowhere, "Mildmay, Isaac wants to
know more about the witch-hunts."

"What?" I said. They'd got to the brandy stage, and I'd relaxed a little, thinking that things were nearly over, so he caught
me completely flat-footed. I'm sure he meant to.

"I'm really very interested," Mr. Garamond said.

I looked at Felix.

"I thought," Felix said, "since you've said so many times that
I don't understand them, that you would prefer me *not* to explain
them to Isaac."

Sure you did, you prick.

"What d'you want to know?" I said to Mr. Garamond.

He laughed a little, but I wasn't sure whether it was at himself or at me. "They really happen then? The Mirador hunts
wizards in the streets of the Lower City?"

"And the Bastion don't hunt down hocuses and kill 'em?"

"But those are traitors." After a second, his face turned an
ugly dull red. "Like me."

"Yeah, well, that's what the Mirador says about the nature
witches in the Lower City."

"That they're traitors?"

"Close enough."

He looked at Felix. Felix smiled and shrugged.

I said, "The Mirador don't like hocuses who don't do as
they're told."

"But what are these nature witches doing?" Mr. Garamond
said.

"I ain't a hocus. Don't know."

"They're practicing blood magic," Felix said, like a dagger sliding between my ribs, and made me admit I did know after all.

"No, they ain't. They just ain't practicing your kind of magic, is all."

"Some of them follow Eusebian precepts," Felix said. I couldn't tell whether that was aimed at Mr. Garamond or me, but I think it hit both of us.

"Why does the Mirador fear them?" Mr. Garamond asked.

"We don't fear them," Felix said, lazy as a cat with its claws sunk in a half-dead mouse.

"But then why . . . ?"

I said, at Felix, "It's heresy, ain't it? That's what you do with heretics. You hunt 'em down and burn 'em."

"Blood magic is a terrifying force for evil," Felix said in this nasty, prim voice like he was a witchfinder himself.

"There ain't no blood magic in the Lower City. There was only Vey Coruscant, and nobody ever came after her anyway."

"What about Celeste Clovis? Benedick Humphrie? Zephyr Wolsey?"

"Zephyr Wolsey wasn't no blood-witch."

"Surely you are forgetting the evidence at his trial."

"I wasn't *at* the trial. But he was a friend of mine, okay? Quit baiting me."

Felix laughed. "You see what a dreadful person I am, Isaac? I can't have so much as a simple disagreement with someone without *baiting* them."

"Dreadful," Mr. Garamond said, and they smiled at each other.

"You can't disagree with anybody without turning it into a war," I said. I knew I should've kept my mouth shut—I'd gotten off pretty light, considering—but I just couldn't lay down under it no more, not in front of Mr. Garamond.

"A violent metaphor," Felix said. "I begin to be frightened of myself."

"Maybe you should be."

"Should I? And why would that be?"

I looked at Mr. Garamond, but he wasn't going to help. He was just watching, his eyes bright and greedy.

"'Cause you do things like this," I said. My eyes were starting to get hot, and I knew Felix would be able to hear how upset

I was. "'Cause you're a prick for the fun of it. Can't you just leave me alone?"

"But you said you wanted us to talk more. When I try to talk to you, you just tell me to leave you alone. What am I supposed to do?"

"If this is your idea of talking, it ain't worth the bother. Just treat me like a fucking dog and be done with it."

Felix opened his mouth and closed it again. You could feel what he had almost said in the air, like the smell of smoke. He said, "Suppose you go on back to the suite."

My heart skipped a beat because I'd heard the Lower City in his voice, plain as plain could fucking well be.

"Okay." I stood up, grabbed my cane. "My lord," I said and bowed to Mr. Garamond, even though he wasn't a lord and didn't rate it. Then I limped to the door.

As I was leaving, Felix said, "Don't wait up."

I walked back alone.

When I came in, Gideon looked up from a diagram he was making with three different colors of ink. His eyebrows went up.

"Yeah," I said. "He sent me back."

Gideon pointed at the chair opposite him. I didn't want to be alone. I sat down.

Gideon made a kind of *come on* gesture.

"I don't know. I don't know what he's pissed off about or why . . ." I thought a second, said carefully, "You know he don't care about Mr. Garamond, right?"

Gideon gave me a flat *I don't want to talk about it* head-shake. And powers and saints, I didn't want to push. I said, "Look. You want to play cards or something?"

He shrugged and nodded, giving me a lopsided smile that said as how I was no good at changing the subject but he wouldn't get on my case about it.

We played cards until the ninth hour of the night. Felix still hadn't come back by the time we went to bed. Gideon lost the last five hands like he'd never seen a deck of cards before in his life.

Chapter 11

Mehitabel

By nine that evening, I was mostly finished moving in, and perhaps messages had been passed along the grapevine of the back hallways, for it was only at that point that Stephen appeared, Hemminge behind him with a tray holding a decanter and two glasses. Hemminge set the tray down ceremonially on the occasional table, bowed to both Stephen and myself, and left.

Stephen poured the wine, handed me a glass, and said, "So, who should I marry?"

I was tired and had a splitting headache, but I manufactured a laugh. "Surely I'm the last person in the world you should be asking that."

"I value your opinion," he said; he wasn't teasing.

"Isn't it a little soon?"

"What? I've seen them."

"You don't want to get to know them?"

He looked at me for a moment with an expression of weariness that unsettled me, then said, "All I could learn is whether they dance well. No romance. Sorry. Political convenience. They know it, too. No sense pussyfooting around it. I hate dragging things out to no point. So who do you think?"

I could appreciate a pragmatic view of the situation. "Lady Enid or Lady Dinah."

"All right. Why?"

"Zelda Polydoria is too young," I said, editing out the fact that Felix Harrowgate said with absolute certainty Stephen wouldn't marry her.

"True," he said, "and I don't want to marry into the Polydorii."

"The Severnii are as poor as a ragman's dog, and I've heard at length from five sources about the hereditary madness of the Otanii."

"Indeed. And Lady Clementine Novadia?"

"Lady Clementine's reputation as a virago is well-established and well-earned—fast work for a girl of eighteen. If you aren't going to marry for love, don't marry her."

His laugh was like a crack of thunder. "I won't, then."

"Which leaves Enid Lemeria and Dinah Valeria. But between them, I frankly do not see a whisker of difference. They are young, pretty, well-bred, and as far as I can tell Philip Lemerius is no better an addition to one's family than Winston Valerius."

"I rather like Philip," he said mildly.

"Yes, I know, and it baffles me."

He grinned briefly, then sobered. "And I don't want a tie to the Valerii, either—although the child seems a nice enough lamb."

"Suitable for sacrifice?"

"Exactly."

"Then marry Enid."

"Just as everyone expects."

"Yes." I'd heard that opinion more than once. Most people had seemed to assume that the soirée was no more than a polite form—and a chance for the other girls to get themselves noticed by eligible young men. Certainly no one was upset by it.

I said, a little warily, for I still had no sense for how he reacted to being teased, "You don't exactly have a reputation for being unpredictable."

It made him laugh. "I don't, do I? Very well, then. The Lemeria it is. And now let's talk about something else."

Talking wasn't what he had in mind; I didn't let myself sigh before I agreed.

Mildmay

I dreamed about Strych and Felix again. I was trying to find Felix and hide from Strych. Only I couldn't tell which one was Strych and which one was Felix, and because it was that kind of dream, every time I thought I'd found Felix, it turned out to be Strych. And the more times I found Strych, the more I knew I had to find Felix so I could warn him, because I knew it was really Felix that Strych wanted to find. Me, he was just going to kill. And Strych kept smiling at me with Felix's face and telling me not to be silly, I'd got it all wrong. But I knew he was lying, and I knew if he touched me, it would kill me. And then there wouldn't be nobody to keep him from turning into Felix for real.

I came awake like falling off a wall. The sheets were sweat-soaked and tangled around me, and I was shaking, like I was a septad old again and Keeper was having to smack me out of my bad dreams.

And I knew what that dream was all about, too. Sometimes Felix was way too much like Strych. I mean, I knew why and everything, but it didn't help, the way sometimes I could see him turning into Strych right in front of me. I'd never had the guts to tell him that. Either he didn't know, and it would tear him apart, or he did know . . . and I didn't want to think about that one.

I concentrated on my breathing and on the basics of getting dressed—doing up the buttons, straightening my cuffs. By the time I was ready to go out, my hands were steady. But I'd also come out of myself enough to hear Felix shouting. I couldn't make out the words, but it wasn't like I needed to.

Blessed saints, I thought. Of all the septads of things I didn't want to do right then, walking out into another fight was right up at the top of the list. But it was either that or stay cowering in here like a mouse who's spotted a cat, so I opened the door and went on out.

I knew in about a half a second I'd've done better to admit I was a mouse. Felix and Gideon were standing in the middle of the room, staring at each other. Felix was still wearing last night's clothes. They both turned toward me, like they thought I was going to attack them. I stopped right where I was because it seemed like they were maybe an inch, inch and a half, from starting to throw magic around, and I didn't want to get in the way of none of that.

Gideon said something to Felix. I could tell by the way Felix stiffened. I thought, praying, that Felix was going to be able to keep himself from answering—that was the only way they could get out of the bad fights—but then he said, "No, I'm *not* bound-by-forms to you, and I'm fucking well grateful for it."

Oh fuck me sideways 'til I cry, I thought. That was the worst sign, the worst ever. Felix *never* swore, never anything worse than "damn." But Gideon was every bit as mad, maybe even

madder, and I stood there and watched and saw Gideon doing
something I hadn't thought you could. He was playing the fight
by Felix's rules, and he was winning. Felix actually backed up a
step, and I saw something in his eyes that I hadn't seen there in
a long time.

I was praying at Gideon to see it too and stop, but he was
past anything like that. I knew what had got him going—it was
that same old fight about Felix cheating on him, the fight they'd
been worrying at like an old bone the past couple days—but
even in the fight that winter where they hadn't spoken to each
other for three days, it hadn't been like this. Because this time
Gideon wasn't stopping. I could see it. He had had enough, and
it got clearer and clearer for me, standing there with one hand
still on the door, that this was everything Gideon hadn't said to
Felix for like an indiction and a half, everything he'd turned a
blind eye to or laughed off or told himself was just Felix—all of
it coming back in Felix's face at once. Felix wasn't mad no
more. He was white as paper and his eyes seemed to be eating
up his face.

"Gideon—"

Gideon stopped him with a gesture, like he was pushing him
away. Gideon looked from him to me, and I saw that right then
he didn't care about me any more than he did Felix. He turned
and walked out the door. We both stood there, staring after him.
Felix said, "Go after him."

"What d'you want me to do?"

"I don't know! Just go after him."

"What about court?"

"*Fuck* court."

I didn't move. I didn't know what was the right thing to do.

Then Felix's left hand went up to his eyes, and he said, "No,
you're right. We have to go. But afterward I want you to go find
him. Maybe he'll listen to you."

"About what?"

The look he gave me was full of poison, and neither of us
said one word more.

🙪

I felt Felix like a fire all morning. If we hadn't had to go to court,
if he'd been able to go after Gideon and talk to him, I think things
might have come out okay. Not great, maybe, 'cause I had a kind

of idea that some of the things Gideon had said were things that you couldn't leave lay once they were out, but good enough to get by on. But we had to go to court, and we had to stand there, and Felix had time to think. And that was bad. I could feel his mood shifting. I think he'd almost been to where he might have said he was sorry to Gideon—something he said even less than he swore—like Gideon had managed to tear off that spiked armor. But the longer we stood there—dunno what was going on 'cause I sure as fuck wasn't listening—the more I could feel the armor going back on, and the spikes getting longer and sharper. By the time court was over, not only was Felix not sorry, he was pissed off at Gideon again.

"He said he was going to Rinaldo and Simon. Come on."

"Felix, I don't think—"

"Nor should you. Come *on*."

He knew how to shut me up. I followed him, my head down and my face burning.

Simon opened the door. "Felix," he said. He wasn't surprised.

"Good afternoon, Simon," said Felix, in that parody of good manners that most especially made my spine crawl. "May I speak to Gideon please?"

"He says that he has said everything to you he intends to," Simon said.

"Indeed," said Felix. "Well, there are some things I intend to say to him. If I can get past his guard dog."

Powers, Felix, could you be any fucking nastier about it if you tried? But I knew the answer to that: he wasn't even warmed up yet.

Simon said, "He's not here."

"Simon, my darling, don't try lying to me. You're very bad at it."

Simon went red. I saw something I'd never gotten in good light before and felt hollow and sick. Fuck, fuck, fuck. I was leaning away from Felix, like that could keep me from knowing whether he knew how Simon felt about him.

Felix said, "I want to talk to Gideon. I would *prefer* to do so without hurting anyone who happens to be in my way, but the necessity won't grieve me overmuch. Unless you think you can stop me?"

Simon and me both knew he couldn't. No hocus in the Mirador could stop Felix. He said, "Felix, I think this is a mistake."

"I didn't ask you what you thought. I asked you to get out of my way."

Simon stepped aside. There was nothing else he could do. I didn't have no choice either. I followed Felix in. Gideon was sitting in a chair by the fire, and he stayed sitting there, his hands folded in his lap. He looked at Felix, and I got to say that it wasn't a look I'd ever have wanted turned on me.

Whatever they said to each other, it stayed silent. Felix started, I think, because I could tell when Gideon interrupted him. Gideon's face didn't change. It was like he'd moved himself into some other place, someplace where he didn't have to forgive Felix or listen to him or care what he thought. I kind of wished I could get there with him, but I knew I never could.

He didn't say much to Felix then. I don't think he had to. It looked to me like there wasn't anything much left to say, and Gideon knew it. Felix hadn't, but Felix never could understand when an argument had to be over, not unless he'd won it. Gideon found the right words this time, whatever they were, because there was a moment's silence—a real silence, with neither of them saying anything—and then Felix said in a weird, flat voice, "Very well. If that is how you feel."

Gideon didn't even answer him. He turned away and looked into the fire. I'd never seen Felix dismissed like that—even people who hated him couldn't ignore him—and there was nothing in my head when we left the room but stupid swear words. Felix didn't say nothing to Simon. I can't think of nothing he could have said, and I'm not really sure he even noticed Simon was still there.

He sure didn't notice me, all the long way back to the suite. I kept up with him as best I could. I wasn't about to ask him to slow down, even though I could hear Rinaldo in my head, nagging at me.

At the door, he turned, his left hand still on the doorknob. I saw what was coming and braced myself. It was a full-force backhanded blow. If I hadn't had Jashuki, I would have been on the floor for sure. As it was, I staggered sideways into the middle of the corridor. I put my hand up to my face, and my fingers came away red.

I said, "Did that help any?"

The look on his face was black and crimson murder. And then, like falling through the cover on a well, I saw something else, something the rage was supposed to be holding back, something he wasn't ever going to admit to Gideon or to me or probably to anybody. I remembered the way he'd been in the Grasslands, how frightened he'd been, and lost, and how bad he'd needed me. And the need wasn't gone. He just couldn't talk about it no more, couldn't get to it through the anger.

He said, "Get away from me, you stupid little rat."

I went. He could've used the binding-by-forms to hold me there, to hit me until I fell down screaming at his feet, and I thought I'd be smart to remember that he hadn't, that no matter how mean he'd been about it, he'd sent me away instead.

And, you know, there wasn't a thing in the world I could do for him anyway. I couldn't make Gideon come back, even if I'd wanted to try. And I didn't, because, as awful as it made me feel, I thought Gideon was right to go.

I had to hunt up Maurice to get my face dealt with. Maurice was all agog to find out what had happened, but I said it was an accident and stuck to it, even though we both knew he knew I was lying.

To get his mind on something else, I said, "You ever go back, Maurice?"

"Back?"

"You know. You got family?"

"Them?" Maurice snorted. "I wouldn't go and they wouldn't thank me." I thought he'd turn the subject, but he went on, almost like it was my fault, "I got out when I was ten. My father was drunk so much of the time he didn't know I was there—even if he's still alive, I doubt he's noticed I'm gone. My mother was no better. My sisters were already whores, and all but one of my brothers was dead, missing, or in the Kennel. That one brother broke three of my fingers once for getting in his way. I walked up here—I would have *crawled*—and I found a man in the stables, and I said, 'Anything you want me to do. I don't care so long as I don't got to go back.' And he said, 'We ain't looking for a boy, but there might be need in the kitchen.' So they sent me 'round and Geburon said, 'I'll find you work but you won't be here long.' He knew what he was talking about. I ain't rightly been kitchen staff since I was thirteen."

He stopped, hearing the Lower City rising up in his voice.

He reminded me of Felix, or, I guess, gave me a look at what Felix had gone through getting his voice to where it was.

"Shit, I'm sorry, Mildmay. I didn't mean to dump all that on you."

"I asked, didn't I?"

"I guess." He gave my face a critical look. "Well, you're no beauty—"

"Never was."

"It's done bleeding, anyway. Just don't go tearing it open on any more 'doors.' "

Powers and saints, I am a shitty liar. "Thanks, Maurice," I said. At the door, I thought, C'mon, Milly-Fox, you owe him this much. I turned back and said, "You and Rollo—don't say *nothing* to Felix except 'yessir' and 'nosir.' I mean, if you don't want your heads bitten off."

His eyebrows went up.

"Gideon left him."

Maurice's jaw sagged open. "You're kidding," he said.

"Nope. Straight up honest."

"Almighty fuck."

"Yeah," I said and got the hell out of there.

It was damn clear that whatever favors Maurice might do me, going to the Lower City for anything wasn't one of them. And since I couldn't very well drag Simon along to a necromancer's house—even if he was still speaking to me, which I doubted like fuck—that meant I was going to have to look someplace else. And Jean-Tigre owed me one and knew it.

I hate cashing in on favors. Generally it makes things worse than they were before. The blood I owed Margot was never going to be off my hands, even if Margot would've let me do anything about it, which she wouldn't. But when you can't solve one problem, you got to think about another. I couldn't do nothing for Felix, but maybe I could figure out what the fuck was going on with Jenny and get Kolkhis and Ginevra off my back along with it.

Jean-Tigre had been one of Kolkhis's buys the same indiction she bought me, a skinny little gnome of a kid. He'd been great as a pickpocket. He had light, fast hands and a sort of—I dunno—invisibility about him. It wasn't that cits didn't suspect him, it was that they just plain didn't notice him. He didn't think much of the life, though, and when we were near our second septad—about

the same time I was getting my stupid face laid open—Nikah
got caught by the Dogs and hanged. That was it for Jean-Tigre.
I'd never known what had happened to him until I came to the
Mirador and found him already in place, the valet of Lord Gerald Malanius. He'd looked long and careful right through me
the first time we happened to bump into each other, and that told
me clear enough where I stood, namely nowhere in Jean-Tigre's
sight.

I didn't blame him for that. I didn't think I'd have wanted to
know me, if I'd had a choice about it, and I didn't feel like I
needed to push myself on him. But I'd never told Keeper Jean-
Tigre was skimming, although I knew about it for a good indiction and a half before he cut and ran. She would've flayed him if
she'd caught him, and then she would've flayed me for not
telling her. He'd begged me to keep my mouth shut and I had,
even though I'd had nightmares, up until the day he left, that
she'd found out anyway. It don't sound like much, I guess, but
between kept-thieves, it was a pretty big sort of a thing. I knew
it and Jean-Tigre knew it, and the way he kept looking through
me like I wasn't there said that he didn't *want* to know it but
couldn't quite turn the trick of forgetting about it either.

I knew where to find him at this hour of the afternoon. Lord
Gerald was a dandy, and I'd heard more than once from the
servants about how he wouldn't let nobody but Jean-Tigre
touch his clothes with an iron. The laundry maids were all
miffed about it, although they allowed as how it cut down on
their work. They didn't like Jean-Tigre, neither, said he put on
airs and talked down at them, even though they knew where he
was from. Lord Gerald might not know, but flashies don't got
to know those sorts of things. From the top, I don't suppose
one level of down looks much different from another. But the
laundry maids were respectable gals from Breadoven and
Archwolf and Dimcreed, and they didn't like a little snip from
Britomart sneering at them. If I'd wanted to make Jean-Tigre's
life a pure misery, I knew right who to go to.

That wasn't what I was after, so I didn't go hunt out Jeanne-
Arlene and Taffy. Instead, I took a wander by Lord Gerald's
suite, and sure enough there was Jean-Tigre in his shirtsleeves,
ironing away on a set of ruffles you couldn't have paid Felix
enough to wear. I knocked on the door after I'd closed it, and
his head whipped up.

"You're getting slow, Jean-Tigre," I said.

"What do you want?" He was sweating, which was probably just the iron, but I didn't think the heat and the weight had anything to do with the way his face was changing colors. By reflex, he'd brought the iron up, though I don't think he knew he had it in his hand.

"I dunno. To talk?"

"You're nuts. I've got nothing to say to you. I've gone straight."

"And I haven't? I ain't an assassin or nothing no more, Jean-Tigre. Just a servant boy like you."

"You are not like me!" For a second, I understood why Felix loved baiting people. I couldn't have hit Jean-Tigre more squarely on the raw if I'd meant to, and there was a mean kind of satisfaction in it. But it wasn't what I wanted.

"Okay," I said. "All I'm saying is there ain't nothing wrong in being seen talking to me."

"You don't really believe that, do you?"

"No." I stood there and waited for Jean-Tigre to work it out. Which he did.

"What do you want?"

"A favor."

"What kind of favor do you think I can do you?"

"You can get back down in the Lower City without getting lynched, is what."

"I'm not going there!"

"Jean-Tigre—"

"No! I don't care what you do to me or who you tell or anything—*I'm not going back there*." He meant it, and I had an awful feeling that if I pushed he was going to try and brain me with the iron.

"Okay," I said, and opened the door.

"That's it?"

"If you think it's worse than anything I can do, you're probably right. Sorry I asked."

"Wait. Mildmay—"

But I'd already closed the door.

᠅

There was one more person I could try. I mean, it wasn't what you'd call *likely*, but from what Josiah'd said, it'd just been me making Hugo twitchy. And, well, maybe he'd be less twitchy if I owed him a favor. Some people are like that.

So I hauled myself over to the Mesmerine, where Hugo wasn't in his room. Fuck, I thought, and went looking for musicians. I found a whole bunch of them together in a big room that might've been a ballroom once. It was their practice room, so there were instruments and pages of music lying around everywhere and music stands like weird wooden flowers. They got real quiet when they saw me. They knew who I was, all right. So I asked 'em as polite as I could where Hugo was. There was another silence. I was wondering if maybe I should point out that I'd find him anyway, sooner or later, or if maybe I should tell them I didn't want to skin him alive, when a fat gal holding a flute said, "He and Axel went to the Queen Madeleine Garden. Hugo's composing." She said that like it was sacred or something.

Fucking perfect, I thought. I thanked them for the information and left. I was halfway up the Mesmerine's funny half-flight of stairs when I heard them start practicing again.

I'd always been grateful that Felix didn't like the Queen Madeleine Garden. We'd been there once, early on, because he said it was famous and beautiful and I should see it. I suppose it was—beautiful, I mean—but the stairs up to it were killers, worse than the stairs to the Crown of Nails, and there were more of them.

The Queen Madeleine Garden was part of the great project of Gustavus the Architect, the second to last Ophidian king. He'd wanted to get out of the Hall of the Chimeras, along of having seen his mother, Queen Eugenie, executed there on a trumped-up charge before he'd hit his second septad. And you can kind of get behind him for feeling that way. So he'd built this new throne room—torn down and rebuilt half the St. Idris to get it just like he wanted it—and he'd put a garden in on the new roof and then given it to his wife to show as how he wasn't going to be like his father. There were stories said he'd even bricked up the Hall of the Chimeras, but they were lies. He just wouldn't use it. So he'd used his throne room, and his son had used his throne room, and then the Cordelii had come along and moved everybody right back where they came from. They used the New Hall for a ballroom for a while, and then they just quit using it.

But the Queen Madeleine Garden had got popular with the court by then, and so Gustavus's throne room, that he'd meant

to replace the Hall of the Chimeras, had turned into a kind of
waiting room, where people could sit who wanted to catch
somebody important but didn't have the nerve or the energy to
go hiking up all them fucking stairs and find 'em among the
flowers. There wasn't no law that said you *couldn't* go up there,
whoever you were, but lots of people acted like there was. So
there were merchants and landlords all sitting around, sunk in
gloom. I walked through them to the staircase and started up.

The stairs to the garden were made of marble. They were
slick. I was glad for Jashuki. The stairs went around in a kind of
square, and every few flights there'd be a bench so you could sit
down and catch your breath. When I had to stop, twice, I
thought about how I'd've run up these damn stairs once—and
not all that many indictions ago.

You can't go back, I thought when I caught myself glooming
about that again. Ain't that what Rinaldo was saying with that
remember you are lame crack? It *happened*. Pretending like it
didn't ain't going to get you past it. So maybe you better fucking quit pretending.

Problem was, neither me nor Felix seemed to be any good
with that at all.

The Queen Madeleine Garden, I admit, is quite a piece of
work. Brumaire ain't its best time, but you can see how things
are laid out, and where the flowers would be if it was spring. It
was cold today, and the flashies were all strolling in their fur-
lined coats and their muffs. It wasn't windy enough to be really
uncomfortable—the St. Idris is lower than the other parts of the
Mirador, so the wind gets blocked—but it still wasn't where
I'd've wanted to go to write music. I figured Hugo probably had
a reason, and when I came in sight of him, I knew what it was.

Josiah'd said Hugo's new flame was a blond boy from Skaar
who didn't cause trouble. And there'd been that crack about him
being too pretty for his own good. But anybody young and not
bad-looking who was in any type of service in the Mirador
probably got some of that, and so I hadn't taken what Josiah
said quite the right way. But I got myself straightened out in a
hurry. Axel knew how pretty he was, and he knew just how to
use it. Axel had wanted to come up here with a lute, because he
looked all romantic and melancholy sitting with it under a bare
tree, dressed in dark brown and with his hair hanging around his
face in long curls. The court ladies were eating it up. You could

tell by the number of them who were sauntering, like they had just come there by accident, up and down that particular stretch of path. Hugo was up here because that was how he got about people he was in love with. I remembered the way he'd come out to Dragonteeth from Nill, just to sit and stare at Austin and get laughed at when he dared to open his mouth.

Hugo was on a bench, about three septad-foot from Axel, with his wax tablets and stylus. He wasn't looking my direction and didn't see me. That was fine, since I decided I didn't want to walk past Axel and through all the promenading ladies to get to him. I retraced my steps, back around the lily pond that had already been drained for the winter, and came up from the other side.

"H'lo, Hugo," I said.

I hadn't been trying to be quiet—fuck I *wasn't* quiet, between Jashuki and the gravel—but he jumped a foot. He managed to say in a kind of a squeak, "Hey, Mildmay." And when I didn't move on, he even said, "Would you like to sit down?"

"Wouldn't mind," I said. Hugo's face said he'd wanted me to say no, but he piled his tablets all to his side of the bench, and I sat down on the other half. I hoped I was hiding what a relief it was. "I wanted to talk to you."

"To *talk*? To . . . m-m-*me*?"

"Calm down, Hugo. I ain't gonna bite you."

His eyes skittered sideways to Axel, but Axel wasn't looking at us. I didn't know him, so I didn't know whether he'd seen me and was pretending he hadn't or whether he was so wrapped up in the show he was putting on that he really hadn't noticed. "Wh-what do you want?"

"Well, I need to ask you a favor. See, I'm trying to get ahold of a necromancer named—"

"A *necromancer*? What do you want a necromancer for? Is this about Ginevra?"

"Sort of," I said. It was easier than explaining.

"Powers, Mildmay! You're not doing yourself any good with this, you know. It's not healthy."

Which I might've bought, except for the part where Hugo was scared shitless just sitting next to me. It wasn't me he was worried about.

"I wasn't gonna ask you to *do* necromancy," I said.

"Well, what right do you have to ask me favors in the first place? What did you ever do for me except get Austin killed?"

Oh sacred bleeding *fuck* this was not what I needed. People were starting to stare at us, attracted by Hugo's voice, which was getting louder as he went. In a moment or two, some of those ladies would have strolled themselves over within earshot. I said, "Look, all you had to do was say no." I got up and left as quick as I could. Hugo could tell the ladies anything he wanted, but I wasn't going to talk to them.

Felix

Someone was sobbing.

I was standing in a room with padded walls and a flagstone floor. My cravat was off, and my coat and boots. My sleeves were rolled up to my elbows. My rings were still on my hands, and they were sticky with blood.

Not my blood.

There was a man crouched on the floor, his hands over his face.

He was sobbing.

It was his blood.

I was in the Red Room of the Two-Headed Beast, and I had only a fever-dream memory of how I'd gotten here. I had no idea what I'd said to this man to get him in this room with me, no idea if I'd lied or told the truth.

It hardly mattered either way, and my arousal was an almost nauseous pain at the pit of my stomach.

It happened like this. Too many times, it had happened like this, the fury burning itself out and leaving me with nothing but a handful of ashes and the sick knowledge of my own evil. But before, at least I'd *remembered* how I got to this burned out desolation.

At least I'd remembered what I'd done.

My last clear memory—I cast back, and then flinched away from it as if it were some physical thing that could be evaded. Hitting Mildmay, taking the worst and most savage kind of pleasure in watching him stagger, in seeing the blood vivid red on his face. Wanting to do it again. Wanting him screaming, wanting him sobbing at my feet the way this unknown man was sobbing now.

I'd sent him away. At least I could say that much for myself.

Yes, sent him away and picked a random victim instead. How very noble.

I closed my eyes, my hands cramping shut on a racking shudder. And what could I say, to Mildmay or to Gideon or to this man bleeding on the floor of the Red Room? *I'm sorry? Could there be anything more pathetically, ludicrously inadequate?*

I crouched down laboriously, my entire groin throbbing with arousal turning fast to agony, and laid a hand gently on the man's shoulder, asking, "Have I broken any bones?"

He recoiled from me so violently he rolled himself over. "No more, please. Please, m'lord, please don't."

I pressed my bloody beringed hands against my mouth, fighting the way that every indrawn breath wanted to become a scream. The man was an experienced martyr—the red silk cravat crumpled beside him was proof enough of that, and he bore a very old tarquin's mark on his left shoulder blade—and I had reduced him to this? Reduced him to begging for mercy like—

Please don't, Malkar—please!

I don't want to. Lorenzo, please don't make me.

I'll be good, Keeper! I swear by all the powers! I'll be good! Please don't!

I twisted, falling from my crouch to my hands and knees, and vomited. I hadn't eaten all day; there was nothing to come up but bitterest bile. The spasm wrenched at me regardless. Finally, panting and dizzy, I wiped my mouth on my sleeve and staggered to my feet; my victim was still hunched tight, still sobbing.

No matter how much I wanted to, I had lost the right to be gentle with him, to be kind. I washed my hands like the thaumaturgical automata said to have been built in Cymellune before it sank, put my coat and boots back on. Arrogance was a poor shield, but it was all I had. I pulled it about me before I left the room and climbed the stairs to tell the bartender to send someone to deal with the mess in the Red Room.

And to assure him I would not be returning to the Two-Headed Beast.

Mildmay

And of course the first fucking words out of Septimus Wilder's mouth were, "What happened to you?"

"I walked into a door."

"Wicked doors you got in this place," was all he said, and I was even grateful to him for letting it go, that's what a sorry piece of shit I was.

I told him about what Cardenio'd said and pulled the paper with the address on it out of my pocket.

"Hey, wait. What makes you think I want that?"

"Figured you could use it to earn your keep," I said.

"Nothing doing. I ain't playing errand boy for you."

"Just for Kolkhis."

He gave me a glare you could've used to kill rats. "That's between me and her."

" 'Course it is. But, see, I can't go."

"Well, why the fuck not?"

"Oh, I dunno. 'Cause they'll be dragging me out of the Sim a decad from now?"

"You got down to Ruthven just fine."

"I brought my own insurance. Which I can't do talking to a necromancer."

"Ain't enough brass on your balls?"

"Fuck you. I ain't starting no witch-hunts. 'Sides which, no necromancer's gonna talk to me with a Cabaline hearing every word." And Kethe spare me from myself, I couldn't keep from adding, "You may be stupid, but I ain't."

That hit him square between the eyes. I'd known it would, along of knowing exactly how Kolkhis worked. He came back fast, though, faster than I could've: "Funny. That ain't how it looks from where I'm standing."

Oh, that's just 'cause you ain't seen what you're standing on. I said, "She fucking you yet?"

"Kethe's cock! What kind of question is that?"

She was, then. "Don't think she cares."

"Why? 'Cause she's still pining for you?"

"No. Because she *never* cares, okay? You can lie to yourself like I did, but she won't care and she never will."

"She doesn't care about *you*, you mean."

"You think you're any different?"

"Least I'm not fucking hideous."

"So she's fucking you for your looks?"

"*No!*" He caught himself short on whatever he'd been going to say, and I finally did the smart thing and shut my fucking mouth.

There was this long silence while we both thought of a

septad different nasty things to say and didn't say 'em, and finally, Septimus said, "Fuck it. I'll go with you."

I gave him the hairy eyeball. He said, "Look. I've got better things to be doing than coming up here every damn night. So if you won't go without a babysitter . . . or ain't I good enough for you?"

"Oh, no, you're just fucking perfect. But when d'you think . . . you want to go *now*?"

He'd opened the secret door and was waiting for me. "She's a necromancer. It ain't like she won't be up."

🙬

It didn't make Septimus like me better when I told him we couldn't use the Arcane. We went by the roofs instead, and I took it slow and careful like somebody's granny instead of the hot shit cat burglar I used to be. We kept to neutral routes and did what we could to stay low. Too many people on the roofs I didn't want to meet, starting with Margot and ending with Rindleshin—and I didn't notice Septimus arguing, neither, although he had plenty to say about how slow I was moving.

We came down the Mousetrap in Scaffelgreen. Septimus quit mouthing off about then, and I didn't ask if he'd ever done the Mousetrap before. What with one thing and another, I figured I'd stomped his pride about as flat as I needed to, and it wasn't like I was enjoying myself anyway. Mousetrap's no joke even with two good legs. But we made it down and nobody broke his stupid neck and Septimus didn't even give me lip about helping with Jashuki.

The ninth hour of the night ain't no good time to be wandering around Scaffelgreen. It's when the apprentice sangermen practice, for one thing—the sangermen say Madame Sanguette never flirts except after the septad-night. The Mousetrap is practically in the ketches' laps—it's part of why people use it, because you can't go hang around at the bottom and wait for the guy you particularly want to have words with. Septimus kind of twitched every time we heard the blade of the sanguette thump home, and I wasn't no better.

And then of course there's all the other people got business in Scaffelgreen at the wrong end of the night, and even with Vey Coruscant dead, there was still plenty of shit you'd sleep better not knowing about. Me and Septimus stuck to the shadows like we were glued there, and we let anybody who wanted it have the right of way. I figured maybe Septimus *wasn't* stupid.

At least Augusta Fenris's house wasn't far from the Theater. Nice little cul-de-sac, granite facing and iron bars everywhere. And sure enough, the house at the end of Barbary Close had lights burning. One way up at the top of the house, and another in the front room. You didn't put out a sign if you were a necromancer—and if you were any good you didn't need to— but that lit front room told them as needed to know that you were open for business.

"Well, now what?" Septimus said, cross and snarky. "Shall we knock?"

"I ain't about to try sneaking up on a necromancer," I said. I climbed the steps—pretending like fuck that I was only leaning on Jashuki because it would make Rinaldo happy—and used the knocker. And I got to say the look Septimus gave me was worth it.

Door got answered pretty quick. A Norvenan lady, tall and big-boned, the way they are, like it's true what they say, that they're all descended from Brunhilde. I knew she wasn't the necromancer right off. She was wearing a sort of pale lemony colored dress, and her hands were perfect. A lady's hands, not a hocus's.

She looked at me and Septimus, and the frown she'd already been wearing got a bunch heavier. "What do you want?" Little bit of an accent—enough to say she wasn't born in Mélusine.

"Can we speak to Mrs. Fenris please?" I said, careful as I could.

"On what business?"

Powers and saints. "I'd like to talk to her about Jen—about Miss Dawnlight."

Oh, it was the wrong fucking thing to say, wrong like the Queen of Swords. "We aren't talking to anyone about Miss Dawnlight. You want to know about her, you get her out of prison and ask her yourself." And she slammed the door in my face.

"*That* went well," Septimus said.

"Shut up." I could've kept that door from closing, and it'd taken a lot out of my self-control not to do it.

He gave me a moment, then said, "So what now? You wanna try sneaking?"

"Oh powers," I said. I was too tired even to be mad. "I s'pose we'd better give it a—"

Thump and jingle and lanternlight out on Forsythia Street, and me and Septimus were off the stoop and into the alleyway between Mrs. Fenris's house and its left-hand neighbor before either of us knew we were moving.

"Maybe we won't try sneaking," Septimus said once the Dogs had gone past. Some parts of Scaffelgreen are too fucking respectable for their own good.

"Fuck this for a teapot," I said—which was what Geburon the cook said when something went so wrong there was nothing to do but throw it out and start over. "Let's go home, and I'll think of something else in the morning."

"You sure?"

"Yeah, I'm fucking sure. C'mon."

"The Mousetrap again?" He was trying to sound like he didn't care.

"I won't make it," I said. Because who was I trying to fool, anyway? "But the Bittersweet ain't far."

And the Bittersweet's easy—so long as you ain't got nobody hanging around who particularly wants to have words with you. We got up it okay, and started back up the city, still doing okay, although my leg was letting me know about it. And then this voice says, slow and drawling, "Well, I'll be fucked," and I was already reaching for my knife, thinking, oh fuck it's Rindleshin, when it finished, "if it ain't Septimus Wilder."

"Conroy Blackhand," Septimus said, his voice nice and level like he wanted to kill something.

"Who's your friend, Sep? Danny off crying somewhere 'cause you gave him the push?" He swung down onto the roof with us. Big, was all I could see, and I didn't suppose I needed to know much more than that. "Or have I got it backwards, and it's Danny given you the push, and this is some molly-toy you've picked up on the rebound? What d'you think, Eris?"

"Oh fuck," Septimus said, only just loud enough that I could hear him. "Can you run?"

"No," I said back, the same way.

"*Fuck*," said Septimus, no louder but with teeth in it.

"Danny Charlock give Septimus Wilder the push? Never happen," said another voice, and three more guys dropped down onto the roof. We'd walked right into 'em, and you don't need to think I was feeling good about it. Stupid, Milly-Fox. Stupid stupid stupid. And being out of practice ain't no excuse.

"So who *is* your little friend?" said Conroy Blackhand. I remembered a loudmouth little kid named Connie Blacksmith—remembered him on account of having had to put the fear of the almighty powers into him to get him to shut the fuck up—but powers and saints, he'd been doing some growing since then. And he must've been talking to Jenny about names.

"None of your business, Con," Septimus said, but he knew as well as I did it wasn't going to do us no good.

Conroy Blackhand said to me, "Has he fucked you yet, sweetheart? Fast and hard up against a wall? We seen you limping."

They all laughed like he'd said something funny.

He was getting closer than I liked, too. I flipped my knife open, said, "I ain't his type. And you ain't mine, Connie Blacksmith, so back the fuck off."

They had a dark lantern, and that got it open in a hurry, while Septimus said very quietly beside me, "Kethe fuck me upside down."

Conroy Blackhand was staring at me like I was the blood-dripping ghost of King John Cordelius. "You must remember me, *sweetheart*," I said and smiled at him.

He did back up, so him and his goons were in a tight little bunch. And it took him a second to get words out: "What're you doing with Mildmay the Fox, Septimus?"

"Well, like he said, he ain't my type. So what d'you *think* we're doing? *Connie?*"

"Asking for trouble," said the guy named Eris. He had a knife, too, and from the way he was moving sideways, trying to spread our target out, he might even know what to do with it.

Four on two wouldn't've been so bad if I hadn't been lame. Fuck, if I hadn't been lame, I could've taken 'em myself. Or just lost myself in the roofs, which would've been easier and less messy. But there I was, lame and tired, too, and there wasn't nothing fancy left up my sleeve, neither.

Septimus said, "You know, we don't have to do this."

"Oh, I think we do," Conroy said. He was starting to grin, and I wished I'd hit him harder back when he was Connie Blacksmith. A lot harder. "I think I owe it to Mildmay the Fox."

"You are such a fucking piece of shit," Septimus said, kind of admiringly. And then he let out this yell—powers and saints, it was like a cat going through a mangle—and jumped Conroy so fast and so hard that he actually took him down.

I did the only thing that was going to make any difference. Closed my knife and threw it, hard, at the dark lantern. Broke the glass, which was nice. Startled the guy holding it into letting go, which was better. And somehow on the way down, the flame died, which was exactly what I wanted. I was over there in two strides, swung Jashuki hard into the nearest set of ribs, and burned my fingers a little getting my knife back. But while I was ducked down, I heard the guy I'd hit land a punch on one of the other goons. So I just slid out of the way, up onto the next roof nearer the Mirador, and waited.

I was backing Septimus to figure it out before any of them goons, and I was right. They were still fighting and hollering and carrying on when Septimus joined me on my piece of roof and said, "However fast you can go, I think now's a good time."

"Okay," I said.

I *couldn't* run, and we fucking well proved it, because Connie Blacksmith and his goons caught on about two steps and a drainpipe shy of where it wouldn't have done them no good, and we spent the last couple hours of the night in the nastiest game of hide-and-seek I'd had to play for a while—me thinking to myself how a couple indictions back, I would've got out of that mess by just slitting Connie's stupid throat, and are you sure this is an improvement, Milly-Fox?

But we could hide better than they could seek, and we saw dawn from the gilded roof of the Banke Haarien's Mélusine branch, which fronted on the Plaza del'Archimago. We were both filthy and bruised and bleeding from scratches we couldn't remember getting. But we were alive and pretty much in one piece.

"Shit," I said, panting. "Some babysitter *you* turned out to be."

Septimus Wilder tried to glare at me, and burst out laughing.

Mehitabel

I knew from the moment the wizards started their procession into the Hall of the Chimeras the next morning that something was horribly wrong. Something had happened. I glanced up at Stephen; from the complete blankness of his face, he had noticed it, too, and didn't like it.

I knew the disaster when I saw it. Felix Harrowgate's hard white face and blazing eyes were unmistakable signposts. I was just thinking, I should have known Felix was in this up to his neck, when I got a good look at Mildmay.

His expression told me nothing, but the ugly, scabbed-over welts on his right cheek told their tale as loud as shouting. Felix had hit him.

Court proceeded normally, if rather uneasily. I was acutely conscious of Felix and Mildmay halfway along the Hall of the Chimeras, and everyone seemed more fidgety than normal. Stephen refused to be rushed, or even to admit knowledge of the problem, and I had to admire his nerve.

As soon as Stephen had left, I started for the door. All around me, the gossip sprang into life, and the only way I could have avoided hearing bits of it would have been to stop my ears and run.

"... Felix looking like death ... went to Simon Barrister, that's what *I* heard ... that poor mute wizard ... so he gets dumped by his piece of Imperial ass ... the Fox tried to protect Lord Gideon and Lord Felix struck him aside like he wasn't there ... never trusted ... pitched a screaming fit in the middle of the Welkin Vault ... see Lord Tomcat on the prowl again, you mark my words ..."

I fought through to the doors and outside, and just when I thought I'd made my escape cleanly, there was a muffled cough at my elbow and I turned to find Lord Philip Lemerius rising from one of the benches.

I curtsied, cursing him in my heart. "My lord."

"Madame Parr," he said with a stiff little bow. "Will you walk with me?"

Oh God. I resisted the urge to say, *I'd rather fuck a skunk*—Corinna's phrase—and instead dredged up the swan-daughter, the version of myself I'd learned to present to Antony. "Gladly, my lord, although my time is limited."

"I know," he said, offering me his arm. "You go back to your theater now, do you not? I will walk you to whichever gate you like."

"Chevalgate, my lord."

He nodded, and we turned in that direction. We walked for some time in silence before he said, most uncomfortably, "Madame Parr, will you do me a favor?"

Swan-daughter, I reminded myself. "I don't know, my lord. What favor would you ask of me?"

He did not turn his face toward me, staring straight ahead as if resisting torture. Finally, he said, "My son."

"Antony, my lord?" I said sweetly. Even a swan-daughter has weapons. "Or Semper?"

His teeth clenched. "Semper. I hear that he is now at the Empyrean."

"Yes, my lord."

"Madame Parr. I do not think acting is a fit profession for him."

"No, my lord? Why not?"

He ignored the question. "If you have any influence with him at all, I ask that you persuade him away from the stage."

"And what am I to offer him in its place?"

"Eh?"

"What would you have him do instead?"

"He can come to me. I can find a place for him in my household."

"A noble offer," I said, and I let myself say it coldly. "It occurs to me to wonder why you have not made it before."

"I am not accountable to you for my actions, madame."

"No, my lord, of course not. But if you ask me to intercede between you and Semper, then I think you must offer me assurances that I will be doing the right thing."

We had reached Chevalgate. I removed my hand from his arm, and we stood facing each other, each aware of the guards not quite out of earshot.

I was a swan-daughter. I was cold and disapproving and perfectly in control. "I will bear a message, if you wish. I will tell him that you disapprove. More than that I will not do until I have greater faith that concern for Semper is at the bottom of your disapproval."

"You are too kind, madame," he said, with a stiff, jerky bow. I dropped him a form-perfect curtsy and he strode back the way he had come. I stood for a moment where I was, until I realized that I was wrenching my gloves in my hands as if they were some vermin I wanted to kill and made myself stop. I put my gloves back on, smooth and serene, as befitted a swan-daughter, and swept out Chevalgate to find a cab.

Mildmay

Felix sent me away the moment court was over. Nothing had changed, and I was glad to get away.

I'd cleaned up before court in Mehitabel's old room, since the one thing I figured I could be sure of was she wouldn't show up there. All her things were gone. It was probably the safest place in the whole fucking Mirador. And there was a bed. But I didn't want to go back there. I sat on one of the benches outside the Hall of the Chimeras and made a sad, stupid list of all the things I did want to do and how many of them I could manage. Which was none. Flashies and hocuses and servants would go by and look at me, but nobody stopped. Finally I sorted it down again, about the same way I had yesterday. I couldn't do nothing about Felix. I couldn't even imagine anything to do. I mean, I tried to pretend I was thinking about going to Fleur or Charles the Dragon or even Isaac Garamond and trying to get them to talk to him or something, but I knew I wasn't. For one thing, they wouldn't have listened to me, except maybe for Fleur. And anyway, Felix would have skinned me with a dull knife. I did think, for a little while, about going to Gideon and begging him to come back, but when I looked at it square on, I knew he wouldn't. If he wouldn't do it for Felix—and it was pretty fucking obvious he was done doing things for Felix—there was no fucking way he was going to do it for me. And it wouldn't've been right to ask him anyway. I couldn't drag Felix out of the pit he was in, that was the long and the short of it, not until he asked me to throw him a rope.

But the bitch of it was that I didn't seem to be able to do nothing about Jenny, neither. Maurice and Jean-Tigre and Hugo weren't going to go down the city for me. Brunhilde at Mrs. Fenris's place wasn't going to help nobody. I was beginning to think there was something wrong with me.

And probably there *is* something wrong with you, Milly-Fox. Nice, normal people don't go around killing folks for money.

And wouldn't that be one of the reasons Maurice and Jean-Tigre and Hugo don't want to go back down the city—'cause it's full of guys like you?

Oh, c'mon, I said to myself, about like I'd said to Jean-Tigre. I don't do that no more. I quit doing shit like that a long time ago.

So you think the leopard can change his spots? I actually brought my head up, because it sounded so much like Felix I thought he had to be there with me. But it was only my own head and yet more stupid fucking questions about things I'd done or hadn't done or should've or shouldn't't've or Kethe knows what all.

I put my head in my hands. I felt like driving it straight back against the wall—that at least might shut the questions up—but I didn't. They'd be waiting when I came round, only I'd have a headache to go with 'em.

And the point wasn't me anyway. The point was Jenny, sitting there in the Kennel, not telling the Dogs nothing. And Kolkhis, sitting there in Britomart not telling me nothing. And nothing I could fucking do about it.

And then I thought about that Brunhilde saying *You want to know about her, you get her out of prison and ask her yourself.* And, you know, back at the start of this whole fucking mess, I'd sworn I wasn't going anywhere near the Kennel, but I should've known better. Because Jenny was there and like I'd said to Septimus, I had insurance.

Except—

"Fuck," I said, out loud and loud enough that a servant going by just about dropped his broom and dustpan. Of all the people in the world who weren't going to want to talk to me just now. Powers and saints.

But finally I said to myself, You can sit here and drive yourself crazy or you can go try. If they say, no, they ain't gonna listen, well, then you'll be right where you are except at least you'll have tried. It's not like things can get worse.

That seemed true enough. I hauled myself to my feet and started for Simon and Rinaldo's suite.

Mehitabel

Rehearsal was bad. Not that anything went wrong, exactly, but Drin was stalking around the stage like a tomcat who smells another cat on his turf, and I couldn't tell whether his black glares were meant for Semper or for Gordeny. Happily, Drin was cast as the villain, so his smoldering malevolence could at least be usefully channeled, but he wasn't acting, and we all knew it.

Beyond that, the key scene between Semper and me was limping. It reminded me of a broken vase. We'd try gluing it together one way, and a piece would fall out someplace else. We braced that spot, and a chip leaped out of the rim. We put that back in place, and the shard we'd originally glued fell out. It wasn't Semper's fault—his other scenes showed that he was an actor perfectly adequate for the part of Edith Pelpheria's doomed husband—and it wasn't my fault. But between us, the thing just wouldn't jell. Jean-Soleil was all but chewing the flats in exasperation, and he finally had the sense to let us go, turning his attention ferociously on Gordeny and Corinna. I jerked my head at Semper, and we fled to my dressing room.

"I'm sorry, Madame Parr," he said, the instant the door was closed behind us. "I don't know what I'm doing wrong."

"Don't apologize, and for God's sake don't call me 'Madame Parr.' My name's Mehitabel—Tabby if you find that too cumbersome."

He blushed up to the roots of his hair.

I didn't sigh, although I felt like it. But I had a duty here, not so much to Semper as to Jean-Soleil, and really not to either of them at all. To Gran'père Mato, who had insisted that all his children and grandchildren and every player who came into the troupe be taught to read so that they could understand the stories they acted out. And to the Empyrean. And to *Edith Pelpheria*, because it was a wrenching, brilliant play, and if we were going to do it, we had to do it right.

"Semper?"

"Yes?"

"Do you understand what that scene is supposed to be doing?"

"I'm sorry?"

"Asline Wren put it there for a reason, you know." What Mildmay called my governess-voice. And I was a good teacher. I'd taught Angora Gauthy how to factor an equation, although it'd taken me the better part of two weeks.

"Oh." He frowned, as if that was an entirely new idea. "Then I guess I don't."

"Well, *think* about it. What do you think it's there for? And sit down while you're thinking."

He sat obediently, his frown deepening. "I guess maybe that's why I don't get it. It doesn't seem to me like it's doing anything."

"Why not?"

"It's the only scene with Edith and Merrick together," he said. "So it seems like maybe it should be showing how much she loves him. But it doesn't."

"No," I said.

"But it can't be showing that she *doesn't* love him, because the rest of the play shows that she *does*. So you're right, Ma—Mehitabel. I don't understand it."

"Do you know why *Edith Pelpheria* is such a famous play?"

"Is it famous? I'd never heard of it."

"Bless the boy, is it famous! Yes, it is extremely famous. Edith is considered one of the greatest female tragic roles."

"Oh. Father Ulixes doesn't approve of plays."

"That's his problem," I said tartly. "The reason that this is considered a great play—and that Edith is so important and so difficult—is the vigil scene in Act Three."

"Oh," Semper said, this time in tones of great enlightenment.

"*That*'s where we find out that Edith loves Merrick, and that's why *this* scene is important."

"I get it! Because it looks like it's establishing that she doesn't."

"Exactly." I shut my mouth and let him think about it.

After a while, when his eyes had refocused on his present surroundings, I said, "Your father asked me to talk to you."

The shutters came flipping down across his face with the speed of lightning. "You know my father?"

"Neither well nor fondly. Nor, ah, intimately." Semper blushed as he caught my meaning, and I forbore mentioning Antony. "But I promised him I'd tell you he doesn't approve of you becoming an actor. He says he'll take you into his household."

Semper said nothing, his face bleak.

I said, "That's all I promised him."

"My mother," he said after a moment. "She loved him very much. She was always watching for him when she knew he was at Copal Carnifex—and sometimes even when she knew he wasn't—hoping he'd come by, just to talk or just so she could see him. He never did, not once in seven years. Even when he took me away, he sent his steward to Moldwarp to fetch me. The first time I ever saw him was in the great hall at Copal Carnifex. It's only about a quarter of the size of the Hall of the Chimeras, I suppose, but the effect is very much the same." His mouth twisted wryly. "Especially when you're seven and scared out of your mind. He looked me over and said, 'I expect you not to shame me at St. Kemplegate.' That was it. The steward whisked me away. I spent the night in the kitchen with the scullery boys and rode to Shatterglass the next day in the carriage with Lady Beatrice's dresser and my—and Lord Philip's valet. They despised me, too." I saw the moment when his mind caught up with his mouth; that look of stark horror would have been hard to miss.

I said mildly, "I have no good opinion of Lord Philip to lose."

"Thank you," he said, blushing again.

"Would you like me to take a message back to Lord Philip?"

He thought about that carefully. "If I wrote a letter . . ."

"Yes, of course. I think I've even got some sealing wax you can use."

His smile was radiant. "That would be splendid. If you're sure you don't mind?"

"Not at all. Now, mind you, I wouldn't care to make a *habit* out of it . . ."

"No, no, of course not. But just a short letter?"

I couldn't help laughing. "Make the letter as long as you need."

"Thank you, M—Mehitabel. I'll go write it now. If I give it to you tomorrow, is that all right?" He darted out, barely waiting for my affirmative.

Something to look forward to, I thought dourly, and went out to tell Jean-Soleil that I thought we had the scene licked.

Mildmay

I knocked on Rinaldo and Simon's door. Rinaldo opened it.

"You," he said.

"Me," I said. "Just me. I mean, Felix ain't around the corner or nothing."

"That is some comfort. Do you wish to come in?"

"Not if you're gonna be giving me the hairy eyeball the whole time. I ain't responsible for Felix being an asshole."

His mouth twitched. "Good point. Come in."

Simon and Gideon were sitting by the fire. They both looked nervous when they saw me.

"Don't get excited," I said. "It's just me."

"Where's Felix?" Simon asked.

"Fucked if I know."

"Get him a chair, Simon," Rinaldo said behind me. "At least, I assume you're staying?"

"Um, yeah, I mean, I . . ." Powers, Milly-Fox, could you sound stupider if you *tried*?

"Do you need something, Mildmay?" Simon said, dragging a chair forward.

"Um, sort of."

"Not to do with Felix?"

"Nah. It's, um . . . well, it's about Jenny."

"Your friend in the Ebastine," Rinaldo said.

"Yeah." I sat down. "I, um, I think I got to go talk to her. But it's gonna take some really fast talking, and I . . . well, I could use some backup."

"You want me to come with you," Simon said.

"Yeah." I didn't let myself wince, because I knew better than that, but I was all tied up like a piece of string inside waiting for what he'd say.

He looked at Gideon, kind of sharp. Then he said, "Gideon wants to know if he can come, too."

"You . . . I mean, don't . . . I mean . . . oh fuck it. Of course you can come. If you want to."

Gideon nodded and gave me something that was almost a smile.

Simon said, "Then I'm in, as well."

"Okay," I said. "Thanks. I'll, um . . . is tomorrow afternoon okay?"

Gideon kind of shrugged and nodded at the same time, and I knew what he meant, but Simon made a face. "It'd be better for me to wait a couple days."

"Sure," I said. "Kennel ain't going no place. I'll come by when I can get away—you know." I got up.

"You don't have to leave," Rinaldo said.

"Yeah, I do," I said. I didn't mean to look at Gideon when I said it, but my eyes slid that way anyway.

"Gideon says he isn't upset with you for anything," Simon said.

"Thanks, Gideon, but I know how Felix would feel about me being here. And, I mean, you can't exactly *want* me around. I'll just go."

Rinaldo said, "You said, accurately, that Felix is not your fault."

"Yeah, but I got to drag him around after me anyway. I mean, I can't get rid of the binding-by-forms. I'm sorry, Rinaldo. I guess I lied."

"No," Rinaldo said. "But I think I understand how you feel. Go if you think you have to. We will see you tomorrow."

"Thanks," I said and left without looking at either Simon or Gideon again.

Mehitabel

I heard the knock, but thought nothing of it until Lenore came in and announced, "Lord Felix Harrowgate, miss."

Oh hellfire, I thought. I put my book down. "Please, show Lord Felix into the sitting room and tell him to make himself comfortable. I'll be with him in a moment."

I hadn't been expecting anyone and so had unpinned my braids and taken off my shoes, and I was glad of the time to collect myself. When I came out of my dressing room, I saw, through the open antechamber door, Felix alone in the sitting room and clearly not expecting me yet. He'd sunk into a chair; his left elbow was propped on the chair arm, and his head sagged against that hand as if it were too heavy for him to hold upright. I had a clear, fire-lit view of his profile, his blue eye clouded and all his habitual façades and masquerades dropped. He looked deathly tired. I backed away from the door before he noticed me; I couldn't deal with that Felix. When I started forward again, I was noisy about it, and by the time I came into the sitting room he was on his feet and smiling.

"Tabby," he said, "do I kiss your hand?"

"No, thank you," I said. "I hardly think that courtesy necessary among friends."

He seemed somehow to brighten. "Do you really think of me as a friend?"

"Of course I do, sunshine," I said, and gave him a real smile. "And anyway, at least I know you're here for *me*."

"I see. Heavy lies the, er—"

"No, don't go on from there," I said, and we both laughed. "Sit down instead and tell me to what I owe the honor."

"Am I that transparent?" he said, with an odd sideways glance at me; the yellow eye was merely mocking, but the blue eye looked worried and anxious.

"I *do* know you. And I believe a lady is supposed to receive her gentlemen callers in the afternoon." I made a very small production out of looking at the clock, and was half alarmed, half delighted when he blushed and bit his lip and looked away.

"Yes, well, no one can suspect me of having designs on your virtue. And I did want to ask you something, but . . . I wanted to find out if you *would* see me."

"I've forgiven you worse things," I said.

His face stayed still, but his hands flinched a little. "Yes, I suppose you have."

"What did you want to ask me?"

"It's about Vincent."

"Vincent?"

"Vincent Demabrien. You remember?"

"Lord Ivo's catamite."

"Yes." Unlike Isaac, he didn't balk at the word.

"What about him?"

"Lord Ivo is disinclined to let him associate with undesirables such as myself."

"And?"

"He won't want to offend you, not now."

That was elliptical, but I thought I saw the light. "You want me to invite Vincent Demabrien here?"

"Would you?"

"Stephen is not going to marry Zelda Polydoria."

"No, of course not."

"Won't this look like, er, collusion between Vincent and me?"

"Will it? Does it matter if it does? The gossip is flowing thick and fast in all directions anyway. Will one more crosscurrent matter? And you're welcome to tell Stephen it's all my fault."

"I'd tell him that anyway. Is this Vincent Demabrien so important to you?"

There was a pause. He'd looked away from me, down at his hands, at the tattoos and garnet rings. When he looked up again, his face was calm and rather remote. "Since I came to the Mirador," he said, "which was when I was sixteen, I have seen no one whom I knew in my childhood. Most of them are dead. Finding Vincent again . . . I don't know. It's like getting a chance to talk with the dead. I don't suppose that makes any sense, but I will be *damned* if I let a two-centime pantomime vulture like Ivo Polydorius get in my way."

I sighed—and let him hear it—and capitulated. "What do you want me to do, invite him to tea?"

"Dinner would be better," Felix said. He gave me one of his blazing smiles, the sort that made even people who knew better forget to distrust him. "My afternoons are so busy."

"All right," I said. "I'll see what I can do."

"You are a saint," he said. "Shall I light candles for you?"

"No thanks." There was another pause, a longer one, and then I said, "Did Gideon really leave you?"

He'd seen it coming; he didn't flinch. "Yes," he said. "I do not think he will be coming back."

"I'm sorry," I said.

"I brought it on myself," he said, with a kind of half-shrug. After a moment, he got his chin up and met my gaze, his left eye glowing like a jewel, his right eye dim and grieving. "Could you change what you are, Tabby, if you wanted to?"

"No," I said.

I knew what he meant.

Chapter 12

Mehitabel

Over breakfast, I wrote a formal letter requesting the honor of Vincent Demabrien's company for dinner on any night in the coming week that he should find convenient. I kept the wording ambiguous, so that, while the letter was addressed to Messire Demabrien, the request might be read as being addressed either to him or to Lord Ivo. Not so much as the faintest hint of Felix Harrowgate got into my careful phrases. I left the letter with Lenore to be delivered and took myself off to the Empyrean.

Semper was waiting for me at the Empyrean's side door, shifting from foot to foot like a child anticipating a present. But it was his letter, which he pressed into my hands as furtively as if it were appointing an assignation. "I'll be sure Lord Philip gets it," I said, and we went backstage together.

Isaac was waiting in my dressing room. I was shocked that he was skipping court, and then I saw the red, swollen welts on his hands.

"What happened to you?" I said as I closed the door.

He didn't answer me. I didn't think he'd even heard me. The words came pouring out of him in a torrent, a babbled account of some argument he'd seen between Felix and Mildmay on Vendredy. I sat down while he was talking and began redoing my hair for Edith. When he was done, he all but wailed: "But what does it mean?"

That Felix is an idiot. "You *must* know he picks fights."

"I mean, what were they fighting *about*?"

"What did Felix tell you?"

"Nothing. He insisted on talking about opera, and then we . . . I mean, until he left."

"Ah," I said, and let the silence hold until I saw him start fidgeting in the mirror. Then I turned. "What happened to your hands?"

He startled, then recovered and said, "Oh, I made a mistake with a spell," with a fine show of carelessness and followed it up quickly with, "Why did Messire Thraxios leave?"

"I would imagine because he got fed up with Felix fucking you."

It was worth it a thousandfold for the way he jerked back and actually hit his head on the wall, even though he pulled himself up and said, "You forget yourself, Maselle Cressida," with all the menace he could bring to bear.

It was, of course, considerable. I smiled at him sweetly and turned back to the mirror. And said nothing.

"Tell me about Vincent Demabrien."

"What about Vincent Demabrien?" I'd finished with my hair, but I stayed where I was. I liked him better in the mirror. It was tempting and all too easy to imagine him trapped there, furious but unable to cause mischief.

"Is his relationship with Felix common knowledge?"

"What relationship?"

A pause, a single beat, and he said, "Felix came to talk to you last night."

I went cold.

"And this morning you sent a letter to Messire Demabrien. Are the two events entirely and innocently unconnected, Maselle Cressida?"

He was smirking at me, damn him.

"Withholding information from me isn't a good idea," he said. "Lying to me would be an even worse one. I expect a sending from Major Goliath tonight, and it would be simplicity itself for me to tell him that Lieutenant Bellamy needs a reminder of what happens to the disobedient. He won't even ask me what you've done."

I hated him. I hated him and there was nothing I could do about it. And I couldn't be sure he hadn't already seen my letter. I didn't think it likely, but I knew all too well how quickly and easily a servant could be suborned if one's pockets were deep.

I said, "Felix asked me to write to Messire Demabrien."

"Yes," said Isaac. "Why?"

If he was watching either Felix or me that closely, he would find out anyway. "I've invited them both to dinner tomorrow."

"Yes," he said again. "Why?

Beneath the vanity-top, where he couldn't see even in reflection, I dug my nails into my palms. I could fence another round or two, but we both knew he'd get the truth out of me, and I didn't feel like providing his morning's entertainment. Not when I couldn't think of a single plausible lie. Not when he was so casually ready to punish Hallam.

"Lord Ivo is being difficult. That's all Felix told me."

"And you accepted that with all complaisance?" he asked, eyebrows rising.

"Felix and I *are* friends," I said mildly, "difficult though that concept may be for you to grasp."

He missed the implied insult, which was safer, though less satisfying. "Well, I shall expect a full report," he said and finally got up to leave.

"Of course, lieutenant," I murmured dutifully. Surely I could think of some good strong lies before I saw him again.

ॐ

There was someone watching rehearsal that afternoon.

I only became aware of him gradually—he was well back in the darkness of the pit—but a play feels different with an audience, and I spotted him near the end, while Drin was trying vainly to tempt me into forgetting Semper and ignoring all the other murders he'd committed. "All for you," the villain keeps saying in that scene, until the claustrophobia of obsession hangs over the stage like a pall.

But there was our audience, a slumped figure near the northeast set of double doors. Probably one of Semper's friends, I thought, and put my mind to the serious business of poisoning Drin.

Afterward, when I went out to check my pigeonhole, there he was, a heavy-built boy of eighteen or so, dark and unremarkable except for his nose, which had not been reset as well as Mildmay's. It leaned crookedly askew, as if it were looking for a wall to prop it up; he must've snored like a thunderstorm.

He was standing in the stage-lobby, looking uncertain and a little frightened, but when he saw me his face smoothed out. *Very* like Mildmay, only not as good at it.

"Excuse me, miss," the boy said, "I need to talk to Gordeny

Fisher." Lower City accent so thick you could slice it, but perfectly polite.

I gave him a hard stare, up and down. He stood his ground, though he wouldn't meet my eyes. "I can tell her you're here, if you'll give me your name, but I can't make her talk to you."

"Would you?" And he seemed sincerely grateful. "My name's Danny Charlock."

"I'll tell her," I said, but I shot the bolt behind me when I closed the door. I didn't like the idea of Danny Charlock wandering around backstage with no one watching.

I found Gordeny in her dressing room, in the last throes of a final fitting for her dual role as the murderer's lover and the heroine's sister (affianced to the murderer and therefore the second to go—the lover hangs on until nearly the end). I waited until Corinna and Mrs. Damascus, the Empyrean's dresser, had finished extracting Gordeny from the pins and cleared themselves away, and then said, as Gordeny slid her dress off the hanger: "There's a young man in the stage-lobby who wants to talk to you. He says his name is Danny Charlock."

I'd picked the moment because I had a good view of her face, and the results were interesting. Her face went quite mask-like, and a little gray. Danny Charlock, as I'd expected, was not her best beau. The first words she found were obscenities, and her Lower City accent, which she'd been striving dutifully to shake, was back in full flood. "Fuck. That motherfucker and his stupid, shitty, gotta-know-everything-you-do head. Help me with these fucking buttons, Tabby, please?"

I helped her, and made her wait while I repinned her hair. "Look, either he'll have gone away—and it doesn't seem like you're very interested in talking to him—or he'll still be there. I shot the bolt."

"Did you? Good."

"Are you scared of him? Cat and Toad will come with you if you want."

She snorted in profound contempt. "The day I'm afraid of Danny Charlock is the day they can bury me for being too lily-livered to live. Thanks, Tabby, but I can handle Danny."

I set the last pin; she stood up, shook her skirts out carefully, and left. I badly wanted to hear her interview with the unfortunate Danny—for I didn't doubt in the slightest that Gordeny could "handle" him—but the stage-lobby wasn't convenient for eavesdropping, and Gordeny hadn't seemed to want my support either. I thought, though, that what she had said was true; Danny didn't frighten her. The question remaining, and looming large, was: what did?

I was still in Gordeny's dressing room when she came back. Her color was heightened, and she had her hand on the door to slam it when she saw me. "You didn't need to wait for me."

"I wasn't," I lied with an apologetic smile. "I'm sorry, I was standing here woolgathering. Everything all right?"

"Oh, yes," she said. "Everything's fine. Danny won't bother you again."

I moved toward the door. Isaac hadn't set me spying on Gordeny; it was time to leave her alone. "Danny didn't bother me."

"After Mildmay the Fox, I don't suppose he would," she said. I kept going, against a sudden desire to argue. And back in my own dressing room, staring at my reflection, I thought that the fact Mildmay had never frightened me was a sign either that I wasn't very bright or that Mildmay had learned, somewhere along the way, to hide what he was from those who wouldn't understand.

"You can't solve that riddle, Tabby," I said to my reflection and started taking down my hair. "Let it go."

But I couldn't dismiss Mildmay as easily as Gordeny had dismissed Danny Charlock. I reassembled the façade of a lady, feeling more and more like the grubby selfish little girl my father had reprimanded for making my baby brother cry. I shrugged into my coat and flung open the door, preparing to stalk back to the Mirador.

Gordeny was in the passage. We both started back with a yelp.

"Oh! I'm sorry, I was just going to knock."

"What is it?"

"Well, I wanted, I mean . . . If I was rude about Danny Charlock, I'm sorry."

"Not that I noticed."

"You see, Danny and me were kids together—"

"Danny and I."

"Right. Danny and I. We were kids together, and I thought he was coming to tell me Mom and Dad wanted me home. But he wasn't." She gave me one of her lovely smiles.

What I wanted to say was, *Gordeny, just how stupid do you think I am?* "Everything all right at home?"

"Oh, yes," Gordeny said. "Danny just wanted to see me."

Poor Danny, I thought. "I hope you told him to come watch you act. I should think he'd be very proud."

She blushed and said, "Danny doesn't like plays, so probably he won't. But thanks!" And she slipped past me down the hall, gone in the darkness of the Empyrean like a fish into deep water.

⤫

Everywhere I looked in the Mirador, there were echoes of the Bastion; certain corners of the Mirador could make me think that I was back in the middle of the Grasslands of Kekropia, trapped again in that vast, windowless ant-hill-cum-tomb. I'd had nightmares for months after I finally escaped the Bastion, nightmares about being chased through its narrow halls by monsters made of dust, monsters made of sheets, monsters made of blood-stained wizards' robes. And Juggernaut always ticking, the Bastion's lifeless, unbeating heart.

On Vendredy, I'd taken advantage of my new status to make Stephen—who complied amiably, even if he found it funny—show me exactly how to reach my suite from both the Hall of the Chimeras and the Seawater Room, a small and elegant parlor that some long-dead hand had lovingly and painstakingly painted in shades of turquoise. I wondered if it had been some homesick wizard from the Imari, longing for water that was not the cruel Sim. The Seawater Room was easy to find from Chevalgate, so I could at last be free of the page boys' bright-eyed curiosity.

"How do *they* do it?" I had asked Stephen in bed later that night.

"Who?"

"Your little noble boys from the sticks. How in the world do they find their way around?"

"They study it," he said.

"You're joking."

"Not at all. I studied it as a child. So did Shannon and Vicky. And even so, the boys don't know very much."

"I thought they could go anywhere."

"May, not can. They only deal with visitors."

"You've lost me."

"It's not that difficult. Suppose you're a visitor to the Mirador—I mean, suppose you're an *ordinary* visitor."

"All right, I'm supposing."

"You go to the Hall of the Chimeras, right? Or the New Hall. Or you have an appointment in a specific room."

"But surely people go other places."

"Like where?"

"Good God, Stephen, I don't know. It just seems like . . ."

"No, not really. If somebody wants a place the pages don't know, they take them to the Master of Pages. Sometimes it's just a mistake."

"And if it isn't?"

"They end up discussing the matter in the Verpine—the visitor, not the page."

"How draconian."

"Saves headaches." And then he had gone on to talk about some other headache, and the subject of the Mirador had been shelved. But I was proud, nevertheless, with a bloody-minded sort of defiance, to be able to reach my rooms from Chevalgate with no guide save myself, and it was in that savage mood that I came into my sitting room and found a letter propped on the mantelpiece. It was from Vincent Demabrien, accepting my invitation for the following evening.

Mildmay

Court that Deuxième was bad. For starters, Lord Stephen stood up and said he'd decided to marry the Lemeria gal, and I swear you could've used Robert of Hermione's face to pickle eggs. Robert was pretty much out the door, and he knew it, and that meant, if I knew Robert at all, that he was going to be looking round for something nasty to do—and he'd like it best if he could do something nasty to Felix, who he hated more than he hated anything else on the face of the world. So that gave me the jitters going one direction, and then when Lord Stephen asked if there was any business, Thaddeus stepped out and said as how he thought the Mirador ought to be more careful about the Bastion's spies, that just 'cause they said they wanted to be friends didn't mean they were going to be playing fair, and as how he, Thaddeus, thought they were all a bunch of liars and cheats and shouldn't be trusted any further than a cat can sling a cart-horse.

Right then I hated Thaddeus about as bad as I hated Robert, because anybody could see that if he'd just gone to Lord Stephen with his concerns, Lord Stephen could have sort of settled the thing without much fuss. But he had to get up and say it in the middle of the Hall of the Chimeras, and within five minutes there were people howling for the Bastion's blood. It made me feel sick, and I wondered if Cerberus Cresset had been good at this particular move.

Things were getting uglier, and I could see Andromachy Sain and the other Eusebian hocuses who hadn't gone back to the Bastion clumping together tighter and tighter, when this voice beside me said, "Thaddeus, that's arrant nonsense and you know it."

Felix pitched it to lift right over the babble clear to the other end of the hall. That trick don't work all the time, but it worked fine just then. Everybody got quiet and was staring at him and I was wishing he could have picked something a little more tactful to say.

Lord Stephen said, "Thank you, Lord Felix. Lord Thaddeus, I understand your concerns. A committee will be formed to look into the matter. Next!"

By that time, one of Thaddeus's friends had got ahold of him, and whatever she said at least made him shut up, although he stood there looking sulky the rest of the time. So now there were two guys out for Felix's blood. Fucking marvelous. And—let's face it, Milly-Fox—those are only the guys at the head of the line.

Mehitabel

Vincent Demabrien had proposed the hour of seven—a little early for dinner, but I gathered that Messire Demabrien had to be grateful for what he could get. In my message to Felix, I had told him he could come early if he wanted, primarily so that I'd have a way of judging how nervous he was. He showed up at six-thirty.

I couldn't have deduced his state of mind from anything else. He was beautifully dressed in a dull, lush periwinkle-blue brocade embroidered with bullion; I wondered if he had chosen it because it gave his right eye more color. Otherwise he wore the clothes of any Marathine courtier; trousers, boots, and snow-white shirt all complete. His waistcoat was unexpectedly sober, dark green without any embroidery at all, the gold wizard's sash like a streak of sunlight across the forest floor. He hadn't queued his hair—he almost never bothered—and the gold rings in his ears were all but lost in the flame. The rings on his hands, the rings that had undoubtedly caused the welts on Mildmay's face, glowed like the eyes of dragons in the lamplight.

He smiled at me as he came in, a wry, nervous quirk of his mouth that couldn't have been less like the way he smiled when he was setting out to charm, and said, "Thank you."

"Don't thank me yet, sunshine," I said, smiling back at him with more warmth than I should have. "There's still plenty of time for a disaster."

It got a better smile, and he said, "You can't possibly make me more nervous than I already am, so quit trying."

"All right. Bourbon?"

"Yes, please." I poured sherry for myself, and we stood before the fireplace like strangers.

"Will you tell me a little about your friend?" I said.

"What do you want to know, beyond the fact that we knew each other as boys and he is the catamite of Lord Ivo Polydorius?"

"If I'm not to try to make you nervous, you aren't to try to shock me. Out with it."

"I don't suppose it *will* shock you," he said with a sigh. "We know each other because we were managed by the same procurer. The term in Pharaohlight is 'stablemates.'"

I didn't have to fake a grimace, and he saluted me with his glass.

"It could have been much worse," he said, his breathy voice light, as if he were talking of someone else. "The Shining Tiger was what they call an upright house, and Lorenzo took very good care of his investments." He took a deep swallow of bourbon. "Malkar found me when I was fourteen and took me to Arabel—which might as well be on the moon as far as Pharaohlight is concerned. Vincent assumed Malkar had killed me—a far from unlikely theory—and I assumed he had died in any one of the ways a teenage prostitute can die in Pharaohlight. Believe me, they are myriad. If Lord Ivo had not been fool enough to think his insipid little rat of a daughter could catch Stephen, we would never have known each other still lived."

"It's like something out of a romance."

"Much of my life is," he said wearily, not responding to my teasing tone.

I picked up his cue and turned the conversation to Stephen's marriage. Since both of us disliked Philip Lemerius intensely, it was a safe topic, and as Felix relaxed, an increasingly entertaining one. He was in the middle of a story about the one ghastly time he'd had the honor to be introduced to Philip's late father when the knock came. Lenore ghosted out to answer the door.

"Vincent Demabrien, m'lord, miss," she said and vanished again.

I hadn't been able to get a very good look at Vincent Demabrien during the soirée, just an impression of a slight, feline body and ink-black hair. Now I saw he was a small man, several inches shorter than I, and fine-boned with it. He was as pale-skinned as Felix and Mildmay, and close up, I could see the lines starting to etch themselves around his eyes and mouth. He was older than Felix, and he looked it. I'd never seen a man who looked so tired.

"Madame Parr," he said and bowed out of pure, reflexive good manners; his attention was all for Felix. "I must thank you for your kind invitation." He had no more accent than Felix did; his voice was pleasant, quiet, unremarkable.

"Thank Felix," I said. "It was his idea." I drifted myself away, ostensibly to consult with Lenore although there was nothing that needed saying, leaving the two of them staring at each other as if their past had deprived them of language. By the time I returned, they'd managed to start a painful, limping conversation about the kings whose busts were in the Hall of the Chimeras. I thought, Mildmay could help, and then wondered where Mildmay was. He and Felix were bound-by-forms; he was supposed to be with Felix unless explicitly ordered otherwise. Yet both times Felix had come here, he'd come without Mildmay. Tact on Felix's part was a possible but unlikely answer; I remembered the rumor that Mildmay had tried to protect Gideon from Felix and then shoved the entire subject hastily out of my head, stepping into the conversation with a question about why Michael Teverius had left the busts in the Hall of the Chimeras. Felix said promptly, "Superstition."

"Beg pardon?" I said.

"Michael was superstitious. Yes, I know, it seems odd in a

man who showed no qualms about personally executing the entire royal family, but the Cabal tried to get him to destroy the busts, and he wouldn't. He wouldn't take out the mosaics either, and for that, at least, I think we can be grateful. Or perhaps it was some perverted kind of family loyalty."

"You've lost me again."

"Michael's mother was a Cordelia. The king he, er, replaced was his own cousin."

"Was he a madman?" Vincent asked.

"Not so far as anyone's been able to tell. He didn't rule terribly long as Lord Protector—only nine years or so—but he ruled perfectly competently by all accounts, and he died quite prosaically of the Winter Fever. No assassination, no suicide."

"But to kill all those people . . ."

"People can do astonishing things when they want something badly enough," Felix said, on which rather ominous note Lenore appeared to announce dinner.

The food was magnificent, and I was grateful for my access to the Teverius chef. Vincent Demabrien relaxed, by infinitesimal but perceptible degrees; Felix expanded like a gaudy flower; and by the time we reached dessert, you could almost have believed it was a normal dinner party.

We returned to the sitting room for coffee. I offered brandy, but neither of them would take it. I poured a jigger's worth for myself and sat down to listen to Felix explaining in his light, polite, deadly voice just why Robert of Hermione was miserable to the point of madness about Stephen's marriage. I was concentrating on what Felix was saying, hoping that it might be information that would please Isaac and thus distract him, so it took me a while to notice that Vincent's attention was divided. He was certainly listening to Felix, but his eyes kept wandering from Felix's face and expansive gestures to the stretch of wall between the fireplace and the dining room door.

Felix noticed very shortly after I did; he twisted to look behind him and, seeing nothing, twisted back to look at Vincent. But instead of being perplexed or annoyed, he was wide-eyed with what might have been comprehension or even fear. "Vincent, do you still see them?"

Vincent, for his part, looked even more alarmed—almost sick. But then Felix's cryptic question seemed to reach him; he visibly relaxed and said, "I forgot you knew."

I'm as willing as anyone to let other people play out their dramas, but my patience has its limits. "Knew *what*?"

They both flinched, almost perfectly in unison, and exchanged an unreadable glance. Then Felix shrugged—he had a particularly irritating way of shrugging that conveyed without any need of words his disavowal of responsibility for other people's short-sightedness and stupidity—and said, "Vincent sees ghosts."

He was all but daring me not to believe him. I looked at Vincent, who made an odd, apologetic little grimace and said, "It is true, but I won't be offended if you don't believe me. Ivo thinks I'm mad."

"Yes, because the Polydorii are *so* noted for their sanity and mental stability," Felix said.

But I'd thought of something else. "Who do you see?"

"Beg pardon?"

I waved my hand at the wall. "You clearly see *something*. Who is it?"

"Ah." His head tilted in a listening gesture eerily reminiscent of Felix in conversation with Gideon. "She says she was very beautiful. Men wrote poems to her. She was Damian Teverius's lover, and she killed herself when he put her aside. Her name . . . I'm sorry, Mehitabel. She doesn't remember."

"Mildmay would know," Felix murmured.

"She killed herself? Here?"

"She took poison. Widow's tea, she calls it. I don't know what that is."

"Hemlock," Felix said.

"It didn't hurt. And then Damian had her removed with the rest of the trash and put a new girl in her place." He shook his head once, sharply. "Sorry. She's very . . . bitter. And she has you confused with the woman who replaced her. It's the nature of ghosts."

"Wonderful," I said. "Is she going to—to *do* anything?"

"She can't," Vincent said, almost sadly. "There's not enough left of her. Just the bitterness."

"Well, that's some comfort." I tore my gaze away from that empty stretch of wall. Vincent didn't look at all alarmed any longer, and I asked, "Does this happen to you often?"

"I always see them. I try to ignore them, but sometimes it's hard. I'm sorry, Felix. I really was—"

But Felix cut him off. There was a wild look in his eyes, as if he'd just had a profound and revelatory idea. The yellow eye seemed to say it was magnificent, while the blue eye said it was dreadful. He said, "Vincent, how would you feel about a small experiment?"

"What sort of small experiment?" Vincent said warily.

Felix consulted his pocket watch. "It can't be tonight. It's late, and I've got other things to do. Jeudy? Could you get away Jeudy?"

"Maybe. But to do *what*?"

Felix smiled brilliantly. "To find out how you see ghosts."

Mildmay

You know, I hated the fuck out of the fact I didn't have nowhere safe to go in the Mirador except Mehitabel's old room. Hated the ever-living *fuck* out of it.

But that didn't change nothing.

I lay there on the bed and stared up at the ceiling and tried not to think about fucking Mehitabel. Which went about as well as you'd expect.

But the third or fourth time I forced my jaw to relax, I realized something funny. It wasn't the fucking I missed—there's plenty of that around, and powers, I got hands, don't I?—and it wasn't even Mehitabel herself. Not exactly. I mean, I *missed* her, but I wasn't lying here pining or nothing. What was wrong with me was that I didn't have nothing to do and nothing to think about. Except me. And everything I'd fucked up.

Because, you know, Mehitabel hadn't trusted me, but why in the world should she have? I mean, sure, I'd fucked her brains out whenever she wanted, but powers and saints, I knew better than anybody that didn't mean nothing.

Hadn't talked to her. Hadn't talked to Ginevra, neither. What had Felix called it? *A persistent motif*. He was fucking well right about that. So what did I think I was doing, talking like I loved Ginevra? What the fuck did I think love was, anyway?

I rolled over and punched the pillow instead of the wall.

Well, okay, maybe I had loved Ginevra. Her death had fucked me up bad enough I could give myself that much. But I hadn't acted like it. I hadn't *tried*. And maybe it wouldn't've worked if I had—there wasn't no sense pretending Ginevra hadn't been exactly what she was—but we'd never fucking know now. Because I hadn't tried. I'd looked at it and decided it wasn't worth the risk. No, Mildmay the Fox don't stick his neck out for nothing. Except for money.

Well, or Felix.

But that ain't the same kind of love, I said to myself, and then I couldn't think of a reason why that ought to matter. If I didn't care about somebody enough to take a risk for 'em, I didn't have no business saying I loved them, whatever I thought that damn word meant.

And I didn't. I realized that, laying there. I mean, I'd thought I'd loved Keeper—Kolkhis like that. Thought I'd been *in love* with her. You know. And if that was what it was, I didn't want no part of it. Certainly didn't want to make nobody feel that way about me. I didn't want power like that.

Well, and you ain't no good at it anyway, I said to myself and settled in to try and sleep. Maybe you should just leave it the fuck alone.

I thought, I can do that. And it was such a huge fucking relief that I never even noticed when I fell asleep.

Felix

I'd worked out the thaumaturgy as well as could be hoped for. Once they'd quit insisting on Death, the Dog, and the Prison, the Sibylline had given me the Unreal City, the Nightingale, and the Wheel. Attempts at clarification had all been threaded through with Death, and I cursed Malkar in my heart. But the Unreal City, the Nightingale, and the Wheel were enough to show me how to proceed.

If I'd read them correctly, of course.

It was both the gift and the curse of the Sibylline, that its symbols, its semeia, could be interpreted in so many different ways. This property made it beautifully flexible as an instrument of thaumaturgic architecture, but frustratingly ambiguous when one was trying to use it for divination, whether of the future or of extant thaumaturgy. Mavortian had laughed at me and claimed that reading the cards was an art, requiring "card sense" just as ordinary card games did, but I had suspected then and suspected now that that had been a smoke screen intended to keep me from seeing that he was no more certain than I was.

But I could put the semeia together in a way that made sense for my purposes. The Unreal City was as good a description as there was for the Khloïdanikos. The Nightingale—"A gift from the night," Mavortian had said. "Balance, generosity, unexpected strength." And that was Thamuris, both in himself and in his relationship with the Khloïdanikos: it was almost always night for him.

The Wheel was trickier. But I'd thought about it, in and around other things, and I thought I understood. The Khloïdanikos had a rhythm, a cycle—"a single day," I had suggested, and that still seemed true, but it wasn't strictly linear. It didn't have to be, as long as the deeper rhythm held. The deeper rhythm was the Wheel, and if I could wed the rubies to the Wheel, it would hold them. If.

I emerged into my construct-Mélusine holding the Parliament of Bees balanced on one palm. The bees were crystalline, faceted, glowing brilliant red as they caught the sunlight. They flew in wary circles around me, returning to their hive periodically: a dance, a ritual. I moved very carefully toward Horn Gate, concentrating on holding the beehive steady. Dropping it seemed like a truly terrible idea.

The bees did not trust me, but they did not attack me, and when we reached Horn Gate, bedecked as it was with wisteria, they became less interested in me, crawling thoughtfully among the trailing blossoms. Thamuris was there almost as soon as I was, his anxiety visible around him in an indigo and cerise tumult.

"Are you—oh. Is that them?"

Neither grammatical nor particularly lucid, but I knew what he meant. "Yes. Come with me. I'm going to need your help."

He followed me, anxious but not arguing, and the bees followed us both. I had chosen a place for the rubies amongst the settled geography of the Khloïdanikos: a patriarchal oak that was ringed by brambles. The brambles had been trained over a trellis to form a gateway and now hung like a curtain. Their flowers were yellow, small and musky, and their thorns were fierce, jealous claws. The oak was strong enough to withstand the last lingering taint on the rubies, and the brambles would contain their malice.

Thamuris held the curtain of brambles aside for me; we were

both bleeding from several long scratches by the time I knelt in front of the oak, the bees flying in their silent circles around my head and hands.

"Guard," I said to the oak, to the brambles. "Hold." I set the beehive that was also a gray wash-leather bag down on one of the cracked paving stones, placed my hands carefully to either side, palms flat against the rock.

The Parliament of Bees. The Unreal City. The Nightingale. The Wheel. I drew the rubies through the symbols, from one to the next to the next, winding them onto the Wheel, ringing them with brambles. I felt it, when it took: a jar against my hands, and the beehive was a wash-leather bag with a shining ruby bee crawling across its drawstrings. I turned my attention toward my sleeping body and knew that the bag was no longer clutched in my left hand.

"There," I said, and got to my feet. "It worked."

I emerged back out of the brambled circle of the oak, and Thamuris let go of the trailing briars. "I wish," he said, "that you would tell me a little more about the wizard those gems belonged to."

"What do you want to know?" I said, starting away from the oak and toward the ruined orchard wall.

Thamuris followed me. "Well, if he were—and I know this is silly, but *if* he were to . . . well, to *manifest*, what would the signs be?"

"That isn't silly," I said reluctantly as we entered the fallow orchard. "If he manifests *himself*, you'll know him because he doesn't—didn't—look in the least Troian. Phenomena . . ." I ran through a rapid mental survey of everything I knew about Malkar, everything I'd watched for in the shadows and dreaded. "He always wore musk—at least when I knew him. He murdered a woman by burning her alive, by magic. He was very old—I don't even know how old. He died by burning. And he was a blood-wizard, as I told you, so anything bleeding, any sign or smell of blood . . ."

"You know a great deal about him," Thamuris said. "And I would guess that he did not leave you these relics in his will."

I had betrayed myself. I should, I thought, have known that I would.

The perseïd tree was still not dead. I reached out and laid my palm on its trunk, feeling the cold of the bark and beneath it the faintest sense of brightness. Of hope? "What is it you want to know, Thamuris?" I said wearily.

"What I've just helped you put in the Dream of the Garden, for one thing."

"A little late to be asking that, don't you think?"

"I trusted your judgment."

"And now you don't?"

"I would like some more information," he said, very levelly.

I turned away from the perseïd tree. "Look. How I know him isn't . . . it isn't relevant."

"No? Then why does the phrase 'death by burning' have such a violent effect on you?"

He was watching my emotions, damn him. And I was failing to control them.

"It *is* how everyone I knew in my childhood died," I said, both to defend myself and for the vicious, unworthy satisfaction of seeing him flinch.

He did flinch, but he recovered and said, "That's nothing to do with this man whose name you won't tell me."

"It doesn't matter. He's dead." Strange, how much of my time I seemed to spend these days telling people Malkar was dead.

Thamuris's breath hitched; I looked at him and saw his eyes widen. "He is your spirit-ancestor."

"No, he is *not*." But if he wasn't, why had I been so eager to find out how to do a thanatopsis?

Of course Malkar—Brinvillier Strych—was my spirit-ancestor, my patron saint. Who else could it possibly be?

Thamuris had quite rightly ignored my futile outburst. "I thought I understood what you were doing, but I don't. You can't treat a spirit-ancestor like a contagion—"

"That's what he is!" The banshee fury of my voice surprised me just as much as it did him, and for the first time in years, my concentration broke, splintered, shattered, and I lost the Khloïdanikos entirely in a nightmare, an old terrible nightmare of the Fire and pain and Malkar's laughter until my own half-shrieking sobs woke me.

Chapter 13

Mehitabel

There was, of course, a soirée in honor of Stephen's impending marriage. Stephen was dining beforehand with the amassed Lemerii, and it was a good thing I wasn't expected to join them, both because I couldn't offhand think of a more dire way to start the evening and because if I had been, I would have been horribly late.

Mrs. Damascus caught me after rehearsal for a final fitting of my costume—at this stage of the game, she took over almost entirely from Corinna. By the time she left, Jean-Soleil, Corinna, and Semper were all standing outside my door. Jean-Soleil looked apoplectic, Corinna anxious, and Semper wretched. Jean-Soleil barely waited for Mrs. Damascus to clear the door before he came in, shutting it behind him with a bang.

"Harlot!"

"Me?"

"Great powers, no! Susan."

"What's she done now?"

"She came calling, all great lady and lah-di-dah, the narcissistic cow." He stomped in a circle, muttering obscenities.

"What did she want?"

"For us not to put on *Edith Pelpheria*, of course. I couldn't make out if Jermyn had sent her or it was her own idiocy."

"It sounds like Susan all the way down. Did she say what ought to motivate you?"

"She said we were being dreadfully cruel to her."

I started laughing, relieved not to have to censor my reaction. Jean-Soleil's mustache twitched, and then he burst out laughing, too. "Thank you, Belle. I was too mad to laugh at her."

"Susan's particular gift is to make people take her most witless actions seriously. She can make a five-act tragedy out of dropping a handkerchief, and for God's sake don't let it get under your skin *now*."

"I couldn't afford to get angry with her before. Have to keep the leading lady happy, you know. You have no idea how great a relief it is to be able to call Susan a harlot at the top of my lungs."

"You might be surprised," I said dryly and made him laugh again.

"I don't think you need to worry about her coming near you. She seems to dislike you nearly as much as you dislike her."

"If that was news to you, it certainly wasn't to anyone else in the Empyrean."

"No? Oh, dear." Jean-Soleil worked hard to believe in the acting troupe as happy family, and in general we did our best not to disabuse him.

"It's all right, Jean-Soleil. She's gone."

"Thank the powers," Jean-Soleil said and left, only to be replaced by Corinna, who wanted to talk about Drin.

"I can't make him stop," I said to her. "You know that. I can never make Drin do anything."

"You made him sleep with you pretty easy."

"Oh, please. You don't imagine I had to *work* at that, do you? Why don't you talk to him? He's scared of you."

Corinna snorted.

"No, he is. He's a lot more likely to listen to you than to me."

"I just wish he wouldn't be such a pig."

"I do, too, but I'm afraid that's past praying for. Look, Corinna, I'll back you up, but I am *not* opening the subject with him."

"Oh, all right, but I'll hold you to that."

"Just not tonight!" I said to her at the door, which she acknowledged with a wave.

I expected Semper to be upset about Drin, too, but he had a different thorn in his paw. He sat down at my invitation, his long, beautiful hands twisting in his lap, and furrows in his forehead you could have planted seeds in.

"What is it?" I said, when it became clear he wasn't going to be able to launch himself.

"I got a letter from my father." He looked up at me. "Is it true his daughter is going to marry the Lord Protector?"

"Yes."

"He says . . . he says it would be a disgrace and a scandal if anyone found out that his son was working with the Lord Protector's, er . . ."

"Lover."

"Yes. Would it be?"

I shrugged, as indifferently as possible. "The Mirador's weathered worse."

He wrestled with it a moment and burst out: "I just wish he'd quit *nagging* me!"

"Lord Philip has managed his family by nagging for years and years. It seems to work. But if it's not going to work on you . . . ?"

"No," he said firmly.

"Then you need to call his bluff."

"Beg pardon?"

I grinned at him. "Come to the soirée with me this evening. I dare you."

His eyes widened. "You can't be serious."

"Oh, I am. I learned this trick from my mother. Meet it head on, and scandal loses most of its power. *And* it cuts Lord Philip's feet out from under him very neatly indeed. So will you?"

He was too smart not to see it. He was grinning, too, when he said, "Yes."

Another complication for an already complicated evening. But more worth it than not. "Then come on, and let's find you something to wear. And I'll write a note to Enid."

✷

Enid's reply came just before dinner. Four words: *How excessively like Father.* I gave it to Semper, who laughed with delight and tucked it carefully into an inside pocket, like a talisman.

Mildmay

I got all the way to the door of the suite just fine, and there I stuck fast, one hand up to knock. After a minute where I must have looked either like a half-wit or a dressmaker's dummy, I let my hand fall again and backed up to the other wall. He'd have to come out sooner or later. It might even be on time, since there was nobody in there to fight with. We had to go to this stupid

soirée together, but there was nothing said I had to put myself in
the way of his nasty temper before then. So I just waited.

After about five minutes, the door opened. Felix said, "Oh,
it's you. I thought I heard *some* buffalo snorting around in the
hall. You might as well come in."

"Might as well," I said. I went in and sat in the chair by the
door, the uncomfortable one for visitors. I was tired of cosseting
Felix and his little airs. I mean, it wasn't like he was the only
person in the world who'd ever had somebody walk out on him.

He said, "You're stubborn as a pig," and flitted into his bedroom to finish dressing. I didn't say nothing, since I realized—
about two inches shy of opening my mouth—that I was fixing
to pick a fight myself. What had been keeping me out in the
hallway was my nasty temper, not his. Powers, I thought, this is
going to be a long fucking night.

"It was clever of you to get one of the servants to come for
your clothes," Felix said, coming out again. "How did you know
I wouldn't yell at him?"

Fuck. He really was on the prowl. Any answer would be the
wrong answer, so I just gave him the truth. "They get paid to
have hocuses yell at them."

Felix's eyes narrowed. I was bracing myself when he flipped
open his pocket watch and said, in this nice, level, lethal voice,
"I promised Fleur I would be on time for this thing if it killed
me. Come on." He snapped it shut again, dropped it in his
pocket, and I followed him out the door, just like I'd done Great
Septads of times before. Some of those times we'd been out for
each other's blood, too.

Mehitabel

The soirée began with the betrothal ceremony, very formal and
restrained; only mannequins of wax and papier-mâché and
clockwork could have managed the thing with less emotion.

That was fine, that was perfect; no one wanted any unbe-
coming displays. Afterward, I circulated, Semper in tow, introducing him left, right, and center. He took it very well, blushed
charmingly at some of the things Phegenie Brome said to him,
was exactly the right mixture of shyness and excitement. Give
him a little time to find his feet, and he'd be cutting a swath
through the Mirador as wide as anyone could wish.

I seized the chance to introduce him to Lord Shannon—one perfect gold eyebrow rose very slightly at the "Philipson," but he didn't comment—and that propelled Semper neatly into the middle of Shannon's theater-mad friends. Shannon himself stepped back a little, watching, and after a moment I said, "He is lovely, isn't he?"

"What? Oh yes." And I realized Shannon hadn't been watching Semper at all. He'd been looking past Semper to where Felix Harrowgate was standing in a knot of courtiers and some of the younger wizards. Felix's face was animated, and he was gesturing widely, clearly in the middle of a story that was, to judge from his audience's reactions, both hilarious and scandalous.

I opened my mouth to say something—I didn't even know what—and Shannon said, sounding amused and regretful and resigned all at once, "He's telling them about the meeting between Evadne Corvinia's second husband and fifth lover. Unless it's the fifth husband and second lover. I could never keep that story straight."

"Oh," I said, with perfect uselessness, but he continued, "I still love him, you know. Isn't that stupid?"

"No, my lord," I managed.

"He hates me," Shannon said, "and after the way I treated him, I deserve it. But I just . . . Do you remember, Madame Parr, in *The Wooden Daughter*, when the old alchemist says everyone has one thing they can't think straight about?"

"Yes," I said, and quoted: "It is a rose planted in your heart, and as its thorns tear you, so does it thrive and flower."

"It sounds rather romantic, doesn't it? But it isn't. It isn't at all. I couldn't forgive him for my own betrayal of him, and so I betrayed him twice. Three times? I can't keep this story straight either." He smiled at me with such aching melancholy that I could almost have been tempted, if he hadn't been Stephen's brother, to tell him about Hallam. My own stupidities, my own betrayals.

I didn't say anything; he didn't expect me to.

"But tell me," he said, turning the conversation with grace and finality, "when are you going to give your recital for Lady Enid?"

I answered—no date was set, since Lady Enid's schedule had become quite complicated—and we fell to talking about what I might perform for her, a conversation that attracted the attention of first one, then another, of Lord Shannon's clique, and brought Semper, too, for he confessed to ignorance of almost all plays, and there was a flurry of recommendations, and squabbles about recommendations, and Shannon shook off his melancholy and was in the thick of the debate, laughing at Semper's polite but manifest bewilderment, when Lord Philip Lemerius came upon us.

It couldn't have been better timed, since Philip probably disapproved of Shannon even more than he did of Semper. And Shannon wasn't a provincial nobody whom Philip could stare down. Philip was expanding like a monstrous rose-colored bullfrog—he shouldn't have let his tailor talk him into the velvet—and for a moment I worried he might go off in an apoplexy. But then he said to his son, "What are *you* doing here?" and I changed my mind. An apoplexy was better than he deserved.

The blank look Semper gave him couldn't have been bettered; I wasn't sure if he was acting or not.

"Good evening, Lord Philip," Shannon said pointedly.

"My lord," Philip said. It came grating out between his teeth as if there were several other things that would have come out more smoothly. "I must ask you to excuse us for a moment—"

"There's nothing to say," Semper said. "Is there, Father?"

Philip choked, sputtered. Finally he said, still grating, "I am *very* disappointed," and turned on his heel and stalked away.

Shannon divided an inquiring look between Semper and me. Semper was turning slow scarlet; I said with mocking precision, "Lord Philip has certain definite opinions on the morality or lack thereof of the acting profession."

"I see," said Shannon. "You know, Semper, I think now would be an excellent time for you to be introduced to my brother. Coming, Mehitabel?"

"I believe I can trust you not to lose the baby," I said.

"Mehitabel!" Semper moaned faintly, but Lord Shannon smiled, his eyes alight with shared wickedness.

"I'll take good care of him. Come on, Semper."

I watched them make their way, in a graceful but unswerving line, toward Stephen and Enid, and turned around smack into Simon Barrister.

We both yelped; we had been standing back-to-back without

knowing it, each of us watching a different playlet. As we exchanged courtesies, I glanced in the direction Simon must have been looking and saw Dinah Valeria and some noble cadet whose name I didn't know, half-obscured behind the bust of King Henry, standing gazing into each other's eyes as if they'd never seen another human being before.

Simon didn't turn. "A happy ending," he said, with a bitter note in his voice that was unlike him. He heard it himself, for he gave me a smile and said, "No matter."

"Simon, I—"

"No, really, forget I spoke."

"Well, I admit they do look a pair of prize mooncalves," I said, and he laughed.

"There's nothing so tiresome as new-minted love. I'm growing old and cynical. Give me some good scurrilous gossip, Mehitabel, and cheer me up."

I told him about Semper, which did the trick nicely, and we were talking about the ghastly spectacle of Philip Lemerius in velours rosace when we became aware of a commotion on the other side of the hall.

"Felix," said Simon, who was tall enough to see over intervening heads. "And—oh powers and blessed weeping saints— Robert with him."

He set off through the crowd without another word; I wondered if he really thought he could do anything to avert the disaster already happening. But I followed him. Out of morbid, vulgar curiosity. Nothing more—because I knew that Felix couldn't be averted from disaster anymore than a cyclone could.

Mildmay

I should've seen it coming.

I'd been looking for trouble from Robert of Hermione for decads, and I knew perfectly well he didn't have no weapons left to use against Felix. And I knew, better than most anybody in that room, that the Lower City only keeps secrets until somebody pays enough for 'em. And I hadn't forgotten about it—it wasn't the sort of thing that ever really drops out of your memory—but it had happened so long ago, and it had been tangled up in so many other things, that I guess I had forgotten it was dangerous.

Yeah, I know. Too dumb to come in out of the rain, that's me.

Felix had been drinking, not hard but steady. He'd got to about half lit early on, and he'd stayed there, not drunk enough that most people could tell. It was letting him pretend he was in a good mood, all charming and funny. He had all his bright, hard armor on, and I thought that as long as nobody tried to find a chink in it, we'd be okay.

And that was when Robert of Hermione said, "You never cease to amaze me, Lord Felix." All smirking and oily, and powers, we weren't okay at all.

"What now?" Felix said, like he was so sick of Robert he hardly even cared.

It didn't throw Robert, not even a little bit. "I have grown accustomed to the way you flaunt yourself in the Hall of the Chimeras, but—"

"Me?" Felix said, turning on him, quick as a cat, quick enough that Robert went back a step without meaning to. "What about you?"

"What have I done?" Robert said, innocent as a baby.

"Shall I recite the full list? To start with—"

"At least I'm not harboring the murderer of Cornell Teverius."

"Cerberus Cresset," Felix said, like a guy puts a hand up to block a punch.

"Oh, him too," and Robert's smirk widened into a grin, all teeth and evil, like this fish from the Imari I saw once in a carnival. At least it'd had the decency to be dead.

There was this sick pause, while nobody said nothing and I could feel things crashing around me like enormous stone vases being dropped from the Crown of Nails to shatter to bits on the granite of the Plaza del'Archimago.

"I should have known," Felix said. His head turned my direction. "Did you?"

I felt like a dog being asked if he'd eaten the dinner roast. "Yeah," I said, because there was nothing else I could say.

He shut his eyes for a second, like he was in pain, and said, "What *do* you think can be done about it, Robert? Bring Lord Cornell back to life? That's necromancy, and don't think you'll escape the heresy charge a second time."

"What? Felix, I—"

Felix turned, looking at Robert sidelong out of his good eye, and it was a nasty look, ears laid back like a horse about to kick. "You're not so lily-white yourself, after all. Or shall I"—and his voice started to rise, playing for the crowd gathering to listen— "shall I tell those assembled about your experiments in the basement of St. Crellifer's?"

"The ravings of a madman."

"You think?" And Felix's smile was worse than Robert's, because it was Strych, exactly like Strych. "There's nothing wrong with my memory, Robert. And I have been very well trained to recognize what you did."

"The Curia consented!" And Robert almost sounded panicky.

"I don't think the Curia had the least idea what you were doing, not really. I could tell them. But I don't think you knew what you were doing, either, or you would have done a better job. You're incompetent, darling, and really I can't think of a worse thing to say about anyone."

Robert's mouth opened, hung that way for a second, and I guess he had the sense to see things were only going to get worse for him—Felix had that look on his face, like a cat wondering if the mouse is good for another round—because he cleared out. No parting shot, no nothing. Just bailed.

And everybody all at once pretended like they hadn't been watching and didn't have the first clue what was going on, and were way more interested in something else besides.

"Damn," said Felix, real quiet, and Simon came up out of nowhere and said, "How comforting to see that Robert hasn't lost his touch."

"Oh, quite. Do you think there's any point in my trying to talk to Stephen?"

"What are you planning to say?"

But just then, we all got to find out. A voice said, "Lord Felix, a word please." It was Lord Stephen, of course, standing a little ways off.

"My lord," said Felix, "I am at your service."

"If only that were true," Lord Stephen said, and that hung there nastily for a moment before he went on. "But let's pretend it is, and that you'll do as I ask. I need to speak to your brother for a moment."

I felt like one of them vases I was talking about had cracked me on the skull.

"Be my guest," Felix said with a sort of lordly little wave. Powers and saints, he was pissed at me.

"Mr. Foxe," said Lord Stephen, with an odd, awkward bob of the head that was something almost like a bow.

That threw me even further off balance, but I managed to say, "M'lord," and give a kind of cautious nod back.

Lord Stephen jerked his head at me, and I followed him—I spent most of my time, it seemed like, following people—back behind the bust of King Paul.

He said, "I do not blame you for being an assassin."

"It was a septad ago," I said, before I knew I was going to say anything. "I mean, I was, and I'm sorry, but I ain't no more."

He looked at me for a while. I couldn't read his face, and I wondered, with a crawling feeling all down my spine, what Mehitabel had told him about me. He was angry behind his good manners, I knew that much, but I couldn't tell if he was angry at me or at Robert or maybe at Cornell or at somebody else entirely.

"I was only going to ask," he said finally, "who hired you?"

Fuck. "I don't know."

"You don't *know*?" I was going to get some of that anger, whether it was really meant for me or not, but after Felix's tantrums, I was really only worried that he'd have me thrown in the Verpine before he remembered he couldn't.

This wasn't the time or the place to talk about thief-keepers and how they worked. I said, "I was hired through a third party."

"How did you do it?"

"With a knife," I said.

"No. Not that. How did you get him down there?"

"I didn't."

"But you killed him."

Shit, I was going to have to explain it anyway. "When I was an assassin, I—well, I was a kept-thief first."

"What?"

The word "assassin" is a bitch, and it never does come out right. I said it again, slower, and this time he got it.

"Yes," he said, like he didn't see where this was going.

"It was my keeper made all the arrangements. I was just like . . ." I shut my mouth hard on the words "a clockwork bear" because I'd have to explain what I meant. "Like a knife or something. She told me what to do, and I didn't ask questions. I did a lot of things I'm sorry for that way, like Lord Cornell."

"And Cerberus Cresset," he said. He was sneering.

"No. I ain't sorry about Cerberus Cresset." And then neither one of us could believe I'd said it.

Lord Stephen decided to ignore it. "So you can't tell me who hired you, and you can't tell me how my cousin was lured out of the Mirador—"

"I can tell you some things," I said, "if you feel like you got to know."

"If you're a knife, I want the person who threw you at Cornell. What can you tell me?"

"The place where I was . . . I mean, whoever planned it, they brought him to me. I was in a place where people could buy boats and get down to the Sim and get out of the city. He was frightened of something when he came there, like he thought there was somebody after him. And there was a guy with him."

" 'A guy'?"

"The servant. The one who gave the story about the guy in a boat."

His eyebrows went up. "You mean that was a lie?"

"Um, yeah. There was no guy in a boat. Lord Cornell was dead before they got out on the river."

"So Drake was part of it. No wonder he wanted to try his fortunes in Vusantine."

Smart of him, I thought, but he'd been smart. Smart and cold-blooded, and I was willing to bet I knew what kind of fortune he'd found. But I didn't say none of that.

"Can you tell me anything else?"

"Dunno. I mean, it was a big plot, but I don't know how they found my keeper or what they paid her or anything like that."

"You didn't even get paid?"

He was mocking me. I shrugged. You don't pay a knife. Or a clockwork bear.

"Tell Felix that if he restrains himself, this doesn't need to become official," he said and stepped out from behind King

Paul. After a minute, I dragged myself together and came out around the other side.

Felix

It was nearly three in the morning before I left the Hall of the Chimeras. I'd wanted and intended to make an early night of it, but after Robert's little playlet, I knew better than to leave the gossip to ferment unsupervised. I talked and danced and smiled at people until my face ached, and Mildmay was always there, politely in the background, like the shadow of death. And politely, like the shadow of death, he followed me when I said my goodnights and started back for my suite.

I hadn't meant to say anything to him. There was after all, as I'd pointed out to Robert, no use. But I was exhausted and half-drunk, and my mouth betrayed me in the middle of the Glasswing Corridor: "Why didn't you tell me?"

"Tell you?" he echoed, as if he were stupid.

"*Tell* me that you'd murdered Cornell Teverius. Come on, Mildmay, wake up in there!" I aimed a halfhearted cuff at the back of his head; he dodged it without really seeming to notice.

"Dunno," he said.

"That's your answer to everything. Did it get you off the hook with Kolkhis?"

I saw it hit home—not in his face, never that, but in the way his stride checked for a moment, as if he were uncertain of the ground.

I said impatiently, "I'm not Kolkhis, and it doesn't satisfy me. You must have a reason."

"Maybe I didn't want to talk about it."

"I'm not asking for a full confession. I'm saying, why didn't you let me know *before* Robert of Hermione told the world?"

"'Cause I didn't think Robert *would* tell the world. If I'd wanted it talked about, I would have told you."

"Meaning that at least you weren't the one who told Robert." He'd meant several other things as well, but I didn't want to deal with them, at least not yet.

"Look. I ain't proud of having killed all them people, and it ain't exactly the sort of thing I go around bragging about."

I stopped where I was and waited until he turned to face me. "Let's clear up a misconception. I'm not asking, why didn't you tell me all the gory details? I'm asking, why didn't you tell me you'd been involved in *both* of the Mirador's big mysteries?"

"*I don't know*, all right? I just don't."

I couldn't quite tell if he was lying or not, but one thing was very clear: "You don't trust me, do you?"

"What? Felix, I—"

I shouldn't have said it, but now that I had, I'd be damned if I was going to let it drop. "You don't. You never have."

"Oh for fuck's sake. I asked you to do the obligation d'âme, didn't I? What's that if it ain't trust?"

"Desperation. You *don't* trust me. You wanted to know how we could help each other. That's your answer, Mildmay. Trust me."

"How can I trust you? Anything I told you, the next time you get mad at me, you'll tell whoever the fuck you're standing with."

I stared at him, feeling suddenly breathless. "You think that?"

"I know how you work. You make fun of me to other people; why wouldn't you betray me, too?"

"Mildmay, it's not the same—"

"It's the same to me, okay? Just the fucking same."

He meant it. I swallowed hard, managed: "I won't do it again."

"Like that helps. You'll just find something else to do, something that ain't what you said you wouldn't, but that works just the same. I don't care. You can be as mean to me as you like, but don't come 'round wondering why I don't *trust* you. Good night, Felix."

He left me there, and I stood as if I'd been turned to stone and watched him go.

Mildmay

I dreamed that night about the cellars of St. Kirban, about standing on the bottom step with a lantern, looking out at the blackness and the water. There were boats on the water, Phoskis's little black boats, and every single one of them had a corpse in it. I spent the whole night looking for somebody I hadn't killed.

Chapter 14

Mehitabel

I'd written to Vincent to tell him he could come early if he (or Lord Ivo) wanted, and he did. "Lord Ivo," he said apologetically, "thinks it an excellent thing for me to cultivate your acquaintance. I haven't, of course, mentioned Felix."

"Well, I'm glad to see you," I said and gave him a strong but nonflirtatious smile. "Come sit down. And would you like something to drink?"

He accepted sherry, and when we were settled, I asked, "Does Lord Ivo find Felix so reprehensible, then?"

Vincent bought himself time by making a very small show of tasting the sherry, but he said quite mildly and without a hint of discomfort, "It's more that Ivo doesn't find Felix useful. The people with whom he wants to ingratiate himself do not care for wizards."

I remembered Antony saying, *The Lemerii do not consort with wizards.*

Vincent continued, "And Felix himself . . ." His shrug was graceful, economical, and very elegant.

"Do you find him much changed?"

"Felix?"

"From what he was when you first knew him."

"In some ways," he said, the somber lines of his face lightening with a reminiscent smile. "He was beautiful—and arrogant with it even then—but . . . He came from Simside, you know. Dreadful accent, and all the poise of a cornered rat. He wears the mask far more naturally now."

"You must have come from a very different background," I said.

Vincent laughed, a light, chilly sound, and said, "Once upon a time, there was a poor but virtuous scrivener who lived in Havelock. He had three sons. The youngest and most beautiful of the three was named Vincent."

"I'm sorry," I said. "I didn't intend to pry."

It was mostly a lie, but partly true, and in any event the right thing to say, because Vincent said in a much more natural tone, "I used to wonder how it was I got into the wrong story, where it was that I should have started having fabulous adventures and ended up in the Shining Tiger instead. I never did figure it out. The story's simple enough, though: my father died when I was twelve. All of his money had been sunk in sending my eldest brother, Jonathan, to the Academy so that he could become a secretary. Jonathan, who really was the sort of eldest brother one encounters in stories, had promptly cut the entire family dead. I know my mother went up to see him after he didn't come to the funeral; she came back weeping and told Conrad and me that Jonathan would help us when he could. She was a very bad liar."

I said, carefully, "You don't have to tell me this."

"It's nothing but old bitterness now, like the last trace of a bloodstain on a sheet. And, you know, no one's ever *asked*. I rehearsed it for years planning what I would say to the young, wealthy, sensitive noble who saw my sterling qualities beneath the hard veneer of whoredom and took me away to his palace in Lighthill. But I was never in that story, either." His smile was bitter and thin, mocking his former self. "My mother was bad at a lot of things, you see. She couldn't find work, she couldn't fight my father's employers for the widow's gift they were supposed to give her, she couldn't seem to understand how to make last what little savings my father had. Conrad was old enough to have helped—he was fourteen—but his love had been for my father, not really for any of the rest of us. He ran away about a month after Father was buried, and I have no idea what became of him. And then, a few weeks later, a man came to the door. I don't know who told him to try his luck with the Widow Demabrien, but it was good advice. He told her a pack of plausible lies and gave her a septagorgon. That was all it took."

He gazed at his sherry meditatively for a moment, then looked up and gave me a brighter smile. "But there are advantages, including a prodigious amount of time to read. I gather your company is putting on *Edith Pelpheria*?"

We were still talking literature when Felix arrived looking white and distrait like something out of a romance. He pulled himself together to be amusing, charming, but his eyes never lit, and his laugh was never quite real. I wondered what he thought of the murder of Cornell Teverius, but even if I'd been feeling cruel enough to ask, he wouldn't tell me.

He said, rather abruptly, out of a discussion of *The Singer's Tragedy*, "Are you ready, Vincent?"

A pause. Vincent blinked, and some of his immaculate coldness returned to his face. "I suppose."

Felix nodded, stood up. "Then let's go. I really do want to try this." His smile was self-deprecating, but it still didn't reach his eyes.

I insisted on going with them. Felix wasn't best pleased, but Vincent seemed grateful in a shy, embarrassed way. I wouldn't have wanted to be alone with Felix in this mood, either.

Despite all Mildmay's disparaging remarks about Felix's sense of direction, he led the way to the crypt of the Cordelii directly and without hesitation. I squashed the niggling worry about whether he would be able to lead us back so easily, and followed him and Vincent between the tombs to the candles clustered in front of Amaryllis Cordelia's wall-vault.

Felix lit the candles with a careless flick of his fingers and quirked a grin when Vincent and I startled. "I *am* a wizard, after all. There's no point in not getting any use out of it."

Vincent was looking around uneasily, and I felt obligated to ask, "Do you see anything?"

"Not yet," he said and moved farther into the circle of candlelight. "Very old places are . . ." He made a gesture, economical and evocative, and I was distracted for a moment memorizing it for use on the stage, the spread of his fingers, the turn of his wrist and how that moved into the set of his shoulders.

"Old places," Vincent was saying, "are slow to wake, to warm. Some places don't respond at all. There's a ruined church at Arborstell that's *always* cold."

"Mikkary," Felix said absently.

"Beg pardon?"

"It's a Kekropian concept to do with the atmosphere—the aura, if you like—of places. I'd not thought about it being antithetical to ghosts, but it makes a certain amount of sense."

"It does?" I said. "I would have thought the two would go hand in hand."

Felix made a dissatisfied noise—not with me, but with himself. "Ghosts *become* mikkary. Oh dear, that made even less sense, didn't it?"

"Yes," I said, and he laughed.

"Give me another couple weeks and I'll be able to write you a monograph. But for now . . . ghosts are the memory of being human. Mikkary is the hatred of the memory of being human."

"That's probably as much as I *want* to understand."

"Yes, well," Felix said and shrugged.

Vincent said, "Tell me again what it is you want?"

"I want to figure out how you see ghosts," Felix said. "It doesn't just *happen*, you know."

"It doesn't?" Vincent said dubiously.

"No, of course not!" Felix started, then brought himself up short. He flashed Vincent a nervous smile I thought was calculated, and said more moderately, "You're sensitive to . . . well, I don't know to what exactly. That's what I want to find out."

"And what do you want me to do?" Vincent asked.

"Give me your hands." Felix extended his own peremptorily, and Vincent took them. "And now—well, have you ever tried to see a ghost on purpose?"

"No, I told you. I try to ignore them."

"Mmph. Try *not* to ignore them, and let's see what happens."

I'd moved around to where I could see Vincent's face, and from the look he gave me, he couldn't tell if Felix was joking or not. I shrugged back; I couldn't tell either.

And then for a while we stood, unspeaking. Felix's head was bent over his and Vincent's hands; Vincent was watching the darkness beyond the candlelight, and eventually he said, sounding almost surprised, "There's a lady."

"I thought there might be," Felix murmured without raising his head. "Does she remember who she was?"

"Amaryllis Cordelia," Vincent said promptly. "She was the lover of kings. She was almost a queen. She died by treachery and poison."

"Oh God," I said, remembering the corpse's stiff claws and staring desiccated eyes. "Strychnine."

"Old herbals call it St. Grandin's Kiss," Felix said, and then to Vincent: "Does she remember who killed her?"

"The court poisoner," Vincent said, and I said, "Grendille Moran."

Felix glanced at me over his shoulder. "You're positively a fountain of knowledge tonight, Tabby."

"You're such an asshole. Stephen was playing tour guide."

"Oh my," said Felix. "And to think I missed it."

"Have you seen what you wanted?" Vincent said sharply.

"What? Oh. Yes. Rather." Felix let go of Vincent's hands.

"Then may we please leave?" Vincent's tone was an odd combination of plea and demand.

"You don't care for the ambiance?" But Felix's fingers flicked out again, dousing the candles and calling his eerie green will o' the wisps into being instead.

"No," Vincent said. "I don't. And if we stay, I think some of the others may start to become restless."

"Then by all means," Felix said and waved us ahead of him out the door—which I noticed he was careful to close behind him as he emerged.

We climbed the white marble stairs, and I thought we all breathed a little easier at the top. Felix started back the way we'd come with apparently perfect confidence. After a minute or so, he said, "So, Mehitabel, tell us about Grendille Moran."

"You make it sound like there's something to tell. Stephen said she was the court poisoner under Laurence. Her suite was somewhere near mine, and she was beheaded there."

"History in the Mirador," Felix said to Vincent's wince of revulsion. "Did Amaryllis know who, er, commissioned her death?"

"If she did, she'd forgotten. She remembered an astonishing amount as it was. More than most."

"Really?" Felix seemed pleased.

"Does that fit in with your theories?" I asked curiously.

"It might. Vincent, how would you feel about another small experiment?"

"What this time?" said Vincent, and I wished I could believe there was any mockery in his resignation.

"I have a great fancy," Felix said, "to talk to a court poisoner."

"You realize it's unlikely anything useful will come of it."

Vincent was right; I didn't like the febrile light in Felix's yellow eye, or the dreaminess of the blue eye. "Just an idea I've got," he said.

"Not tonight," Vincent said. "I have to get back."

"No, of course not tonight. But tomorrow?"

"Felix, I don't—"

"You're probably right, and nothing will happen. But come to Mehitabel's suite anyway, and we'll talk about it."

"All right," Vincent said, his gaze dropping as if intransigence were too heavy a burden. "I'll get away when I can."

"Marvelous," Felix said.

We said nothing more until, astonishingly, Felix had brought us back to my rooms, where Vincent murmured "Good night," and left.

Felix sighed. "At least it's time he doesn't have to spend with Ivo Polydorius."

"Do you know Lord Ivo?"

"Only by reputation. He'd packed up bag and baggage and left the Mirador before Malkar brought me here, a chronological serendipity of which I have often been glad. He is *not* a nice man, and I have a horrible feeling that he and Malkar would have been bosom friends."

"Why does Vincent put up with it?"

"What else could he do? There isn't much market for whores in their thirties." The vulgarity jarred me, and I saw that bitter whiteness had come creeping back into his face.

"Felix, are you all right?"

"Me? I'm fine. What is there in my life to complain about?"

I refused to be drawn, saying only, "You look tired."

"Tired I grant you. I'm going home to bed. Enjoy your evening, Tabby." A barbed wish from Felix, but I let him go with a simple good night. If he was looking for a fight, he was going to have to look somewhere else.

Mildmay

Let's be frank. Except for court—a nightmare and I ain't saying another word about it—I spent the day hiding, down in the levels of the Mirador where nobody lived but rats and spiders and feral cats. Nobody was going to want to talk to me, and I didn't want to see the difference in people's faces. There was nobody I could think of in the Mirador who wouldn't care, nobody who wouldn't think that what they knew made me somebody different. Maybe it did make me somebody different, but if so, that'd happened a long time ago and it wasn't Cornell Teverius had done it, neither. It was a nobody named Bartimus Cawley.

Cawley had been a neighborhood boss in Pennycup, one of

the septads of unimportant little crooks that keep the Lower City running. Cawley had been stupider than most, a pigheaded, greedy prick without the basic smarts to understand when he was in over his head. He started pushing the boundaries of his half-centime kingdom, taking over a couple guys to the south of him, and then he thought he knew what he was doing and he did two stupid things at once. One was he started pushing into Scaffel-green. The other was he started expanding his line of business. From being a fence and a shylock and a part-time extortionist, he thought he'd hit the big time and be a drug dealer.

Drugs are a pretty brisk trade in the Lower City, between phoenix and spiderweb and roseblood, and the sick part is that there really is always enough business to go around. But Bartimus Cawley didn't just want to deal. He wanted to be a big mover, what dealers call a spider, and he didn't have enough sense to see you couldn't start off at the top. So he knocked over Pennycup's biggest spider and set himself up in business. For a decad or two, he probably thought he got away with it.

But the guy he was pushing in Scaffelgreen was bigger than he thought, and meaner, and the drug dealers were pissed off, and somebody knew Kolkhis and knew she had another assassin coming up—and maybe owed her a favor. Bartimus Cawley was such a fuckup, I guess they figured they could stand the risk. If Kolkhis couldn't take care of him, somebody else could.

I was a couple months past my second septad. My face had healed up as well as it was going to—the scar was starting to go from bright red to dull white, which was better in a sad sort of way—and Kolkhis had been training me to kill people instead of just robbing them blind. I wasn't the first kid she'd trained that way. When I was little, her assassin had been a girl named Lettie Harbinger, but Lettie got careless and got dead when I was still about two and a half indictions away from Jenday and his knife. Kolkhis hadn't picked anybody out after Lettie died, and we'd figured she was waiting for somebody in particular to get old enough to do it. I'd never thought she'd been waiting for me, and I still ain't sure she was. But she'd figured out she could make me do whatever she wanted, and maybe that was all the particular she needed.

So she'd trained me up good, and she sent me out to kill Bartimus Cawley. I guess as far as first targets go, Cawley was about as easy as you could ask for. He was stupid and he was fat, and I didn't have no trouble getting to him or getting him dead. There wasn't even a moment where I thought I couldn't do it or nothing like that. I climbed up to his window—second storey, he was at least smart enough for that, but what good does that do you against a cat burglar?—found him in bed, snoring like five alligators in a fight, and got a garotte around his neck without him even knowing I was there. It was only afterward, standing there staring at his purple, swollen face, that I thought, You can't take that back. I could be sorry now if I wanted to be—and I thought maybe I was—but it wasn't going to make Bartimus Cawley less dead. Nothing was going to make Bartimus Cawley less dead, and it was my fault.

I went back out the window, went back to Britomart and told Keeper I'd done what she wanted. Then I did some other things Keeper wanted—any successful job made her horny, same way the sun rising makes the world full of daylight—and it was only when she was asleep that I crawled out of bed and went somewhere private and cried until I puked.

But then Keeper was so pleased with me that I thought maybe it was a good thing I could kill people, and we got more commissions, and people started calling me Mildmay the Fox and I started liking it. I got to where I was proud of killing people, proud of being able to get at people nobody else could get at, being able to kill people in ways that nobody else could manage. I kind of lost track of what it meant, that thing I'd understood about Bartimus Cawley, who was in a lot of ways not worth my caring.

But it came back around and bit me, the way stuff you don't think about right most always does. It wasn't somebody I killed that did it, either, although Kethe knows what I did to Griselda Kilkenney should've made me stop and think. It was stupider than that. It was the way Keeper said "Milly-Fox."

Now, I'd always hated that nickname, which she started using within two days of people starting to call me Mildmay the Fox. But it wasn't until I was halfway to my third septad that the *way* she said it started to bug me. I'd tried and tried to pretend to myself that it was, you know, loving, that if she'd known how I felt about it, she would've quit, but one day—I don't even remember what she said—it hit me that there wasn't no love in her voice. Nothing but meanness.

At first I'd been pissed off, and I lay awake half the night imagining fights with her I'd never be brave enough to go through with, not if I lived a septad of Great Septads—what right did she have to sneer at me? I was Mélusine's top assassin. But then, somewhere around the ninth or tenth hour of the night, when all the thoughts in my head had started to go in ruts, and it was eating further and further into me that Keeper wasn't proud of me, and she didn't love me, and I didn't know what I could do to make her love me, make her proud of me, I started thinking maybe she was right. Maybe there was nothing to be proud of in being the city's best assassin. Sure, I could kill people, but plenty of people died every day without my help. And, I mean, the people I killed were dead, and it was my fault they hadn't gotten to live any longer, and what the fuck was the good of that?

And then I thought, Sacred bleeding fuck, Milly-Fox, have you been killing people all this time because you thought it would make Keeper love you?

That was what did it, right there, although it took me a lot longer to get enough guts together to walk out. I might be good at killing people, but it wasn't nothing to be proud of being good at, and it wasn't nothing I *wanted* to do when I looked at it head on. I'd done it because Keeper wanted me to, and that was a shitty reason. What was worse was that Keeper didn't care that I was doing it for her. I would have died to please her, and it was hard to realize that I *couldn't* please her, that nothing I could do would ever be good enough, and she hadn't even fucking noticed that I was trying.

So I'd stopped. I don't suppose cat burglary was any great moral victory, but at least nobody was dying no more. It had taken me a long time to see how much of myself I'd killed along with Bartimus Cawley and Griselda Kilkenney and Cornell Teverius and all the rest of them and how much of that was just as dead as they were. There was a lot of stuff in myself I couldn't bring back to life by saying sorry, either. Which I figured was about what I deserved.

What I hated most was the way the assassin wouldn't fucking lay down and die. I kept saying I was done with him, and it was like the world was just going out of its way to prove me wrong. I couldn't pretend I wasn't the guy who'd killed Cornell Teverius, even if the person I'd been when I'd done it wasn't the person I wanted to be anymore, and it was that person, the assassin, that everybody saw when they looked at me. And every time I saw that fucker in their eyes, I hated him more.

Gotta put your money where your mouth is, Milly-Fox. You want to stop being that guy, you gotta *stop*. No fucking backsliding.

I knew what I really meant, even if I didn't have the guts to say it outloud to the spiderwebs. No more giving into Felix. Make him use the binding-by-forms, and make him use it hard. Because I knew that was the real problem. I didn't kill for myself—never had. I'd killed for Kolkhis, and then I'd killed for Felix. And it wasn't the killing I couldn't quit, neither. It was the doing what I was told.

You know how sometimes you can be going along and do something or say something, and suddenly you *know* yourself? I mean, it's like you're looking at somebody else, and it's just so fucking clear you want to hit something.

I sat down right where I was and made these noises like a coyote having a conniption fit in a sack, and I can't tell you if I was laughing or screaming or maybe both. It was a long time before I could get myself upright again, too, and I was glad there wasn't nobody around to watch.

Because fuck me for a half-wit dog. People'd kept asking me why I'd let Felix cast the obligation d'âme on me, and I'd kept giving them these shitty answers, and all the time the reason had been *right fucking there*.

Why'd I asked Felix to cast the obligation d'âme? Because let's keep that straight, too. I hadn't *let* him. I'd *asked* him. And why? Because I'd needed somebody to tell me what to do, and I'd wanted it to be him instead of Mavortian von Heber. Or Kolkhis.

And boy, don't that just show I don't have no business making decisions in the first place?

So I could put it all off on Felix. Just do what I was told and not have to think about it. Not have to be responsible for who I was. That's why I'd done it. That's why I'd asked Felix to cast the obligation d'âme on me.

And the bitch of it was, it didn't even work. I still had to live with my shitty decisions. I was still *me*.

So maybe I'd better make that somebody I could stand to live with.

🙊

But life don't stop just 'cause you've decided to make big changes. I still had to show up for court with Felix the next morning, like I did every morning. We weren't talking to each other after what I'd said on Troisième. On Quatrième, he hadn't so much as looked at me, although I couldn't quite figure whether it was because he was mad at me or because he was afraid I was mad at him. Today, he wouldn't look me in the eye, but when the Lord Protector dismissed the court and people started moving, he hung back long enough to say, "You can come back to the suite if you want." And then he swanned out before I'd figured out how to answer him. Which was probably for the best, all things considered. I didn't know if it meant that he'd taken in any of what I'd said, but at least he'd forgiven me for saying it.

Mehitabel

Today we began full dress rehearsals; the premiere of *Edith Pelpheria* was only two days away. All that afternoon, there was no room in my head for anything but Edith, and as always, that was a blessing.

I did notice that we had an audience again, sitting in the same seat Danny Charlock had chosen last time. Gordeny saw him, too; I could tell by the way she abruptly stopped looking past the edge of the stage.

No business of mine, I reminded myself when I was offstage again, and managed to believe it for the rest of rehearsal and while listening to Jean-Soleil's barbed commentary.

But as soon as Jean-Soleil was done, Gordeny went flying off the stage; I knew she was racing through the maze of backstage corridors to the stage-lobby, where she was most likely going to tear strips out of the hapless Danny Charlock. And I was following her—though more slowly and with a plausible excuse. I did, after all, have a right to check my pigeonhole.

Sure enough, when I came through the stage-lobby door, there were Gordeny and Danny Charlock. They both swung around as the door opened, and whatever they'd been saying was lost.

"Miss," said Danny politely, with a bob of the head.

"She's *Mehitabel Parr*, numbnuts," Gordeny hissed. "Ain't you heard of her?"

I couldn't tell from Danny's abashed expression whether he had, and had never expected me to be so plain, or he hadn't, and had no idea of who I was or why he ought to be impressed by me.

"Don't mind me," I said and crossed to my pigeonhole, which actually did have something in it.

"Tabby, tell Danny there ain't nothing wrong with me being an actress," Gordeny demanded.

"Why should there be anything wrong with you being an actress?" I looked at Gordeny, but she was looking at Danny. I raised my eyebrows at Danny.

He was looking mulish. "It ain't right."

"It ain't none of your business," Gordeny said. "Nobody's died and made you king that I know of."

"Gordeny, I'm just saying—"

"And I heard you say it the first time. And I know it ain't you saying it anyways. You go on back, Danny, and tell Septimus Wilder that if he wants to say something to me, he should have the guts to come say it himself."

"Septimus didn't send me," Danny said, but a stone statue could've seen he was lying.

"'Course Septimus sent you," Gordeny said, with a toss of her head she must have copied off Corinna. "I ain't so dumb I don't know that. You tell him, Danny. Go on."

He went, slinking off like a scolded dog. I was still standing there, turning that sealed envelope over and over in my hands. Gordeny turned to me.

"Don't bother lying to me," I said, not raising my head.

"Tabby, I—"

"Just don't. And for the love of God watch your grammar," I said waspishly and left her there.

ॐ

I recognized the crest sealing the envelope, and that alone was enough to make me uneasy. Why would Ivo Polydorius be writing to me?

I could think of several answers to that question, none of them good. I opened the envelope reluctantly. Ivo Polydorius affected a peculiar green-black ink and highly ornate capitals.

After the usual salutations, the letter read:

> It is very kind of you to take an interest in Vincent. Certainly your patronage can do him nothing but good in the Mirador's eyes. I would be greatly pleased for Vincent to have access to wider society; in particular I feel that the circle of Lord Shannon Teverius would provide him with the cultural and philosophical discussions so sadly lacking at Arborstell. Anything you can do to effect an introduction to Lord Shannon for Vincent would be most appreciated by both of us, and I would of course do in return any favor which lies within my scope.
>
> Your most obedient servant,
> Ivo Polydorius

Now that, I thought, was a very odd letter. I reread it in the hansom on the way to the Mirador, but found no enlightenment, and then set it aside, mentally as well as physically, to prepare for dinner with Stephen.

Stephen and I dined alone that evening and spoke very little. I didn't think he'd care about my worries—except the ones I was most emphatically not going to share with him; his preoccupations remained behind his stone face. But the silence was amiable—I didn't feel, this time, like I was being tested.

"Plans tonight, Mehitabel?" Stephen asked as we rose from the table.

"A small social gathering," I said lightly. "I've persuaded Felix to join me."

Stephen smiled; we'd be safe from interruptions from him. "Good. I won't have to worry about him brooding on the battlements, then."

"Brooding on the battlements?"

"His favorite pastime. I prefer it to pitching tantrums in the Hall of the Chimeras—which he has also done a time or two—but it makes me uneasy."

"Afraid he'll jump?"

Stephen snorted. "Hardly. Afraid he'll amuse himself by

pitching centimes over the edge. Or decide to go roof-walking and I'll have to send the Protectorate Guard to get him down. Like a cat."

I laughed. Stephen wouldn't hear it was fake; he'd never heard my real laugh. "I'll come to you later."

"Good," he said and kissed me. "I've got the bigger bed."

Felix

I spent the afternoon alone with the *Influence of the Moon*. Clef had been right; I found Ynge's theories both enlightening and provocative. Understanding Vincent's odd gift in terms of a noirant sensitivity was suggesting some very intriguing possibilities—even more intriguing than I had originally imagined. We would see this evening if I was correct.

It was ridiculous of me, but with Gideon and Mildmay gone—driven away—I found my suite too empty. I could not work there. I sat instead in the Archive of Crows, and the silent, disinterested scholars meant I did not have to be alone with myself. Ridiculous to feel the emptiness of my rooms like a killing weight. Ridiculous to find myself turning half a dozen times a day to say something to Mildmay. Ridiculous to feel, every time, a sharp, blinding pain like grief.

So I stayed away from my rooms, except at night when I came back to toss restlessly, unsleeping, in my massive bed. I did not make the mistake of seeking out the Khloïdanikos again.

Not a single wizard asked me where I was or what I was doing. They were probably just grateful I was somewhere else, where I didn't have to be noticed or dealt with.

That, too, was a lonely feeling, even though I knew with mathematical precision the exact degree to which it was my own fault.

Which was to say, entirely.

It astonished me how much I missed Mildmay. And it irked me because I could not fathom it. That Gideon's absence should be painful, I understood—was even a little relieved by, for surely it showed there was a limit to my monstrosity. But why my silent, glowering, disapproving brother should feel so weirdly necessary . . .

It is the obligation d'âme, I told myself firmly. But I knew I was lying.

The truth was, he was right and I was wrong. We understood each other, needed each other, in a way that had nothing to do with the obligation d'âme and everything to do with our childhoods and my madness and the hurts he guarded and would not speak of. All the clever words in the world didn't matter, all the barriers we put up against each other, turn and turn about. The obligation d'âme was not what bound us together; it was merely the manifestation of a much deeper, darker, wordless truth.

I had denied that, again and again. I had mocked him, embarrassed him, reviled him, used him uncaringly in one and another of my petty little wars. Even after I had sworn I would not, I betrayed him—oh, in small ways, nothing like forcing him to murder a blood-wizard, so it was easy for me to ignore. It was amazing that his trust was all I had forfeited.

How many times? I asked myself, leaning my hot face against the cool stone of the wall on my bad side. How many times are you going to have to learn this same, simple, stupid lesson?

I didn't have an answer.

Mehitabel

I couldn't get back to my suite until eight, and when I did, Vincent was there, sitting in the chair nearest the fire. I sat down in the chair across from him and said, "I got a rather odd letter today. From Lord Ivo."

Vincent said nothing for a moment. "What does he want of you?"

"Here." I handed him the letter. As he read it, his face became stiller and stiller, until it was as lifeless as a mask. He handed the letter back, and I thought only his phenomenal self-control had kept him from throwing it into the fire.

"What does he want?" I said.

"To humiliate me," Vincent said.

I said nothing.

"Oh, he's right enough. I *would* like to meet Lord Shannon, and even more to meet Athalwolf Toralius, the poet, who I know is a friend of his. But introduced by you, with what I am so clearly marked"—and he spread his hands so that his long black nails gleamed in the firelight—"that defines me in ways which Ivo has no desire to allow me to escape."

"Shannon isn't like that," I said.

"Maybe not," Vincent said in polite disagreement.

"What do you want me to do?"

"As Ivo asks you, if you will. I am used to humiliation."

"I can tell Lord Ivo I have no influence with Shannon."

"No, he'll know it for a lie."

"All right. But I'm doing it because you've asked me to, not because Lord Ivo did."

That got his beautiful smile. "Thank you, Mehitabel."

"Do you attend court?"

"Yes, although well to the back. Ivo and Lord Stephen do not care for each other."

"Then catch me afterward. It will have to be quick, because I have to get to the Empyrean, but I can introduce you to Lord Shannon. But you know Felix won't like it."

"That is far more Felix's problem than mine."

I raised my eyebrows at the unexpected ruthlessness.

"I am sorry," he said. "I did not mean that as harshly as it sounded." And he firmly turned the conversation to Athalwolf Toralius's poetry. I'd read some of it over the winter, so we kept the conversation from flagging until Felix came, but I don't think either of us had more than about half our mind on it. And Felix was preoccupied, frowning. His blue eye seemed cloudy with grief, but the yellow eye was sparking, dangerous.

"What is it you want to try, Felix?" Vincent asked as we started for Grendille Moran's suite.

Felix shook himself a little. "Call it a practical application of rather abstruse theory."

"All right," I said, "but what are you going to *do*?"

"You don't want the theory, do you?"

"Not especially."

That got me about half a grin. "If it works, I'm going to make us—you and me—briefly able to see ghosts."

He didn't seem to be kidding. "Maybe we'd better have some of that theory after all, sunshine."

He made an exasperated noise, halfway between a sigh and a snort. "All right. Imagine that magic has a kind of polarity, like a lodestone, and call the two poles noir and clair. Clairant magic is magic involved with life and light, with straightness and cleanliness. Noirant magic is the magic of labyrinths, of things that are tangled and lost and dark."

"And dead," Vincent said, and Felix gave him an approving nod.

"Exactly."

"But is any of this *true*?" I asked. "You said, 'imagine.'"

He grimaced. "It doesn't work quite like that. Let's say that it *can* be true."

"You're the wizard," I said lightly, to hide how uneasy the idea made me.

"Magic is all about metaphors. In any event, one way to understand Vincent's ability to see ghosts is as a . . ." He broke off, searching for a word. ". . . a receptiveness to certain manifestations of noirant energy. What I want to do is tap into Vincent's ability—redirect the noirance, if that makes any sense—and—"

"Could you make it stop?" Vincent's voice was harsh, eager, maybe not quite sane.

I *saw* Felix come back to the world, with a startle and a wince. "Vincent, this is just theoretical. I don't even know if—"

"But could you make it *stop*?"

There was a pause, long enough that Felix's answer was obvious before he spoke, and Vincent's shoulders slumped fractionally. "Not without knowing what made it, er, start in the first place. And even then—it's not something someone did to you, it's something you were born with. It might be the equivalent of ripping out your eyes. Or your heart. And it would be gross heresy, of course."

He didn't sound like that would bother him; I said, "Isn't this heresy, what you're doing here?"

"Well, the trial would be interesting, let's leave it at that. Tabby, are we not *there* yet?"

Mocking plaintiveness. "Down this side-hall," I said and waited a beat. "Brat."

I startled a laugh out of Vincent, and was glad to hear it; Felix just beamed at me beatifically. "I gather you have the key?"

"Yes." I unlocked the door with the key Leveque had given me. The hinges of the door did not squeak. I'd brought a lantern, and Felix's witchlights were clustering around his head like tame stars. We went in.

The suite had been stripped at some point, probably long ago. No hangings remained, no furniture, no carpet—nothing to give a sense of what Grendille Moran had been like alive. The rooms were dark and desolate and bone-cold; we explored them in a clump, with Felix's witchlights darting and wheeling into the corners to get rid of the shadows. Then we returned to the first room, and Vincent said, resigned, "What do you want me to do?"

Felix said, "Do you see anything?"

"Traces," Vincent said, with a half-shrug.

"Good," said Felix. "Then all I want you to do is relax and hold still." He came up behind Vincent, the eight-inch difference in their heights emphasizing Vincent's slightness, and placed his fingers against Vincent's temples, his rings gleaming evilly against the blackness of Vincent's hair. Vincent might have flinched a little, or it might just have been the cold in the room.

At first it seemed only as if the shadows in the room were darkening, the air getting colder. But then I began to see patterns in the shadows, patterns that weren't stone and cobwebs. They were inchoate as they emerged, things that might have been faces, might have been hands. They coalesced gradually, becoming clearer, and then Felix said, "Grendille Moran, are you there?"

The pattern snapped closed, as if, until that moment, any one of a number of ghosts might have shown themselves and spoken to us. But now there was only one, a figure in an old-fashioned, narrow-skirted dress, her shoulders ending in a ragged stump, her head cradled in her hands, like any ghost out of a lurid folktale.

She hadn't been a beautiful woman when she was alive; her jaw was too heavy, her eyes too small. But she'd clearly been a woman with appalling force of character; the heavy jaw was almost balanced by the uncompromising line of her mouth, and those small, flat, gray eyes reminded me of the one time I had come face to face with a rattlesnake somewhere out in the Grasslands to the west of the Bastion.

I am Grendille Moran, she said, although the lips of her severed head did not move, and I didn't think her words were audible, exactly. *What do you want of me?*

Vincent's eyes were shut, but he had relaxed a little against Felix's hands. Felix didn't seem to have turned a hair. He said, "We are seeking the truth."

A dangerous pastime, Lord Wizard, she said. If a dead rattlesnake could be amused, she was. *What truth do you seek?*

"The truth about Amaryllis Cordelia's death."

The truth is that she is dead, as I am. What more do you need?

"Who killed her?"

I did.

"Who put her in the crypt of the Cordelii?"

The man who hired her death from me. It was the safest hiding place in all the Mirador.

"Who had her stone engraved?"

I did. That lying stone at Diggory Chase angered me. The stonecarver was dying. There was something growing inside him, a poisonous child. I gave him a quick and painless death, and in return he made sure that she would not be forgotten.

"Why?"

Because she belonged there, and the man who paid me to kill her knew it as well as I did. That, of course, was why he killed me.

"What do you mean?"

It was foolish of me, but I had not imagined that he would notice. Her lips quirked in something I was loath to label a smile. *It did not occur to me that Wilfrid Emarthius would make pilgrimage to his victim's tomb.*

"Who?" I said.

The ghost's eyes cut my direction, a dreadfully unnerving trick. *Wilfrid Emarthius, Amaryllis's husband. He had her killed, but he had the guts to kill me himself.*

"But why would Wilfrid want Amaryllis dead?" Felix asked.

She was profoundly unfaithful to him, the ghost observed dispassionately, as one who has noticed that this provokes rage in others. *Laurence and Charles were far from her only conquests. And he saw his way to power through Charles's advisors. Amaryllis would never listen to him. If she controlled Charles, there would be nothing in that for Wilfrid. He had good reasons, my lords and lady, I assure you.*

Felix said, "Why did you care whether Amaryllis was forgotten or not?"

The ghost shrugged; even Felix seemed a bit taken aback at how that maneuver looked with no head above the rising shoulders. *She deserved better than to die at the behest of her paunchy toad of a husband. She was beautiful and vibrant. I wanted her remembered, and I see that I have succeeded.*

"Did you kill Laurence for her?"

Me? the ghost said, her eyebrows going up. *No, that wasn't me. I think—*

Suddenly, Vincent reached up, jerking Felix's hands free of his head even as his knees buckled, and he collapsed onto the floor. Grendille Moran vanished like a popped soap bubble, and the thought that she might still be there, observing, sent a cold shudder the entire length of my spine.

"Vincent?" Felix said. He went down on one knee. "Did I hurt you?"

"Too much," Vincent said in a thin, strained voice, not moving. "I'm sorry."

"I'll be in the hall," I said and escaped.

The corridor was blessedly uninteresting. I stood and thought and composed about half a letter to Antony in my head—knowing he wouldn't believe any of it, knowing I'd probably never send it—before Felix and Vincent came out.

Felix said preemptively: "Wilfrid!" He was supporting Vincent with a hand under the elbow, and Vincent was leaning into him, shivering a little.

"Which will teach us never to judge a man by his name," I said, following his lead.

"Yes, indeed. Here we were thinking he was a poor, put-upon rabbit, when all the while he was the mastermind."

"And a paunchy toad into the bargain."

"Lock that door again, Tabby, would you? My mental picture of Wilfrid Emarthius never quite included him beheading Grendille Moran."

"I imagine hers didn't either. She looked to me like a woman it would be difficult to catch off-guard."

"Oh, very," Felix said, and we started back toward my suite. He was still supporting Vincent, and Vincent obeyed his guidance like a blind man.

"She must have found her head, though."

"Her head?"

"Stephen said it turned up somewhere unlikely several days later."

"How fittingly grotesque. And who do you suppose *did* murder Laurence?"

"What's to say it wasn't Amaryllis herself?"

Felix considered that. "Well, nothing, I suppose."

"Do you think Grendille Moran would admire anyone not smart enough and tough enough to do her own dirty work?"

"A very cogent point."

Vincent said, his voice rather shaky, "What a profoundly unpleasant woman."

"She *was* a court poisoner," I said.

"Grendille Moran would have been nasty as a nun," Vincent said. "Powers and saints. Well, at least now I can *imagine* how Ivo could be worse."

That killed the conversation, and we were silent the rest of the way back. I opened my door, calling to Lenore to bring the brandy from the sideboard, and made Vincent sit in the chair nearest the fire. He was still shivering. I took the opposite chair, to act as a buffer between Vincent and Felix—and if I'd been asked who I was protecting from whom, I wouldn't have been able to say.

We were still silent. Lenore poured brandy. Felix brought a glass to Vincent before taking one for himself; I knew it for an apology, and wondered if Vincent could read Felix well enough to see that.

Vincent knocked the brandy back, shuddered profoundly, and shut his eyes. He stayed that way for some time, and finally I asked, "Are you all right?"

"Thank you, yes."

And I didn't want to know, but I was asking all the same, "What happened?"

Vincent hesitated, looking at Felix. But Felix was staring into the depths of his brandy. Vincent said, "It was—I know this sounds mad, but it was being able to *share* it—not being the only one, not seeing things other people don't see, hearing voices other people don't hear. It was too much. I . . . I'm sorry."

"Don't be sorry," Felix said. "It was hardly your fault." Another almost apology.

"Are you never free of them?" I said.

"They don't hold together well outside—although I go to graveyards only when forced. Most buildings have them. Arborstell was unpleasant, but the Mirador must have more ghosts than rats." He paused and said in a smaller voice, looking at his hands, "It *amuses* Ivo to have a mad catamite."

Almost before Felix and I had time to realize we didn't know

what to say, his expression became wide-eyed with horror. He
pulled out a pocket watch, flipped it open. "Powers! Ivo will kill
me!" And he fled, like a child whose cruel schoolmaster will
cane him for being late.

Felix said, "I had better go, too."

"Stephen will be waiting for me," I said.

"Give him my best," Felix said flippantly, as smoothly and
reflexively as a master swordsman parries a thrust, and was
gone.

I knocked back the last of my brandy and went dutifully to
present myself for Stephen's pleasure.

Chapter 15

Mildmay

It felt weird being back in Felix's suite. I mean, everything was the same—Gideon hadn't even gotten his books off the shelves—but nothing seemed like it was quite in the right place. I poked around the sitting room for a while, just looking at things and trying to decide why I thought the table belonged about half an inch to the right and Felix's favorite chair a cat's-whisker closer to the wall. But finally I sat down, in the other chair by the fire, and just sort of waited for Felix. I didn't want to go to bed without seeing him. That felt even weirder.

It was the fifth hour of the night when Maurice came in, and he just about had a spasm when he saw me.

"Where have you *been*? Me and Rollo had a bet on that his lordship had killed you and stuffed the body up the chimney."

"I been around," I said. "Felix ain't killed nobody."

"Well, thank the powers for that. You coming back for good?"

"Less'n he throws me out again. It's the binding-by-forms, Maurice. I go where he tells me. What're you here for, anyway?"

"Taffy begged me, on bended knees with tears in her eyes, to come get his laundry tonight. She says if he looks through her like that one more time, she's going to break down in hysterics. And she says she'll probably die of them, because he won't notice."

"He ain't here," I said, "so go on and do Taffy's job for her."

He made a face at me in a friendly sort of way, then ducked back in the hall and got the little wheeled cart the laundry maids used.

"I didn't know Taffy was scared of Felix," I said.

"Oh, we all are," Maurice said over his shoulder, going into

Felix's bedroom. "Except for the ones like Rollo who have a crush on him."

"Oh." Poor Rollo, I thought. I knew for a fact Felix couldn't tell him and Maurice apart.

When Maurice came back out, he said, all at once, no lead up or nothing, "Is he okay?"

"Yeah," I said. I think so, I thought. "It's just rough on him, Gideon leaving, you know."

"Yeah," Maurice said. "Love's a bitch." He sighed and stretched. I could hear his spine popping. "Gotta get on. But I'm glad you're back."

"Thanks, Maurice." He shut the door behind him. I hoped I was glad, too.

Felix came in a little later. His stride kind of hitched when he saw me, like he hadn't really expected me to be there, but then he came on over to his chair like it was what he'd meant all along.

We didn't say nothing for a while. Felix just sat there, staring into the fire, and I was about to give up and go to bed when he said, "Were you really friends with Zephyr Wolsey?"

"Yeah."

Another long silence, only now I was scared to move. Then he said, "Do you hate me?"

"Do I *what*?"

"Do you hate me?" He was still staring at the fire.

"No."

"That's it?" He glanced at me and then away again.

"What more d'you want? I don't hate you."

"Nothing, I suppose. Go to bed, Mildmay. I'm not fit company."

I went. I got up enough nerve to say, "Good night," at the door to my room.

"Good night," he said without looking round. He was staring into the fire again.

☙

I dreamed about the labyrinth in Klepsydra that night, cold stone and water dripping everywhere. There were voices calling me from all directions: Ginevra, Kolkhis, Strych, Mehitabel, Simon, Maurice, Josiah, Septimus. I even heard somebody I knew in the dream was Gideon, although I couldn't remember what

his voice had sounded like anymore. I was listening for Felix,
trying to hear him through all the noise, but his voice was really
faint, like he was really far away or hurt or something, and I
didn't find him before I woke up.

Mehitabel

After the official proceedings of court were over, and the three
Teverii had disappeared, I went in search of Vincent and found
him, standing by himself against the bust of King Cyprian, just
as a page trotted up and said, "Lord Shannon says he'll see you,
madame. In his suite."

"Thank you," I said; the boy darted off again. "It's all right,"
I said to Vincent's suddenly ashen face. "I sent him a note. He
knows I'm bringing someone."

"You think of everything," Vincent said.

"It's a knack. Come on. I don't have much time."

"I'm sorry to put you to all this trouble," Vincent said when
we were free of the Hall of the Chimeras.

"It's not trouble, just tight scheduling."

"You are very kind, Madame Parr."

"Oh for God's sake. Mehitabel. Please. Or Tabby if you like
it better."

"I . . ." He went rather pink.

"What?"

"Nothing," he said hastily, and although I was sure that wasn't
true, I really didn't have time to pry it out of him. We were already at Shannon's door, and I needed to get to the Empyrean.

I knocked. Shannon's dark, handsome servant—whose name,
I'd learned, was Jean-Arpent, a Lower City boy for sure—
opened the door promptly and bowed us in, saying, "His lordship is expecting you."

I thought for a moment that Vincent was going to bolt, but he
didn't, following me staunchly into Shannon's sitting room.

Shannon rose to greet us, exquisite as always. "Mehitabel,"
he said, bending over my hand. "Who is your friend?"

"My lord, may I present Vincent Demabrien?"

"Charmed," Shannon said and extended his hand.

I could see the grimness behind Vincent's polite façade as he
extended his own. Those long lacquered nails were a badge that

everyone in the Mirador knew how to read. But if Shannon noticed—and I was sure he did—he didn't show it. "Any friend of Mehitabel's I know to be a person worth meeting," he said, with a smile that would have charmed a slab of granite. Its effect on Vincent was almost literally staggering; he still looked a little dazed as he accepted Shannon's offer of a chair.

"Won't you join us, Mehitabel?" Shannon said.

"I have to go. We open tomorrow. Are you coming?"

He smiled at me warmly. "I wouldn't miss it for the world."

"I'll send you a ticket," I said to Vincent, and then to Shannon, "Vincent is very fond of the theater." Because I might have been raised, as I'd told Mildmay once, to think bear-baiting a fine sport, but I didn't have to play by those rules. I certainly didn't have to give Ivo Polydorius what he wanted.

And then, with a sweeping curtsy, I left, not quite running on my way to Chevalgate.

Mildmay

After court, I told Felix I had something I had to do. He was still worried about me hating him or something, because he didn't so much as ask me what I was doing, just let me go. I was glad of it, even though it was worrisome, because if he'd asked, I would have had to tell him I was going to the Kennel with Gideon, and either one—I mean, either the Kennel or Gideon—would probably have given him a screaming fit.

But he didn't ask, and I got away clean, got back to Simon and Rinaldo's suite, where Simon and Gideon were waiting for me.

Simon said, "I admit, I'm learning more about Mélusine than I ever expected to."

"It pays to have a native guide," Rinaldo rumbled sleepily from his enormous chair. "You must tell me all about it when you return."

"Yes, yes, but now you wish we'd leave because we're postponing your nap."

"I shall not rise to that or any other bait of your casting," Rinaldo said, without opening his eyes, and Simon was grinning as we went out the door.

We didn't make this cabbie happy, neither. Simon said as he

climbed in, "I'm also getting a wonderful education in arguing with fiacre drivers. Tell me, is there anywhere in the city they *will* go without argument?"

"Most anywhere north of the Mirador," I said. "It's the Lower City they don't like."

"Is there anything north of the Mirador worth seeing?"

"Prob'ly not."

Simon laughed. "I shan't bother, then."

We got to the Kennel, and Simon bribed the cabbie, and I said to the Dog on duty at the door, "I want to talk to Sergeant Morny."

His eyes just about bugged out of his skull—I don't guess I did look like the sort of person who'd be wanting to talk to Morny instead of Morny wanting in the worst way to talk to me—but he got himself pulled together and said, "Who should I say is asking?"

And just for the pure poison joy of it, I said, "Mildmay the Fox."

"Gracious, what an effect you have," Simon said when the Dog had bailed in a hurry.

"I'm the guy who killed Cornell Teverius," I said. "Ain't you heard?"

Stupid, nasty thing to say, I know. But there were so many things I was pretending hadn't happened by not ever talking about 'em. It was like that old story about the boy and the dam, how he can stop one hole with his finger, and another with his foot, but then there's a third, and a fourth, and a fifth, and finally he just gets washed away. That's what happened with me and that crack about Cornell Teverius. I hadn't meant to say it. It just burst out.

Simon said, "Mildmay, I didn't mean—"

"No, I'm sorry. I shouldn't've said it. It was stupid."

"Gideon says that you are allowed the occasional outburst."

As much as I could tell, they both just looked worried—like they were worried about me. "It . . . I mean, it really don't matter to you, does it?"

"What?"

"That I . . . I mean, I *did* murder him. It ain't a lie."

"I didn't think it was. I *had* grasped the idea that you were an assassin."

"But . . ."

Simon shrugged. "I might feel differently, I suppose, if the victim had been one of my dearest friends, but Cornell was not a nice man. And when you sit in the Bastion for seven years, waiting and waiting for someone in the Mirador to remember you're alive and care enough to try to get you out . . . it changes the way you look at some things."

"I guess it would, at that." So I'd been wrong. There were people in the Mirador who didn't care what I'd done. They were willing to let me get past it. All at once, I felt less like somebody with big hobnailed boots was jumping up and down on me.

"You got me out," Simon said. "That makes it difficult for me to pass judgment on you."

"Fuck, Simon, I ain't no saint. I didn't do it . . . I mean, it wasn't for you, or nothing."

"I know that." His smile was sad and gentle. "But you did it all the same."

"Right," I said, and the Dog came panting back to say as how Sergeant Morny would be happy to see us. We followed him into the Kennel, up a staircase that had been wedged into the thickness of the outer wall, and then into a rabbit warren of passages, the sort of thing that people do when they realize one big room ain't no good, but a bunch of little rooms would be just dandy. Sergeant Morny was in one of those little rooms, cheap boards on three sides and the stone of the outer wall on the fourth.

"Mr. Foxe," he said, polite and surprised and a little worried all at once, "what brings you here? And, um, who're your friends?"

I elbowed Simon to make him get his hands out of his pockets. "You remember Mr. Thraxios. And this is Lord Simon Barrister. I want to talk to Jenny Dawnlight. You still got her?"

"M'lord," Morny said, with a bob of the head at Simon. "Since she won't tell us who the body is or what she was doing in Laceshroud, we're hanging on to her. We won't be able to much longer, since we don't have the space, but I don't like it when weird things happen in the cemeteries. It's always bad news."

"If I can get her to tell you what you want to know," I said, "will you let her go?"

Morny looked at me, one eyebrow going up.

"What she was doing was criminal anyway, so if you ain't holding her along of it being a crime . . ."

He laughed, a bass snort like a bull getting ready to charge. "You're sharp. And you're right. We can't hold her for digging up dead bodies when there's a whole damn guild in Ruthven we aren't saying boo at. So, yeah, if you can get her to cough up a name or a reason or *something*, we'll let her go."

"What about the corpse?"

Morny rolled his eyes. "Powers. Let me tell you about that corpse. See, we don't know who it is, and the Laceshroud people say it isn't theirs, and they say we can't bury it there, 'cause we don't have burying rights in their cemetery. But we can't bury it anywhere else, since we don't know who the poor bastard was or whether he can go by rights in consecrated ground—but I hate to stick somebody in the Boneprince who doesn't deserve it."

"Yeah. What're you gonna do?"

"*I* don't know. Sit on it 'til it hatches is what it looks like. But you wanted to talk to Miss Dawnlight."

"Yeah."

"Come on, then," he said, getting up with a grunt.

As we followed him down another staircase, Simon said in my ear, "Gideon says he's entirely convinced you're plotting something."

"Tell Gideon he's right."

"Are you going to get us arrested?"

"They can't arrest you—you're a Cabaline. And they can't arrest me. And they won't arrest Gideon, 'cause Gideon ain't gonna do nothing but take Jenny out to the fiacre. Don't worry so much."

The look Simon gave me was just this side of a smack across the ear, but we came out on the ground floor then and had to catch up with Morny. He was sorting through his keys. "Okay," he said, "you go on in and talk to the young lady. If you can get her to cough up any information at all, I'll let you take her off our hands."

"You got a heart as big as all outdoors," I said, to see how he'd take it, and he grinned, which I figured meant they really didn't want Jenny no more.

"Go on with you," he said, unlocking the door to Jenny's cell.

"Y'all stay out here," I said to Simon and Gideon. "I'll try and not take too long."

"Please don't," Simon said pointedly, and I gave him a kind of a shrug for an apology as I went into Jenny's cell.

Morny closed the door behind me and I tried to pretend like I didn't mind. "Hello, Jenny," I said.

She hadn't looked around when the door opened. She'd just stayed on her cot, her face pointedly turned toward the back wall. Jenny'd always been good at playing the tragedy queen, and part of me was glad to see she hadn't lost her touch.

But she whipped around like a snake at the sound of my voice. She didn't look like I remembered her. The smallpox had caught her, probably last summer when the outbreak in the Lower City had been so bad. She was lucky to be alive, but she'd lost teeth, and her face—well, nobody was going to call her pretty no more.

"Mildmay?" she said, like she thought she was seeing a ghost.

"Yeah. Me."

"What are you doing here?"

"Long story," I said. "D'you mind if I sit down?"

"No, 'course not." She watched me limp across to the cot. There wasn't anywhere else to sit. She moved a little farther toward the back wall. I sat down. "Did the Dogs arrest you?"

"Nah. Nothing like that. They got you, though."

"Are you narking?"

"Don't tell me nothing if you don't want to," I said.

"Okay." She bit her lip, a coquette's trick that didn't work no more. "Why're you here?"

"I want to trade favors," I said.

"Favors? What kind of favors?"

"I know who you're working for," I said. "If you'll help me get in to see her, I'll get you out of here."

"You're crazy."

"Maybe. You want to stay in here 'til your brain rots out your ears?"

"How can you get me out?"

"If you'll tell the Dogs your corpse's name, they'll let you go."

"I can't do that!"

"Sure you can. It beats me telling them your necromancer's name."

"You wouldn't."

"I might."

"Mildmay, you can't do that. You don't know what they'd do to her."

"Nothing much. And they sure ain't gonna do nothing to your stiff, Jenny. Come on. I mean, I admire you standing mum all this time, but it ain't doing you no good."

"But she *needs* that body."

"Did I say she wasn't gonna get it?"

She gave me a long, suspicious look. "I ain't as dumb as you think I am. You ain't got that kind of pull."

"Nope. But I got a plan."

"A plan?"

"Jenny, trust me."

"Oh, fuck you," she said. "Why should I?"

"Well, it beats the fuck out of your other options," I said, and it made her laugh.

"Okay, okay," she said. "I don't want to stay here if you're gonna get me out. The guy's name was Littleman. Luther Little-man, if you got to know."

"All right, then," I said. "We're gonna go out there, where Sergeant Morny and a couple of my friends are waiting. One of 'em's going to take you out to the fiacre. He's a nice guy, but he's mute, so don't expect no conversation."

"What about you?" she said. She was still smelling a trap, and I guess I don't blame her.

"Me and my other friend are gonna go spring Luther Little-man," I said.

5⋒

It went off just like it was supposed to. Morny said, "Littleman, huh?" but I could tell it didn't mean no more to him than it did to me. Jenny just about fainted when she saw one of my friends was a hocus from the Mirador, but she kept her head, and I was able to get her and Gideon moving without looking funny. Me and Simon followed more slowly with Morny. Morny and me were sort of talking about Luther Littleman—or I guess a better way to say it is that we were pretending to talk about Luther Lit-tleman, since neither of us wanted to tell the other guy any-thing. When we got to the staircase that would take him back up to his office—and he had to be itching to get up there and start

his men nosing around after who Luther Littleman had been before he got into Laceshroud—I said, "You must be wanting to
get shut of us. We'll be fine from here," and stepped back onto
Simon's foot.

"You've been very helpful." Which was a nice way of not
agreeing with me right up front. But it was a hike from here to
the doors and back again, and he had *other things to do* written
all over him. "I'll bid you good afternoon then," he said with a
funny sort of bow. "My lord, Mr. Foxe." He started up the
stairs. Simon and I started for the front door. But I tugged him
aside at the first cross-corridor.

"Are you *mad*?" he demanded, but in a whisper. "What do
you think you're doing?"

"I told Jenny we'd get her stiff out. So we're gonna. Come
on."

"You *are* mad. How do you think you're going to do that?"

"Well, strictly speaking, I ain't. You are."

"ME?"

"Keep your voice down, would you? This place is crawling
with Dogs."

"Merciful powers, Mildmay, it's the *Ebastine*. What on earth
do you think—"

"Look. They got Luther Littleman in a box down in their
morgue. All you do is go in there and say you're collecting him,
and it's a piece of cake. Just keep your hands where they can see
'em, and won't nobody ask questions or nothing."

"I can't do that."

"Sure you can."

"Why can't *you* do it?"

"For one, I ain't a hocus. For another, they know who I am.
Simon, all they'll see of you is your tattoos."

"But what about when Morny figures out he's gone?"

"What about it?"

"Mildmay!"

"He don't got jurisdiction in the Mirador. He can come ask
you why you made off with Mr. Littleman, but that's it. Oh, and
I guess he can tell Lord Stephen he's pissed at you, but that
don't matter."

"And what am I supposed to tell Lord Stephen?"

"Anything you like. I mean, I wouldn't say nothing about

me, if I was you, since he don't like me, but I'm sure you can come up with something. Come on, Simon. I promised Jenny."

"We're *both* mad."

"All you got to do is say you want the corpse Guinevere Dawnlight was caught with in Laceshroud. They'll give it to you."

"How can you be sure?"

"I'm sure. Trust me, Simon."

"I can't believe this. All right, all right. I'll do it."

I'd kept him moving while we wrangled, so it was only a couple more minutes before we found the morgue.

"Go on," I said. "And keep your hands out of your pockets."

"Powers," Simon said under his breath. But he took his hands out of his pockets and walked into the Kennel's morgue.

The next septad-minute lasted an indiction and a half, but when Simon came out he was carrying a latched box. We started away from the morgue at what I guess you might call a fast saunter, and he said, "That was amazing."

"What?"

"You were right. I said what I wanted. They looked at my hands, and they went and got it. Didn't ask my name, or what I wanted a corpse for, or *anything.*"

"You can say thanks to Cerberus Cresset and the rest of the witchfinders if you want to. That's what they're scared of."

"But no one in the Ebastine could possibly be a heretic."

"Neither could some of the people the witchfinders burned. It's hard to get over being scared about that."

"No wonder you don't like wizards."

"I never said that."

"Oh, *please*. Give me credit for some intelligence."

"I like you," I said. "And Rinaldo and Gideon."

"I didn't say you—"

There were footsteps coming. There were no doors along this piece of hall, no place to hide. If it was Morny, we were sunk.

"Don't look guilty," I hissed at Simon, just in time to get his chin up before a Dog came around the corner. He looked surprised to see us, but me and Simon kept walking, and I saw him notice Simon's tattoos, at which point he got very interested in his own feet and stayed that way until we were out of sight.

"Powers and saints," Simon said. "I wasn't cut out for a life of crime."

"It's okay," I said. "There's the doors. Just walk past the guys on duty like you own the world, and we're outta here."

Simon came through like a champ. When I asked him later, he said he'd just imagined how Felix would handle the situation, and that carried him out the door, down the steps, and into the fiacre like Luther Littleman wasn't even there. I just followed him and did my best to look like everything was Simon's idea. The Dogs didn't ask no questions.

"Where to?" Simon asked when I'd closed the fiacre door. "The cabbie will want to know."

"Where d'you want to go?" I asked Jenny.

"Me? I thought . . . I mean, you're letting me *go*?"

"Sure, I told you, I want to talk to your boss, not make your life a misery."

"Powers," she said. "Okay. Um." Her eyes lit up, and for a second she was the girl I'd known, back before we'd both fucked up our lives in our different ways. "Tell him to take me to Scaffelgreen Theater."

"You'd better do it," I said to Simon.

"Not again," Simon said, but cheerfully. "Er, what am I to do with . . ."

"Give him to Jenny. He's her stiff."

"Luther Littleman, miss," Simon said and gave Jenny the box before leaning forward to fight with the cabbie through the trap.

Jenny's eyes got wide. "You mean . . ." She undid the catches and took a hasty look at the contents of the box. "Mildmay, you're a *saint*."

"Nah. Like I said, I want to talk to Mrs. Fenris. I want to know what she wants with Luther Littleman."

"I'll do my best," she said. "Miss Gussie's a little . . . I mean, she's real shy. But I can manage her most of the time."

The fiacre started with a lurch, and Simon sat back. "There's other ways I can get at her," I said to Jenny, "but they ain't gonna be good for somebody who's 'shy.' "

"I'll talk to her, I said. Honestly."

"*Honestly*, Jenny, you're a liar and always have been. I'm just saying, don't go forgetting what you owe me."

"I *won't*."

Gideon swung his foot sideways into my ankle. He was right, and I held my tongue.

Simon said, "The cabbie's not at all happy with me. Where did I just tell him to go?"

"Public scaffolds," I said.

"Powers," Simon said. "You're going to get me murdered yet."

"Nobody in the Lower City is stupid enough to touch a hair on your head. Jenny, when you've got an answer from Mrs. Fenris, send a message to Simon. Simon Barrister."

"Okay," Jenny said. She was looking at Simon through her eyelashes in a way that had probably been sexy once but was now just sad and shy. "I'll tell Miss Gussie."

"And you should probably promise her," Simon said, "that the Mirador has no, er, official interest in her. I'm just doing a favor for Mildmay."

The look Jenny gave me was sort of awed and sort of resentful, like if I was so grand that I had hocuses doing favors for me, why hadn't I got her out of the Kennel a decad ago? But neither of us wanted to start arguing again, and she just said, "Okay. I'll tell her."

We didn't talk on our way through the Lower City. Jenny sat hugging the box like she was afraid Simon might take it away from her again. Simon and Gideon might have been talking, but it was hard to tell, since they were both looking out the fiacre windows, one on each side. And I thought, since I didn't want to pick a fight with Jenny, maybe it would be better if I just kept my mouth shut. Me and Jenny never had been able to go more than a septad-minute or so without arguing, and it seemed like all the things that had changed hadn't changed that.

Scaffelgreen Theater's this big open square like the Plaza del'Archimago, only in the middle are the gibbets and scaffolds and Madame Sanguette instead of the Mirador. And maybe that ain't so big a difference as you might think. The fiacre pulled up right on the edge, like the cabbie was afraid if he got any closer, the ketches would come out and hang him and his horses.

Jenny said, "Thank you. I mean . . . thank you."

"Just talk to Mrs. Fenris for me," I said.

"Our pleasure, Miss Dawnlight," Simon said, like she was a real lady, and held the door for her. "Will you tell the cabbie please to take us back to the Mirador?"

"You got it. And I *will* talk to Miss Gussie, Mildmay. I promise." Simon shut the door. A moment later, the fiacre started rolling again with another nasty lurch.

"He hates us," Simon said.

"He'll be shut of us soon enough," I said.

Mehitabel

Before rehearsal, Jean-Soleil had a very pointed and public word with Drin about upstaging other actors and generally being an asshole. Drin was dark with embarrassment by the time he was done, and Corinna nodded when I glanced at her. It would do the trick.

And it did. Not that rehearsal went smoothly—there was no such thing as a smooth rehearsal the night before an opening—but at least problems were no longer being *caused*. They were simply happening, and thus could be fixed. And both Gordeny and Semper improved tenfold simply from not having Drin stepping on their metaphorical heels.

"We might pull this off after all," I said to Corinna afterward, and she lifted her skirt to show me the saint's medal pinned to her petticoat.

And then I went to my dressing room, where I found Isaac Garamond practically clawing the walls.

"Where have you *been?*"

"Doing my job, Lieutenant Vulpes. Why are you here?"

He was pacing the room in a distraught way. "I don't know. I wanted to talk to someone, to . . . oh, I don't know!"

"What in the world is the matter?"

"I hate him, you know. I can't stand his eyes. How can people bear looking at him?"

"Felix?"

"Yes! I can't stand having him look at me. I can't stand *him.*"

"Sit down," I said. Because whatever I thought about Isaac Garamond, nobody would benefit from a wizard being discovered in strong hysterics in my dressing room. "Take a deep breath. What's happened?"

"Happened? Nothing's *happened*, that's the problem. Do you know what it's like to have Louis Goliath staring at you in your dreams?"

"I'm happy to say I don't."

"You should be happy. He wants to know why I'm not getting anywhere, and I can't tell him. I don't know. *I* don't know what's going on behind those goddamned spook eyes of his."

"Pity the poor spy," I said, and I said it scathingly.

"You don't understand."

"Nor do I want to. Is there something I can *do* for you, lieutenant? Or did you just come to whine?"

"Bitch," he said vilely and flung himself out of the room.

"And good riddance," I said after him, though under my breath. At that moment, I wished him and Felix much joy of each other.

Mildmay

Me and Felix weren't talking to each other. I think we both figured it was safer that way. I was fine with silence, but Felix was getting more and more fidgety, and so I was glad when somebody knocked on the door.

It was Fleur. I'd noticed the way she'd taken to standing farther away from Felix than she had, and had been wondering if it was because of me and Cornell Teverius. But the first thing she said cleared that up—and made me a sight less glad to see her. "What have you been doing to Gideon?"

"Fleur!" Felix said. "How delightful to see you! Please, come in."

"Don't play games with me." She did come in, but not very far. "What made him leave you?"

Felix folded his arms and glared at her. "What business is it of yours?"

"Felix, I am your friend. I'm not going to stand by and watch while you destroy yourself." It was a pretty thing to say, and I knew she meant it—she was all flushed and wide-eyed and earnest—but, powers and saints, she didn't have a clue.

Felix just kind of sneered at her. "Are you attempting to bring me to an understanding of my wicked ways? I know what I am. So does Gideon. That's why he left. Your crusade is useless."

"What's *wrong* with you? You used not to be like this."

That made Felix laugh, but not in no nice way. "I've always been like this. I just used to be better at hiding it. Good night, Fleur."

She stood her ground. "Are you trying to make enemies of everyone in the Mirador?"

"No. I'm trying to tell you that I don't want to talk about it. If you really want to be my friend, leave me alone."

Her look was pleading, but Felix wasn't budging an inch. "Very well," she said, "but, Felix, you know if you *want* to talk to someone—"

"Yes, yes, I can come to you. I'm touched, really. Good *night*, Fleur." He all but shoved her out the door, and he slammed it behind her. I sat there and tried to look like I hadn't understood a word they'd said.

He stared at me, daring me to say something. I was nowhere near stupid enough for that. Finally, he said, "I'm going out."

"Okay," I said. I wanted to ask him where he was going, but I'd been wanting to ask that for months.

"You must be solid rock from ear to ear," he snarled and slammed out of the room.

I knew he'd said it only to hurt me—not because he believed it or anything—but it was a long time before I was able to make my hands unclench.

But I figured since he wouldn't be back for a while, I might as well make the most of it, and went over to the Altanueva and St. Holofernes, where Septimus was getting better at looking like he was waiting for a girl. Fidgety instead of bored half to sleep.

I told him about getting Jenny out of the Kennel and the corpse's name and how I didn't know yet what Mrs. Fenris wanted Luther Littleman for, but Jenny was going to get me a meet. "Unless Kolkhis don't need to know," I said, not real hopefully, but there was always the outside chance—not that she didn't want to know, but that she didn't want *me* to know.

Septimus said, "Um," and looked down at where his fingers were rubbing over a chipped spot on St. Holofernes's toes.

"Yeah?"

"I, um. I ain't told Keeper."

"Ain't told her what?"

"Well, anything. Since you said the resurrectionists didn't know anything. I told her about that."

I knew I was staring at him like he'd sprouted wings and started barking, but I couldn't fucking help it. "Why the fuck not?"

"Um," said Septimus and got even more interested in St. Holofernes's feet.

"Look, I remember what she does when she catches you holding out on her, so what the *fuck*?"

He looked up at me, real quick, and then away. "I, um . . . oh *shit*. I don't know what to do."

"You could start by answering my question," I said, and only realized after it got out of my mouth that it was exactly what Felix would've said. I sighed. "C'mon. Let's sit down."

I sort of slid down the wall, hoping like fuck I'd be able to get up again. But it was worth it, because after a moment, Septimus sat down next to me, and a moment after that, he said, "She really fucked you over, didn't she?"

I didn't need to ask who he meant. "She's pretty pissed at me."

"I don't mean *that*. I mean . . . I dunno. But she really fucked you *over*. I remember when you left."

Oh powers and saints. "You got a point here?" I said and hoped like fuck that he was avoiding eye contact hard enough he wouldn't see I was turning red.

"She said you failed her, but you didn't, did you?"

"No," I said, because I hadn't. Not once.

"Did you ever, you know, do something for her you wish you hadn't?"

"Yeah," I said and kind of laughed, because that was such a *nice* fucking way of putting it. Weren't hardly any teeth in it at all.

And he shot me this look, sideways but meaning it, and said, "How d'you know?"

"Sorry?"

"How d'you *know*? How d'you know you're gonna wish you hadn't done something before you fucking do it?"

"Um," I said, but he wasn't stopping for answers.

"I been staying away from her so she can't ask and I won't have to answer, but I can't keep that up forever, you know? I mean, it's okay for now, 'cause she thinks it means you ain't got no place and I don't want to tell her, and she's got other shit to do. But sooner or later, she's gonna want to *know* and I don't know what to do. I don't know how to *handle* it."

Oh, kid, there was your first mistake right there, thinking anybody could "handle" Keeper.

I said, "What is it she's wanting you to do?"

He really wasn't looking at me now, staring down at the floor like he was welded in place. But his voice was still steady. "I'm new—she was training Kelso until he got his stupid self offed last Thermidor. So she ain't telling me everything yet. But she's got something big, something with *backers*, and I think . . ." He ran down for a moment, but he got the clockwork going again. "I think she's after the Lord Protector."

"Mother*fuck*," I said.

"Yeah," Septimus said, unhappy like a cat in a rain barrel. "And I don't wanna do nothing like that. I don't wanna do nothing that *big*. I don't wanna be like you." And then he seemed to hear himself and said quickly, "No offense."

"Nah, it's true. You *don't* wanna be like me. I mean, look at where it gets you." I waved a hand at myself. Nothing but scars, one way or another.

"That ain't what I meant. You're a legend, and I don't want to be one. Not like that."

I didn't ask him why he'd let Kolkhis train him in the first place, along of knowing the answer, down in my bones. I didn't want to be a legend either.

"Well, anyway, I can promise you you don't want to go after Lord Stephen. You won't be a legend, you'll just be dead."

He was going to get offended, but I said, "Lord Stephen's got more protection on him than Cerberus Cresset did. And Miriam's gone."

"Miriam?"

"The hocus who made it so I could kill Cerberus Cresset and not be dead before I touched him." She'd died the winter after I killed Cresset, and she hadn't taught no other hocuses how to work that spell.

"Oh."

"Kolkhis didn't mention that part, huh?"

"I told you, she ain't giving me all the details yet. I ain't even sure Lord Stephen's the hit."

Except I was willing to bet he was sure. Because he was a smart kid, and Kolkhis might not ever *tell* you much, but she purely did love to hint. I said, "What d'you want to do?"

He gave me a sort of wild-eyed look. That ain't a question kept-thieves get asked much.

"C'mon," I said. "You can't just hide from her forever."

"Yeah. I know. But." He chewed on his lip, still giving me that wild-eyed look. "I think maybe this Jenny thing has something to do with the other thing."

"How d'you figure that?"

"I dunno. It just . . . well, it's the only major thing Keeper's got right now, and I mean, why else would she *care*?"

"About Jenny?"

"Yeah, and the corpse. It ain't like Keeper's into necromancy or anything."

Or like she gave a rat's ass about Jenny. "So you think Jenny's stiff has something to do with offing Lord Stephen?"

"I think it *might*. And I don't want to tell Keeper anything without knowing."

"You know I got reasons for wanting Kolkhis to get her answers."

"Yeah. And I mean . . . I just want to *wait*, that's all. I hate trying to make decisions without enough information, you know?"

I didn't say it, but that all by itself was a sign he should take himself away from Keeper, and do it soon. Anybody who talked about making decisions that way . . . him and Keeper were just a war waiting to happen. And I was kind of surprised they hadn't gotten into it already.

I said, "Yeah. I waited this long. I can go see Jenny's necromancer and see if she'll tell me anything. But you can't put it off forever, right?"

"Yeah." He heaved a sigh sounded like it came all the way up from his boots, and got up. "Thanks."

"It's okay." And before I'd decided whether I was enough of a sissy to ask for some help, he reached down a hand, like it wasn't no big deal. He didn't say nothing about it, and I didn't, neither.

He opened the secret door, then turned back all of a sudden and said, "Look, if you get something about, you know, about *that*, and you need to reach me, I got a message drop in Pennycup. The gaslights on Furnival that don't work no more. Third from the corner of Antimony, river side of the street, the lily on the south side of the base is loose. Anything you put in there, I'll get it quick. And Keeper don't know a thing."

"Yeah, that's great. Soon as you tell me how I'm gonna get to Furnival Street without getting fucking lynched, I'm all over it."

"Kethe's cock, I'm trying to do you a favor here!" He sounded kind of raw, like it actually bothered him I was being a prick. Like he cared what I thought.

"Shit, I'm sorry." I scrubbed a hand over my face. "Thanks. I'll remember."

"Okay." And then he went back through the secret door and I went back to the suite. Where Felix wasn't. And I thought about trying to get to bed, but there was just no fucking point, so I was still sitting up, playing Hermit's Pleasure, when he came back around the ninth hour of the night. His waistcoat was unbuttoned, and his cravat was in the pocket of his coat.

"What are you doing up?"

"You didn't say I had to go to bed."

He gave me a look that was pure poison. He wasn't drunk, and if he'd been doing phoenix, I couldn't tell.

"Now I am telling you. Go to bed."

He didn't hit the obligation d'âme, but I knew he meant it.

At the door of my room, I stopped and looked at him. I didn't want to ask, but I couldn't think of no other way to show him I cared about him. "Where were you?"

It didn't make him angry. He just said sadly, "Nowhere you want to know about," and walked into his bedroom. He locked the door behind him, and there was nothing more me or anybody else could do. He'd put himself out of reach.

৩৹

Tickets for *Edith Pelpheria* came before court.

"Two tickets," Felix said, taking them out of their envelope. He was himself again, like last night hadn't happened or something. "How kind of Mehitabel."

"I don't much want to go," I said.

"Nonsense. It's a great play, and you would be stupid to miss it."

"Really, I—"

"Besides, committee meetings are one thing, but I can't show myself to the adoring masses without you. And *I* want to see it."

"Powers, Felix, I don't—"

"Your absence would be remarkable and conspicuous—as mine would be, for that matter. We are noted patrons of the Empyrean. No one will eat you, Mildmay."

"Oh, okay," I said, because he would get what he wanted anyway. He always did.

"Excellent," he said and tucked the tickets in his waistcoat pocket.

He must have decided, sometime when I wasn't looking, that it was time for things to get back to normal. Today, he didn't lose track of me after court, and so I had to go off to the Lesser Coricopat and another fucking Curia meeting. Everybody got so quiet when I walked in behind him that you'd've thought they'd fallen down a well. Fuck me sideways 'til I cry, I thought, but I put myself behind Felix's chair and I stood there like I was a statue or something and pretended I couldn't see the way Lady Agnes Bellarmyn and her cronies were looking at me. I didn't watch the hocuses to either side of Felix sliding their chairs away sideways either.

And then Lord Giancarlo came in and gave me a nasty look under his bushy gray eyebrows same way he always did, and Felix leaned back and tilted his head toward me. I bent down, and he said, just loud enough for me to hear, "Don't waste your time caring what these twits think about you." Then he straightened up again, all attention and innocence for Lord Giancarlo, and I straightened up, too, and felt like every bone in my body was only half as heavy as it had been a minute ago. No matter how much I tried to keep myself from caring what Felix thought, and no matter what I might say to him about trusting him—and no matter how true that was—I couldn't keep from feeling right now like the only thing that mattered was that Felix didn't hate me, that he was on my side against the whole fucking Curia. If he'd asked me to fly around the room right then, I would've tried.

I didn't pay no attention to the Curia meeting after that, except for noticing that Felix was on his best behavior, and even Lady Agnes couldn't draw him. I saw Lord Giancarlo's eyebrows noticing that, too, and I knew he was wondering what horrible thing that meant Felix had in store for him. But if Felix was plotting anything nasty for the Curia, he didn't spring it on them before the end of the meeting, and he furthermore got us out of there before Lady Agnes could catch him.

We spent a while in the Archive of Thistles, and I was still feeling so happy I didn't even mind being bored, and then we went back to the suite, and Vincent Demabrien was waiting for us—I mean, for Felix. The look he gave me said he'd've been happier if I'd been off drowning myself in the Sim or something.

"Vincent!" Felix said. "Good afternoon—well, evening I

guess," with a look at his pocket watch. "What can I do for you?"

"Madame Parr was kind enough to send me a ticket for *Edith Pelpheria*. Ivo hates the theater, and he said I ought to find my own company for the performance. He didn't say I couldn't go with you."

"Marvelous!" Felix said, and I felt everything inside me curdle and go brown. "Mildmay and I will be delighted to share our box, won't we, Mildmay?"

"Sure," I said. Felix shot me a glare, and I said, "I mean, it's nice that you can come, Mr. Demabrien."

"Thank you," Mr. Demabrien said. He wasn't fooled a bit.

"I've got to change," Felix said. "Can you two entertain each other for twenty minutes?"

"You mean thirty," I said. "Or forty."

"Mildmay leaves me no discretion," Felix said to Mr. Demabrien, laughing. "But I will be as quick as I can." And he vanished into his bedroom.

I could feel Mr. Demabrien looking at me, and I didn't much like it. I would have gone into my bedroom and shut the door, except that would have pissed Felix off, and it was such a relief to have him in a good mood again that I couldn't do it. So I stood there and looked at the floor and hoped Felix would be quick. And Mr. Demabrien was nice enough not to say nothing until Felix came out and it didn't matter anymore.

Felix had the charm running full bore that evening. Him and Mr. Demabrien talked about all sorts of things over dinner, and he left me alone, which was about all I was asking for. They talked about poetry and philosophy, about magic some, too. They skirted around their childhood a little, enough for me to pick up that they knew each other because they'd been managed by the same pimp, the Lorenzo that Felix had told me about once. There was that mystery cleared up, and I never had thought Mr. Demabrien could've been a kept-thief. I sat and listened and minded my manners and wished I could've joined the conversation.

We left for the theater in plenty of time. Felix liked watching the crowds before the play started, and he only liked being late for things when it was on purpose. In the fiacre, him and Mr. Demabrien talked about the Empyrean. Mr. Demabrien had been to plays once or twice before he took up with Lord Ivo, but he'd never sat in a box before. Felix got to explaining the system, where he hired the box by the indiction but got tickets for each play separately, mostly through Mehitabel. The Empyrean's main revenue was in the hire of the box anyway. It didn't matter to them so much whether Felix came to see the plays.

At the Empyrean, things were like they always were, with the ushers getting all round-eyed and nervous at Felix and Felix pretending like he didn't notice. I thought sometimes he came to the theater as much for that as for the plays. He liked people making a fuss about him, and the people at the Empyrean didn't have no secret plans or nasty traps they were waiting for him to fall into. They were just all excited that he was Felix Harrowgate and he tipped like it was going out of style.

We got up to the box, and Felix and Mr. Demabrien took the front chairs. I sat behind Felix and to the side, with about as good a view of the stage as anybody could want. They could have squeezed three chairs across the front of the box—Felix had offered to once—but I liked being back a ways, where I was harder to see and there was a fighting chance people wouldn't notice me at all. Especially tonight. I'd never figured out, and I'd never liked to ask her, whether Mehitabel could see into Felix's box from the stage. If she didn't see I was here, so much the better.

Felix said to Mr. Demabrien, "How many of the people in the boxes do you recognize?"

"The fat lord in the box closest to the stage is Lord Humphrey Bercromius, and I know I've seen some of the others before, but I don't know their names. Ivo doesn't go around introducing me to people."

"Well, if you're going to stay in the Mirador, you need to know who these people are. And Ivo doesn't show any signs of leaving."

"No. I don't know what his plans are."

"Here. The man sitting next to Lord Humphrey is Winston Valerius, his son-in-law. You won't see Charlotte Bercromia Valeria around—she's dying of consumption somewhere south of St. Millefleur—but Dinah Valeria was one of the girls presented to Stephen last Mercredy. The woman in the box with them is Humphrey's other daughter, Susannah. She's the mistress of Alder Sophronius, and has been for years and years. If his mad wife ever dies, they'll most likely be married the day after the funeral. You might have heard of the wife, actually. She was a Polydoria before the marriage, but I can't remember which branch of the house she belongs to. Claudine is her name."

"No, I have heard no talk of Cousin Claudine, but it seems unlikely somehow that I should."

"Oh, they still told the most hair-raising stories about her when I first came to the Mirador. She tried to kill Alder three times before he had her locked up in the Dower House at Singsby."

"That sounds like one of Ivo's cousins, all right."

"Now, in the first box to the left of Humphrey and Winston, the excessively well-bejeweled lady is Sabrina Anastasia. She was . . ."

I quit listening. Felix hated Sabrina Anastasia—I never had figured out why—and I'd heard his version of how she'd come to catch Lord Matthew Anastasius too many times already. She was one of maybe a double-septad people in the Mirador who'd managed to marry up instead of just getting a flashie protector, and what I thought was, more power to her. And her and Lord Matthew seemed happy together, which was more than you could say for a lot of flashie marriages. Or anybody else's marriages, come to that.

The house was pretty full and getting fuller as I watched. The pit was already packed, and the doors to boxes kept opening and flashies kept coming in. I was braced for it before I heard the door to the Teverius box next to us open. Felix glanced over, and I saw his eyebrows go up. "Lord Stephen *and* Lord Shannon. Gracious."

"Is that so odd?" Mr. Demabrien asked in an undertone. "I understood they were both fond of theater, and Lord Stephen is, er . . ."

"Yes, but they don't often come *together*. They don't get along very well."

"No?"

"They have almost nothing in common," Felix said and went on to a piece of gossip about Lord Cecil Demellius that would probably have gotten him called out for slander if Lord Cecil had heard it. I was kind of surprised—Felix usually didn't miss an opportunity to say nasty things about Lord Shannon—but glad of it, too.

Like they'd been waiting for Lord Stephen, it was only a

minute or two later that the curtain went up. I started out telling
myself that it wasn't going to hurt me any to watch Mehitabel
on the stage and I should just enjoy the play, and it was only
when the curtain came down for the intermission that I realized
I'd forgotten about five minutes in that I had anything to be unhappy about. And I was even more amazed to realize that I
didn't care, that I *wasn't* unhappy, that watching Mehitabel on
stage didn't have a thing to do with how I felt about her otherwise.

After a while, Felix said, "They should have gotten rid of
Susan Dravanya a year ago."

"I always thought that was a terribly weak scene," Mr.
Demabrien said. "Reading it, it looks like a piece of nonsense."

"It takes an actress to make you believe it," Felix said. "She
is magnificent. I was dreading the night-vigil scene, because I
didn't think she could pull it off, but . . ."

"You could *hear* her façade crack," Mr. Demabrien said.
"Great powers, I think I still have goose bumps."

"I may have to go to the opening at the Cockatrice, just to
laugh loudly at this scene," Felix said and told Mr. Demabrien
all about Madame Dravanya and the rivalry between Mr. Aubert
and Mr. Jermyn. I sat and waited for the curtain to go up. I
wanted to know the rest of the story.

Mehitabel

The performance went off like a miracle, like that ideal performance you dream about but never, ever reach.

Beforehand, when I was putting the finishing touches to my
maquillage, there was a knock on the door and Penn the doorman's voice, "Begging your pardon, miss, but there's all these
flowers." I got up and opened the door, and there was Penn,
practically invisible behind a mound of tawny, golden, bronze,
white chrysanthemums.

"Good God, Penn," I said.

"I know, miss, but I couldn't very well put 'em in your pigeonhole, now could I?"

"No, no, of course not. Here. This corner will do."

"They set somebody back a gorgon or two," Penn observed
and returned to his door.

They certainly had; chrysanthemums were about the only

things blooming this time of year, and that made them dear. I found the card tucked among the stalks; the message was a quote from *Cyprus Askham*, another of Asline Wren's plays: "In her such perfection we behold, As would make any man turn saint." The signature read, quite clearly, *Shannon Teverius*.

I must have sat there staring at those foolish, magnificent chrysanthemums for a good five minutes, until Mrs. Damascus came in to lace me into my costume. It wasn't that I hadn't received flowers before—there had been several bouquets already when I'd arrived at the Empyrean, most of them silk—it was that these flowers, this amazing gaudy panoply, came from a man who had no interest in getting me into bed. There were no strings, no coded messages. Just . . . chrysanthemums.

That was when I started to lift out of myself, the way I could do sometimes, for my very best performances. Out of myself, and into Edith Pelpheria, where I stayed for hours, only coming back slowly, by degrees. Jean-Soleil told me later we took eleven curtain calls; I could only have told you about the noise, the sea of faces, Shannon and Stephen standing together in one box and Felix and Mildmay standing together in the next with Vincent beside them. But I still felt like Edith Pelpheria's ghost, and I drifted like a ghost from the stage to my dressing room, from my dressing room to the largest rehearsal room, where someone's benevolence had provided champagne and canapés. It seemed like half of Mélusine was there, laughing and drinking and conversing raucously. After my first glass of champagne, I found Shannon to thank him for the flowers.

"I should have had them gilded," he said.

"Don't be silly. They're beautiful, and they wouldn't be nearly as fine if you'd smothered them with gold." We were both a little drunk, and I knew better than to try to say anything serious. But I could see that he was pleased.

Semper was standing in the middle of a cluster of Shannon's friends. I didn't know if he was molly, but he was clearly being courted, and clearly enjoying being courted. Jean-Soleil and Drin were in another corner, singing something that was probably both abstruse and obscene, while Jabez and Levry were doing bits of the comic cross-talk from Clerkwell's *Artème* and laughing uproariously. Corinna was holding court among her lordlings. Cat and Toad, lured down from their Firmament, were sitting on the rump-sprung settee, hand in hand like children.

Gordeny Fisher . . . I looked around just in time to see Gordeny slipping silently out the door.

I was a little drunk. And I was suddenly tired of the stifling din. Other parts of the theater would be cool and quiet. I didn't have to take Gordeny's path any farther than the first cross-passage.

Of course I followed her. All my worst, Bastion-trained instincts came surging up, and I slid off my shoes and trailed along behind her with no more noise than a whisper of skirts, inaudible under the clatter of her heels. I tracked her through the maze of passages until she came out onto the stage. I stopped in the shadow of the flats, wondering what brought her here. I was almost expecting her to start declaiming the night-vigil scene to the empty pit. And if she had, I would've crept away again and left her to her dreams.

But she said, in a hard, peremptory voice, thick with the Lower City, "Well, Septimus? I got your message and I'm here. Where the fuck are you?"

"So you ain't too lah-di-dah to talk to an old friend," a voice said from the pit. It was a voice as Lower City as Gordeny's own. Its owner vaulted up onto the stage, a thin, wiry boy with a mop of dark hair and dark, blazing eyes.

"Is that what you want?" Gordeny said. "To talk?"

"I guess I don't rightly know what I want, Gordeny. That's why I wanted to talk to you."

"I'm here," she said, with a wide, mocking gesture.

"You and your airs," the boy said.

"My airs are my own business. I got a job, Septimus. They're paying me here, paying me to be an actress."

"Don't you miss me, Gordeny?"

"Maybe," she said, with such indifference that the boy swung around to stare out at the empty auditorium.

"You're such a *bitch*."

"Powers, Septimus, am I trying to make you do anything? Am I telling *you* to get out while you can?"

"Not this time."

"Yeah, well, I figured out just how fucking well that worked," she said, and her own bitterness streaked her voice like copper showing through gold wash.

"Gordeny—"

She cut him off, her voice suddenly fierce. "If you're drowning and you see a way to get out, are you gonna stay in the water just 'cause somebody else says you oughta be enjoying the swim?"

"It ain't like that."

"Maybe not for you. Maybe you got something in front of you better than what I was seeing. But I found what I want, and I ain't giving it up. Not for you. Not for nobody."

She meant it. That flat, intransigent voice didn't even leave a loose thread to pull, a way to coax or cajole, to threaten or coerce. He could kill her, her tone said, but he couldn't make her go back with him.

He was smart enough to hear it; his shoulders slumped. "Then I guess we got to say good-bye, huh?"

"I can't see we're going to do each other any good," she said.

"Kethe's *cock*, Gordeny, is that all you can think about? Getting ahead? What if I ain't talking about 'doing good'?"

"You?" She laughed, hard and brittle and cruel. "You know, I think we had this conversation already, only it was the other way 'round. 'But I can learn stuff,' " and her mimickry of him was painfully good. " 'I can meet people, important people.' "

"Well, maybe I was wrong!"

The auditorium caught and echoed his shout, and they both flinched.

But after a moment, he went on, picking his words, struggling. "I been thinking. And I seen some stuff . . . I dunno, consequences, I guess. And I ain't sure . . . I'm thinking maybe I should get out."

Gordeny's applause was slow and sarcastic and terribly audible. "What do you want me to do, Septimus? Reward you?"

He wheeled around and grabbed her hands. "Fuck it, don't love mean *anything* to you?"

She got her hands back and stepped away, as neat and economical as a cat. It was all the answer she needed to give; I could see some of her expression, upset now and sorry, but not budging. And she didn't love him. He would have given her the world right then, if he'd had it in his hands to give, but it wouldn't have made the slightest difference.

"I'm sorry, Septimus," she said after a while.

"What fucking good is that?"

"None. But I can't give you what you want." She sighed, and her own shoulders sagged. "I think maybe you oughta leave."

"Maybe I ought. You ain't gonna change your mind, are you?"

"No."

"Well, if you do, you know how to get ahold of me," he said, and I admired him for trying to sound cheerful and nonchalant. He vaulted off the stage again and disappeared into the darkness.

"Good-bye, Septimus," Gordeny said, standing alone in the light of the sconces that hadn't been extinguished yet. She was still standing there, staring out sightlessly into the pit, when he'd had time to cross the distance from stage to auditorium doors three times over, and I slipped away, out of the flats and through the door into the Empyrean's rabbit warren.

Drin's voice said out of the darkness, scaring me half to death, "I was right."

"God, Drin! Are you trying to give me a coronary?"

"I was right," he said, taking no notice. "She's in a pack."

That was hardly the only interpretation of Gordeny's conversation with Septimus Wilder. Trust Drin to choose the simplest and most damning. "Maybe. And even if she *was*, why, by the seven sacred names of God, does it matter?"

"Do you want the Empyrean to become a pack hangout?"

"I hardly think that's likely."

"She lied, Mehitabel!"

"*Maybe*. And if she did, judging by you she had good reason."

"She lied about her family, and the saints only know what else she might be lying about. Why do you suppose she's really here?"

"To be an actress, you idiot. Look—"

"Mehitabel, we have to tell Jean-Soleil."

"No," said Gordeny Fisher behind us. "I'll tell him. But I want to tell Mr. Baillie something first."

I moved out of the way.

"Now, Gordeny," Drin said nervously.

"I've had about all of you I'm going to take," she said. "I'm going to go to Jean-Soleil and tell him the truth. Which is that I know some people who ain't all that nice. That's *all*. I'm not a pack-rat and I'm not a hooker or a pusher or whatever the fuck it is you think I am. If he throws me out—"

"He won't," I said.

"*If* he throws me out, you win. But if he lets me stay, I want you to quit with the fishy looks at me—and the fishy looks at Semper, for that matter. Okay?"

I wished there were enough light for me to see Drin's face; I was willing to bet he looked like he'd just swallowed a live frog, and I would have dearly loved to see that look on Drin Baillie's face.

"*Okay?*"

Fundamentally, Drin was a coward. He mumbled agreement and fled.

"There," said Gordeny with great satisfaction.

"I'm sorry I was spying," I said.

"It don't matter. Doesn't. I mean, it's not like there's any big secret. I got an ex-boyfriend who's into some nasty shit. He won't bring it here. And it doesn't *matter*."

"Only to Drin," I said.

That made her laugh, and we were able to start back toward the party.

"Don't tell Jean-Soleil tonight," I said. "He'll be too drunk to pay attention. Catch him Neuvième. He gets back at ten on the dot. And, er . . ."

"I won't say anything about Drin. I don't figure he's going to be a problem anymore."

"No, you've fixed him. And Jean-Soleil will know anyway. It's just unkind to make him admit it." We'd reached the re-hearsal room. I smiled at her. "Now go on in there and enjoy being Madame Fisher."

She smiled back and dropped me a curtsy. "Madame Parr."

We went into the light and babble together.

Felix

Mildmay went to bed as soon as we got back to the suite. He remembered his manners enough to say good night, but his eyes were inward-focused and exalted, and I wouldn't have gotten any sense out of him if I'd tried.

He went into his little room and shut the door, and Vincent and I stood awkwardly staring at each other until I remembered my own manners and asked, "Will Ivo be expecting you back, or can you stay for a little?"

Vincent consulted his pocket watch. "Ivo said he wouldn't

wait up for me. If I stay an hour or so, he'll have gone to bed and I shan't have to deal with him at all."

"And you can, er, trust him? Brandy?"

"Yes, please. And, yes. Ivo, in his way, is quite scrupulous. He doesn't lie to me."

I poured brandy, brought him a snifter, and we went to sit in the chairs by the hearth. "What *does* . . . no, I'm sorry. It's no business of mine."

"What does he do to me, you were going to ask?" He smiled, wry but real. "You never did have any tact."

"Guilty as charged," and I smiled back at him, wanting him to like me.

"It's not as bad as you think," he said, looking down into his brandy.

My eyebrows went up. "No?"

He gave me a sidelong quirk of a smile. "Not quite. Ivo isn't a tarquin, you see."

"Ivo . . . *isn't* a tarquin?"

"No."

"But—"

"Ivo," Vincent said with great precision, "is a martyr."

After a moment, I realized I was staring and looked hastily away.

"In the bedroom," Vincent said, in that dry precise tone like a man dissecting his own heart, "I am Ivo's tarquin. Out of the bedroom, I am Ivo's catamite. Do you see?"

"You said he was jealous," I said slowly.

"He is. Fearfully jealous. And he hates . . ." He swallowed brandy. "He hates himself for needing what he needs. And he hates me for giving him what he needs. But at the same time, it is *need*, and so he will not give me up. Because he can control me."

"You've had a long time to think about this."

"Oh, yes. And no one to talk to about it. Because even if I could trust anyone at Arborstell to listen and not betray me, none of them would understand. But you do, don't you?" And his pale eyes caught me, like an iron spike through my chest.

"I . . . Yes. I do. But how—" My voice was all breath and much too high. "How can you tell?"

"Oh." His eyes widened. "Oh, I'm so sorry. I just meant that you were at the Shining Tiger. I didn't mean . . ."

"Damnation," I said, and lowered my face into my hands.

"It doesn't matter," Vincent said, very gently. "You must know I won't tell anyone."

"Yes," I managed.

"And," he said, more cautiously, "it doesn't matter to *me*. Powers, Felix, you can't think I'd hold a . . . a difficulty like that against you."

"No." But I felt as if I were naked, and the scars on my back were burning with imaginary gazes. I drew a deep, shuddering breath, forced myself to sit upright again. I had to move this conversation away from myself. "Vincent. You don't have to stay with him."

"Felix—"

"You can come to me. I won't . . ." I swallowed hard. "I will swear an oath on anything you like not to lay a finger on you."

"I wouldn't have been worried," he said, but he was leaning away from me, just slightly. "Do you desire me?"

"I—"

"And do you desire me because you want a tarquin? Or because you want to tarquin a tarquin?"

"Vincent, I wouldn't—"

"But you would want to," he said, wary now, like one of the half-wild cats which lived in the interstices of the Mirador and preyed on mice and rats and cockroaches. And somehow he was standing up, with his chair between us.

"I *wouldn't*."

"I believe that you believe that," he said with terrible kindness. "I think it will be better if I say good night now. Thank you for the loveliest evening I've had in as long as I can remember."

I stood up, but did not dare to approach him. "Vincent, please don't—"

"I don't hold it against you," he said. "But I'm not going to talk about it any longer. Good night."

He left, swift and silent, and I sat down again. After a moment, I reached for my brandy glass.

Part Four

Chapter 16

Mildmay

When me and Felix got back after court, there was a letter on the mantelpiece.

"It's for you," Felix said. "From Simon."

He was suspicious as fuck, but he handed it over. I opened it. It was Gideon's writing inside. All it said was *FENRIS TO-MORROW SUNDOWN*. I crumpled it up and fed it to the fire before Felix had a chance to ask. He'd for sure know Gideon's handwriting when he saw it.

"What was it?" Felix said.

"Oh, um, me and Simon kind of got plans for tomorrow evening. Is that . . . I mean, d'you mind?"

"You're going to go see Gideon," he said. He wasn't asking, just telling me, like I'd got the date wrong.

"Yeah," I said.

"No, I don't mind. I can amuse myself, you know." And when I didn't say nothing, he said, "I'm not *that* much of a monster. And I'm not angry at Gideon anymore. He did what he had to do. It's all right, Mildmay."

It wasn't, since of course what he meant when he said he wasn't angry was that he was trying not to be angry. So I was just as glad when he said, "I'm going out. Back for dinner probably." And he bailed like he thought I was going to try and stop him.

Furthest thing from my mind, let me tell you.

Couple hours later, there was a knock at the door. Oh powers, please don't let this be Fleur again.

It wasn't. It was Mr. Demabrien.

"He ain't here," I said.

Vincent Demabrien, who looked so much like Keeper it made my skin crawl, stared straight through me and said, "I need to talk to him."

"Then you'll have to try back later, 'cause he ain't here, and I don't know where he is." And I was closing the door, along of really not wanting to talk to Mr. Demabrien, when he moved, fast and sudden and forward instead of back, and I gave way because he wasn't any kind of a threat, and I might not want to talk to him, but that didn't mean I wanted to hurt him.

"Mr. Demabrien—"

"I *really* need to talk to him." And he looked wild enough around the eyes that I believed him.

"I heard you the first time. I ain't hiding him in my coat, you know."

He colored a little. "I didn't think you were. But can't you find him?"

"In the Mirador? Yeah, I s'pose, if you got a month or two to spare."

"No, I mean the obligation d'âme."

"I'm sorry. What?"

He went even redder, but he didn't back down. "In the stories, the esclavin can always find the obligataire."

I said, short and ugly, "Well, I can't."

"Are you sure? Have you ever tried?"

"I just *can't*." I wasn't going to give into the binding-by-forms like that. "Look, you can leave a message and I promise I'll tell him as soon as he walks in the door. I ain't trying to spike your wheel or nothing."

"I'm not . . . it isn't . . ." And then, all in a rush, "It's just that I've seen another ghost, and I *really* need to talk to him about it."

It took me a moment to believe that I'd heard him say what it sounded like I'd heard him say. "A . . . *another* ghost?"

If I'd thought he was embarrassed before, it wasn't nothing compared to the way he was embarrassed now. "He didn't . . . I thought Felix would have told you. I . . . I see ghosts. Felix has been . . ."—his mouth twisted—". . . doing experiments."

"And ain't that just like him," I said. Because I knew how Felix got, and I knew it was just Mr. Demabrien's bad fucking luck he'd gotten in the way.

His face went kind of slack, like I'd thumped him over the head or something. Powers. I wasn't going to ask what he thought of me, that he was surprised I could feel bad for him about getting pinned by Felix like that, so I pretended like I hadn't noticed nothing and said, "What d'you want me to tell him?"

"Tell Felix . . ." He took a deep breath. "Tell him that Magnus needs his help."

"Needs his *help*?"

"He needs to be laid."

For a moment, I heard him wrong, and I was going to say, *I know Felix will fuck anything in trousers, but even he's gonna have some trouble with that one.* But Mr. Demabrien said, "He said Felix tried to help him before, so I'm hoping he'll understand the situation better than I do."

And then I did remember, back before Strych, Felix telling me about this ghost he'd talked to when he was crazy. "Okay," I said. "I'll tell him. I even sort of know what you're talking about, so . . . it'll be okay."

Which was a stupid thing to say, but Mr. Demabrien didn't seem to mind. He left looking almost happy, and it wasn't 'til Felix came back and just about had a brain-strike when I told him Mr. Demabrien'd been looking for him that I figured it out.

They'd had a fight—or, looking at Felix trying to act all nonchalant and shit while I told him about the ghost, maybe not a fight exactly. But a something. Felix was good at those. And now Mr. Demabrien didn't want to talk to Felix, and Felix kind of didn't want to talk to Mr. Demabrien and kind of really did.

I was glad when he took in what I was telling him, because all at once he quit being flustered and started thinking again, and that was a lot easier to deal with. Well, what I mean is, once he started thinking, there wasn't anything *needed* dealing with. Just Felix muttering under his breath and pawing through his old notes. And I could sit there and watch and not have to worry that he'd catch me at it.

Felix was weird about being watched. For one thing, he almost always knew. He didn't mind—fuck, he *loved* it. But when he knew, which like I said was mostly, he'd . . . I dunno. He'd perform. Nothing major—half the time I swear it was just him pretending like he hadn't noticed—but always some kind of performance, and you know, I couldn't even begin to imagine how tired it must have made him.

But sometimes he did forget, when something got him worked up enough, and I knew he'd forgotten now, because he wasn't muttering loud enough for me to hear him. So I watched, and I was grateful for it—just a funny little chance to see who Felix was when *he* wasn't watching.

And if I wished I could get to know that guy better—well, I sure wasn't stupid enough to say so.

᠀

My dreams were patchy and bad, Strych and Kolkhis and the Duke of Aiaia who'd cut out Gideon's tongue playing this crazy game of tag in and out of the pillars of St. Kirban's flooded cellars. I had a hard time shaking the dreams, too, so that I went half the day feeling like I wasn't really awake, like I might turn around in the Hall of the Chimeras and find Strych grinning at me. I'd had a terrible time with that after we got back to the Mirador two indictions ago. I'd keep looking behind me in corridors, and it got to where it was hard to open doors for being afraid he'd be waiting on the other side. I never have liked mirrors, but I couldn't look in one for months without my eyes cutting sideways to check for his reflection. It had passed off, the way most bad frights do, and half of my trouble that Huitième was just plain tiredness at the thought it might start up all over again.

Felix said on our way to the Grenouille Salon, "Are you all right? You look white as a sheet."

"Yeah, I'm fine," I said. "Just bad dreams, you know."

"You dream about Malkar a lot."

"Yeah, I do. Him and Keep . . . Kolkhis."

"Let me ward your dreams tonight. Just so you can get some rest."

"That would be great," I said, and I was about as alarmed as Felix at how tired I sounded.

"I'll do it, then. I won't forget."

"Thanks," I said. I wanted to say more, I don't know what, but he waved it off, and then we were walking into the Grenouille Salon, and I wasn't about to say anything in front of all them kids.

They were all *real* quiet that afternoon, like they were afraid Felix would bite them. I couldn't help wondering what he'd been like last time and what he had or hadn't said about why I wasn't there with him. He was talking about spells of locking and unlocking. He started with doors and went on to secrets, and about there he lost me. But it made me think about Strych's workroom and the spells on the door there. And that got me thinking about Strych again, and every time one of the kids shifted, I was afraid they were going to turn around and smile at me with Strych's mouth.

Get a grip on yourself, Milly-Fox, I thought, but I couldn't help it. It wasn't that Strych was everywhere I looked. It was that he was *about* to be everywhere I looked, like he was biding his time, waiting for just the right moment to tap me on the shoulder and say, *Really, with that scar it's a wonder you can talk at all.* I couldn't shake him off, and it seemed like this was about the stupidest night I could have picked to go traipsing off to visit a necromancer. But when Felix suggested after class that maybe I should cry off, I couldn't do that, either. I couldn't tell Felix why—the whole tangle with Jenny and Luther Littleman would just make him feel like the Lower City was crawling up into the Mirador to get him—and I think I left him feeling like the real reason I wouldn't cry off was I'd rather spend my time with Gideon than him.

Once I got the answers, I thought, heading to Simon and Rinaldo's suite. When it's just a story, then I can tell him.

Simon and them were glad to have me show up early, because Rinaldo had this craze for a four-handed version of Long Tiffany called Hogram's Key. It was enough to give a counting machine fits, but I didn't mind it so long as we didn't play for money. And it kept my mind off Strych pretty good, aside from having to keep an eye on the door in case it started to open or he just walked through it or something. Powers and saints, I don't know.

Simon told me he'd gotten a letter from Augusta Fenris. "Bad handwriting and worse spelling, but she says she'll meet us in a bar called the Lady's Lapdog in Dragonteeth."

"Powers," I said.

"What?"

"I been in the Lapdog before."

"What's wrong with it? Is it dangerous?"

I snorted. "Worst you got to look out for in the Lapdog is the fleas." It was a pretty smart choice, looking at it from Mrs. Fenris's point of view. If I had anything nasty in mind, I sure wouldn't be trying it there. Too many flashies. But fuck me sideways. If I was risking my neck going down the city, it seemed like I ought to at least get a shot at the beer at the Hornet and Spindle out of it.

We left in plenty of time, me and Simon and Gideon. Simon didn't have near as much fuss with the cabbie this time around. They take flashies down to Dragonteeth and Candlewick Mews all the time, and he probably figured he knew what we were after. In a weird way, I kind of wished he was right, even though I wouldn't have touched the sort of gal who hung out in the Lady's Lapdog with a septad-foot pole. But it would've been nice to be doing something normal.

"You don't need to have him wait," I said as we got out, and Simon paid him off. There ain't no lack of fiacres and hansoms in that part of the Lower City in the evening, and it'd even be okay to walk if we had to. In Dragonteeth, leastways most of it, if you yelled for help, the Dogs would come.

The Lapdog was about like I remembered it. It was Ginevra's sort of bar, all gaudy paint and watered wine, and it was full of flashies wearing what they thought they should wear to go slumming and Lower City kids wearing what they thought they should wear to catch flashies. There was a table free in the corner, and we sat down.

"Do we want anything to drink?" Simon said.

"No," I said, "but we'd better get something or they'll try and bounce us."

"I like your use of the word 'try,'" Simon said and flagged down a serving girl. He ordered wine for him and Gideon, and I asked for bourbon, like I had in the Stag and Candles, to remind me of Felix. Thinking of him did more for my nerves than the alcohol would.

The Vigor Street Clock hit the first quarter of the first hour of the night, and Jenny came in with Augusta Fenris.

I could see right away what Jenny'd meant by "shy." And she really did mean it, not just that Mrs. Fenris was scared of the Mirador like any sane hocus would be. She was tallish and skinny and stooped, with straw-colored hair and light-blue eyes, like the Brunhilde me and Septimus had bounced off of down in Scaffelgreen. She was probably around her sixth septad. And she looked scared to death.

Jenny towed her over to our table, and they sat down, and we said names all around. Jenny ordered gin for her and the necromancer, but I noticed when it came that Mrs. Fenris didn't drink it, just sat and blinked at it with her pale-lashed eyes. Simon and Jenny did a kind of hard-cased small-talk act while Mrs. Fenris sat and looked at her gin, but finally she sort of shook her head, like there wasn't no point in waiting no longer, and said, "What did you wish to speak to me about?"

I'd worked out an answer for that. I said, "I want to know why you want to talk to Luther Littleman."

She blinked at me, but I could see her brains working behind her harmless-looking eyes. She was silent until she'd figured out what she wanted to say, and then she said, "The patterns of power in Mélusine shifted in the first indiction of the reign of Narcissus. I am trying to ascertain why, and therefore I am interested in the doings of Mr. Littleman's quondam master."

Since she hadn't hurried, I didn't either. I looked at it from a couple sides, and then said, "Did Mr. Littleman used to work in Dassament?"

"Yes," said Mrs. Fenris.

"Then I think maybe I'm interested in what he has to say, too. Is that okay?"

She looked at me, and looked down at the gin she wasn't drinking, and then looked back at me. She knew who I was, all right. She thought about it for a good long while, and then she said, "I suppose so. Will you come now?"

"Yeah," I said.

Simon said, "I think it would be better if Gideon and I did not come."

"What?" I said. I could tell by the look on Gideon's face that him and Simon had already had this out, and he didn't like it.

Simon had been keeping his hands pretty much out of sight, but he put them on the table now. He said, "I have neither love nor respect for the Mirador's policies, but I have sworn oaths. Up until now, I have heard nothing but hearsay about Mrs. Fenris's habits and activities, and nothing in my oaths compels me to take notice of hearsay. Were I to *witness* an act of, say, necromancy, that would cast things in a rather different light."

"I appreciate the distinction," said Mrs. Fenris, "and I would not wish to cause a crisis of conscience. Let hearsay remain hearsay."

"Where is it we're going?" I said. "Am I likely to get set on before I can find a hansom?"

"Ah," said the necromancer. "Do not worry. I have no desire to see you come to a sticky end, and I will pledge myself to see that you get back to the Mirador safely."

"Thanks," I said. She might not be able to spell, but she sure did talk like a book.

"I don't want to get anybody burned," Simon said to me, like an apology.

"No, you're right. Y'all go on. I'll come find you when I get back and you can have the rest of the 'hearsay.' "

Simon made a rueful face. "Gideon thinks I am a coward."

"You can come if you want," I said to Gideon. "You ain't sworn no oaths."

He smiled and shook his head, with a kind of shrug. If he said anything, Simon didn't tell me what it was. They left together, and me and Jenny and Mrs. Fenris looked at each other.

"What now?" I said. "I mean, if you got something nasty planned, you might as well spring it."

"I ain't no double-crosser," Jenny said.

"Your actions in Dassament were to me personally a great source of relief," Mrs. Fenris said, which I thought was a neat way of getting around saying she'd been praying for indictions Vey Coruscant would choke on a fishbone and die.

"All right, then," I said. "If I'm gonna act like a half-wit dog, I might as well *do* it. Wherever you need to go, let's go."

"Very well, then." She stood up, and Jenny and me followed her out of the Lady's Lapdog and down the block to a livery stable, where there was an ugly old black coach and two brown horses waiting. Mrs. Fenris held the door for Jenny, and then took the coachman's seat like she was used to it.

She looked down at me. "You may take your pick. I am sure both Miss Dawnlight and I will be equally glad of your company."

I wasn't so sure of that, but I also wasn't sure my leg would get me up there with her. "I got a thing or two I need to say to Jenny," I said and climbed in after her. Mrs. Fenris handled the horses like she knew what she was doing, and we rattled off.

Jenny and I sat across from each other in the dark. Mrs. Fenris drove west, toward the Road of Chalcedony. After a little while, Jenny said, "What did you want to say to me?"

I hadn't particularly wanted to say anything to her, but fair was fair. "Just thanks," I said. "And I'm sorry you had to stay in the Kennel so long."

"It wasn't so bad," she said. "If you ain't pretty they mostly leave you alone."

"Was it smallpox?" I hadn't meant to ask—hadn't meant to say anything about her face at all. Don't know how the words got out.

"Yeah," she said. "Last summer. Miss Gussie found me when I was most of the way to dead, laying out on the street like last year's rubbish. She saved my life."

"Powers, Jenny, I'm sorry."

"No," she said. "I'm better off. You were right."

"I was . . . sorry, what?"

"You probably don't remember," she said, with an uncomfortable little laugh. "We had this big fight—I guess it's a septad ago now, and you said as how I shouldn't waste my time with the packs, that if I wanted to be a whore I should just go to Pharaohlight and sign a contract."

"Fuck. I didn't say that, did I?"

"Something like. I was mad at you for indictions, and the more I saw that you were right, the madder I got. Sometimes I'm really stupid, you know? And if it hadn't been for the pox, I'd still be over there in Candlewick Mews, pretending that what I was doing wasn't turning tricks."

"Jenny, I'm really sorry. I didn't have no right to say that kind of stuff."

"It don't matter now. It's all an old story. And you get what you pay for, you know?"

"Yeah," I said and touched my scar. It was dark. She wouldn't be able to see me do it.

"So where are we going?" I said after a minute.

"Dunno. The box is under your seat, so probably wherever Miss Gussie thinks she can get what she wants out of it."

"Thanks," I said.

"Mr. Littleman sure can't hurt you now."

"Yeah, but did I want to know I was sitting on top of a dead guy?"

"Sorry," she said, but she didn't sound it.

"What kind of stuff does Mrs. Fenris have you do?" I asked. I was wondering what kind of a job it was, being a necromancer's assistant. "I mean, aside from digging people up."

"She's only had me do that the once. And seeing as how I fucked it up, she probably won't have me do it again. Mostly I keep track of things for her, like where all her books are and when she needs to go buy more stuff. And I run her household."

"Is it just the two of you?" I knew it wasn't, and it was mean of me to ask like that, but I really did want to see if she'd lie.

And I was surprised when she didn't. "Nah. She's got a widowed sister, and her and her little boy live with us."

"And Mrs. Fenris is supporting them just on necromancy?"

"Nah. Anna Medora takes in washing and does fancy embroidery and stuff like that. So we get by."

"That's good," I said and kept to myself my idea that what Jenny really meant by "running" Mrs. Fenris's household was doing whatever errands and chores the Brunhilde, meaning Anna Medora, wanted her to. Jenny never could keep from making up stories about herself, and I was even kind of glad to see the smallpox hadn't beat that out of her.

"Yeah," Jenny said.

We were quiet for a while, until it struck me how long we'd been driving.

"She ain't planning on going out of the city, is she?" I said.

"Maybe," Jenny said. "I don't ask her questions about what ain't my business."

There was more to Mrs. Fenris than met the eye if she could teach Jenny that and make it stick, but my problem was the obligation d'âme. It said I wasn't supposed to go no farther from Felix than from the Mirador to Carnelian Gate, and it started pulling at me if I did. I could stand it—I'd stood worse—but I was worried that Felix would be able to tell somehow. And I knew he wouldn't like me going out of Mélusine without telling him. But I couldn't shout at Mrs. Fenris to turn around now, especially not for a reason like that, so I just sat and watched the storefronts and banks and townhouses going past us along the Road of Chalcedony.

A little later, Jenny said, "Why're you so interested in Luther Littleman?"

"Dunno," I said. "Just a hunch."

"You're sure going to a lot of trouble over a hunch."

"That's what made me a great assassin, darlin'."

I'd meant to offend her, and it worked. She snorted and didn't say nothing more. That was good, because I thought we were about to the limit of where me and Jenny could talk without getting in a fight, and if we really were driving all the way out of the city, I didn't want to spend the time fighting with Jenny. Silence was better.

They don't close the city gates no more, along of how nobody's dumb enough to attack with the Mirador standing up like a sore tooth. The Dogs don't even bother people much unless they think they got a reason, and about the only reason they care for these days is smuggling. They didn't bother us at all.

We didn't go far outside Mélusine, although I started to feel it, that place inside me where the obligation d'âme had hooked on. But we were barely past the end of the St. Grandin Causeway before the coach stopped.

Jenny and I got out as Mrs. Fenris was coming down from the coachman's seat. She said, like she was continuing some conversation, "The strongest places for necromancy are cemeteries, but they are also the most dangerous, and I will not practice my arts in the Boneprince. Second strongest are crossroads." She waved an arm around.

I recognized where we were. I'd been here before on business for Kolkhis. The Road of Chalcedony was starting to dwindle down into an ordinary sort of road on its way south to Verith and St. Millefleur and—I guess if you followed it far enough—down to the sea. This was where it crossed with the Gracile-Wraith road. From here, you could just barely see the lamplight at Chalcedony Gate, and so it was a good place to do stuff you didn't want an audience for.

"Get the box, Jenny," Mrs. Fenris said. "Mr. Foxe, my best advice to you is to stay back a bit."

"I won't get in your way," I said.

"Good." Jenny came back with the box and a lantern. She gave Mrs. Fenris the box. Jenny lit the lantern and stood holding it while Mrs. Fenris went looking for the edges of the roads and paced off the space where they crossed. Mrs. Fenris didn't put the box down until she'd figured out the exact center of the crossroads, and she spent a good five minutes aligning the box, although I couldn't tell with what. I took a reading from the stars for my own satisfaction, but she sure wasn't aiming for true north. I held to my promise and stood back. Truth is, I didn't want to get near what she was doing.

When she was satisfied, she opened the box. Luther Littleman's skull gleamed in the lanternlight. Calmly, matter-of-factly, like she did it every day—and for all I know, she did—Mrs. Fenris pulled out a knife and cut an X across the base of her thumb. It wasn't no big gash or nothing, just enough to drip a little blood into the box with Mr. Littleman. Then Mrs. Fenris said, "Luther Littleman. Speak to me."

What do you want?

I nearly jumped out of my skin. Not that I hadn't believed Mrs. Fenris was a necromancer and not that I hadn't been expecting her to call up Luther Littleman's spirit—but she did it so damn casually, the same way she'd told Jenny to get the box. I'd been expecting her at least to do stuff with chalk the way Felix did. But she didn't seem to need to.

"Cycles, Luther Littleman. Cycles in Vey Coruscant's workings. The first indiction of the reign of Narcissus, the last indiction of the reign of Narcissus." 20.1.7 was the indiction I'd killed Cornell Teverius, so you'll understand if I twitched a little. And 20.1.1 . . . It took me a moment to place it, and when I did I twitched again, so it was good nobody was looking at me. 20.1.1 was the indiction Gloria Aestia had been burned for treason.

The ghost said to Mrs. Fenris, *I don't remember. I am cold and tired. Let me rest.*

"You can remember if you try," Mrs. Fenris said severely. "You were her servant. You witnessed her actions. You kept her house. What was she doing?"

Why should I tell you? What will you give me?

Carefully, Mrs. Fenris squeezed another drop of blood from her hand. This one fell on Luther Littleman's skull, making a dark, wicked stain just over the left eye socket.

Blood, said the ghost. I was beginning to be able to see it, a kind of misty lump just over the box. *Blood is hot. Will you give me more?*

"Answer my questions."

What do you want to know?

"The first indiction of the reign of Narcissus. What was Vey Coruscant doing?"

Many things, said the ghost, and the eye sockets of its skull seemed almost sly. *She was a busy woman, my master.*

"What magics did she work?"

I wouldn't know, the ghost whined. *I was only her manservant. She did not tell me things.*

"Luther Littleman, do not lie to me. I know what you were and why she had you killed."

You are hard. I want to rest.

Mrs. Fenris gave the ghost another drop of blood. Now I could see its outline, a nondescript sort of guy, the kind you'd pass on the street and not even notice.

"I've seen the pattern. The first indiction, the last indiction, a fallow septad. Now we're in the first indiction again. So tell me about her magics."

My master is dead.

Mrs. Fenris made a huffing noise that was almost a laugh. "So are you, Luther Littleman. And you will tell me what I want to know."

First indiction, last indiction. The Rabbit and the Snake. The Snake came late at night. She was cold and beautiful and she clawed my face open when I tried to kiss her. The Rabbit came in the day, and he couldn't sit still, he was so frightened.

"What was your master doing with these people?"

Plotting for power, of course. She wanted power, my master, more than love or riches. She wanted to rule the city, and she thought she could.

"Through the Rabbit and the Snake?"

And her own magic. She worked many great magics. First indiction, last indiction. And yet they came to nothing.

"Why?"

The ghost was clear enough that I could see him shrug. *Who can say? The stars were against her, perhaps. And she could never control the living as she could the dead.*

"Who couldn't she control?"

The Golden Bitch, said the ghost, and all three of us—the living people, I mean—startled back.

"Gloria Aestia?" Mrs. Fenris said in something that was nearly a squeak. "Your master was plotting with Gloria Aestia?"

The Rabbit came from the Bitch, the Bitch and her dog-pack, and not all the dogs died with the Bitch. First indiction, last indiction.

"Who did the Snake come from?"

Oh, the Snake didn't come from, *for all her airs. The Snake came* to, *and she came when called.*

"What did she do for your master?"

She arranged things. She could make people appear and disappear.

"Such as who?"

Oh I name no names. First indiction, last indiction. People appeared and disappeared, in and out of the mouth of the Snake.

I hate people, even dead ones, who go out of their way to show you that they know something and ain't telling. Luther Littleman had clearly been a first-class prick when he was alive, and I could see why Vey Coruscant had liked him.

Mrs. Fenris knelt there and thought for a while. The ghost's eyes were fixed on her hand and the blood starting to clot there. Finally, she said, "What magic was she working, that she thought would bring her power?"

Blood, said the ghost. *She was seeking to turn the power of the Mirador from the bloodline of the Teverii. First the Golden Bitch and the Golden Whelp, and then the Other Child. Her magic could do much. But it could not do everything. Thus the Rabbit. And the Snake.*

Fuck, fuck, fuck. I had the cold spooked-out horrors crawling up and down my spine now, not over the ghost himself—he wasn't nothing compared to the dreams I'd been having—but over what he was saying, what Vey Coruscant had been doing.

"Why did she want Lord Shannon to be the Lord Protector?" Mrs. Fenris asked.

I could have told him if the ghost hadn't said it. *Because he was malleable. He was but a child, and he was more like his mother than his father. My master could not influence the Lord Protector, save in his weakness for beauty, and she could not touch his heir. She could gain no hold. But the Golden Whelp would have been different.*

Powers and saints, she hadn't been the only one to think so. It had sure been his mother's plan, hers and Cotton Verlalius's, to make Lord Shannon another Puppet King.

"And the, er, Other Child?"

A fool, the ghost said. Well, that was Cornell Teverius, all right.

So now I knew. The thing I'd never wanted to know, and now I knew. Mrs. Fenris was still talking to the ghost, but it was all hocus stuff, and I lost it for a while along of being too busy trying not to puke.

The Other Child was Cornell Teverius. There wasn't nobody else it could be. And that meant Vey Coruscant had been the buyer behind the job at St. Kirban's. I'd killed Cornell Teverius for Vey Coruscant.

Small fucking world, huh?

And Kolkhis was the Snake. It was a good name for her. Suited her. And she'd been working with Vey Coruscant for two septads. Maybe longer. Powers and saints, I *really* didn't want to know this.

I concentrated on Mrs. Fenris talking to the ghost. It was better than listening to the inside of my own head. I didn't understand more than half of what she was talking about—cycles and tides and Kethe knows what all—but I got the part about why she was digging around now, even though Vey Coruscant was dead and you'd think that'd be the end of it. There was a pattern—first indiction, last indiction, like the ghost kept saying. First indiction of the reign of Narcissus, 20.1.1, and the last indiction of the reign of Narcissus, 20.1.7, and then what Mrs. Fenris called a fallow septad, but now it was 20.3.1, and there was a new pontifex, Valentine after Berenger, like it'd been Berenger after Narcissus, and she was afraid the pattern was going to start up again. Or her magic said the pattern *was* starting up again. I couldn't tell.

And I thought of Septimus saying he didn't want to assassinate Lord Stephen, and I knew, cold as cold, that Mrs. Fenris was right.

Mehitabel

Stephen had a formal dinner that evening, the sort at which a light of love's presence was not at all the thing; he came to my rooms beforehand, and I spread myself out on my bed and tried not to think about Mildmay with only middling success.

But afterward, sitting propped against the headboard, Stephen said, "I get the feeling I'm not very good at this."

"Sorry?" I said.

He gave me an odd little smile, and I was shocked to see he was embarrassed. "What I mean is, it's not doing much for you, is it?"

"My lord, I assure you—"

"Oh, stop it."

Startled, I closed my mouth hard.

He looked down, pleating a corner of the sheet very carefully. "You're the second woman I've ever had sex with, and Emily didn't know any more than I did."

"But—"

"I was not going to be my father," he said flatly. "And being the heir to the Protectorate ... it's like being a wolf in a menagerie cage, you know. Everyone *watches*. I could have gone to Pharaohlight, but I couldn't have gone without the entire court knowing about it before I even got back. And by the next day, the stud report would be circulating, too. I'm not like Shannon. I couldn't face it."

Silence. Finally, I said, "You trust me not to bear tales."

"You said you have your own kind of honor." A one-shouldered shrug. "I believe you."

"Thank you," I said.

Another silence. He said, glaring at me, "What I'm trying to say is, will you teach me?"

Wonders will never fucking cease. "Yes, my lord," I said. "C'mere."

He rolled to meet me, and he was beginning to smile.

∂

I dined alone and told Lenore she could have the evening to herself, settling in with a romance called *Astraea* that Stavis had lent me. But I had barely begun to sort out the characters when there was a knock at the door. I cursed under my breath, took my spectacles off, and answered it. Felix.

I raised my eyebrows at him; his smile was rueful. "Mildmay has deserted me, and the Mirador is lonely tonight. May I come in?"

"You could do better than me, sunshine."

"You underestimate yourself, Tabby, my love," he said; I made a face at him, and he laughed. "Please?"

"How anyone ever says no to you, I can't fathom," I said and stood aside.

"Some people find it quite easy," he said, but waved aside the bitterness before it had a chance to collect. "Don't mind me. I don't seem to have any control over my tongue these days."

"*That* never used to bother you," I said, sitting down again.

The blood showed beautifully beneath his pale skin when he blushed. "So I'm trying to do better."

"You astound me, sir," I murmured and made him laugh again. "But really, Felix, why me? When you could—"

Another knock at the door.

"If it's Stephen, I'll go," Felix said.

"It won't be."

It was Vincent. "I'm sorry, Mehitabel, but Ivo wanted privacy to fight with Manfred, and I couldn't think . . ."

"Enough of this incessant apologizing," I said. "I wasn't busy, and it's just Felix with me."

Vincent hesitated, but then came in and sat down. He asked Felix, "Did you get my message?"

"About Magnus?" said Felix. "Yes, thank you."

The atmosphere was thick, almost choking. There was something between them. There had always been something between them, but this was different. This had edges sharp enough to draw blood.

"Who's Magnus?" I said—anything to keep away silence—and poured brandy all around.

"Magnus *was* a Cordelian prince. One of Sebastian's sons, I think." Felix's voice was light, brittle. "I tried, two years ago now, to lay him, disperse him, but apparently I failed."

"He was very grateful that you'd tried," Vincent said. "But he was hoping you could try again. He is . . ." Another of Vincent's graceful gestures, eloquent of frustration. "Not in pain, since he has no body to feel pain with, but—"

"Something like pain," Felix finished. "I've failed him twice, you know. Can you imagine how horrible that must be? To be trapped and in pain and the person you ask for help—the only person you *can* ask for help—keeps making all the right noises but never *does* anything?"

"He doesn't blame you," Vincent said; he sounded anxious, and I was right there with him. "He isn't angry."

"Maybe he should be!" Even Felix seemed startled by that outburst. He blinked, manufactured a smile from somewhere, said, "Well, maybe this time I can get it right for a change. I've been combing my notes, all the books I have, trying to find out what went wrong. I need another day or two."

"Felix," Vincent said gently, "you aren't answerable to me."

Felix's flinch was visible in the sudden agitation of the brandy in his glass. He covered with an airy gesture, said lightly, "Well, tell him if he comes to perch at the foot of your bed tonight. Or whatever it is ghosts do."

That was deliberate provocation, but Vincent did not rise to it. After a moment, a nervous swallow of brandy, Felix began to talk about the thaumaturgical theory of laying ghosts to rest, his voice like a frail, brave boat on a heavy sea. Vincent was watching Felix carefully; Felix was . . . not looking at Vincent, and his color was high. He lost the thread of his remarks. Regrouped. Lost it again and stood up, abrupt and gawky as a colt. "I should go."

"You don't have to," Vincent said.

"Yes," Felix said with a painful smile. "I do. Good night, Tabby."

He was gone before I could stand.

"What the fuck?" I said.

"My fault," Vincent said. "I'm sorry."

"Vincent, I've warned you before . . ."

"Oh, powers." A reluctant smile warmed his eyes. "All right, I'll try to stop. But this *is* my fault. Felix made me an offer last night, and I turned him down."

"Felix made a pass at you?" I said, incredulous.

"No, actually. He offered me"—his mouth twisted—"his protection."

"He . . ."

"If I left Ivo."

I couldn't read either his face or his voice. "Which isn't likely?"

"No." That sat between us a moment, and then he said, more softly, "Not unless . . ."

"Unless what?"

"It's pure foolishness." The motion of his hands curling into fists—loosely because of those long nails—caught my eye and I knew.

"You don't want to trade one bed for another."

His breath released in a sigh that sounded painful. "Yes."

"And you think Felix would . . . ?"

"I don't think he would *intend* to. But, yes. Yes, I do."

Because Felix was my friend, I wished I could have said Vincent was wrong. But I couldn't.

Mildmay

This time it was me waiting for Septimus, and I didn't have to fake being eager as fuck to see him, neither.

I'd got Mrs. Fenris to write the note for me—*COME LIGHT*

A VOTIVE AS SOON AS POSSIBLE—and Jenny'd put it in the drop, and they'd taken me back up the city. I'd had them leave me a couple streets away from the Plaza del'Archimago, along of how it'd be better if the guards didn't get a look at either Mrs. Fenris or her coach, just in case. I picked Livergate to come back in through, because the guards there wouldn't ask questions. Livergate was where they put the young guys, and though they'd see me, and know who I was, and tell anybody who was interested all about it, they wouldn't have the nerve to say nothing to my face. And that was good enough for now.

And then I went up to the Altanueva and settled in to wait for Septimus. Because I didn't know what the fuck to do about what the ghost had said, but I knew I had to tell Septimus before I did anything. Because he needed a chance to get clear.

I didn't have to wait nearly as long as I'd thought I might. He hadn't been lying about his system being good. It wasn't even the fifth hour of the night when the arch behind St. Holofernes shuddered, and Septimus came through.

"You got something."

"Yeah, fuck, I got something," and I told him about Luther Littleman and the patterns and Gloria Aestia and Cornell Teverius and the Snake and the Rabbit, and he listened, listened hard, and muttered, "fuck," between his teeth whenever I stopped for breath.

And when I was done, he paced halfway down the hall and back and said, "Fuck, you're right. Vey fucking Coruscant. And I know you're right, because I've seen this Rabbit guy. Seen him talking to Keeper. Seen him in the past two *months.*"

"Fuck me sideways. You got a name?"

"Yeah, but . . ."

"But *what*?" I said, when he didn't go on.

"What're you gonna do?"

"Fuck, do I *look* like I got a plan?"

"It's just . . . are you gonna tell Keeper?"

"If I was gonna tell Keeper, I should've done it, what, three days ago? When you were begging me not to."

He winced. "I just meant—"

"No, I ain't. If you'll tell me who the Rabbit is, I'm gonna go shake him until the rest of the story falls out. And if you ain't, then get the fuck out of my way."

"Slow down." He had both hands up, palms out. "I didn't

mean it like that. It's just, if you don't tell Keeper, she won't tell you who got your gal killed."

"Yeah." And I felt the weight of that, too. But I could carry it. "I'll cope."

"No, I mean, that's what I'm trying to tell you. It's the Rabbit."

So there was a slow count of seven where I couldn't even figure out what the fuck he was saying, and then it, I don't know, everything suddenly fucking *fit*. It was like having a tree grow from a seed to a giant in about half a second in my head. "Hugo Chandler. Are you sure?"

And I'd wondered how Kolkhis knew Hugo.

"Yeah. Keeper said . . . well, she said some stuff."

She always did love to hint.

"Okay. Thanks. You want to go to ground for a decad or two. Don't go back to Britomart."

"You couldn't pay me enough." He gave me a once-over. "You okay? I mean—"

"Oh, I'm fine," I said. "Take care of yourself, Septimus."

And I left him there to put whatever plan he had into action. Guys like him always have a plan.

I didn't. Except for the part where I was going to tear the lights and liver out of a rabbit. Hugo fucking Chandler. I'd never thought about him twice. He looked like a rabbit, and he acted like a rabbit, and I'd never even thought about the possibility that he wasn't a rabbit inside—or, he wasn't as much a rabbit as he made himself out to be. He was a weedy little guy I could have taken apart with one hand tied behind my back, and so I'd never even wondered if he might be lying to me. He must have been laughing at me all this fucking time. Him, Hugo Chandler, fooling Mildmay the Fox, and Mildmay the Fox, sitting there taking it, trusting as a fucking lamb.

Well, I was done with that shit.

Felix

I felt filthy—not merely untrustworthy, but rotten with depravity, oozing monstrosity, as if I would contaminate anything I touched.

I stood at a cross hallway, trying wearily to decide what to do. I could not bear the thought of returning to my rooms, not until I was certain Mildmay would be there; seeking out any of my so-called friends would merely get me more sanctimony and disapproval, and I'd had as much of that as I could stand. There were places I could go in the Arcane, even barred as I was from the Two-Headed Beast, men who would plead with me to hurt them. I'd proved that already.

But it wasn't enough. I'd proved that, too. I couldn't trust myself, and I'd been painfully aware of that the nights I'd tried it. I'd pleased the men picked up in one bar and another in the Sim-tainted depths of the Arcane, but I'd kept remembering that last night in the Two-Headed Beast, and I hadn't been able to release my cramped control over my own desires.

It was no wonder Vincent didn't trust me.

I repulsed myself, and with Malkar dead, there was really only one place I could go.

Isaac Garamond was not pleased to see me. He was untidy, flustered, harried, and he tried to tell me he had an appointment elsewhere. But I could see it was a lie, and I could see the desire he hated in himself sparking, catching, starting to burn. He hadn't got the information his masters wanted from me, but he'd certainly learned a few things about himself.

I smiled at him as the words caught and crumbled in his throat.

"All right," he snarled. "Come in."

"Thank you," I said, and pulled the door gently out of his grip to close it.

Chapter 17

Mildmay

I knocked on Hugo's door. He was a stupid rabbit and opened it. Two seconds later, he was pinned against his bedroom wall with my knife at his throat, and the door was closed.

"Mildmay," he said, gasping because my hold on his collar was choking him. "W-w-what—"

"That's what you're gonna tell me," I said. "Vey Coruscant, Hugo. You're going to tell me all about her."

"She's dead!"

"Yeah, I got that part." I increased my leverage just a little, tilting his jaw up with the flat of my knife. His breath was sour. "But before she was dead, you had shit going on with her. You told her how to find Ginevra."

"I didn't!"

"Don't fucking lie to me. You *did*. And you know what the sad part is? I don't even care. It bit you on the ass, didn't it?"

"Austin wasn't supposed to die," he said in this horrible watery whimpering voice.

"Yeah, well, that's what you get when you fuck around with Vey Coruscant. Even if you are in good with her." I shook him a little, to be sure he was paying attention. "You used to run messages to her. From the Mirador. And now I understand you're running messages to Kolkhis. And I wanna know who your boss is."

"How'd you find out?" he said in a panicky little whisper.

"I got my sources. Who is it?"

"I can't tell you."

"'Course you can, same way I can cut your throat. Or, you know, pop your eyeball like a cherry tomato."

He was a clever rabbit, but he was a rabbit. "Lord Ivo! Him and Lord Robert and some other lords—I don't know all their names, I swear!"

"Fuck me sideways 'til I cry," I said. That sure explained how Robert had known about Cornell Teverius. "Is this the truth? I'm tired of you lying to me."

"I swear it! I swear it! Anything you like!"

And it probably *was* the truth. I realized, standing there with Hugo's breath sobbing inches from my face, that this was too big for me. If Lord Ivo'd been tangled up in trying to get Lord Shannon on the throne once, and if he'd been laying low for two septads but he'd come *back*, and then Lord Stephen hadn't married his daughter, and Kolkhis was involved again . . . I wasn't anybody who could handle the trouble this looked like it was going to be. Somebody else needed to be told.

Felix? Yeah, but not now. I needed somebody people would listen to, not argue with for an hour first. Lord Stephen? Yeah, but I needed somebody who'd listen to me, and I didn't think Lord Stephen would. Not now. Then all at once I thought of Lord Giancarlo. He didn't like me, but he was a fair-minded man, about as fair-minded as a hocus could get. I knew without having to wonder about it that he'd listen to me, and he was the chairman of the Curia. Lord Stephen would listen to him.

I shifted my grip from Hugo's wrist to his collar. "Come on, Hugo. Let's see if you get better at spilling your guts with practice."

ᔑ

I stood and hammered on Lord Giancarlo's door for what felt like an hour before he opened it. He was in his dressing gown, his thin gray hair all up on end.

"Mr. Foxe? What on earth?"

"Sorry to disturb you, m'lord, but I'm afraid of waiting." I dragged Hugo in and kicked the door shut.

I'd judged Lord Giancarlo right. The eyebrows went up, but he said, "Clearly you have something to tell me. I am listening."

"Talk, Hugo," I said, and Hugo talked. I'd told him lies about Lord Giancarlo all the way up from the Mesmerine, about how he was the meanest, toughest hocus in the Mirador, about how Cerberus Cresset had answered to him, about how he was more powerful than Felix and I'd seen him turn a man into a dog for looking at him wrong. Hugo believed it all, and I'd gotten him more scared of Lord Giancarlo than of either me or Lord Ivo. He told him everything, more even than he'd told me, details about

how they'd got rid of Lady Dulcinea, about how Vey and Lord
Ivo turned against Gloria Aestia and Cotton Verlalius when they
realized how stupid and dangerous they were. He even talked
about the plot to kill Cornell Teverius. It was weird listening to it
from that side, how they'd decided to try with Cornell, along of
him being both greedy and not very bright, but how he'd gotten
too cocky and started shooting off his mouth, and how Lord Ivo
had written to Robert to say he'd betray them before they could
get him the Protectorate, and so Robert had sent Hugo down the
city again. And then details about how Lord Ivo'd moved back in
and it was like nothing had changed and how Hugo'd gone to see
Kolkhis twice, and I remembered thinking that the Guard would
know if Hugo was leaving the Mirador and wanted to just die of
my own stupidity. Lord Giancarlo was scowling like the end of
the world, but he took notes and asked for dates and details, and
I knew he wasn't making the mistake of not taking the information seriously just because it came from a rabbit. He got everything out of Hugo there was to get and then got his valet to run
for the guards to take Hugo down to the Verpine, the prison under
the guard barracks.

"I must go to Lord Stephen," he said to me.

"You don't need me, do you?"

"No, if you do not wish to come."

"Lord Stephen, he ain't exactly . . ."

"I understand. You have done the Mirador a tremendous favor, Mr. Foxe. We will not forget."

"Thanks, Lord Giancarlo," I said. I could feel my face going
red. "Well, good night."

"Good night, Mr. Foxe." As I left, he was throwing on his
clothes.

                              🙘

I went to Simon and Rinaldo's suite. Them and Gideon deserved to hear first.

"Did you find what you were looking for?" Simon asked as he
let me in.

"Yeah, and then some." I looked around. "Where's Gideon?"

"He got a message from Felix and went out. Come on, Mildmay! Don't sit on it—what did you learn from the necromancer?"

I gave them the rundown of what Luther Littleman had said,

and then of what Hugo had said. Rinaldo applauded with delight when I told them about dragging Hugo to Lord Giancarlo. "I would have paid money to see the look on Giancarlo's face."

"It was mostly the eyebrows," I said, and he boomed with laughter.

"What's going to happen?" Simon asked.

"I dunno. Lord Giancarlo was gonna go talk to Lord Stephen, and I guess it depends on how much Lord Stephen believes."

"Stephen will listen to him," Rinaldo said. "He has hated Ivo Polydorius since Dulcinea died."

"Why?" I said.

"There were . . . words spoken at her funeral that would have gotten Ivo a challenge if Stephen had been older. Gareth was fond of Dulcinea, but he never loved her as her children did. And perhaps he was already beginning to look at Gloria Aestia. He accepted Ivo's apology, and they remained on amiable terms until Gloria's execution. I now see why Ivo was so desirous of leaving the Mirador at that time, and why he picked that clumsy fight with Gareth."

"Clumsy?"

"I had thought Ivo was unnerved—we were all unnerved. He said something stupid to Gareth about Shannon's place in the succession, and Gareth exploded. Although perhaps it *was* genuine clumsiness. That question must have been very near and dear to Ivo's heart."

"So he left," Simon said, "and then Gareth died and Stephen became Lord Protector—"

"And I suppose it must have seemed like there was very little point in returning. They had tried an open coup once and failed. Better to wait, bide their time. They must have been ecstatic when Stephen married Robert's sister."

"Shit," I said. "Her kid, they could've done most anything they wanted."

"Exactly. But then she died, and Stephen did not marry again, and Shannon *was* his heir. And the Polydorii tend to be good at waiting."

"Mrs. Fenris said something about a fallow septad."

"I don't pretend to understand heretical thaumaturgy," Rinaldo said. "But I do understand politics. Ivo would pass his schemes on—not to his wastrel son, but I'm sure there are other young Polydorii who cleave a little closer to the true line. But then Stephen announced he was getting married again, and Ivo got nervous. *No one* could have imagined Stephen would marry Zelda. But it gave him an excuse."

"Powers," I said. "That's nasty."

"That's the Polydorii," Rinaldo said.

Simon yawned. "If you find Gideon in Felix's suite, tell him he can come back or pick up his things, whatever he wants."

"I will," I said and left. It was really Gideon I wanted to tell the story to anyways, and if him and Felix were together, I could tell it to both of them. That felt like a good idea. It was the first time in a decad or more that I'd really been happy about going back to Felix's suite.

But they weren't there. Felix's bedroom door was open and everything. I stood for a minute in the middle of the sitting room sort of going, *What the fuck?* to myself, but then I figured that maybe Gideon'd wanted neutral ground for whatever it was Felix had to say to him, and I couldn't blame him for that.

So I got the cards off the mantel and started laying out another round of the Queen of Tambrin. I could wait.

Mehitabel

Even after Vincent left, I couldn't settle. The romance seemed stiff and nonsensical, my bed uninviting. I couldn't get that little pained smile of Felix's out of my head.

Finally, I said to myself, "There's nothing wrong with being worried about a friend," found my shoes, and went to see if Felix was all right.

My nerve nearly failed me when I reached his suite. It was ridiculous, I told myself; I wasn't afraid of Felix and never had been. I knocked.

And Mildmay opened the door.

We gave each other a good blank look, a fast silent mutual agreement to pretend neither one of us was embarrassed, and I said, "Can I talk to Felix for a minute?"

"He ain't here," Mildmay said.

"No?" I said, and my mind was immediately thronged with foolish images of disaster.

Mildmay saw my distress, for he added, "Off with Gideon somewhere."

Oddly, this did not help. "With *Gideon*?"

The tiniest hint of a frown. "Yeah. Sent Gideon a note and all."

"When?"

The frown was getting less subtle. "Dunno. I mean, Gideon'd gone out when I got over to their place, say, an hour and a half ago?"

"But, Mildmay, an hour and a half ago, Felix was with me. He said you'd deserted him, and he was lonely. And he left because—oh, never mind. But it wasn't to meet Gideon. I'm sure of that much."

"What the *fuck*?" Mildmay said, more or less under his breath.

"I'm trying to think of an innocent explanation," I said tightly.

"Well, either Gideon was lying to Simon, or Felix was lying to you, or . . . I hate the fuck out of all of these, y'know?"

"Yes. Where would he go?"

"Felix?"

"Gideon could be anywhere." He nodded reluctantly. "Look, Felix wasn't . . . when he left me, he was . . ."

"He was in a mood," Mildmay offered.

"That'll do. Where would he go?"

"Dunno. But—you think we'd better find him, don't you?"

I was remembering Isaac Garamond pacing my dressing room in a frenzy. "Yes."

"Okay. Will you check around with his friends? You know, Fleur and Edgar and them?"

"All right. What are you going to do?"

"I got another idea," he said, grimly enough that I decided I didn't want to know.

As for me, I'd go to Fleur Masterton and Edgar St. Rose if I had to, but I thought I'd start with Isaac Garamond.

Mildmay

So, you're Felix, you're in a mood, and you've got the whole fucking Mirador laid out like a quarter-gorgon whore in front of you. Where do you go?

I'd thought of the battlements right off, but even Felix wouldn't go up there all by himself in the dark. Thought of the

Arcane, seeing as how he was like one big raw twitchy bruise every time anybody mentioned it, but if he was down there I couldn't go after him nohow. Fucking binding-by-forms. If he'd gone to one of his friends, Mehitabel'd find him, and that was better than me going round like a sheepdog who's lost his only sheep.

And then I thought of something else. And I know I only thought of it because I'd had Strych in my head all fucking day, but, you know, it made too much sense. It's the sort of thing Felix *would* do, and the thought of him down in that nasty little room all by himself gave me the creeping crawling screaming horrors. So even if I was wrong, I had to go look.

I took a lantern, because I was starting to wonder if I was crazy, but I wasn't going to be stupid about it. Didn't have no trouble finding my way, neither. Only ever gotten lost the once in my whole life, and there's a couple different ways that wasn't my fault.

So I found the door again, the one Felix had hexed shut, and there it was, open maybe a quarter inch. Fuck, I thought, because I hadn't wanted to be right, and tried to get ready to talk Felix down from wherever he was at.

Gideon was the first thing I saw when I opened the door.

Somebody'd lugged a chair down, and he was in it, facing the door, a lantern by his feet. And he was dead. It wasn't suicide, and it wasn't an accident. People don't get strangled without somebody meaning it to happen. His face was swollen and dark. It took me a moment to figure out what was wrong with him, why he didn't look like all the dead, strangled people I'd seen in my time, and then it hit me, so hard my knees buckled, and I ended up on all fours, gasping, trying not to cry and not to puke. His mouth was sagging open, but there was no tongue sticking out.

Kolkhis had taught me how to be cold, and I needed it right then, even though I hated it. Hated myself for it. But it got me back on my feet, and got me close enough to the thing that had been Gideon to take a good look.

He'd probably been dead an hour or so, though I wasn't no expert on that end of things, and whoever had done it had taken some pains with the body. Same way you don't get strangled by accident or because you decide to do it yourself, you don't sit there and let somebody get their knot all tidy behind your ear. He hadn't died with his hands folded all neat like that, neither.

There was a piece of paper under them, like Gideon was a paperweight or something. I couldn't see most of the message, but the signature was in plain view, and it was one of those words I didn't have no trouble with: *Felix*.

Fuck, fuck, fuck. But Felix wouldn't've killed him like this. First thought that got through that wasn't purely obscene. Garotte's a sneaky sort of thing, all cold and planned out in advance. Felix wouldn't do it like that. Beat him to death, sure, or knife him even, or just fucking magic him to death. But not creep up behind him with a strangling wire.

And then I thought, Felix wouldn't've brought him here to kill him anyways.

And then I thought, Mehitabel said Felix wasn't going to meet Gideon.

And then I saw the hair tangled in Gideon's fingers, long and red and curly, and I knew with the trouble somebody'd taken over arranging Gideon's hands, that hair hadn't got left there by accident either.

This was a frame-up. Somebody wanted Felix dead, and they couldn't kill him themselves, along of the spells Cabalines all got hung on them. I was the only guy who'd ever murdered a Cabaline despite all that, and nobody'd been asking me how I did it recently. Only people who ever had asked were Felix and Gideon and Mavortian von Heber. And two of them were dead.

I bit down hard on my knuckles, and got thinking again.

Gideon wasn't a Cabaline. They wouldn't let him swear their precious fucking oaths. And he wasn't real big, and he wasn't no fighter. Easy. And with Felix wandering around like a thunderstorm, you just rig your murder a little, and hey presto! like Jean-the-Wizard always says in the pantomimes. Because who's going to believe Felix when he says he didn't do it? Especially when they find the body in a room only Felix knows about . . .

"Fuck," I said under my breath, but hard enough that it hurt my throat. I had to find Felix, and I had to find him right fucking now. There was no time to fuck around with guessing and asking, because this room was a trap, and I didn't figure the guy who set it was planning to just *wait* for somebody to come along and wonder what the awful smell was. He'd've found a way to spring it, and it was only the purest, stupidest luck that I'd gotten to it first.

I got myself back out into the hall, not thinking about it until

I was pulling the door shut on Gideon's dull, bulging eyes. "I'm sorry, Gideon," I said, as fucking useless as anything in the world has ever been.

I didn't latch the door. Left it just like it had been. Because it was proof—I mean, not great proof, but *something*—that somebody'd wanted the body found. And if Felix *had* killed Gideon, he would've shut the door and hexed it again, and not in no little way, neither.

You got to find him, Milly-Fox. And there ain't no time to be nice about it, neither.

I shut my eyes for a second.

I'd been leaning away from the binding-by-forms as hard as I could for—well, for a while. Because when I was stuck in the Bastion with Simon and Rinaldo, it'd nagged at me 'til I wanted to smash my own brains out just to make it stop. And then I hadn't wanted Felix in my head, and I hadn't wanted to deal with it. And I'd just sort of shut it down. Felix had used it on me, but I hadn't used it back on him. I'd even quit hearing his voice all through my dreams the way I had at first.

"Fuck," I said out loud. "You did it to your own self, you sissy." And instead of ignoring the binding-by-forms like a headache, I gave it some room, and all at once, something fell open in my head, and I knew where Felix was. Could've got to him blindfolded.

Couldn't run, but I had Jashuki, and I was moving as fast as I fucking well could.

Mehitabel

There was light showing under Isaac Garamond's door, so I knocked. Knocked again harder when there was no answer. Tried the handle. Locked, of course, and I didn't have Mildmay's way with a hairpin.

I pounded on the door, making it shudder in its frame, and at last heard signs of life from the other side.

"Who's there?" Isaac's voice, and I supposed I could understand why he sounded rather cautious.

"I need to find Felix. Is he with you?"

"Cre . . . Meh . . . M-Madame Parr?"

Oh, very smooth, Lieutenant Vulpes, I thought, and repeated, a bit louder, "I have to find Felix."

And blessedly, Felix's voice, more muffled than Isaac's, "I'm here, Tabby. What's the matter?"

I wish I knew. "I need to talk to you for a minute."

"Can't it wait?"

"No, it damned well can't. *Now*, sunshine."

"Well, unless you want to see me in *all* my glory—oh. Thank you, darling."

A few moments later, the door opened. Felix was wearing a dressing gown clearly meant for a much shorter man, with a good couple inches of his shirt showing at the cuffs; I didn't want to know if he was wearing anything else. "So," he said, one eyebrow up, Felix at his worst, "what is it that is so terribly urgent?"

"Have you seen Gideon tonight?"

"Gideon?" Both eyebrows up now. "Darling, surely you *noticed* the very messy and unpleasant end of our affair?"

"Cut it out," I said impatiently. "Have you seen Gideon? Yes or no."

"No, of course not." He was frowning now, quite like Mildmay. "What's this about?"

"Well, the thing is, sunshine, Gideon left Simon and Rinaldo's suite several hours ago—to meet you."

"To meet *me*? But I—"

"Apparently, you sent him a note."

"I didn't!" And that bewildered, almost childlike indignation I judged was genuine. "What in the world is going on?"

"Let me in, and we can try to figure it out."

"What? Oh. Yes, of course." He stepped out of the way.

Isaac Garamond's suite looked as uninhabited as a hotel room, and Isaac himself looked dreadful, his face almost gray and sweat standing on his forehead and lip. I felt a sinking certainty that I hadn't been wrong, that this was malice, and he was at the back of it. He'd taken the opportunity to get dressed, and he shoved Felix's trousers at him as soon as the door was closed. Felix put them on by reflex and shrugged out of the borrowed dressing gown, still frowning at me. "Why don't you explain things from the beginning? What does it have to do with you anyway?"

"I was worried about you," I said, and he had the grace to look a little ashamed of himself.

I told him the whole; he listened attentively, his frown

deepening, while Isaac fidgeted around the room, growing visibly more anxious by the second.

"And I got a servant to show me the way here," I finished. "I'm sorry I was right."

Isaac flinched; Felix didn't even notice. "But how did you know?" he said, his gaze moving from me to Isaac and back again, and that was when someone began pounding on the door like the drummer for the Day of Judgment.

"Felix!" Mildmay's voice, raw and frantic. "Felix, open this motherfucking door!"

Felix moved like a puppet toward the door, and for a useless, cowardly moment, I wanted to tell him to stop, as if there were any way we could hold off the catastrophe and grief I could hear in Mildmay's voice.

Mildmay

Mehitabel'd got there ahead of me, and it wasn't 'til a lot later that I even started wondering how. Right then, I didn't care, except hoping she'd already explained things because I couldn't. All I could say—all I could get out around the stone wedged in under my breastbone somehow—was, "Gideon's dead."

Felix's face slammed shut like a door. "If this is a joke—"

I said over him, "He's dead. Somebody strangled him in Strych's old workroom."

"Malkar's workroom? But I—"

"Yeah, I know. You hexed the door. Somebody unhexed it."

"But—"

Mehitabel's breath hissed in hard. She was looking at Mr. Garamond, and he'd gone this funny clay sort of color.

Felix—powers and saints, I couldn't stand to look at him, because he knew he had to hold himself together, and at the same time, I could see the howl building up, and it was going to win sooner or later. But he looked at Mr. Garamond, too, and said, "Isaac? Is there something you ought to tell me?"

"Nothing. I didn't expect—"

"Your hands were burned," Mehitabel said. "You said it was a spell."

"Did he?" Felix said, and it would've just been the tone he used when he was baiting people, except there was this edge in it like splintered wood. "Well, Isaac?"

"I don't know anything about Messire Gennadion's workroom. I didn't even know he had one." And he added primly, "I'm sorry for your loss."

"You *liar*," Mehitabel said, and I hadn't even thought she knew Isaac Garamond, never mind hating him like black poison. The funny thing was, she didn't faze him a bit. He just smirked at her, like it didn't matter what she thought.

But there was something else. "Felix," I said, to get his attention back on me, "whoever did it's trying to frame you. They left stuff to make it look like it was you. Can you prove where you been all evening?"

Powers, the look in his eyes. He was about an eyelash away from just completely losing his shit. But he tried to answer me: "I was with Mehitabel. And then I came here. I don't know what time . . . ?"

He looked at Mr. Garamond, and Mr. Garamond said, still prim and nasty, "I have no idea. And I certainly don't know what you might have been doing beforehand. You didn't want to *talk*." He sneered at Felix, and I wanted to kill him for it.

But that sneer—that look on his face—I'd had Strych in my head all damn day—and now I wasn't fighting the binding-by-forms no more, and I don't know if that was what did it, or it was something else, but all at once the whole fucking thing came back at me, and I *knew*.

I probably would've passed out on the spot, but I had about half a grain of sense left in my stupid head and sat down. Hard. Staring at Mr. Garamond and not thinking about nothing except my breathing, because it was too hard and too fast, and there was this ugly sort of hitch in it.

"Mildmay?" Felix said, and powers, I could hear the worry in his voice, even though he shouldn't've been bothering about me at all. He touched my shoulder. "Mildmay?"

My throat was locked up, and my hands were balled into fists so tight you could see every scar on my knuckles standing out against the bone. And I wrenched my head over and heaved a breath in somehow, like trying to breathe rocks and broken glass, and got out, "He killed him."

Felix's fingers cramped on my shoulder, hard enough to bruise. "How do you know?"

"'Cause . . ." Another breath, worse than the first one. "'Cause he was with Strych, in the Bastion."

"I thought you didn't remember any of that."

"It just came back at me. Fuck it, Felix, d'you think I'd tell you if it wasn't true?"

"No." But he wasn't thinking about me anymore. "Was spying not enough for you, Isaac?"

"Spying? What are you talking about? Good God, Felix, can't you recognize a farrago of lies when you hear it?"

"Oh, I definitely can," Felix said. "Did you murder Gideon?"

"Of course not!"

But he was lying. We could all hear it—even Mr. Garamond himself, because when I finally quit being such a fucking coward and looked at him, I've never seen a guy with more guilt on his face.

"You murdered Gideon," Felix said, in this horrible, quiet, perfectly calm voice.

"I swear to you . . . I was with you!"

And that was when his nerve broke, once and for all, and he bolted for the door.

I was moving probably before he was—enough knife fights'll do that for you—and I took him down hard. Got him pinned, twisted to look at Felix and see what he wanted, and Felix said, still in that horrible, quiet, perfectly fucking calm voice, "Kill him."

It was a command, all the binding-by-forms behind it, and my hands were closing on Mr. Garamond's throat before I even caught up with myself. But then there was Gideon and Bartimus Cawley and even, Kethe help me, Vey Coruscant, all dead and strangled, and I thought, clear and cold and about as calm as Felix, I ain't doing that no more.

I said, "No."

Mehitabel said, "Killing him won't help anything," and she almost pulled off her old governess-voice, too.

"I want him dead," Felix said, between his teeth, and Mr. Garamond was lying limp as a rabbit with his pulse hammering against my fingers, and I wanted him dead, too. I wanted him dead so bad I could taste it, copper and bile in my mouth, and it would've been the easiest thing in the world to just let my hands close that fraction of an inch more.

I said, "No."

Felix's voice went up into a shriek, "I want him *dead*!" and the binding-by-forms was falling on me like a wall, and it was the hardest thing I've ever done in my life, but I straightened my fingers away from Mr. Garamond's throat and said, "No," for a third fucking time.

"Damn you!" And he was there, trying to shove me aside, to get at Mr. Garamond himself, and that was when the Protectorate Guard broke down the door. Guess they figured it wasn't no time for good manners. They yanked Felix off me, and me off Mr. Garamond, and Mr. Garamond up on his feet, and there was Thaddeus de Lalage in the middle of them, looking smug enough to bust. And I saw Esmond, who hated Felix, and Thibaud, who hated me, and just in case that wasn't enough, there was Agnes Bellarmyn kind of hovering in the doorway.

"Felix Harrowgate," Thaddeus said, trying to sound sort of grand and awful, but it came out spiteful and way too happy, "you are under arrest for treason against the Mirador and the murder of Gideon Thraxios."

And they were kind of shoving us toward the door, and I was trying to turn to get eye contact with Mehitabel, along of how they were way more likely to listen to her than me, when Mr. Garamond opened his stupid fucking mouth and started shouting, "They were going to kill me! They killed Gideon Thraxios and—"

Felix turned. Me and the guards all ducked on reflex, that's how bad his eyes looked. But I don't think he even saw us. I can't do magic and I can't feel it, but I swear I felt something, like getting pushed out of the way by the biggest fucking invisible hand you ever heard of, and I know I saw it hit Mr. Garamond. He stiffened all over, lurched backwards half a step, and then fell down, not like a person but like a tree. And then I think he went into convulsions, but there were too many guards in the way, and I ain't sure.

"Oh my God," Thaddeus said, and at least he didn't sound happy no more. "What did you do to him?"

"What he deserved," Felix said like death.

I saw the look the guards gave each other, but I couldn't move fast enough.

"Sorry about this, m'lord," Thibaud said, not sounding sorry a bit, and thumped Felix across the back of the skull with his sword hilt.

Felix went down.
I went batfuck insane.

Mehitabel

Thaddeus de Lalage, that stupid, self-righteous *asshole*, would not listen to me. After the guardsmen had subdued Mildmay—it took six of them and two were limping and one nursing a sprained wrist when they finally dragged him out—I tried to tell him the truth about what had happened. He had his own ideas, though, and everything I said was met with the same superior smile and condescending, "Felix is a very plausible liar, you know."

Actually, I knew no such thing. I'd watched Felix hide and evade and dance around various truths for all the time I'd known him, but I'd almost never seen him outright lie. And when he did, he did it badly. But Thaddeus wasn't going to listen to that, either. And when I insisted, he said, "Josiah, would you escort Madame Parr to her chambers and see that she rests? I believe she's a little overwrought."

"What Lord Thaddeus means," I said to the politely hovering guardsman, "is that I'm confusing him. All right, I'm coming."

The guardsman, Josiah, was a nice young man; he obeyed orders but didn't make a fuss about it. I caught him glancing at me sidelong once or twice, and at my door, I stopped and turned to face him. We were of a height. His eyes were brown and steady, and they seemed kind.

"Did you have something you wanted to ask me?" I said.

"You said Lord Felix didn't do it," he said.

"He didn't."

"You got proof?"

"Oh, do I ever," I said bitterly.

"You think Lord Stephen'll listen to you?"

I gave him my best and most dubious look, and he offered me an apologetic half-smile.

"Mildmay and me are sort of friends. And I ain't got nothing against Lord Felix."

I considered him a moment longer, but there was no guile in his round face, and, really, it wasn't like I could make things worse. "I think Stephen *may* listen to me. If I can get to him."

Josiah nodded once, sharply, like a man making up his mind. "Come on then."

"You can get me in?" I said, having to break into a trot for a moment to catch up with him.

He grinned at me, a sweet, sunny grin missing half a dozen teeth. "Don't tell nobody, but I got an in with the guards."

Mildmay

In case you were wondering, the Verpine ain't no luxury hotel. It's deep enough in the Mirador that you can feel the Sim, and it's all bare stone, and oh yeah, they don't give you light unless you got somebody wanting to talk to you. And it smells just exactly like the Kennel.

It was a while before I came 'round, and it would've been longer if it hadn't been for the obligation d'âme jumping up and down on me. Felix was in trouble—I mean, I *knew* that, because it didn't take no brains to see it, but the binding-by-forms was telling me all about it, too. They'd done something to his magic, which I supposed—making myself think about it logically because otherwise I was just going to beat myself to death on the bars like a sparrow against a windowpane—actually made some sense. Without his magic, Felix wasn't no kind of a threat. But the binding-by-forms didn't care if it made sense, and it didn't care about the bars and the walls and the locks. It just kept clanging in my head like an alarm bell.

They'd taken Jashuki—at least, I couldn't find it, and I wouldn't've left it where I could reach it if I'd been them, either—so I had all the time in the world to test my bad leg. Thanks a lot, Thaddeus. Upshot was, I could get by without a cane, but I was going to get by a lot better with one.

And, you know, every fucking time I let my guard down, even a little, I'd find myself pressed against the bars of the cell like I thought I could push my way through them or something.

The fifth or sixth time that happened, I gave up and just stayed there, grabbing onto the bars so hard the rough iron of them bit my hands. I kept seeing Gideon, the smile he'd given me when he left the Lady's Lapdog, kept thinking that while I'd been scaring the shit out of poor, stupid Hugo Chandler, Gideon had been dying, choking and strangling with Isaac Garamond's wire around his throat. And, Kethe, I knew just exactly how it would've happened, the way his fingers would have scrabbled at the wire and at Mr. Garamond's hands, the way he would've twitched and struggled and then gone limp, just another sack of dead meat.

If I'd thought I could've run into the bars hard enough to knock myself out, I would've done it.

But finally—I don't know how long it was, my time sense was fucked to Hell and back—the door at the end of the hall, the one where you could see the light around its edges so you knew you hadn't gone blind, opened, and two guards came in, kind of half dragging and half carrying Felix between them.

"Away from the door, Fox," one of them said, and I backed up. They unlocked it, and shoved Felix in, and they didn't even stop to sneer before they went back out and shut us in the dark.

Where we belonged, I guess.

I could hear Felix breathing, unsteady and harsh, and when I was sure the guards were gone, and not going to come bouncing back in or something, I said, "Felix? You okay?"

"They think Gideon was a spy," he said in this thin little voice, and powers, he sounded lost. "I kept trying to tell them he wasn't, and they wouldn't listen."

"But why would Gideon be spying? It don't make no sense."

"I don't know. Some notion of Thaddeus's, I think. They think—" He broke off, and I could hear him trying not to giggle. We both knew if he started, it wouldn't stop 'til he was screaming. "They think Gideon suborned me, that he was like a spider, sitting and waiting, and I was running around finding things out for him and trying to recruit other spies. They think that's why I was interested in Isaac. And they think . . . they think—" It nearly got away from him, but he fought it back down. "They think I killed him because I didn't know any other way to get free of him."

"How fucking dumb can you get?" I said.

"Oh, my past history more than supports the theory," he said, his voice dry now but still shaky and still full of splinters and shards.

"You mean, because of Strych?"

"And certain . . . aspects of my relationship with Lord Shannon."

"It's still dumb."

"Thank you," he said, and he sounded like he meant it.

We were silent for a minute, and I was just about to ask him if his head was okay, when he said, "Is . . . is this the Verpine?"

"Yeah," I said, and tried to hide how gut-punched I felt that he had to ask.

"I was here once before."

"Before?"

"When I broke the Virtu. They put me down here. I remember the dark."

We were silent again, because I didn't know what the fuck to say, then he said, "Mildmay?"

"Yeah?"

"Do you think it's dark, where Gideon is?" And, powers, his accent had gotten away from him, and his voice was barely more than breath, and he sounded so fucking *lost*.

"Oh, sweetheart," I said, and my voice broke. "C'mere." We found each other in the dark, and I hugged him, and for once he didn't go stiff or shrug me away, but hugged me back.

"I don't want him to be in the dark," he said into my shoulder. "I don't want him to be afraid."

"His White-Eyed Lady was waiting for him," I said. "She'll take care of him. She'll help him rest."

"Do you think so? Really?" He was crying, the way you learn to cry when you're a kept-thief and you don't dare make any sound about it. But I could feel his tears soaking into my shirt.

"Really," I said, and held him against the dark.

Mehitabel

Stephen did not exactly look on me with favor when Josiah had sweet-talked me past the guards on duty outside his study.

"Mehitabel, I am extremely busy, and—"

"Shut up and listen," I said.

His jaw sagged a little, and I threw myself into speech before he could muster himself to have me evicted. "I was a spy for the Bastion. Up until about quarter of eleven tonight. No, yesterday, it must be past midnight by now."

"It is," Stephen said grimly. But he flicked his fingers at me to continue.

I told him the whole thing. About Hallam and Louis Goliath and Isaac, about what I'd done and hadn't done, what I'd seen, what I knew. I laid out every piece of the puzzle, every link in the chain, and Stephen sat and listened with perfect concentration.

"Felix didn't kill Gideon," I said finally. "Isaac did."

"To get Felix convicted of murder and executed."

"That seems the logical conclusion."

"Pity we can't ask him," Stephen said, his voice as dry as salt and ashes.

"Is he . . . ?"

"His mind is gone," Stephen said. "Whatever Felix did to him, it's not the sort of thing you get over."

I shivered.

"And so you may clear him of murder, but I'm afraid there's still the gross heresy to deal with."

"Oh," I said. Stupidly, I hadn't thought past Gideon.

He sighed, deeply. "There will have to be a trial. Will you testify?"

"If you're going to kill him anyway, why does it matter?"

His basilisk stare turned me to stone where I stood. "Because it is the truth. Will you testify?"

"You burn wizards for heresy, don't you?"

"Yes."

"God." I wrapped my arms around myself in a useless parody of a hug. "Is there any way . . ."

"He's made a man into a drooling, weeping, mindless wreck, and you're pleading for him?"

"That same man is one you would only have executed. Do you burn spies, too, or just hang them?"

"Revenge and justice are not the same."

"The end results look pretty damn similar," I snapped. "And, oh, by the way, are you going to execute me? I'd like to know before I make dinner plans."

"You haven't committed a capital crime," he said, quite mildly all things considered. "Will you testify?"

"In front of the court? Will you provide the rail for them to run me out of town afterward?"

"In front of me, Giancarlo, and one other, whom you may choose."

I stared at him, wishing I could basilisk right back at him. "Is this because I'm sleeping with you?"

"Yes," he said, perfectly unashamed. "And because you

chose to come to me with the truth. And because I'm going to be ruining enough lives in the morning. Your Mr. Foxe was very busy last night."

"He's not mine," I said. I'd heard rather more than I'd wanted to about the downfall of Ivo Polydorius and Robert of Hermione while Josiah was arguing with the guards.

"In any event, you acted under duress." A pause, and he added with the first sign of discomfort he'd shown, "I will see if there's anything I can do about Lieutenant Bellamy."

Maybe Thaddeus was right. Maybe I *was* overwrought. Tears were suddenly burning in my eyes, in the back of my throat. "Thank you," I said, and it came out more hoarsely than I wanted.

"There may be nothing," Stephen said, as if trying to evade my gratitude. "Go get some rest, Mehitabel. And tell me who you want as your third witness. Oh—it has to be an annemer."

I expected the decision to be a difficult one, but the answer was there, waiting for me. "Lord Shannon."

Stephen's momentarily dumbfounded expression was very nearly worth the mortification of having had to tell him the whole sordid story. The smile I gave him as I left was almost real.

ᔕ᙭

I lay on my bed, unsleeping, the rest of the night, reciting *Finuspex* and *The Tragedy of Horatio* to myself to keep from having to think. A little after six, Lenore brought tea and toast and a message telling me to meet Stephen, Shannon, and Lord Giancarlo in the Attercop. A page would come at seven-thirty to show me the way.

I rose, washed, dressed, ate, all of it like a machine in one of Mélusine's manufactories. Lenore—silent, watchful, but nonjudgmental—pinned my hair up and unearthed the black gloves I'd bought for the funeral of Corinna's Aunt Constancy. She gave them to me, and I realized I was wearing the same dress I'd worn to that funeral, too: plain gray wool with jet buttons and an underskirt trimmed with black lace.

I wondered where Gideon would be buried.

The page was the brown sparrow-child I'd seen once before. His name—he told me shyly when I asked—was Garnet Aemorius. He had just turned thirteen, and he thought the Mirador

was the most fascinating and beautiful place in the world. I
hoped he'd be able to go on thinking that.

The Attercop was a small room, paneled in cherrywood. Its
only decoration was the carpet, which I recognized as Lunness-
make, bold in cranberry and gold and kingfisher blue. The men
were waiting for me; even Shannon was dressed somberly, and
Giancarlo of Novalucrezia looked as if he hadn't slept for a
week. Even his eyebrows were drooping.

Stephen poured me a glass of water. I thanked him with a
curtsy and then pulled myself up, assuming the swan-daughter,
drawing on Edith Pelpheria and Jacobethy and every other
strong-willed woman I'd ever played. Even Aven, God bless her
crooked black heart. "My lords," I said, "I was a spy for the
Bastion . . ."

                          ༺༄

It was no less wearing to tell it a second time. I tried not to look
at either Shannon or Lord Giancarlo as I spoke; Stephen's
basilisk stare was oddly comforting. When I had done, Lord Giancarlo said, "Thank you," and Shannon got up to hand me to a
chair, as he would for a real lady. He didn't say anything, but
the brief, warm pressure of his fingers on mine was message
enough.

I sat, still playing the swan-daughter, while they consulted in
voices low enough that I couldn't quite hear them. At least they
believed me, I said to myself.

Finally, Stephen said, "Well, we'll do what we must." And,
to me, "Will you come see justice done tomorrow?"

"I hope so," I said, and he gave me a tight smile for the quib-
ble.

Chapter 18

Mehitabel

I went back to my suite because I couldn't think of anything else to do, and it seemed possible I might sleep. But I found that a letter had been delivered while I was gone.

Vincent Demabrien's lovely, lucid hand:

> *I don't know how much you know about Marathine jurisprudence, but it is very likely, from what I understand, that Felix will be sentenced to death. If that happens, the ghost of whom we were speaking last night will never find rest, for I don't believe anyone other than Felix can help him.*
>
> *Does it seem callous at this juncture to be worried about a boy who is already dead? I don't know. But I'm sitting in Ivo's study, waiting for the guards to come and take me to the person who will be deciding how I am to be judged in the catastrophe of Ivo's horrid machinations, and all I can think of is that poor, hurting ghost. And, I admit it, of Felix. Who would never murder a lover in cold blood, and who may have to die drowning in this ugliness. It is ridiculous and romantic of me to think that any benefit might come of his last deed being a good one, and yet I sit here and the idea will not leave me alone.*
>
> *And there's nothing I can do. Probably, there isn't anything you can do, either. But it seems to me possible that you might think of something. At least, I know that you will understand what I mean, and maybe knowing that will help me feel not so fucking awful about this whole stupid, pointless, evil mess.*

And if I am wrong, and there is something I can do—
anything *I can do—please let me know.*

Even his signature was beautiful and clear, as beautiful and
clear as that completely uncharacteristic word, *fucking*.

I read the letter twice, and I thought about atonement and
second chances, and the ghastly thing Felix had done.

And then I called for Lenore and told her I wanted to talk to
the guardsman named Josiah. Because I thought Vincent was
right; I *could* think of something.

Mildmay

Me and Felix both startled awake when the door at the end of
the hall opened again. Felix sort of moaned, deep in his throat,
and pressed his face into my shoulder. And then he woke up
properly and was suddenly two feet away, and I didn't need to
be able to see him to know he was blushing. Because, you know,
powers and saints preserve us all from having to admit we're
grieving.

It was Josiah, and Cleo with him, both of them kind of
frowning, and Josiah said, "Mildmay, that actress you were seeing, did she talk you into doing weird shit all the time and you
couldn't figure out how?"

"Um," I said.

"Because, I'm telling you, this is some weird shit, and I
don't know *how* she talked me into it."

"You'd do anything for a sob story and a pair of pretty eyes,"
Cleo said.

"Then I don't know how she talked *you* into it."

Cleo snorted. "I told you. I believe what she said."

"Which is what, exactly?" Felix said, and if he'd been close
enough, I would've smacked him for being snotty.

"Well," Josiah said, "Madame Parr says as how there's a
ghost you need to lay, and she wants to know if you can do it tonight."

I expected Felix to laugh or rip Josiah a new asshole or
something, but he made this funny little choked noise and said,
"Yes."

"And, um. We're supposed to ask you what you need."

"Well, for starters," I said, "you could get me my cane."

Mehitabel

Later, I had no memory of the performance. Absolutely none. All I remembered was, in the second intermission, getting a note in Felix's looping scrawl, written on cheap paper with a cheaper pen, saying, *Tabby, thank you, midnight is the best time, will you come?*

I hadn't been sure he would want to see me, really hadn't been sure he would want me there. But I wasn't about to turn him down.

We had to meet in the Verpine, there being quite drastic limits to what Josiah was willing to do. I'd never been there before, and I found myself hoping profoundly I'd never have to go there again as Josiah's friend Cleo—massive, scowling, but perfectly comfortable with the idea of laying a ghost—escorted me down the stairs to the room where Felix and Mildmay were waiting.

After a single, searing glance, I couldn't look at Felix. His hands were manacled, ringless. His shirt was torn and his hair was hanging in lank tangles. I had never seen him so disheveled, so far from his usual state of catlike neatness. His face was gray beneath the streaks of dirt. His eyes were red-rimmed and sunk in their sockets, his lips bloodless. In his blue eye I read crushing grief, in the left a darkness that might have been fury or simple insanity.

Mildmay was behind him, looking just as disheveled but much calmer. His head was up, his eyes bright and intent, and it occurred to me that I hadn't seen him this focused since . . . since we'd brought him out of the Bastion. He didn't seem at all thrown by seeing me, either, simply gave me a nod and turned his attention back to Felix.

Felix was looking at me; it took him two tries before he could manage to say, "How did you know?"

"Know what?"

"How much this mattered."

"You told me, sunshine," I said, and watched bewildered as he flushed a painful red. "In any event, it was Vincent's idea. I just organized."

"Vincent?"

"He wrote to me."

"He would understand," Felix said, sounding vague and rather lost.

"We should get going," Josiah said uneasily. "'Less y'all're gonna change your minds."

"No," Felix said. "This needs to be done. Mildmay?"

"Can't you take the manacles off first?" I said to Josiah. They were ugly, crude things, and I could see the welts they were rubbing against the bones of Felix's hands.

It was Felix who answered, his voice unwontedly gentle: "Thank you, Tabby, but they can't. These keep me from—what's the word you used?"

"Hexing," Mildmay said.

"Thank you, yes. *Hexing* everyone in sight and . . . well, I don't know what I'd do then, but no doubt something ghastly."

"But if you can't do magic . . ."

"This isn't about magic."

Even Mildmay was staring at him, and he made a noise that might almost have been a laugh. "We really do need to get going. And I promise you don't want to hear the theory involved. Especially since it's fifty percent guesswork."

"Powers," Mildmay said. "Well, c'mon then." He didn't go back up the stairs, but led us—Felix and me together, with the two guardsmen bringing up the rear—through a series of storage rooms and out again into a hallway I'd never seen before. At one point during our progress, as Mildmay nonchalantly forced the lock of a three-quarter sized door hidden in the shadow of a flying buttress, Cleo muttered, "Fuck me hard." I pretended not to hear, not wanting to embarrass him, but I was a little heartened by the evidence the guards hadn't known about this route either.

Felix asked Mildmay about the buttress, and Mildmay said promptly, "There's a bunch of 'em. Holding up the Vielle Roche. They didn't want to fuck with it, so they just built around 'em."

"You mean that was once the outer wall?" I said.

"Yeah. Vielle Roche is the oldest part. The Tiamat"—with a wave around to indicate that was where we were now—"'s Ophidian."

"How do you know?" I knew better than to ask, of course, but there had been so many times I hadn't asked, and I'd regretted it when I'd thought I'd never get another chance.

And Mildmay just shrugged, the movement stiffer and truncated from what I was used to because he was leaning on his walking stick, and said, "I learned a lot of stuff when Kolkhis was training me."

Which wasn't an answer, but I let myself be distracted. "I've never heard you say her name before."

That got me a glance over his shoulder, just enough lift to his eyebrows that I knew he was teasing—or as close as he got—when he said, "I been practicing."

He led us easily, steadily. Josiah and Cleo clustered up closer and closer, and we had to stop several times for one person or another to recover from a sneezing fit. The dust and cobwebs and mikkary were painfully thick in these abandoned rooms, and Felix said, "I'm glad Vincent isn't here."

"He would have come," I said, uneasily uncertain whether that comment was meant to be taken at face value, "but Lord Ivo's household is still—"

"Lord Ivo's *household*?" Felix interrupted me, his voice suddenly sharp. "What's happened to Lord Ivo?"

"Powers," Mildmay said resignedly. "I didn't get a chance to tell you."

"Tell me what?"

It was strange to hear the thing from Mildmay's perspective, described in blunt, brutal words and with the eerie flat finality of fact instead of the breathless murmur of speculation. Felix listened to it all, his face going blanker and blanker in the light of the lantern Cleo carried, and when Mildmay was done, he said, "You must have been making excursions into the Lower City for weeks."

"Only a couple times," Mildmay said.

"And you didn't tell me any of it."

"I didn't want to upset you."

"Yes, and you picked such a foolproof method of going about it, too."

Josiah, Cleo, and I all pulled back involuntarily from the bitterness in Felix's voice, but Mildmay said, just as bitterly, "If I'd told you, you wouldn't've let me do it."

"Of course I wouldn't let you do it, you suicidal half-wit!"

That might be as close as Felix would ever come to saying *I love you*, and I could tell from Mildmay's startled, reflexive glance at Felix's face that he knew it.

"Oh never mind," Felix said after a moment. "You seem to

have saved the city while I wasn't watching. I shouldn't be churlish about it."

Felix's rather rueful admiration seemed to distress Mildmay even more than his anger had. "It ain't like that."

"No? How would you describe it, then?"

"Um," Mildmay said, and then with obvious relief, "There's the stairs to the crypt."

It was a mark of how hard Felix was working to keep his façades in place that he let Mildmay redirect his attention without another word. I'd watched them do that particular dance more times than I could count, and while Felix often accepted the new topic, I'd never seen him do it without a pointed comment—a warning that he would be returning to the uncomfortable subject later. And then I remembered, looking at the rose-entwined skeletons serving as caryatids at the stairhead, that there might not be any "later" for Felix.

And honestly, the knowledge that I'd done everything I could was no comfort at all.

Mildmay

Josiah and Cleo didn't like the crypt. They stayed by the door—Cleo stayed in the doorway, like he was afraid he'd get locked in if he gave it the chance to close.

Josiah tossed me a box of lucifers, though, and I lit the candles somebody'd put around Amaryllis Cordelia's tomb. It wasn't like it was enough light, but I didn't figure broad daylight would be enough light for this place, and the candles were better than nothing. And better than trying to talk Cleo out of the death grip he had on the lantern, too.

Felix went prowling up and down the rows of tombs. Mehitabel came and stood next to me. After a moment, she said, "I did the best I could. I told Stephen everything."

"Everything?"

"Oh God," she said, and she told me, barely whispering so Josiah and Cleo wouldn't hear. It didn't take her long, and I listened and thought about how much it explained.

When she was done, I said, "You gonna be okay?"

"I'm sleeping with the Lord Protector," she said, and I was surprised at how bitter she sounded. "I'll be fine." She glanced sideways at me and burst out laughing, her real laugh, making everybody else jump. "I love the look you get when you're try-ing to decide if you have to ask someone a personal question. I'm fine—in no danger, and Stephen's promised to see if he can help Hallam."

"Is Hallam your fella?" I asked, and I guess we were both surprised at how jealous I *didn't* sound, because she gave me a really beautiful smile and said, "Yes. I'm sorry, you know. I should have told you—"

"You couldn't. I get that. And, I mean, I figure I was worse, calling you Ginevra and everything."

"I *shouldn't* have told you that."

"Yes, you should," I said, and suddenly I really wanted to make her understand. "It was a shitty thing to do to you, and you shouldn't've had to put up with it. And I think I needed my ass kicked about it anyway. You know, to get over it."

"Have you?"

"I'm getting better. Getting better about a lot of things." And without even meaning to, I was looking for Felix.

He was standing by one of the tombs, resting his hands on it to take the weight of the manacles off his wrists, and when he saw me looking at him, he said, "Can we move the candles over here?"

"Sure," I said, and me and Mehitabel moved them. Felix just stood there, head down, until we were done, and then he said, in this nice even voice, like he was talking to the kids in the Grenouille Salon, "Ephreal Sand calls the world of the spirit *manar*, and magic is only one of the ways to reach it. I don't think I've ever actually used magic to disperse a ghost."

"But that big maze we drew down here—"

"Was ritual. Like I said, another way to channel *manar*. Maybe even a better way."

"It didn't do Magnus no good."

"There's a blockage," Felix said. "In the flow of what Ynge calls noirant energy. I learned how to see it from observing Vin-cent."

"Who doesn't do magic at all," Mehitabel said, like this was all starting to make sense to her.

"Exactly." Felix gave her a tired smile. "Now if I had access to my magic, I could remove the block by brute force, but I don't. I'm almost glad of it—I think a ritual will be less disruptive."

"Disruptive to what?" Mehitabel said.

"Remember what Vincent said the last time we were here," Felix said, and Mehitabel shut her mouth in a hurry. "Tabby, do you have a stickpin or the like?"

Mehitabel did—pretty thing set with citrines—and handed it over. I decided I just wasn't going to wonder if Lord Stephen had given it to her.

Felix looked at it a second, and then jabbed it into the vein in his left wrist.

"Good God, Felix, do you have to?" Mehitabel said, and she sounded every bit as spooked out as I felt.

"I think so," Felix said, watching his blood drip onto the top of the tomb. "I need power to remove the block, and, well, this is what I've got at hand. So to speak."

"But isn't that dangerous?"

He shrugged a little. His hair had fallen forward, so I couldn't see his face. "I've done worse things."

"Not what I asked, sunshine."

"It doesn't matter. Just let me do this."

And Mehitabel held her tongue.

After a little while, he started using the pin to draw patterns in the blood, muttering under his breath. He was using his right thumb to stanch the bleeding. Me and Mehitabel were both trying like fuck to look somewhere else, so I didn't see most of it, but I knew when it worked all right, because, powers and saints, it was like a thunderclap, and then there was just this afterimage, blurring into nothing almost before it was there, a hawk-faced boy, trying to smile, his hands spread like he was giving Felix a blessing.

Felix just stood there, rubbing his fingers like they hurt, and blinking hard. After a long, long moment, he said, "I'll have to remember that one. So as not to do it again."

"It worked, though, right?" I said.

"Oh yes. He'll rest now." Felix brought up his hands to rub his eyes, wincing as the manacles shifted on his wrists.

"That's good," Mehitabel said gently.

"Yes. Will it make you think of me more kindly, Tabby, when . . ."

When I'm dead, he meant, but he couldn't quite make himself say it.

"I think kindly of you now, sunshine," Mehitabel said, still so fucking gentle, and Felix's calm cracked like an eggshell.

The next second he was back in control, just daring us to try and say anything. Mehitabel kind of looked at me like she was waiting to follow my lead, but I didn't have the first fucking clue what to say.

Felix only gave me about a heartbeat anyway before he said, "I expect we'd better get back. I don't want to get our guards in trouble."

"Yeah," I said.

Josiah and Cleo were both staring at Felix like he was gold-plated, and I wondered how long it'd be before the story was all over the Mirador. But that was okay—maybe it would balance out all the other shit.

I blew out the candles.

Felix and Mehitabel helped.

Mehitabel

I'd never seen the Hall of the Chimeras in its role as a judicial court before, and it wasn't improved. I planted myself where I had a good view of the dais, and waited, surrounded by the chatter of the courtiers and wizards. They were anxious, alarmed, indulging in spectacular gossip. The rituals of the Mirador were disrupted, and it was almost funny how bereft her denizens were.

The Curia came in first, followed by Stephen's Cabinet. They flanked the dais, grave-faced as owls. Stephen, Shannon, and Victoria entered through the door behind the dais, and the background mutter increased sharply as the court realized Robert wasn't with them. They were all three as unreadable as stone.

Stephen dealt with the—relatively—simpler matter of Ivo Polydorius and Robert of Hermione first. The rabbity musician, the one who had brought Cardenio to me two years ago—I couldn't even remember his name when I saw him—gave his testimony in a flood of words, babbling and sobbing. Mostly, it made no sense to me, since he was talking about things that had happened many years ago, and I didn't recognize most of the names. But Ivo Polydorius kept recurring, like a cork bobbing in a rain-butt, and the deepening grimness of Cabinet and Curia said clearly that the other names were evil company.

Robert of Hermione was brought out next, sweating and sal-

low. But he was still vilely confident; he'd had Stephen's protection for a long time, and his narrow self-interest was of the
sort that never understands what will make other people snap.
He was too frightened to lie, but his words were all weasel
words, and it took repeated, hammering questions to get the
truth out of him. Robert hadn't been a member of the first con-
spiracy, the one which resulted in the death by burning of Gloria Aestia, but he'd been enticed in after his sister's death, when
he could no longer rely on her soft good-nature to get him
preferment. He'd been in the thick of the plotting around Cornell Teverius, and although he couldn't be driven to say so outright, his animosity for Shannon had been a large factor in the
decision to involve Cornell. It was appallingly clear that Robert
didn't care *who* held power in the Mirador, as long as he got his
share.

When they were done with Robert, there was a long silence,
thick as mud. Everyone was watching Stephen, who was sitting
slumped, bearlike, his eyes hooded and lowered. Whatever he
was thinking about, he didn't like it. Finally, he said, "Let's
have Lord Ivo out here."

At his side, Shannon said, his voice thin and harsh, "May I
speak?"

"What do you want to say?"

"I knew nothing of this plotting. I do not want the Protectorship, and if anyone had approached me to offer it, I should neither have accepted nor remained quiet. There is no evidence I
can produce, of course, since one cannot prove a negative, but
even if you burn me for treason, I will die avowing that this was
none of my doing and none of my wish."

"You are heard," Stephen said. "Does anyone doubt Lord
Shannon?"

People did, of course; human nature alone would have en-
sured that, even if there hadn't been, as Shannon said, such a
hideous dearth of evidence. But it wasn't the sort of thing anyone would say out loud.

"Then let it be known," said Stephen, falling into the formal
cadences of a proclamation, "that I place full trust and confidence in my brother, Shannon Teverius. His loyalty to the Protectorate has never been in doubt, and it is not doubted now." He
and Shannon exchanged a glance; Stephen's face was, as always,

uninformative, but I saw relief and a shy, surprised kind of pleasure on Shannon's. "Bring out Lord Ivo."

I'd never seen Lord Ivo before. He was a straight-backed
man in his early sixties, with a narrow, sardonic face and bright,
hooded eyes like a raptor's. He radiated self-will like the rank
smell of a fox, a sense that in all his life he had done only and
always what suited him. He wasn't frightened, although he had
to know he was defeated.

His determination was to bring as many people down with
him as he could. Unlike Robert, he made no attempt to weasel or
to whitewash himself, admitting freely to his league with Vey
Coruscant, their plotting which had begun with the death of Lord
Ivo's cousin Dulcinea, to all the intricacies and betrayals of the
intervening years. His evidence was clear, cogent, complete—
and damning. He named his confederates, both nobles and wizards, and he gave the name of every single person who had ever
turned a blind eye to what he did. But he didn't lie. He exonerated
Shannon, when he could have dragged him down with no more
than an equivocation. Lord Ivo, too, had his own sense of honor.

When he was finished, that clear, dry voice, like dead twigs
snapping, fallen silent at last, Stephen brooded again, while the
court shifted uneasily and nobody made eye contact with anybody.

At last, Stephen said, "Lord Ivo Polydorius, Lord Robert of
Hermione, you are guilty of treason. The sentence for treason is
death." Of all the people in the Hall of the Chimeras, only Lord
Ivo didn't flinch. "Does anyone speak in defense of these persons?"

There was a terrible silence. Ritualistically, Stephen asked
the question two more times, and the silence just got deeper. I'd
been told of trials in the past—Felix and Mildmay had gotten
on the subject one night—in which clemency had been granted.
The most notable was Felix's own trial, when the Virtu had
been broken. They had left him alive, Felix had said snidely,
because they couldn't solve their jigsaw puzzles without him.
Intellectual aggravation, not clemency. But there were other trials: the trial of Lord George Cledentius, at which his wife had
cast herself weeping at the feet of Lord Malory Teverius; the
trial of Lord Polycarp Aemorius, at which the head of the Curia
had stood up and declared his belief that Lord Polycarp's trea-

son had been justified. It wasn't uncommon for traitors to be
forgiven, or their sentences commuted. But it needed someone
to speak for them. And no one spoke.

"Very well," said Stephen. "For the smaller players in this foul
game, Lord Alaric Gardenius, Lord Walter Malanius, Lady Do-
lores Malania, Lady Parsanthia Ward, Lord Michael Otanius—
and the go-between, Hugo Chandler—my judgment is this: they
are to be stripped of land, title, and privileges, and to be banished.
After Samedy, Dai twenty-fourth, 2283 *ab urbe condita*, if they
are found within the borders of Marathat, they shall suffer the
fate of their leaders. Lord Ivo Polydorius, Lord Robert of
Hermione, my judgment on you is that at sundown, Jeudy, Dai
twenty-second, you shall be taken into the Plaza del'Archimago
and there burned, as Gloria Aestia was burned."

Lord Ivo looked vaguely bored. Robert threw himself forward, grabbing at Stephen's feet, pleading and crying, invoking
Emily Teveria as if she were some patron saint. Stephen sat un-
moved, merely waving for the guards to come and pull Robert
back.

"One last favor for my dead wife," said Stephen, when
Robert was quiet again. "A merciful death for her brother.
Robert of Hermione, you shall die under the sanguette." The
flat finality of his voice silenced Robert at last. Stephen looked
away from Robert and said, "The dynastic line of the Polydorii
passes to Lord Crowell Polydorius. Lord Crowell, the house of
Polydorius is now your problem." A noble near me, with Lord
Ivo's bones, but without the cruel brightness in his eyes, bowed
in acknowledgment, and Stephen sighed. "Take the prisoners
away. Grant them every courtesy due their rank."

Robert and Lord Ivo were taken out. The "courtesy of rank"
often extended itself to the means of suicide being left handy,
and I hoped someone would manage it this time, too. I had no
desire to watch anyone be burned, not even Ivo Polydorius.

Stephen sat up straighter; the day's business wasn't done.
"Bring in Felix Harrowgate."

Felix looked even worse than he had the night before. He
was unraveling, strand by strand, and I hated that there were
so many witnesses to it. From the frown in Mildmay's face as
he followed, he hadn't been able to help. The guards jerked
Felix to a halt before the dais. He seemed almost unaware of
his surroundings, but when Stephen said, "Felix Harrowgate,"

he said, "Yes, my lord," his voice as clear and level as ever. Only I thought I detected a hint of the Lower City in it, a trace of Mildmay.

"Did you murder Gideon Thraxios?"

God, Stephen, must you be so tactless? Felix's flinch was visible, but he said, "No, my lord."

"Did you destroy the mind of Isaac Garamond?"

"Yes, my lord."

"Why did you do that?"

"Because he murdered Gideon Thraxios, whom I loved. Because he was a spy of the Bastion, and a confederate of Malkar Gennadion."

"Oh my God!" Thaddeus, shouting. "Don't tell me you're going to swallow a pack of lies like that!"

"Lord Thaddeus," said Stephen, "be silent. Felix Harrowgate, what proof do you have?"

Felix hesitated. But then he said, in arid defiance, as one who knows he won't be believed, "The word of my brother."

"Mr. Foxe," said Stephen.

"M'lord," said Mildmay.

"What evidence do you have for your claim against Isaac Garamond?"

"M'lord," Mildmay said again. And he told him, the whole thing, repeating himself patiently when Stephen asked. I was disconcerted by how hard Stephen found it to understand Mildmay. I hadn't realized before how acclimated I'd gotten to Mildmay's drawling, diphthonged vowels and slurred consonants.

"You say that you 'remember' Isaac Garamond. Can you be clearer?"

There was a pause. Everyone but Felix was looking at Mildmay. Felix's head was down; I couldn't tell if he even heard the voices around him. Mildmay was struggling for words. Finally he said, "Two indictions ago—as maybe your lordship remembers—I got . . . trapped by Brinvillier Strych. Or Malkar Gennadion, as some call him."

"Yes," said Stephen, almost kindly.

"He kept me awhile," Mildmay said, and I winced at the wealth of things left unsaid. "And I saw Mr. Garamond there with him in the Bastion, helping him." His head went down for a moment, but he got it back up and said, slow and careful, "Helping him torture me."

"Why haven't you mentioned this before?"

There was another pause, as long as a hard winter. Mildmay said, "Strych hurt me pretty bad, and I . . . I dunno. I wasn't letting myself remember what he done, so I couldn't remember none of the rest of it neither. But it came back at me anyways."

"My lord!" Thaddeus again. "Clearly this story is an invention. This creature has been coached by his brother to incriminate their victim."

I saw the spark in Mildmay's eye and didn't blame him. There were worse epithets than "creature" Thaddeus could have used, but it was hard to think of one.

"Lord Thaddeus, open your mouth out of turn again, and I'll have you removed," Stephen said. "Mr. Foxe, do you stand by your story?"

"Ain't a story. But, yeah, I'll swear it's true."

"Very well. We have other evidence, taken under Protectorate Seal, which confirms what Mr. Foxe has said. And—Lord Thaddeus, if you would not mind speaking *now* to tell us how you learned of the location of Gideon Thraxios's body?"

"An anonymous message under my door," Thaddeus said sullenly.

"And once you'd found the body, you went to Isaac Garamond's rooms because . . . ?"

"I knew there were spies in the Mirador. One of my . . . former friends in the Bastion sent me a message with the caefidus. And I knew"—he finished in a burst of defiance—"they were trying to suborn Isaac Garamond!"

"And you did not come to anyone with your evidence," Stephen said, dismissing Thaddeus de Lalage with one comprehensive glance. "Felix Harrowgate, from this evidence, you are guilty neither of murder nor of treason."

There was a rustle of whispers among the Curia; they were thinking of the husk of Isaac Garamond. The envoys from Vusantine were in a huddle and seemed to be arguing.

"However, you have committed gross heresy on the person of Isaac Garamond. Do you deny this?"

"No, my lord," Felix said, not looking up.

"The sentence for gross heresy is death," Stephen said, and Felix agreed, "By fire." He didn't sound as if the idea upset him.

"Does anyone speak in defense of this person?" Stephen said.

Lord Giancarlo said, "Surely we must admit there are extenuating circumstances."

"Would you say I was mad with grief, my lord?" Felix said with sudden savagery. "Will you send me to St. Crellifer's with my victim?"

"Felix, hold your tongue," Stephen said. "Lord Giancarlo, even if we admit extenuating circumstances, it doesn't change what he did."

"Not all heretics must be burned," Lord Giancarlo said stubbornly.

"Yes, and Felix is living proof. However, there are no loopholes here. What he did is gross heresy, and the sentence is death by burning."

Lord Giancarlo coughed politely and said, "There is also the matter of what happens to the esclavin when an obligataire is executed under the Mirador's laws."

I saw Felix stagger, as if Lord Giancarlo's words were a blow, and he said with sudden urgency, "There's no need to enforce that particular law, surely? Given that he couldn't have . . . that he didn't . . ."

The principal among the Tibernian envoys stepped forward out of their huddle and said, "Lord Stephen, I propose, on behalf of the Coeurterre, an alternative."

"You *wh*—" Stephen caught himself. "I beg your pardon, what did you say?"

The Coeurterre didn't mark its wizards as the Mirador did, but they did wear rings, so the Tibernian who spoke next was their wizard, his gems flashing in the candlelight. "Felix Harrowgate is a noirant wizard of such great power that his sudden death—here, where he has done his greatest working—would do untold damage to the balance of energies."

I remembered Felix explaining about noirant and clairant magic, so I at least had a very vague idea of what the Coeurterrene wizard meant, which put me several streets ahead of most of the other people in the hall.

"Then what do you suggest I do with him, gentlemen?" Stephen said, moving his glare from Lord Giancarlo to the Tibernians.

"Send me to Kekropia," Felix said wearily. "The Eusebians will take care of the problem for you."

"Felix, shut *up*!" Mildmay said, quite audibly.

"Well?" said Stephen, not even glancing at Felix.

"We recommend exile," said the principal envoy.

"Where to?"

The principal envoy coughed politely. "The High King, Aeneas Antipater, has recently been in negotiations with the Convocation of Corambis. Their wizards are interested in our theories of magic, and their own orthodoxy does not regard the working of magic upon persons as anathema. They have ways of binding a wizard's power, as well, so that you would not need to worry that this might happen again."

"You wouldn't need to worry about that anyway," Felix said. "My lord, please, am I to be a performing bear now?"

"You have no room to object," Stephen snapped at him, and Giancarlo struck in, "Remember the *legal consequences* of your execution."

By which he clearly meant Mildmay's fate, and Felix knew it, for he gave Mildmay a wide-eyed, unreadable look, then turned back to Stephen and said, "I am your lordship's performing bear, then."

"You certainly are," Stephen said, with a kind of grim unwilling fondness that almost—*almost*—made Felix smile. "Very well. My judgment is this: you are stripped of your title and privileges as a wizard of the Mirador. You will travel to Corambis—you may have two horses and provisions for the journey, and I imagine we can find a map—and there present yourself to the judgment and discipline of the Convocation of Corambis and its wizards. You may not return to the Mirador or its territories unless summoned. Do you understand this judgment?"

"Yes, my lord," Felix said.

"Does anyone speak against this judgment?"

No one did.

But at least Felix was alive.

Felix

How did one pack to go into exile?

The guardsmen stood stolidly by the door, distancing themselves from me with every breath they took. Mildmay, ever-practical, had said, "I'll deal with the clothes. You're gonna want some books, aren't you?"

I supposed I would.

I stared at the shelves blankly for some time, then went into my bedroom. "How many?"

"What?" said Mildmay from one of the wardrobes.

"How many books?"

"Um." He straightened up to look at me. From the frownline between his eyebrows, he didn't like what he saw very much. "Well, you can't take them encyclo-whatsits."

The *Encyclopédie de la Philosophie Naturale* in twenty-eight volumes. The first thing I'd bought with my stipend as a wizard of the Mirador.

"No, of course not," I said.

"Well, a septad. If they ain't too big. Is that okay?"

"Seven," I said.

"Yeah. Seven. Felix? That okay?"

"What? Yes. Yes, that's fine."

I went back to the bookshelves. Seven books.

I went back to the bedroom. "Do I count the Sibylline as a book?"

"Do what?" said Mildmay.

"The Sibylline. My cards. Do they count as a book?"

He stared at me for a second, but I couldn't tell what he was thinking. Then he said, "Nah, they ain't that big. I can always stick 'em in my coat pocket or something. You don't have to count them as a book."

"Okay," I said, and went back to the bookshelves.

Seven books.

I touched the spine of the *Geomantica*, the book Mariam Lester—one of the original Cabalists—had finished on her deathbed. But it was a quarto volume and nearly seven hundred pages long. The Ynge I could take, though, and I put it on the table.

That was one.

Six left.

I stared at *A Treatise upon Spirit*.

I went back to the bedroom. "What about Gideon's books?"

"Gideon's books?" Mildmay said. "Felix, do we got to take this coat?"

Red-violet and lavish with bullion. "I don't care. What about Gideon's books?"

"What *about* Gideon's books?"

"What happens to them? If I don't take them?"

"Well, fuck, Felix, why're you asking me? *I* don't know. What's gonna happen to *your* books?"

"They'll . . . they'll be put in one of the libraries. Probably the Archive of Cinders. That's where they put heretics' books."

"Then that's what they'll do with Gideon's books."

"But . . ."

"What?"

"Nothing," I said and went back to the bookshelves.

To punish myself, I put Ephreal Sand on top of Ezrabeth Ynge. There. That was two. I could take five of Gideon's books.

I picked the *Principia Lucis* because Gideon had considered it the greatest theoretical work on thaumaturgy ever written; *A Treatise upon Spirit* and the *Psukhomakhia* because I had made him happy by finding them for him; the new *Concerning the Thaumaturgy of Wood* because it was the book he had been reading when . . .

That was six. I searched the shelves, looking for the book that Gideon himself would most have wanted to take. And I knew, my breath hitching with something that was not quite pain, when I found it. Nahum Westerley's *Inquiries into the World's Heart*. I'd never seen Gideon reading it; he didn't need to. He could quote long passages of it from memory. But he'd insisted on buying a copy all the same, and I knew, I *knew*, that that was the book he would have chosen.

I put it with the others and sat down at the table to wait for Mildmay.

I did not open any of the books.

Mildmay

It was raining when we came out into the Plaza del'Archimago, and it rained on us all the way down the Road of Corundum, out Corundum Gate, and onto the road going north that the map said would probably get us headed the right way for Corambis. Probably. Felix rode ahead of me, and I let him. I had the map and the money. It wasn't like he could ditch me even if he wanted to.

Every septad-foot farther we got from the Mirador, I felt like another length of chain fell off me. Or like there was somebody in my head, going along a row of windows and throwing the shutters open. Even the rain was the most purely beautiful thing I'd ever seen.

Three miles or so beyond the city gates, about the time it stopped raining, there was a carriage drawn up at the side of the road and a man standing beside it. Somebody'd hung an overcoat over the crest on the door, but I hoped Lord Shannon didn't think he was in disguise or anything. Not with hair like that.

I didn't think Felix was going to stop, and maybe he didn't want to, but he reined in just opposite the coach. "Lord Shannon." There was absolutely fuck-all nothing in his voice.

"Felix," Lord Shannon said, "I brought you your rings."

There was a long silence. Felix said, "Why?"

"Restitution. Atonement. Because they are *yours*, and I would not have them destroyed or worn by another."

"I am no longer a wizard of the Mirador," Felix said in his dead stone voice.

"These were not given you by the Mirador, and we have no right to take them away. It is all that I can do for you, Felix. Will you not accept it?"

"Give them to Mildmay. Or take them back and give them to your boyfriend. I don't care." And he rode on.

Me and Lord Shannon traded a look. We'd never liked each other, and now we never would, but that wasn't what mattered here, and we both knew it.

I could see him brace himself before he said, "Will you take Felix's rings, or will you spurn me as I deserve?"

"I ain't no good at holding grudges," I said.

"Thank you." Shannon handed me up a small, neat, oilskin packet, tied and sealed like he was planning to send 'em to the Emperor in Aigisthos. "I strung them on a chain, so I know they're all there."

I stuck the packet in an inside pocket, where it'd be safe. "M'lord," I said.

"Ride on," he said. "He needs you."

I gave him the best kind of bow I could and rode after Felix.

I glanced back once. Shannon was still standing in the road, watching. I raised a hand, and I saw him wave before I had to look back ahead.

Felix didn't wait for me, so it took me a while to come up with him. And he didn't say nothing, and I didn't say nothing, and it started raining again, and suddenly, I thought, Fuck it. "Felix."

"What?"

"Just making sure you're in there."

He didn't even twitch.

Come on, you prick. Give me *something*. "It could be worse, y'know. Lord Stephen could've decided to burn you anyway."

He looked at me then, and his eyes were like lightning. "*And I would have said thank you.* So just *shut up* about how things could be worse, all right?" He drove his horse forward again.

And I followed him.

There wasn't nothing else in the world I could do.

Mehitabel

I went back to my suite, not because I wanted to go there, but because if I went to the Empyrean with this much time before the performance, I'd have to talk to people. And I couldn't bear the thought.

Lenore must have been listening for me, because she came out into the hall to meet me. "Miss, I hope I done right, but that Mr. Demabrien who visits you?"

"Yes?" I said. And here was another whose life was in ruins.

"Well, he came and he said he didn't know where else to go, but Lord Crowell threw him out, and he thought . . . Well, I reckon he didn't know *what* he thought. So I said he could sit by the fire, and I got him some tea. Is that okay?"

"Thank you, Lenore," I said, and meant it. "That is absolutely 'okay.' You did the right thing."

She gave me a shy, brilliant, stunning smile. "You want some tea, miss? And I can see if they'll make sandwiches or something."

I supposed I should eat. Vincent probably should, too. "Yes, please. That's a good idea."

And she bobbed me a curtsy and darted away. I went in to face Vincent.

He looked dreadful, his face naked of maquillage and a livid bruise starting on the right side of his jaw. He dredged together a smile as I came toward him and said, "I promised not to apologize again, but I do hope you don't mind."

"Not a bit. Who hit you?"

He shrugged a little. "I was only a proxy for Ivo. It doesn't matter."

"Is that the extent of the damage?"

"Oh, yes. It was a blow in passing."

"Were you at the trial?"

"If I hadn't been, I would've been out of the way faster, and Crowell wouldn't have had to suffer the indignity of having to throw me out."

"Vincent—"

"I know. Sorry. Yes, I was at the trial. No, I don't have the least idea what I'm going to do now." His smile twisted and became ghastly. "Do you suppose, if I'd said yes to Felix, this might not have happened?"

"It doesn't help to think that way."

"No, I know that." He pressed the heels of his hands to his eyes.

"Have you slept?"

"Powers, since when?"

"Last night will do for a start."

"No. I was too busy being questioned."

"Vincent, they didn't—"

"Oh, I'm exonerated," he said. "They decided I was an innocent cat's-paw in Ivo's machinations against—for? it's very hard to tell—Lord Shannon. Which is fortunate, since it's the truth. Ivo kept his life in a series of very small boxes."

"So you're free," I said.

He snorted. "I suppose that's one word for it. I'm thirty-five, I've been a whore all my life, and I may wish myself the very best of luck in finding a new patron. Who's going to want Ivo Polydorius's leavings?"

He had a point. "Well, what would you do if you had the choice?"

"Cut off my sex and go into a monastery," he said, with such weary disgust that I was afraid he wasn't joking.

"You're not obliged to explain yourself to me," I said, and

held up a hand when he opened his mouth to apologize. "But you can't sit in front of my fireplace forever unless you're willing to earn your keep."

He became perfectly still, as wary as a cornered cat. "And what did you have in mind?"

For a moment, I heard Felix in my head, so clearly it was almost as if he was in the room: *Darling, please. I'm not that desperate.* But I didn't say it. I said, "I'm thinking I need a secretary."

"A . . . secretary."

"Between the Empyrean and the Mirador, yes. Someone to make sure I'm on time for things, handle correspondence, block importunate would-be suitors. You know, the usual."

"And you think I'd suit you?"

"You write a fair hand. And good God, Vincent, what else do you have to do?"

"I've never—"

"You'll learn," I said, and managed to say it cheerfully.

"Do you make a habit of taking in strays?" he said as Lenore came in with the tea tray.

"Huh," I said, thinking of Lenore, and Mildmay, and Semper and Gordeny. And even Corinna. And Hallam—please, God, let Stephen be able to help him. "You have a point."

We dealt with the tea and sandwiches; I was appallingly hungry, now that I thought about it. Lenore ghosted away again.

Vincent said, "Are you quite sure?"

"If it doesn't work out, you'll at least be in a better position to find some other job. And, yes, I like you and I believe I can trust you. Which I think are more important in a secretary than prior experience."

"You're a determined woman," he said—dryly because he was trying to distract me from the fact that he was blushing.

"Mule-headed is the word you're looking for," I said kindly, and nearly made him choke on his tea. "Come on, Vincent, are you betting on the dogs or the ponies?"

"All right!" he said. "I'll quit fighting against the miracle."

"Good man," I said. "Come with me to the theater tonight, and I can introduce you around. Corinna Colquitt will flirt with you, but don't mind that. She always flirts with Felix—"

My voice broke, as sudden and hard as the descending blade of Mélusine's vicious sanguette.